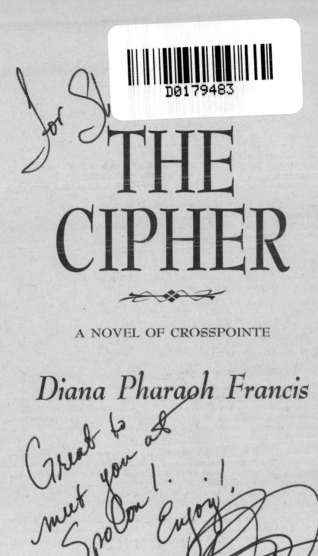

THE CIPHER

A NOVEL OF CROSSPOINTE

Diana Pharaoh Francis

Great to
meet you at
SpoCon! . .!
Enjoy!

RoC
A ROC BOOK

ROC
Published by New American Library, a division of
Penguin Group (USA) Inc., 375 Hudson Street,
New York, New York 10014, USA
Penguin Group (Canada), 90 Eglinton Avenue East, Suite 700, Toronto,
Ontario M4P 2Y3, Canada (a division of Pearson Penguin Canada Inc.)
Penguin Books Ltd., 80 Strand, London WC2R 0RL, England
Penguin Ireland, 25 St. Stephen's Green, Dublin 2,
Ireland (a division of Penguin Books Ltd.)
Penguin Group (Australia), 250 Camberwell Road, Camberwell, Victoria 3124,
Australia (a division of Pearson Australia Group Pty. Ltd.)
Penguin Books India Pvt. Ltd., 11 Community Centre, Panchsheel Park,
New Delhi - 110 017, India
Penguin Group (NZ), 67 Apollo Drive, Rosedale, North Shore 0632,
New Zealand (a division of Pearson New Zealand Ltd.)
Penguin Books (South Africa) (Pty.) Ltd., 24 Sturdee Avenue,
Rosebank, Johannesburg 2196, South Africa

Penguin Books Ltd., Registered Offices:
80 Strand, London WC2R 0RL, England

First published by Roc, an imprint of New American Library,
a division of Penguin Group (USA) Inc.

First Printing, November 2007
10 9 8 7 6 5 4 3 2 1

For Tony, always and forever

Acknowledgments

I've had some of the best fun in my life writing this book, and there were a lot of people who helped me. In particular, Alex Zecha, James Fraylor, the crew of the *Lady Washington*, Megan Glasscock, my friends at the Roundtable, and Lucienne Diver. And at Roc, my amazing editor, Liz Scheier, and copy editor extraordinaire, Michele Alpern, and all of those whom I've not met, but helped me make this a book and get it out to readers.

Additionally, there are places in life you cannot go and things you cannot do without the support of others. I couldn't be a writer—I couldn't be sane—if it weren't for Tony, Quentin, Sydney, my parents and the rest of my (lunatic) family, Megan, Kenna, Christy, and many friends who I know in person and in cyberspace. And most importantly, I couldn't do this if readers like you didn't pick up my books and pass them around.

I know readers will want maps, glossaries, and other fun information about the ongoing tales of Crosspointe. Come visit my Web site at www.dianapfrancis.com for all that and more.

Thank you to all, and I hope you enjoy.

Chapter 1

There were some days that deserved to be drowned at birth and everyone sent back to bed with a hot brandy, a box of chocolates, and a warm, energetic companion. Today was without question one of those days.

The cutter lurched over the chop, shimmying from side to side in a stomach-twisting quadrille. Rain pebbled the deck and sails. Water sheeted across the bow and swirled around Lucy's feet, too great a flood for the scuppers to handle. Her socks were soaked and she could hardly feel her toes. She ought to have had her boots majicked against the weather like her cloak. But it was a bit more majick than she could take.

Cold eeled deep inside Lucy. Her insides quaked with the penetrating chill and her muscles clenched against it. She tightened her arms around her stomach, wishing she'd eaten a better breakfast and thinking longingly of her forgotten flask of tea.

A few minutes later she heard a shouted "Heave to!" Sailors scrambled up the shrouds to reef the handful of bellied sails. The men at the poles dug sharply into the churning water as the cutter heeled to starboard.

"Sorry, ma'am! Weather's too heavy. Can't take you all the way in to shore. We'd be swamped or bilged. Gotta put you ashore on the arm."

The mate didn't wait for her response, which was just as well. She ground out a string of epithets. She had plenty in store. She'd grown up on the docks among

people who lived too close to the edge of life to be
bothered with hoity-toity manners. Or any manners at
all. She rubbed her cold fingers over her cheeks and
pressed them against her mouth to stop the torrent. She
was on duty. She had the reputation of the customs office to think about. Not to mention her own. She didn't
need witnesses to her fears. Which were entirely irratio-
nal. But knowing that did not settle her stomach or
loosen the tension that shook her hands.

The deck dropped and the cutter yawed sickeningly
to the side. Lucy gasped and grappled a bench for balance, her feet sliding. The sailors shouted and clung desperately to the rigging. The boat rolled to the other side.
She sucked in a harsh breath, bracing against the wall,
her legs spread wide. The wash of black waves sounded
hungry and loud above the rush of the wind. Clamping
down on the whimpers crowding her throat, she bit her
lips together so that she tasted blood. She jeered silently
at herself, hoping everybody was too busy to notice.

She straightened with an effort, clinging to the back
of the bench. The cutter righted itself again and continued its lurching way. Lucy's gaze flicked to the strand
of wards glimmering like green pearls beyond the mouth
of the harbor. The Pale. Their glow didn't quiet her nau-
sea. Just because in four hundred years the fence of tide
and storm wards had never failed to keep *sylveth* out of
the harbor, it didn't mean that today couldn't be different. And Lucy didn't want to be in the water when it
happened. Not that the cutter offered safety against *sylveth*. Nothing did.

She shivered and her throat jerked as she swallowed.
She'd seen for herself what raw *sylveth* could do. She
closed her eyes against the memory. But she couldn't
halt it any more than she could stop the storm.

The day had been fine, the black sands sparkling in
the sunlight, the air redolent with spring. Ten-year-old
Lucy and her family were on a picnic during one of their
few summer retreats. Robert had been teasing her again.
She stalked off, leaving all three of her brothers in peals

of laughter. She didn't know how far she walked. She only remembered coming around a jut and stumbling over something soft and sticky.

She had stared at it for long moments, unable to decipher what it was she was looking at. Then a hollow sound slowly filled her ears. Grains trickled past as she stood, unable to tear herself away, recognition creeping over her with insect feet.

It was *sylveth* spawn, born of majick. Whether it had originally been human or animal or something else entirely, there was no way to tell.

Its skin was cratered and spongy, its gray expanse dotted with weeping protuberances. A ten-foot tentacle with orange suckers all along its length erupted from one side of its jellied mass. On top was a turgid frill, fanning across the surface like tree fungus. It smelled like rotting potatoes, burnt fish, and hot butter. The entire length of the creature jerked and twitched as if something inside were trying to escape. More ghastly than anything Lucy could have dreamed of—it was *breathing*. It might once have been a piece of ship debris, a horse, or even something as prosaic as a laundry tub. Or a sailor who'd fallen prey to a *sylveth* tide.

In its raw, unaltered form, *sylveth* wormed through the Inland Sea in silvery skeins of destructive majick. Whatever it touched it *changed*, and rarely for the good. The Pale was the only thing that kept Crosspointe safe from its warping. But the *sylveth* sent regular reminders to wash up on the beaches so that no one ever forgot the danger lurking in the sea.

When she could convince her legs to respond, Lucy had run. Ever since that day, she hated *sylveth*, even worked *sylveth* that the majicars promised was safe enough to handle. If it wasn't, they said, the Pale would never let it through. But there were centuries of gossip and rumor that argued otherwise. About babies turning into giant insects and tearing apart a herd of cows, about houses walking off with the families inside, about rugs transforming into rabid flying creatures and hunting farmers in their fields. Fireside tales to frighten children. Everybody knew it. Almost everybody. Lucy's gut refused to believe it. Not that what she thought made any difference. Worked *sylveth* was the most valuable commodity Crosspointe had to export; it was one entire leg of the three-legged stool making up Crosspointe's economy. Being in customs guaranteed she not only had to be near it; she had to handle it.

Lucy fingered the pendant hidden under her clothing. Even if she hadn't been a customs inspector, she was a Rampling—and loyal down to the toenails. Before she was three minutes old, the crown majicars had put a *sylveth* cipher around her neck. Every Rampling got one, made of the strongest protective majick available. A shield, a badge, a brand, a collar—it couldn't be removed, not by anyone, not even her. The only thing worse than the pendant against her skin was letting anyone else see it.

Her hand dropped to her side. In Crosspointe, it wasn't the *sylveth* you had to be afraid of; it was the spells that were attached to them. She eyed the frothing waves. She hated *sylveth*. But somehow, unbelievably, *stupidly*, she still craved . . .

She didn't dare finish the thought.

The crew rowed closer to the quay, singing a rhythmic chantey in time to their strokes. The cutter bucked and pitched. She watched as a seaman climbed nimbly up on the rail. He stood swaying, a line caught in his fist. The prow swung toward the quay and he tipped forward in a headlong fall. Lucy caught her breath. But the fall turned into a graceful leap. He landed easily, spinning about to snub the mooring line around a waiting bollard. As the rowers heaved against the waves, the seaman hauled in the slack.

At last the cutter jolted against the tarred hawser bumpers. The gate rail was lifted away and a plank tossed down over the last few feet. Seamen lashed it into place, though it bounced and slid loosely on the quay-

side. The tide was going out, making it an uphill climb
from the deck. Waves broke over the gangplank and the
cutter heaved away from the quay. Lucy considered the
narrow bridge skeptically. It might hold a half-grown
child, but she was bigger than that—more like a well-
grown horse.

"Hurry! Can't hold here long!"

Lucy grimaced. She should have stayed in bed. The
wind and rain slapped her face as she hesitated. Beneath
the slender bridge, the water churned like black ink. On
the other side, the seaman waited, holding out a blunt,
rough hand. Two quick steps was all.

She took a firm hold on her satchel, refusing to look
down. She cautiously slid her foot out on the slick wood.
As she did, the cutter yawed wide. She slipped, falling
hard to one knee. The captain caught her under the arm,
helping her up.

"We'll get you a safety line!" he shouted.

"Never mind!" Lucy hollered over the wind, shrugging
him off. She lifted the strap of her satchel over her
shoulder and thrust herself onto the gangplank. It shim-
mied and drooped. Her bruised knee buckled as fire
flared up her thigh. She flung herself upward at the seaman, snatching at his outstretched hand. He caught her
fingers, his callused grip powerful. For a moment Lucy's
feet dangled over the water and then he swung her easily
up onto the quay. Unmindful of her dignity, she stumbled and grappled a piling, her body quivering.

He didn't wait for thanks, but released the mooring
line and sprang back aboard. The gangplank was hauled
in and the cutter shoved off.

Lucy pushed herself upright, hunching into the wind
and shuffling toward the harbor terminal. Her cloak
fluttered up and spume fountained across the walkway,
soaking her uniform surcoat and trousers. She swore
again, thinking longingly of her bed.

She passed a host of vessels filling the slips lining the
quay. They were mostly cutters, tugs, and lighters in the
employ of the harbor or customs. They pitched from

side to side, the lanterns hanging from the riggings winking like frenzied fireflies. A group of sailors trudged past
Lucy, laughing and jostling one another. They moved in
that rolling gait so typical of seamen, hardly seeming
aware of the storm.

Inside the anonymity of her hood, Lucy snarled at
them for their calm indifference. But then, sailors spent
most of their lives beyond the Pale. Lucy stumbled, her
throat closing. Fools.

She worked her way up the quay to the harbormaster's terminal. Stern-faced Hornets in charcoal uniforms
trimmed in saffron and emerald guarded the entry. Lucy
paused long enough to show her customs badge. They
nodded and waved her on.

She hesitated, turning to gaze out through the mouth
of the harbor. Merstone Island rose mistily out of the
ebony water like a sleepy ghost. Beyond were the vast
black waters of the Inland Sea. She had a lot of friends
out there. Her chest tightened. She did her best to avoid
thinking about them. Else she'd chew her fingers to bits
with constant worry. But in a gale like this . . .

Unwillingly, she thought of Jordan. His ship ought to
be coming in soon—she'd expected him more than a
sennight ago. She frowned, her jaw jutting out in defi-
ance against her sudden fear. He was an excellent captain. Few were better. He'd been sailing since he was a
boy. He was too careful, too cunning to be caught by
sylveth or any of the other dangers the Inland Sea had
to throw at the ships that dared its depths.

She tried to make herself believe it. But even the most
brilliant captain didn't have a chance when the sea un-
leashed its fury. Braken's fury. Lightning flashed, sending jagged spears of white light across the entire sky.
Her eyes closed against the knife-bright glare. Hard on
its heels, thunder *cracked*. The air shook with the angry
concussion. Lucy swallowed hard. And the sea god was
pissed.

Abruptly she spun about and headed for the doors.
Once she was submerged in work, she wouldn't be able

to stew about Jordan or anything else. Besides, he was too arrogant, stubborn, and obnoxious to allow himself to be changed by *sylveth*. She allowed herself to take comfort in the thought, but promised herself she would strangle him if he let himself be hurt. He was, after all, her best friend. She had a right to beat him up for letting himself get into trouble.

She stepped into the vast maple and marble entry, the sounds of the wind dying as the doors swung closed. Footmen stood ready inside, taking Lucy's dripping cloak and offering her a towel. She took it, her lips thinning as the burn of majick closed around her like a cloak of nails and nettles. Her scalp prickled and her mouth tasted like polished metal.

The footmen watched her, curious at her immobility. She forced herself to walk deeper inside. It wasn't easy. The harbor terminal was thick with majick, far more than most places in Sylmont. That was one of the reasons she avoided coming here as much as possible. The biting pain did not fade, but every step Lucy took was firmer as she adjusted to it. The hurt was all too familiar and nothing she could not handle once the initial shock had passed.

A footman trailed after her at a discreet distance, wiping up the watery trail she left on the parquet floor. Marble pillars marched along the walls and rose like a scattered forest throughout the entry in support of the ornately plastered ceiling. Lucy shifted the strap of her satchel on her shoulder, dabbing at her dripping forehead with the towel.

Halfway across the room she paused, her attention snagging on the dramatic sculpture set up on a pedestal shaped like a thirty-two-rayed compass. A larger image of the compass was inlaid into the floor. The sculpture depicted the sea god Braken carved in ebony. His fluid, muscular body lay prostrate at the silvery feet of the Moonsinger, Meris. Black waves washed over her feet—like pleading hands, like shackles. She stretched her hand down to her lover, but her eyes were turned up-

ward toward the featureless figure of Hurn, the Hunter,
carved in translucent green windstone. Meris's face was
a study of longing and pain and violent passion. It was
without a doubt the most moving rendition of the terrible triangle Lucy had ever seen. She never passed by it
without stopping, caught by the threat of impending
tragedy in the piece.

Thunder boomed again. Lucy eyed Braken's prone
form with foreboding. The sea god's love for Meris was
furious and vengeful, not to mention desperate. The
Moonsinger could not seem to choose between him and
the mysterious Hurn. Their jealous arguments turned
into vicious storms that scoured the world and churned
the black waters of the Inland Sea.

That sort of passion was entirely alien to Lucy, though
she liked men plenty, and had had her share of lovers.
But she never got so attached that she lost her mind.
Turning away, Lucy briskly walked away toward the
sweep of green jasper stairs on the opposite side of the
room. But she'd hardly gone two steps when the thunder
clapped again. She froze in place as the pillars bracing
the roof vibrated, making a guttural grating noise. Her
gaze lifted uneasily to the ceiling as dust filtered through
the air. Silence fell like a shroud.

Then between one breath and the next, a skin-chilling
siren ripped apart the stillness. The sound galvanized
Lucy. She gathered the length of her dripping surcoat
and pelted up the stairs, taking two at a time. Clerks
and servants joined her on the steps, their faces set and
pale. They flowed upward to the harbormaster's office—
in reality a gallery that took up the entire length of the
third floor. The seaward wall was constructed entirely of
floor-to-ceiling windows. On the interior wall stretched
an enormous map of the harbor. All the docks were
carefully delineated—red, pink, and orange for government docks, green for private, and blue for foreign ownership. Pinned into the occupied slips were various bits
of paper with the ship's name, owner, and status. These
corresponded with files held in the banks of cabinets

filling the vaults on the second floor. Spiraling brass ladders led down into the vaults at intervals along the gallery. Desks and tables crowded the rest of the space and an army of clerks bustled about, shuffling papers, scratching with pens, and making adjustments to the map. Or they would have been, if they weren't all clustered at the windows, staring out at the harbor.

Lucy pushed through the crowd, looking for Hammond Wexler, the recently appointed harbormaster and yet another Rampling—a third or fourth cousin. The siren continued to wail, its majickally enhanced tones echoing across the harbor and through the streets of Sylmont. It drowned the buzz of voices and the pounding thud of Lucy's heart.

She found her gray-haired cousin bent over a spyglass atop a tripod just inside the window. He wore a closely fitted dark blue uniform with parallel rows of gold buttons rising up over his chest and circling around his shoulders. Gold piping trimmed his back-turned sleeves and ran down his pants legs. He wore a pocket watch and chain across his slender waist and a collar of office around his neck. Like Lucy, his royal pendant was hidden beneath his clothing. As she approached, he straightened, his craggy face bleak.

"Braken's eyes," he grated.

She didn't bother with any niceties. "What's happened?"

His gaze flicked to her and then back to the rainstreaked windows. There was little enough to be seen. Though the morning had begun to brighten, the pounding rain and gray mist obscured the southern headland across the harbor. Merstone Island could no longer be seen at all.

"Knucklebones. A weir's grown up in the channel. We're corked tight as a wine bottle. Wind is blowing straight at us. Well above forty-five knots. Ships will rip out their keels on the weir before they even know it's there." He paused, the muscles of his jaw flexing. "You're just in time, cousin. You're senior customer on-site. Better open the sheds. Take whatever you need from the terminal. I suggest you hurry."

He spun about and strode away, not waiting for her reply.

Lucy pressed her palm against the cold glass of the window, feeling heavy and frozen, helpless. Ships were coming. This close to Chance, there could be dozens just out of sight beyond the curve of the horizon.

"Sweet Meris, please don't let Jordan be on one."

Chapter 2

Despite the urgency of the siren and Wexler's orders, Lucy paused to look into the spyglass. She adjusted the eyepiece, twisting a small dial along the side. She caught her breath and recoiled as the knucklebone reeds reared up, seeming only a handbreadth away from her face.

"It *is* a spyglass, after all," she muttered, bending to look again.

The white stalks pricked from the water, their stems articulated like skeletal fingers. Some were short, like wheat stubble. Others stretched up twenty feet or higher. They seemed fluid and soft as seaweed as they fluttered and waved beneath the might of the gale. But Lucy knew better; they were sharp-edged and harder than iron. When ships ran up onto a weir, the reeds did not break; they did not give at all. They appeared and vanished wherever they pleased without rhyme or reason, making them nearly impossible to avoid and causing more wrecks than anything else on the Inland Sea.

Lucy slowly swung the spyglass from side to side. The weir ran along the edge of the tide wards, blocking the entire mouth of the harbor. They filled Merstone Strait to the shores of the majicars' island on the north side and marched down out of sight behind the southern headland. It was a disaster.

Lucy straightened blindly, then spun about with sudden purpose. She had work to do.

The crowd of clerks pressing against the window was

silent and tense. Lucy's gaze swept the room with sharp calculation. At last she lit on a clerk bending over a large book, rapidly making inscriptions. His shirtsleeves were rolled up over his elbows and ink stains blotted his fingers. Pinned to his collar was a master clerk's brooch. Beside it was a silver pin shaped like a compass rose set on an obsidian disk and struck through by an anchor, the latter indicating he was the harbormaster's personal assistant.

Lucy strode across the room, stopping beside him. His hair stood on end like he'd been running his fingers through it, and the corners of his mouth were drawn down in deep grooves.

"I need to borrow some of your people," she said, not waiting for him to acknowledge her. "A dozen senior clerks, no one junior. I want your most trustworthy. I'll need carriages to take us to the salvage sheds. Customs will reimburse the costs."

He straightened, staring down at his hands clenched around his pen. When he spoke, his voice was strained. "I shall arrange it. Is there anything else you require?"

"Hot food. We'll have everything else we need. How soon can you get it done?"

"No more than half a glass. If you like, I'll have someone escort you downstairs. You'll want to eat."

Lucy hesitated.

"There's nothing you can do for now."

He was right. It would be wise to get something in her stomach. Once the salvage began, she'd have precious little time to eat. And she certainly didn't want to wait at the window and watch helplessly.

"Very well."

She followed a young apprentice to a small salon. The warning siren continued to sing its eerie song, the sound muting only slightly as they descended into the building. Her guide yanked the bellpull and ordered tea from the flustered servant who answered the summons.

"It will be here in a moment, miss," the apprentice said, twisting her fingers together. The girl mumbled through lips that refused to open. Accustomed to registering details, Lucy glimpsed pinkish teeth and a tongue the color of garnets. There was also a black burn mark on her right index finger that was not hidden by the ink stains. She smoked bloodweed, an addictive stimulant that many apprentices leaned on to complete their work. However, its side effects were both embarrassing and debilitating with long-term use—like wetting oneself, for instance. Lucy sniffed. The girl did not stink. Nor did she struggle with door handles. But the irony was that if she kept it up, she'd no longer be able to do the work for which she'd started taking the drug in the first place. Lucy gave a mental shrug. No one began taking bloodweed without knowing the cost. And the girl had a right to be stupid. Everybody did.

The subject of Lucy's inspection hovered near the door in jittery silence until Lucy couldn't stand it any longer and dismissed her. The girl rushed out, no doubt to return to the vulture watch at the great gallery windows.

Lucy's tea arrived, served with cold pork sandwiches, sliced pears, an assortment of hard cheeses, and a plate of nut cookies. She could hardly swallow, but knew she had to. The next hours would be frenzied, with little opportunity to eat or sleep. This close to Chance, each day promised two or three dozen ships. Even though some would see the warning beacons and veer away, too many would run up on the weir. The potential devastation was enough to make Lucy's throat hurt. She picked at her food, counting each time she chewed and swallowed. She hardly noticed when she burned her tongue on the steaming tea.

When the warning siren changed to an emergency signal, she leaped to her feet, nearly overturning the table. It pulsed in short, hard blasts, blaring like a donkey's bray.

She was out of time. With or without the clerks and carriages, she had to open the salvage shed.

* * *

"No! That isn't Trilby and Sons—that's Daily and Tripp. Check the box markings and go slower if you have to. If they are loose goods or you can't read the markings, put them in E section and we'll figure it out later."

The journeyman clerk nodded, his mouth pinching. Lucy watched him wiggle the barrel back up onto the cart and go in search of the proper cargo stall.

"Check his sheets. Sloppiness is a crime in customs. Make sure the salvagers are logged and the cargo lots tagged solidly. The only reason we get salvage volunteers and don't lose goods to theft is because the reward is worth more than sitting around watching or stealing," she said to the woman trailing her. Rebecca Rae was a master clerk. She towered above Lucy, with a narrow, beaklike nose and a sharp chin. Her skin was pale, like grass hidden all summer beneath a rock. She was extraordinarily competent, and Lucy made a mental note to recommend Rebecca Rae for customs work.

Leaving the clerk to follow her orders, Lucy continued along the aisle, inspecting the flurry of activity with a gimlèt eye. Much of the wrecked tramper's cargo had washed through the weir and had been collected and deposited. Processing it was slow and the harbormaster's inexperienced clerks made a lot of mistakes. The salvage was becoming chaotic as goods were piled up haphazardly and sloppily documented and recorded. She hoped her own people arrived soon.

She stopped short when the ship-in-trouble siren began its pulsing roar once again. *Not again.* Her lips tightened. *Not the* Firewind! *Mother Moon, not Jordan's ship.* She jerked about as Rebecca Rae joined her again.

"Damn. That's another one coming. I'll have to open another shed and pray to Chayos the gods come to their senses soon."

"Yes, ma'am."

"I'll take half the crew and get started. You'll have to stay here until one of our majicars shows up. Regulations require that every open shed have a customs inspector on-site—there's too much danger of smuggling and theft otherwise. So I want you to stay and keep an eye on things. Don't leave until it is sealed. Got it?"

"Yes, ma'am."

Lucy nodded. Good woman. No blathering on with stupid questions. Yes, when this was over, she'd hire Rebecca Rae for her own team.

She'd nearly forgotten about the gale. It was blowing as hard and wet as earlier in the morning. Waves crashed against the tide wall, geysering high into the air. The rain pecked and the wind roared. She'd not put on her cloak and by the time she'd struggled to the second shed, she was drenched through. She grasped the lock in one hand, groping for her seal with the other. A powerful gust shoved at her. She staggered, clinging to the door handle for balance.

She jumped when strong hands closed around her waist, a short, muscular body bolstering hers from behind.

"Better tie an anchor to your ankle or you'll be kiting off to the Root." Hig's voice was welcome.

"It's about time you got here. Help me get this open," she shouted.

Hig bulled her forward, bracing her as she unlocked the door. Dozens of other customs clerks clustered around them, helping to block the wind. When the lock was sprung, Hig and Gridley shoved the doors open. Lucy took a towel from the shelf inside the door, wiping her face as she rapidly fired off orders.

"Peep and Lester, stoke the furnace. Did you bring a majicar?"

"Brithe, at your service, ma'am."

His voice was cool and almost brusque. Lucy glanced up at him assessingly. Her eyes fell on his *illidre*—a focus for majick made of *sylveth*. It hung on a chain of gold, silver, and copper woven together like a serpent; the clasp was a snake's head biting its tail. The *illidre* was a smaller snake coiled around the chain. It was dark blue with oranges and reds glinting from within as they caught the light. Facets suggested scales and enhanced the fiery glitter. Lucy eyed it distastefully. It wasn't a cipher; it didn't radiate majick. For the moment. But as soon as he worked his first spell—it was like being attacked by hordes of wasps. She shuddered, her lip curling involuntarily.

"Something wrong?" the lanky majicar demanded.

Lucy tore her gaze from the *illidre*. Brithe was probably close to thirty-five years old. He was skinny with straw blond hair, a narrow chin, and fish-belly pale skin. His mouth was wide and compressed; his eyes a milky gray. It was an arrogant face with little in it to like. At the moment, he looked distinctly infuriated. She swore silently at herself. Majicars hated their service terms and more often than not had to be bullied into doing the duty they were legally bound to do. What was she doing antagonizing him during a salvage?

"Yes," she said, reaching out to give Brithe a perfunctory shake of the hand, seeing the flash of humor in his eyes at her bluntness. "I'd appreciate it if you'd overlook my rudeness. I'm usually better behaved," she said.

Brithe examined her a long moment before nodding. "Today you're entitled, I think. As I said, I am at your service."

"Thank you. And well met, sir. I'll ask you to accompany Hig next door. Seal the shed as soon as you can. We'll work on sorting and inspecting its contents later. Hig, send the rest of the crew over here. Master clerk Rebecca Rae is sweeping up. She's good."

Hig leered, rubbing his square, callused hands together. "Is she, now?"

Her senior customs clerk was shorter than Lucy by four inches, and Rebecca Rae was taller than her by equally as much.

Not that Hig would be put off by the difference. Lucy rolled her eyes.

"Do *try* to remember we are in the middle of an emergency. And since I'd like to recruit Rebecca Rae to our team, I'd appreciate it if you didn't entirely put her off the prospect."

"I'll be a pussycat," he promised solemnly.

Lucy knew better. "One of these days I am going to hire a majicar to rot off your favorite bits so I won't have to worry about you tomcatting anymore."

He grinned and gave a little salute. "And deprive the women of Sylmont of my affections? You'd have a riot. Now, if you don't mind, sweet Rebecca Rae is waiting for me." He turned to leave and then paused, frowning, his voice dropping low. "Was it wise, leaving the shed without certified customs supervision?"

"There wasn't any choice. Besides, Rebecca Rae is a bonded master clerk and has been solid all night. Given the circumstances, it was the only thing to do." Except that it was entirely against policy and she could be suspended and fined for it. Lucy gave a little shrug. It was done. She waved Hig and Brithe away, concentrating on the business at hand.

The day passed in a frenzy of activity. Four more ships cracked up on the knucklebones before night fell. Salvagers hauled in recovered cargo from the destroyed vessels. Some of it had survived inside casks and crates. Far more were loose goods hauled in tumbled jumbles inside duffels and makeshift sacks of sailcloth and net.

Customs teams continued to arrive throughout the day. The first wreck had been a three-masted schooner; the next were deep-bellied four-masted clippers carrying twice the freight. The salvage piled up quickly. Even with so many customs teams, it was difficult to log the goods, much less keep them organized. Shed after shed was filled and sealed.

Lucy oversaw the salvage with unrelenting energy and zeal. She threw herself into the work, ignoring her own worries and the increasingly vicious bite of majick. It permeated the air, inhabiting the recovered cargoes in the shape of weak ciphers and majicked commercial goods. Many of the sailors, stevedores, and lighters carried traces of majick as well. But Lucy had learned to tolerate the pain and refused to let it get in the way of her work.

The gale began to subside as dusk fell. But still the salvage continued to flow in. Lucy was completing a report to her supervisor, Alistair Crummel. She folded it and pressed the circular tip of her seal against the paper. A jolt ran up her fingers and the mark on the page shimmered with a green flame. It was shaped like a crescent moon inside a triangle and ringed by a series of numbers and letters in minuscule black script that identified the seal as hers. Only she could activate it.

She handed the report to Ellen Bagnot, her junior clerk. "Make sure Alistair gets this tonight. He'll be waiting for it."

"As ye wish."

"Not exactly what you were expecting on your last day, was it?"

"Not so much, no, ma'am."

Lucy smiled. "At least it's been a memorable ending to your customs career. Though it still escapes me how you could want to attach to a Chancery office in Ospredale." Lucy grimaced at the word *Chancery*.

" 'Tis a good position, ma'am," Ellen said quickly. "Close to m'family. I haven't seen them in nigh on fifteen years since I apprenticed. Ye know I wouldn't of taken it else, and ye don't need to worry none. I won't be having nothing to do with the crown case. I wouldn't never hurt yer family that way," she said fervently.

"You just do the job they ask of you and don't worry about the Ramplings. Most of us don't remember not having to work to eat. We've been mired in this Chancery suit for more than fifty years, and whatever you do or don't do, we'll be sunk in it for another hundred, or until the family goes bankrupt. So don't balk if you're told to work on the case. None of us will take it amiss."

"Yes, ma'am. I mean, no, ma'am."

"Now go and be sure you put that report into Alistair's hands yourself." She grasped Ellen's hand firmly.

"We'll miss you. I wish there was time to celebrate your leaving properly."

The other woman flushed and bobbed her head before scurrying off. Lucy went in search of Hig. She'd not gone more than a dozen feet when she was struck by an agonizing sensation like toothy saw blades raking hard across her skin. She staggered, letting out a soft moan before biting down on her lip, tasting blood.

But challenging the ripping pain was a spurt of eager hunger. A cipher. A *true* cipher.

She forced herself to straighten, to appear as if nothing were wrong. She scanned the shed. Near the opposite wall Hig and Peep had their heads together over a stack of crates. Neither seemed aware of the overpowering majick that had suddenly blossomed inside the shed. Of course they didn't notice; nor did Brithe.

Lucy swung around jerkily, seeking the source like a flower following the sun. It felt like it was coming from the front right corner of the building. A steady stream of dockworkers, sailors, and lighters continued to trudge in, loaded with the dripping remnants of the ships. Lucy ignored them, following the flow of power upstream with slow, deliberate steps. The pain grew with every stride. But it didn't compare with the frantic hunger that had seized her the moment she felt its enthralling touch. The inside of her mouth and the bottoms of her feet started to itch mercilessly. Eagerness made her breath come sharp between her lips. She'd never encountered any but true ciphers that did that to her.

She told herself to stop, to turn around, to ignore her gut-churning want. She didn't listen. She knew it was stupid. The cipher would likely kill her in a long, painful ordeal. Or worse. Much, much worse. But she couldn't help herself.

Four hundred years ago, Errol Cipher had created the first ciphers. His—true ciphers—were far more powerful than those produced by majicars today, even the one she wore around her neck. He'd made most of them to torment those he hated. True ciphers were usually things

of innocuous appearance, like spoons or hairpins or shoe
buckles. Most people had no way to detect them until
they attached, and then there was no way to remove
them until the spell ran its course. Or the wearer died.

Lucy filtered through the throng of salvagers. They
were dripping wet and exhausted. They hauled in their
heavy loads of flotsam with grim faces. She nodded to
those who caught her eye, but she didn't stop.

She was close now. She edged past the long tables of
clerks registering and recording the salvage. Drawn by
the throbbing power of the cipher, Lucy circled around
the haphazard stacks of goods. She ran her fingers over
wet bolts of cloth, several bales of draggled furs and
dripping hides, clay jars of spices and delicacies, bundled
lengths of unfinished wood, ruined shoes, bronze and
porcelain decorative ornaments, and dozens of casks of
wine. The number and variety of goods were endless—
hidden in barrels, chests, and caskets, stacked in crooked
aisles fifteen feet high and ten feet across.

Lucy wandered deeper into this pillared forest, finally
finding what she was looking for in a collection of
stacked bins where small, odd items went to keep them
from getting lost. She paced around to the left, stopping
abruptly, catching her breath sharply as cold cut deeply
into her lungs. She tugged the top bin aside, pulling until
she'd opened a gap into the bin beneath it. She craned
her neck, peering inside. There was a jewelry box carved
from windstone; a wet, floppy straw hat with long crumpled feathers attached; a collection of ivory combs and
brushes; a battered silver teapot with one cup; and an
assortment of decorative bead masks. And there was one
small wooden box made of roughly finished pine held
together with cheap brass tacks. A flat band circled it
with a customs tag identifying the date, the time of day
the box had been logged in, the salvager, and the customs official who'd accepted it.

A gabble of loud voices made Lucy start. She jerked
her head up, breathing a silent sigh when the voices died
and no one disturbed her. Woodenly, she turned back

to the box. Hot *want* demanded that she snatch it and smuggle it home. Her stomach roiled. *Absolutely not!* She was a customs agent, not a thief, not a smuggler. But then—what? Move it where she could keep an eye on it until she could buy it? Her body twitched at waiting, at the thought of possibly losing it. No, that wouldn't do either.

Hardly aware of what she was doing, she reached into the bin, hesitating a finger's breadth away. As a rule, true ciphers were dangerous only once they touched human skin. She'd be handling only the box. Even so, she hesitated, then chided herself. Someone had clearly packed it inside the box without suffering harm.

Lucy brushed the top of the box. The wood was rough, a splinter piercing her index finger. Oh, how she wanted to take it! But everything she was rebelled at the idea. It was against the law. And she wouldn't, *couldn't*, break the rules she lived her life by. But a snide voice inside ridiculed her. She collected true ciphers. *That* was against the law. Taking this one was no different. But it was.

Reluctantly she pulled back. She'd mark the box so that it could not be released without her making a personal inspection. Then at least she'd know to whom it belonged. From there, she'd see about buying it. No one else would know its real nature, and given the rough packing, the cipher was probably nothing valuable. It was the best she could do without stealing it.

Suddenly the top of the box erupted, spattering Lucy's arms with splinters. A chain thrust up like the head of a cobra. It swayed in midair, inching upward above her head. Lucy stared at it in blank shock, fear freezing her in place. The chain was as long as her arm. It was made of *sylveth* disks, each the size of a dralion, and hooked together by heavy silver links. The disks were a dull gray, like rainwater, lacking the usual telltale glimmer. There was no clasp.

The chain gave a wriggle.

Lucy gasped, her heart contracting. She bit her tongue,

telling herself to get away. Slowly she slid her left foot behind her.

The chain wriggled again.

Panic blistered through her veins. She flung herself backward. Too late. The chain darted like a striking snake and snapped itself around her left wrist, spinning like an anchor chain around a capstan and coiling up her arm to the elbow. The *sylveth* disks flared incandescent white. Lucy turned her head away from the brilliance, holding her arm extended.

Her skin went cold, like she'd dipped her arm in snowmelt. The chill washed up her shoulder and around her neck. It swept over her head and down to her ribs, thighs, and feet. For a moment, she felt encased in an icy shroud. The cold sank through her skin into her muscles, into her bones. She felt as if something were twisting tight inside her, the pressure making her choke. She wanted to cry out, but a part of her recalled where she was; that she dared not be discovered. She clamped her lips together and sealed them with her teeth.

The cold turned suddenly scorching. The heat erupted outward. For a moment, Lucy thought she smelled cooking meat. Then suddenly it was gone, and with it the bright light.

She crumpled to the floor, her breath huffing between her lips in short, wheezing pants. She grasped at the shreds of her own equilibrium, examining herself. Her skin wasn't melting from her bones. Her legs weren't turning into frog legs or horse tails. She ran her fingers over her face and scraped her nails across her scalp. She was still herself.

Relief made her giddy.

The scuffle of feet and the sound of masculine voices made her realize how she must look, sitting on the floor. She glanced down. The cipher encircled her left arm from wrist to elbow. The *sylveth* disks now shimmered with the rainbow light of soap bubbles. She pushed at it. It didn't budge. She pushed harder, scratching bloody rents in the skin between the links. Still it didn't move.

"No, no, *no!*" she muttered, continuing to scrabble at it, though she knew it wouldn't come off. Errol Cipher had created this trinket to never relinquish its grip. Not until the spell had run its course. Not until she'd suffered the torments and humiliation that the ancient majicar had woven into its length.

Of course, it might be one of the good ones.

A harsh bark of laughter tore at her throat. Not all of them were curses. A few, a very slim few, were gifts. To grow hair on a sterile pate. To protect from harm. To give precious skills. But this was not one of those. It was stupid and wishful to think so. About as stupid as digging for it in the first place.

The voices drew closer. Lucy glanced up and then frantically pulled at her rolled sleeve. She yanked it down just as two men strolled between two of the pillared stacks. Her mouth dropped open as relief rushed over her.

Jordan.

He was home. . . . He was safe.

Chapter 3

Jordan gaped, then leaped forward.

"Lucy! Are you all right?" He gripped her hand and helped her to stand, one arm circling her waist as she swayed.

Jordan's face was narrow, with sharp cheekbones and a patrician nose. Damp clung to the dark stubble shadowing his jaw. He was bareheaded and ruddy, wearing his hair in the fashionable coif typical of ships' captains and officers—chin-length in front and fastened in a pigtail high on the back of his head, the hair around his collar and above his ears shaved close. The gale had picked it loose and now tendrils of black hair clung to his forehead and cheeks. His oilskin overcoat dripped a wet trail on the floor. Beside him was a man Lucy didn't recognize. He was not quite as tall as Jordan, with broad shoulders and a lean form. His face was square and tanned, his features blunt. His eyes were a pale brown; his walnut hair was streaked gold from the sun.

"Are you hurt? What's happened to you?"

Lucy pushed Jordan away. He held tight. She made a growling, annoyed sound, twisting to see his face.

"What's happened is that you're drenched and intent on making me equally so. And what in Meris's name are you doing here? Why aren't you out on the *Firewind*?" Her voice was accusing.

"What, you'd rather I was trying to run the weir? And in such heavy weather? I thought we were friends."

"So did I. How long have you been in port?"

He looked slightly abashed. "Five days."

"So nice of you to send around a note, you know, just to say you're safe so the rest of us don't have to worry about you."

His eyebrow flicked up. "Who knew you could sound just like my mother?"

"Just at the moment I'd like to see you racked on the weir," Lucy said, shoving herself away. She caught her breath, recalling the cipher. She pulled her arm close against herself to hide it.

Jordan frowned.

"Did you fall? Are you all right?"

"I stumbled is all. I'm fine."

But her knees started to buckle, giving lie to her words.

"Come on, then, you need to sit down."

He started to guide her back toward the center of the building. Lucy resisted.

"No, there are some tables on the west wall. It's closer."

"As you wish."

Jordan and his companion assisted her to a table. There were no chairs, but a cask served well enough. Lucy sat with a sigh. She held her arm close against her ribs, hoping they would not notice the cipher beneath her sleeve.

"You aren't going to faint, are you? If that's even possible for you."

Jordan knelt before her, taking her right hand and chafing it in his. His fingers were callous and warm. Lucy watched him intently, grasping his fingers, not yet able to let go of her fear and worry for him.

He looked up at her, frowning. "You know, you look like you've been keelhauled."

"Aren't you a charmer? Please, don't stop. I can

hardly get enough of such flattery. Maybe if I had known you were safe, I wouldn't have been yanking my hair out with worry." It came out weakly, without any of the usual force.

He smiled, though it didn't ease his frown. "Sorry about that. I forget sometimes that anybody worries about me. And now it seems I need to worry about you. What have you done to yourself? Let me see."

Before Lucy could object, he'd taken her left hand in a gentle grip. He turned it over. Lucy sucked in a breath, unable to pull away. Jordan glanced up sharply.

"Does that hurt?"

Lucy said nothing, her face taut. She wanted to jerk away, but he was already pushing up her sleeve, exposing the *sylveth* chain. A strangled sound tore from her throat. Stricken, she stared at Jordan.

"You should have a doctor look at this. There's no bruising or swelling, but clearly you are suffering a great deal of pain."

Lucy stared. "What?"

He glanced down, running his fingers lightly over her forearm, probing gently as he did. Lucy watched, stunned relief making her queasy. His fingertips slid *through* the cipher as if it weren't there. He couldn't see it, couldn't touch it.

Lucy smoothed her hand down over her arm. The heavy silver links were cold and hard to her touch. The gray *sylveth* disks, by contrast, were quite warm. Hastily she rolled down her sleeve again. Her heart pounded. She felt like she'd won a reprieve, but from what? The danger of the cipher clung to her like her own shadow. Mordant humor twisted her lips. But at least it was hers now. Whether she liked it or not.

"How do you feel?"

Jordan's voice brought Lucy back to the present.

"You're the one touching me—how do you think I feel?"

He grinned and lifted her hand to his lips. "Sharp as teeth, as always, dear Lucy."

She squeezed his hand hard. "It's good to see you, Jordan. I—"

She broke off, pulling her hand from his and splaying it hard against his chest. "You're hovering like a starving vulture. And you smell like a whore who's been swimming in perfume. It would be no wonder if I did feel faint with that stench."

He grinned as she shoved him away. "Perhaps you need to eat. Seems like you're in the mood to gnaw on something. I'd as soon it wasn't me."

Sudden hunger made Lucy's mouth water. But she didn't relish the idea of walking back through the shed. She wasn't sure that her trembling legs would support her.

"If you would be so kind as to fetch something, I would be grateful. There's a temporary mess set up in the back."

"As my lady wishes," Jordan said with a mocking bow and extravagant flourish. "Ah, but I am forgetting my manners. Lucy Trenton of the customs service, I'd like to introduce Marten Thorpe, master of the *Ravenstrike*. I should warn you that he is considered of dubious reputation and you should not let your guard down for a moment. Not that you are not perfectly capable of fending for yourself, a fact that I am sure Marten shall discover if he becomes too forward. And Marten, I have known Lucy since we were children. She is very much like a sister, only I actually like her. I should not wish you to impose on her good nature. Or even her bad one."

"By all means, I shall behave myself," Marten said with an upward flick of his brow.

Left alone with Marten Thorpe, Lucy eyed him narrowly. She'd heard of him, of course. He had a reputation for being quite a ladies' man, and for being something of a gambler. It was this last that made Lucy's expression severe. Gambling was illegal in Crosspointe, and doing so demonstrated a disappointing lack of integrity, not to mention brains. If she ever was assigned to inspect the *Ravenstrike*, she'd go over the ship with a fine-toothed comb. He also had the reputation of being one of the finest—or possibly luckiest—sea captains on the Inland Sea. He'd never lost even one ship in his career. And even though he'd been a captain for only ten years, such a feat was nearly unheard of. Not with all the dangers of the Inland Sea.

"Do I have spiders hanging out my nose?" he asked her, propping himself against a tall crate. Despite his wet clothing, he appeared at ease, as if he were sitting on the deck of his ship.

"I don't believe so," Lucy answered. "Though I am curious, is this a usual occurrence for you?"

"Not at all. However, your expression suggested that I might be infested with noxious creatures."

"Not observably, no," Lucy said. She could see why he was well liked. He had an easy air and his speech indicated intelligence. Which meant that he had brains enough. What he lacked was integrity. She turned her head, hiding her repugnance. She wondered that Jordan would keep his company.

"Ah, I see you disapprove of me," he drawled in an offhand way.

"I did not say so."

"Your face is quite expressive. Might I inquire as to how I've offended you in the mere minutes we've known one another?"

Lucy cocked her head at him. He looked back, his brown eyes impudent. She shrugged.

"Let's just say that your reputation precedes you," she said.

His eyebrows rose. "Your delicate sensibilities are affronted by my liaisons with women, is that it?"

Lucy shook her head. "Not at all. I do not castigate people for their adventures in the bedroom. Otherwise I'd never be friends with Jordan."

His gaze turned speculative. "No? Then do enlighten me; what do you find so abhorrent as to cause such a look?"

"If you want the unvarnished truth . . ." Lucy waited for his nod, which he gave readily. "Very well, then. I am a customs inspector, Captain Thorpe. And I have a deep respect for the law. But you flaunt it. You're a gambler. And it is my experience that men who gamble are like knucklebone reeds—only the barest hint of their true character is revealed above the black waters. What shows may appear beautiful, but it is equally treacherous. As for what is hidden below—well, that part of the man's character is too often corrupt and cancerous."

"And this is your opinion of me? Based on what, I wonder."

"As I said, your reputation precedes you. If I am incorrect in my understanding, I apologize. But I doubt my opinion can matter to you."

"No, indeed. I am fascinated. Would you care to know my impression of you?"

"Not really."

Lucy could imagine well enough what he saw when he looked at her. She had no illusions about her looks or her own reputation. She was short, the crown of her head barely coming to the top of his shoulder. Her auburn hair was pulled back severely and anchored tightly to her head. Even the gale outside had not done much to loosen the coif that her jackdaw lady's maid had fastened so securely in the early hours. Which was just as well. Lucy's hair was coarse and ridiculously curly. It hung to her hips, its weight barely keeping it from standing out like a peacock's tail. Dressed as she was in the saffron yellow customs surcoat, Lucy knew she looked like a lit candle. A plump one. The surcoat made her skin look sallow, and her lack of cosmetics didn't help. Her eyes were an indeterminate smoky blue and probably looked red, squinty, and small with lack of sleep. She had no cheekbones to speak of, and a stubby nose. At least she had good teeth and a merry smile, though absolutely no inclination to demonstrate either at the present moment. Add to her unprepossessing appearance her reputation as a narrow-minded, unrelenting mad dog when it came to customs . . . She wasn't a particularly appealing package.

"No?"

His tone was mocking. Lucy's hackles went up. She didn't back down from challenges.

"By all means, if you'd like. Let it not be said I could not hear the hard truths about myself."

He paused, his eyes running over her from head to foot. Then he shook his head. "No. One day perhaps. But not today."

"I don't suppose we'll meet again after today. Unless I happen to have the inspection of your ship."

It was his turn to shrug. "Maybe the gods will smile upon me."

Meaning what? That he hoped she wouldn't ever inspect his ship and catch him smuggling? Or that he hoped they'd meet again?

"Shall we speak of something else, then?" Lucy did not wait for his response. "What's going on out there?" She waved her right hand at the wall, indicating the harbor and the storm. "Are there any survivors at all?"

Marten's expression altered. Gone was the affable rogue. In his place stood the captain who'd guided ships through the worst storms on the Inland Sea. Who'd outrun *sylveth* tides and maneuvered safely through the gauntlet of dangers on the black waters. He appeared suddenly grave. His eyes had an inward, haunted expression. It was a familiar look among sea captains. Lucy's opinion of him rose a small notch.

"A few have made it through the weir. Crawling over the wreckage and the bodies of their mates. Most won't survive their wounds. It's difficult for even majicar healers to close wounds caused by knucklebones."

Lucy nodded, toying absently with her necklace. "And the rest?"

"Unvarnished truth?" he asked in that same deadpan voice.

Lucy nodded, tensing.

"There's a *sylveth* tide rising."

The breath went out of her. She tipped her head back, closing her eyes. "What are the gods thinking?"

"Thinking? Oh, no. This is mindless fury. Braken and Meris. Hunger and tease. Jealousy and passion. They fight their vicious battles and we get caught in the middle."

Lucy raised her head, surprised. "I'd not have suspected you to be a believer."

He smiled, losing a little of that hardness. "I am a sailor, Miss Trenton. I have to believe."

Just then Jordan returned, carrying a tray of food and a carafe of tea. Lucy's smile of thanks faded as she watched his silent, grim approach. His lips were pulled in a rigid white line, his movements jerky. He set the tray down with a hard thunk. The dishes jumped and clattered. Saying nothing, he reached for the tea, filling the mug halfway. Reaching into the pocket of his coat, he pulled out a silver flask. He opened it and filled the cup to the rim.

"Jordan! What are you doing? She can't handle so much!" Marten pushed to his feet, reaching out to stop the other man.

The look Jordan turned on his friend could melt iron. He handed the cup to Lucy.

"You're going to want this."

Lucy held the cup a moment, staring up at him. His black eyes were stormy, swirling with hard-held emotions she couldn't read. A rush of anxiety filled her. *What had happened?* Jordan was one of the most level-headed men she knew. He rarely lost his temper, and bad news only made him calm. He was a rock.

"Trust me, Lucy. You'll need this. Drink it all."

She nodded and drank. The liquor had cooled the tea so that she could swallow it quickly. The liquor burned her tongue and throat and trailed fire down into her stomach. She forced herself to finish.

"What was that stuff?" she gasped, pressing her hands

to her abdomen. A furnace roared inside. Her head swam and her vision turned fuzzy. Her muscles felt soft and fluid.

"Meris's tears," he said with a thin smile.

"Meris's—what?" she said, slurring her letters.

"The liquor of the sea. Don't worry, things will settle in a moment. They'll just seem . . . farther away."

"What's going on, Truehelm?" Marten demanded.

Jordan grimaced. "Weir's gone. The customs majicar has just been called out to help the cordon with the spawn and no more majicars can cross to the mainland until the *sylveth* tide disperses. Lucy is the senior government official on-site. She's going to have to handle the retrieval and decide—" He broke off and glanced at her. "I'm going to stay with her until it's done."

Now Lucy found Marten's gaze settling on her, his eyes heavy-lidded as if he were half-asleep. It felt like he was looking inside her, measuring her. And she suspected he found her lacking. Her heart pounded. She opened her mouth to take a breath and found she couldn't. Her tongue felt swollen and her body unwieldy. She sagged when at last he turned back to Jordan.

"I'll come too. Keep that flask handy. What you gave her won't be nearly enough."

Chapter 4

Jordan was right. Lucy needed Meris's tears—it kept her sane.

Pewter clouds scudded across the night sky. Sand swirled in stinging clouds. Lucy wrapped her face with a handkerchief, her two escorts buffering her against the wind as she pushed her way down to the salvage docks. She knew what had to be done. She'd learned the protocols early in her apprenticeship and suffered twice-yearly drills since. She knew exactly what to do, if only she could bring herself to do it.

The first order of business was to draft a knacker gang. A silent crowd had gathered, waiting. There was a healthy wage to be earned in the grisly business. Lucy selected a cadre of mostly seasoned sailors who were not likely to panic. Their bleak faces and blank gazes said they knew all too well what was coming.

Next she led them to the black building at the end of the row of salvage sheds. It was set well apart on a rocky shelf high above the tide, its sides square, its roof domed with silver ridge beams ascending from each corner and fusing at the top. The doors were made of ebony. Fine silver wires crisscrossed the entire exterior in a complex pattern. The building radiated cold and darkness that had nothing to do with the storm or the night and everything to do with majick.

As she approached, Lucy marveled at the numbing strength of Meris's tears, which dampened all but a slight *zing!* at the power emanating from the building. Even unlocking the doors was painless. She might as well be wearing thick leather gloves.

Once inside, Jordan and Marten helped her distribute the protective gear. It included trousers, a tunic, gloves, a hood mask, and stockings that slid over the boots and the cuffs of the trousers. They were made of a black material, soft and clingy—almost silky. Lucy turned a mask over in her hand, wondering how such light material could possibly shield against *sylveth* spawn.

"Are you well, Miss Trenton?"

It seemed to Lucy that there was a none-too-subtle note of condescension in Marten's voice, as if her hesitation was fulfilling his rather low expectations of her competence in this situation. Her back stiffened and she glared at him.

"You're looking fatigued, Captain Thorpe. Perhaps it would be wise to retire someplace less hazardous. I should not like to see you harmed because you took foolish risks."

She went back to work with aggressive energy, hearing Jordan's chortle and a sound from Marten that was anything but happy.

The members of the knacker gang donned their gear quickly. Even their eyes were covered, the majicked material becoming transparent to the wearer. The group of forty looked very much like a mob of thieves about to go on a spree. Lucy was the last to dress, skeptical of its ability to protect her. Becoming aware of Marten's appraising gaze, she pulled the garments on, feeling only a faint tingle of majick. She frowned, looking at Jordan.

"Meris's tears—what has it done to me?"

"It's deadened certain reactions so that you can think. Don't you feel well?"

She considered herself. In fact she felt energized. The sensation of being drunk had passed, and now she felt clearheaded and calm. Nor did she have a tormenting headache from being inside the majicked building and wearing the bespelled clothing.

"I'm well enough," she answered finally.

The next order of business was to supply the knacker gang with weaponry and collection containers. A selection of clubs, hooked poles, nets, mesh scoopers, and various ropes hung on racks along the north wall. The containers were piled from smallest to largest, ranging in size from small jars to shipping containers designed to carry furniture or carriages. Lucy hoped the latter would not be necessary; she didn't know if the knacker gang could handle *sylveth* spawn that big without a majicar's help. Everyone chose what weaponry they wanted and lugged a pile of containers out to the beach in readiness.

Lucy searched the black brine. The waves rose black and thunderous, capped with white foam. Half a league away the watery green lights of the Pale bisected the strait. Beyond them *sylveth* coiled like a predatory mass of shining sea snakes. It spread through the strait, besieging Merstone Island, preventing the majicars from coming to help the body collection. Lucy glanced at the knacker gang, like assassins in the gloom. There didn't seem to be nearly enough of them.

"Meris be merciful."

Sylveth was the source of Crosspointe's great wealth and power, but it was also its curse. In its terrible raw form, it flowed through the Inland Sea, snaring ships in its snaking coils and streaking nets. Anyone it touched, it *changed*. Usually in dreadful, monstrous ways. Ships had been known to transform into living beasts. They dived out of the skies and surged from below.

Lucy tried to imagine what it would be like to be aboard a ship that suddenly turned into a vicious sea beast. To become your erstwhile ship's first meal, or else be dumped into the *sylveth* and be transformed yourself. She scowled. It was too early in the season for *sylveth* to swarm Crosspointe. There was still another seven sennights until Chance, when *sylveth* ruled the sea and winds, spreading its taint from shore to shore. Protected by the Pale, Crosspointe was the only safe harbor on the Inland Sea.

The problem was, the Pale kept the *sylveth* out, but not the things it spawned.

It was not long until the shredded bodies of the dead began to wash up onto the headland shore. At first they were just normal body parts. An arm, a hand, a head, a pair of barefoot legs. The wounds were ragged, meaty, and bloodless. It was difficult to connect the pieces with the idea of a man or woman. Most crew contingents were comprised of one or the other, superstition arguing against two sexes sharing the same ship. The *Vacubyr*, the last to fall prey to the knucklebone weir, had been crewed by women.

The knackers collected up the remains quickly and efficiently. They put them in sacks and bins to be sorted out later. Lucy edged closer; to help or just to witness the tragedy, she didn't know. Jordan grabbed her arm.

"Keep back. Let them do their job. It's going to get plenty ugly soon. You're going to want your strength when it does."

He was right. Before long, things got worse—the collection turned to capture.

Things swam on the inky waves. They came crawling over the sand. Shambling, wriggling, shivering, twitching, scrabbling, burrowing. Tiny, like fleas. Bigger, as large as a cow, and every size in between. None were alike. Lucy's stomach flipped as she watched. Fear razored through her lungs. Beside her, Jordan and Marten tugged on their masks, securing them. She checked her own, yanking it down more firmly. She made sure her gloves and stockings overlapped her sleeves and the cuffs of her trousers.

The knackers formed two loose lines on the beach. As the creatures came on shore, the hunters ran to catch them. No one wanted even one to get loose in Crosspointe. It happened, of course. Inevitably the creatures washed ashore from the open sea, wreaking certain havoc until they were captured or killed. A constant patrol was kept against them. Even now the waves were carrying spawn into the harbor. The cordon that kept salvagers from making off with what they'd rescued would hopefully keep the spawn from reaching ships or shore. It was more difficult to stop them in the water, which was why Brithe and likely every other majicar on the mainland had gone to help. Ordinarily, they would be stationed all along the beach and across the harbor. But the majicars were trapped on Merstone and no spells could keep boats safe from a *sylveth* tide.

More and more of the creatures came. Some were near helpless on land, seemingly without bones to animate their limbs. Others were fast. Some shook out wet wings and leaped into the air. The knackers swooped with clubs, hooks, nets, and scoopers or grappled with their gloved hands. The latter made Lucy gasp, her stomach knotting with fear.

When the knackers called for the majicked crates and caskets to contain their captured prey, Jordan and Marten responded. They waded into the fray, helping to shove the unwilling creatures into the containers. The lids were made so that anything inside couldn't escape.

A knacker ran past Lucy, grabbing a scaly thing that rippled and bobbled flaccidly over the ground. It had a long tail that twisted and bent like something sentient. The knacker grabbed the prehensile appendage and yanked the thing into the air. A sound erupted from it, almost beyond hearing—a noise like a rumble from deep underground.

Lucy saw the knacker's lips move as he called for help. But everyone else was busy fighting their own battles. She reacted without thinking, snatching up a casket and circling it with her arms, holding it tight to her stomach. She dashed forward. The rain at least had done that much—it hardened the sand, making it easier to walk on.

The creature dangled from the knacker's fist by its tail. Now that she was close, she could see that the scales were really eyes. The hair on her arms and legs prickled. Thousands of human-shaped eyes in all shades of green, brown, blue, and gray blinked and rolled. Its skin was smooth and pink, freckled with glowing white spots. Suddenly it began to pulse and roil, as if its skin contained something fighting to escape. Fighting *hard*. Lucy took an involuntary step back.

The knacker was less cautious than she and retained his grip, though it was a struggle. The beast was heavy and difficult to hold, jerking from side to side, so that he nearly dropped it. Lucy thrust forward, remembering the container she held. She almost lost her nerve when the tail began to shrink and a dozen nubs appeared on one side of its flabby body. These quickly grew into thin legs, each ending in a limp human-shaped hand, as flaccid as the rest of its body.

The knacker gripped the stump of the tail and pushed the creature at the mouth of the casket. Lucy held it tight under one arm, reaching out to help. She grasped one of the limp arms and was surprised at the strength she felt beneath its skin. It pulled against her. Wicked talons erupted from the fingertips. Startled, Lucy almost let go. Her hand shook and she steadied it with an act of will. All the creature's eyes seemed to be looking at her. They blinked separately from one another, resembling a flurry of carrion-moth wings.

Then with a speed that left her breathless, spines erupted from the eyes. They launched like porcupine quills, ratcheting hard against the black protective clothing. The knacker yelled and jerked as several found the flesh of his arm, exposed in the struggle. Instantly the spines drilled into his muscle. He swore, plucking at them with his free hand, still holding tight to the creature's stubby tail with the other. As fast as the spines had erupted, now long pointed tongues wriggled out in their place. They flickered in the air as if seeking.

Lucy could see the moment they honed in on the bloody arm of the knacker. The creature lunged and she

almost lost her grip on its leg. Or arm—whatever it was.
She saw the tips of several tongues lap at the free-
flowing blood. The eyes all spasmed wide and then filled
with a brilliant orange color that seemed to glow in the
storm gloom. Simultaneously the movement inside
turned frenzied. The body of the creature swelled, its
skin stretching like a bellied sail.

Panic seized Lucy as the bloated beast wrenched
harder, its strength seeming to double. She yanked it
toward the mouth of the cask. The knacker stepped sideways so that he faced Lucy with the twisting creature
between them, and gave a strong push. The *sylveth*
spawn had grown nearly larger than the cask. They battered it with the flats of their hands until they forced it
inside. The lid snapped shut and Lucy staggered backward, relief coursing through her. The knacker dropped
to his knees, clutching his arm. The spines of the creature had nearly disappeared into his flesh, which was
turning purple and black.

Suddenly Jordan and Marten were there. Jordan
grasped the wounded man under the arms and dragged
him back toward the shed row. Marten took the cask
from Lucy and stood it with the other full containers
before dragging her away from the capture lines. His
hand on her elbow was firm and brooked no argument.
Not that Lucy wanted to argue. Still she looked behind
her. This was her job. She ought to be out there.

Jordan settled the knacker against the shed, examining
his arm. The wounded man's face was rigid and pale.
He rocked back and forth, bouncing his head against the
wall as he moaned and whined in desperate pain. As she
drew closer, Lucy realized that the spines had entirely
disappeared under his skin. Worm-shaped bits of white
and red bone and marrow shavings curled from the
holes. Lucy pressed a hand to her mouth as bile flooded
her tongue. The knacker's legs spasmed and kicked,
tears and snot running down his cheeks and chin.

Jordan and Marten exchanged a somber look. Marten

nodded, turning Lucy away. Sudden understanding hit her. She jerked back around. Jordan had his cutlass in his hand.

"It has to be done," Marten said close to her ear, gripping her arm again. "We don't have time to get him in a box."

The truth of his words was undeniable. A majicar could have stopped the spines from burrowing clear through his body and dispersed the poison already blackening his hand. But they didn't have one. And there was no time to fetch a spawn container. It had to be done. But Lucy wasn't going to hide.

She thrust Marten's hand aside and sank down beside the injured man. He was shuddering, his teeth rattling together. His eyes rolled back in his head. Lucy started to pull her mask off, but Jordan shook his head in warning. She complied with his silent order.

Marten and Jordan pulled the knacker down onto his back and extended his injured arm across the wind-scoured rock shelf, rolling up his sleeve. The cutlass wouldn't cut through the protective shirt. The putrid blackness had nearly reached his elbow. Above it was a livid ring where the flesh puffed slightly. Marten yanked off his belt, sliding it around the knacker's bicep and tightening it down to cut off circulation. He glanced at Lucy, his mask hiding his expression. Her teeth ground together. No doubt he fretted she'd faint in the middle of this butchery. Deliberately she moved around so she held the injured man's head in her lap. She clutched him tightly, praying to Chayos that Jordan's first stroke would cut cleanly through the arm.

Marten straddled the knacker, pinning his right hand and lying across his chest to immobilize him before nodding to Jordan. The other man swung his blade down in a smooth arc. The knacker's body jerked and he screamed, spittle spraying from his mouth as the cutlass bit deep into his flesh. Blood vessels burst in the whites of his eyes. His body heaved, his heels thumping wildly on the ground. Marten struggled to hold him still. Jordan didn't pause, but raised his sword again. Lucy couldn't help but watch in hypnotized horror as blood trickled down the steel blade. Again he struck, this time cleaving through the bone and striking rock. Jordan flung his sword to the ground and snatched the severed arm in his gloved hands, running to toss it into a collection crate as the knacker's heart's blood spurted and pooled on the rock.

The wounded man thrashed beneath Marten. His screams were awful. Lucy clutched his neck. Rocks filled her throat and tears rolled down her cheeks. She wanted to stanch the flow of blood or offer better comfort. Do something, *anything*, to actually help.

A sudden memory galvanized her. Abruptly she scrambled up. She ran past Jordan to the black building. Just inside the door was a tall cabinet. Lucy grasped the two handles and yanked the doors wide. The shelves were lined with jars, bandages, vials of powders and pills, blankets, bags, and pegs holding different-colored stone talismans on leather thongs.

Lucy snatched up a jar with a red wax seal, a stack of bandages, and a yellow talisman. Hugging the items to her chest, she fled back out into the wind. She returned to find Jordan tying off the wound with a strip of cloth torn from his waistcoat. Marten had taken Lucy's place by the head of the knacker, who twitched weakly against his agony. The pool of blood had spread, salted with blown sand. Lucy stumbled, her eyes snagging on it. *There was so much.*

Tearing her gaze away, she fell to her knees next to Jordan. She passed him the jar. As he cut away the sealing wax, she unraveled the bandages. Jordan held the jar while Lucy dug her fingers into the cold, sticky ointment inside. A businesslike detachment overtook her as she quickly slathered the green goo on the stub of the knacker's arm. He moaned, a spasm rippling down his body. Lucy ignored it, daubing more on before wrapping the wound tightly with bandages. When she was through, Marten lifted the knacker's head to help her ease the amulet around his neck.

Within an instant, the man slumped against the ground, unconscious. Lucy sat back on her heels with a heavy sigh. He probably wouldn't live. But the amulet would keep his body from shutting down in reaction to the injury and help him fight any remaining poison. The ointment and bandages would keep him from losing any more blood and prevent infection.

Jordan and Marten carried the man back to the salvage shed to put him in the care of Hig. Deliberately she adjusted her mask, gloves, and socks and returned to the beach. When the two men returned, Jordan offered her another drink of Meris's tears. Lucy refused.

The capture continued until nearly dawn. Lucy left a handful of knackers on the beach to guard against any stragglers and ordered the captured *sylveth* spawn to be hauled back to the black shed. Inside, she saw to the wounds of the other knackers. Several had lost their masks in a particularly difficult capture. Lucy had to order a man's ear removed and a woman had breathed in something that was colonizing her insides. Threads of gray unwound like spiderwebs beneath her skin and her two front teeth had lengthened into tusks. With a cold dispassion, Lucy settled a black amulet around the infected woman's neck and ordered her sealed inside one of the black crates. The amulet would hopefully slow or stop the changes to her body until the majicars could have a look at her, and the box would contain the trouble if not.

Next Lucy passed out vouchers authorized with her seal, thanking each of the exhausted, grim-faced volunteers. When all the capture gear had been returned and everyone cleared out, Lucy resealed the black building. Dawn was just breaking as Jordan and Marten accompanied her back to the busy salvage shed. Despite their company Lucy felt remote and alone. The horrors of the night gnawed at the edges of her calm, and exhaustion dragged on her. But she had no intention of letting either man see her weakness, and outwardly adopted a mask of brisk control.

Jordan interrupted her when she turned to bid him good-bye, his voice rough and worn.

"Surely you aren't returning to that mess?" He gestured at the bustle inside. "You need to rest."

Lucy lifted one shoulder. "Until my replacement arrives, there is work to be done."

In truth she didn't want to go home, didn't want to sleep. Or dream. And most especially she didn't want to suffer Blythe's smothering ministrations and questions. She sighed. She had to have a lady's maid; her mother insisted it was only proper. Lucy had settled on Blythe, who was an outspoken cousin several times removed. When she'd hired the other woman, Lucy had been explicit and specific. She wanted a lady's maid who would help her dress, oversee the running of her home, and leave her alone as much as possible. But Blythe was like a dog with a meaty bone. And Lucy was the bone.

"Try not to push yourself too hard. I've got to shove off. They'll let us cross the cordon soon, and we're due to pull the *Firewind*'s rigging. Marten, are you coming?"

"Aye. I want a bed and meal myself."

Jordan pushed his draggled hair from his forehead. He was gritty and dirty. He glanced up. "It'll be fair weather today."

Lucy followed his gaze. The clouds were breaking apart, and the rain was a bare sprinkle. The wind had lightened considerably, though the sound of it still roared in her ears.

A clatter of wheels and horses' hooves signaled the arrival of a four-horse barouche. The seal of the customs service was emblazoned on the door. The carriage pulled up, the footman dropping off from behind and hurrying to let down the stair. A bald, portly man in a saffron surcoat that matched Lucy's emerged. A fringe of gray hair circled the back of his head, and his round face was clean-shaven with drooping eyes and a plump, moist smile.

"Ah, Lucy, my dear! You look dreadful."

"Hello, Henry. It's very good to see you."

He shook out the folds of his cloak. "Right, then. You're relieved. The carriage will take you home. Report to Alistair the day after tomorrow—after you *rest*." His voice mocked the last word. He'd overseen knacker gangs before. There was no such thing as rest after that, only nightmares and cold sweats. He scuttled inside without waiting for her reply.

"Well then, I suppose I am going home. In high style, it appears," she said sardonically, gesturing at the coach. The carriages were usually reserved for higher-ranking customs officers. She'd ridden in them occasionally, but only as a guest of someone else. She thought of the long trip back into Sylmont and the soft cushions within. She went and fetched her satchel and said good-bye to Hig. He merely grunted and shooed her away. Outside only Marten waited for her.

"Miss Trenton, I hope I might impose on you—would you allow me to accompany you back into Sylmont?"

Lucy looked at him in annoyance. For all the damage the wind and sand had done to his clothing, face, and hair, he still looked ridiculously unruffled and collected. She, on the other hand, felt sand scraping in every crease and crevice of her body, and expected she looked like a rag doll tossed in the rubbish heap after years of hard use. She wanted to refuse him and ride away in solitary luxury. She sighed. But she couldn't. His help in the night had been too valuable.

"Very well," she said, and went to get in.

He followed her, settling on the opposite bench. Lucy took a folded blanket from the stack on the seat and spread it over herself before leaning into the corner and closing her eyes as the carriage jolted into motion. She started when she felt his hands on her arms. Marten finished tucking the blanket around her, his dark eyes glinting at her obvious annoyance.

"Are you quite comfortable?"

"Quite. But there's no need to make idle conversation. I surely do not expect it."

"You are a bit irritable, though," he said, tilting his head. "But then it's been a difficult night. I suppose you are to be forgiven."

Lucy stiffened, anger heating her up faster than the blanket. She caught herself before she retaliated. That would only feed his insolence. She forced herself to relax back against the cushions and feigned a yawn, covering her mouth with her hand.

"Since it is highly unlikely that we will find ourselves in company with one another again, let us end this acquaintance on a quiet note. Wake me when we arrive back in Sylmont, won't you?"

And with that, she closed her eyes and pretended to sleep. But in the quiet of the carriage, her eyes closed, she again became sickeningly aware of the cipher's cold weight on her arm. *Stupid, stupid, stupid!* Why had she gone searching for it? For certain death? But she knew why. And in the silent darkness of the carriage, she could not run away from the memories. She was trapped between Marten's mocking curiosity and her own past.

Chapter 5

Lucy had been four years old when she had first realized that unlike anyone else, even majicars, she could detect the presence of majick. No one believed her. They thought she was just trying to get attention with the new baby in the house. She defended herself by pointing out the spells she sensed, but they only laughed. There was so much majick about, spells tucked into every corner and cupboard of Sylmont, that she could point anywhere and likely hit one. Her brothers teased her until she was driven to silence. She promised herself one day she'd prove it to them.

The opportunity came when she was nine. Her father owned a small trading company. Lucy had been chasing after one of the cats who kept the rats at bay through the warehouse when she sensed the stranger's arrival. Majick engulfed him. Its presence was so powerful that it made her eyes blurry and her legs shake. She hadn't known then how to control her reactions, how to tolerate the pain of strong majick. She watched him in awe. Her brothers laughed at her, thinking it was because of his finery and his handsome features. But Lucy couldn't see any of that.

He was a stranger to her family, a stranger to Sylmont. And, she realized gleefully, he was the proof she'd always sought. She could identify on him more than a dozen different spells. Then she didn't know the word for them. She could point each of them out, though not what they did. Her curse was that she could sense majick, but she couldn't tell what any spell was actually for. But that didn't matter. All that was needed was that he would corroborate their existence, and then everyone would know she was telling the truth.

Always cautious, she approached him in a quiet moment when the warehouse was largely deserted. Better to be sure he would cooperate rather than have him deny her and make her the butt of her brothers' bottomless amusement.

"Your pardon," she squeaked, and chastised herself for sounding like such a baby.

He halted, turning, one eyebrow lifted. "Yes, child?"

Lucy swallowed, steadying her breath.

"Come on, then, out with it. What do you want?" He lifted his chin, his nostrils flaring slightly, the corners of his mouth curling downward.

Licking her lips, she said, "The spells you wear—I wondered . . . that is, I hoped—"

She fell silent at the look on his face. Incredulity and something else. Something that made Lucy's skin turn cold. She took a step backward.

He followed. "Where are you going, little girl?" His voice was soft and sibilant.

Lucy stared up at him, fixed in place by the diamond glitter in his eyes. She pressed against a pallet piled high with small crates roped together. He bent over her, bracing his hands on either side of her head. Lucy heard herself whimper.

"Why, my dear, is something the matter?"

He reached up and traced a long white finger down the side of her face, across her cheek, and over her mouth, rubbing back and forth over her lower lip. She felt the tingle of majick through her skin and tasted it on the back of her tongue, like wood ash and wire.

"Now tell me, just how did you know about my ciphers?"

His breath smelled of anise and caraway. A gold pin gleamed on his collar. It was square with a complex design molded into it. Lucy's eyes crept back up to his. Somehow, she knew not to tell him the truth. *He* would believe her. And that would be very bad indeed. She scrambled for something to say, something convincing.

"I . . . I just thought . . . you dressed so fine . . . you just must have majick and my brothers . . ." She halted. His finger didn't leave her lips.

"Yes, your brothers . . . ?"

"They make fun of me and—"

He shook his head. "You are a very bad liar, my dear." His voice hardened. "Tell me how a chubby, snot-nosed, carrot-headed child like you knows about my ciphers. It would serve you to speak quickly, before anyone interrupts us."

His hand crept down lower, beneath her chin. His fingers tightened slowly around her throat. He squeezed, his long, polished fingernails cutting into her skin.

Lucy's panic lit a fire inside her. She wrenched herself from side to side, knocking her head against the crates and kicking out at his knees. He grunted and jerked back as her heavy-soled boot connected.

"You little bitch," he ground out, his hand smashing against her face.

Pain exploded along Lucy's cheek and behind her eye. She sobbed and struggled harder, seeing him cock back to strike again. She kicked out again. He made a high, whining sound and doubled over, clutching his cods as her foot struck. She scrabbled away, dodging in and out of the maze of goods. She ran as fast as she could, to the back of the warehouse and out a side door. She sobbed, her face aching. Her teeth felt loose in her jaw. She pressed the back of her hand against her lips and realized her nose was bleeding.

Behind her she heard the thump of feet and a scrape of metal. Fear streaked through her. She ran along the alley and back to the storage yard and dived into the graveyard of empty shipping containers. She threaded between them, hunching low and swallowing the sobs that tore at her throat. Her heart pounded in her ears so that she couldn't hear anything else.

It wasn't until after dawn the next morning that her brothers found her. She'd taken refuge in a hollow beneath a massive storage container, one large enough to hold two carriages. In the night she'd reached a state of exhaustion where fear no longer suffocated her. But what came then was utter humiliation. That she should have blundered so stupidly. That she'd let him touch her, that she'd just *stood* there and babbled nonsensically and then run away like a mouse from a cat. Her stomach burned with shame. She had wanted so badly to prove her talent, to prove she wasn't lying, that she hadn't considered the danger. And when all was said and done, what was the point? What use was this talent? More like a curse. It gave her headaches and made her sick to her stomach and what was it good for? She couldn't actually do anything majickal.

When they discovered her cowering in her hole, she did not tell them the truth. She told them that a man had attacked her, that she'd run and hidden. It was a dockrat, she said. No, she couldn't remember his face or his clothing. No, she'd gotten away before he'd had a chance to do more than grab and hit her. They believed her lie when they wouldn't believe her truth. They hugged her tight and praised her. She never mentioned her ability to sense majick again. Not to them, not to anyone else.

She did not see the stranger again. She did not learn his name. And she never forgot the ciphers. They became her obsession. And not just any of them. True ciphers. The most dangerous of all.

She sighed, her eyes burning. Then, as now, she'd gotten herself into the mess without any help. Only this time, there was no place to hide, no one to rescue her. She was doomed.

Chapter 6

Lucy thrashed, her legs tangling in the sweat-dampened sheets. She jerked upright, jamming her blankets against her open mouth and biting into the wool to stifle the sounds tearing from her raw throat. Her screams slowly faded to ragged panting. She lowered the blankets, glancing at the door connecting her apartment to the one her lady's maid shared with her husband. Since Lucy had come home Blythe had done nothing but fuss, bemoaning the state of her clothing, skin, and hair. She scrubbed Lucy raw and force-fed her an entire bottle of camphor oil. "In case ye caught yer death, goin' out in the wind and the weather, irresponsible girl."

Lucy groaned, pressing the heels of her hands against her burning eyes. She heard a creak and stiffened. No doubt Blythe was pressing her ear against the door. Thank the gods she'd had sense enough to bolt it.

She swung her legs over the edge of the bed, donning her dressing gown and splashing water on her face. The cold liquid was both shocking and soothing on her hot flesh. She dried herself, glancing at the windows. Moonlight sent a column of light through the open shutters. The remnants of the sunset still gleamed in the western sky. Lucy sighed. She'd hardly slept. But tired as she was, there was little hope she'd start anytime soon. Her stomach rumbled. She went into her sitting room, where a tray of biscuits, cheeses, and roasted nuts waited for her on the sideboard. A majicked pitcher of cold sweet tea sat beside it. Lucy poured herself a glass, savoring it as it soothed her throat. She picked at the food, eating a few bites before the memory of her dream intruded and she lost her appetite.

She paced restlessly. So long as she didn't close her eyes, she could avoid remembering. She took up the candle and wandered into her office. Her desk was made of walnut with slender legs and hammered brass trim. A stack of correspondence sat in the middle. She hadn't had time to deal with it properly in almost a sennight. Now was as good a time as any to do so. Better, in fact. If she was catching up with it, she couldn't think about the *sylveth* spawn.

She tightened her robe and sat in the leather chair, touching her candle to the wicks of the two brass lamps on either corner of the desk. She set aside the newspapers and a rectangular package of books containing copies of the latest novels by Veprey and Amy Eden. She hesitated, tempted to return to her bed and read through the night. The books would be a pleasant distraction. She sighed. The mail first.

There were several letters from her solicitors and eight more from trading consortia looking for investors. Three more wanted to interview her for potential employment, and six more were bills of accounting. She set all of them aside. The pile that was left included a thin note from her best friend and business partner, Sarah Nettles, two with the delicate handwriting of her mother, two with no return address and a bold script that she didn't recognize, and a dozen others from friends and family. Lucy smiled at them with tired pleasure. A feast to be savored.

She started with Sarah's note. It was written in a quick, shorthand style, asking Lucy to come round as soon as she could. They were partners in Faraday, a chic pawnshop on fashionable Glamley Street. Lucy was a silent partner, far preferring that Sarah have the responsibility of running the place. It was a well-wrought partnership. Lucy's only obligation was inspecting and

evaluating the goods that people brought in to pawn. It
wouldn't do to be caught selling smuggled or stolen
merchandise.

Lucy set the letter aside with a pleased smile. Sarah
was marvelous company, with a ready wit and a sharp
tongue. It was just the thing to take her mind off her
nightmares.

She next took up one of her mother's letters, holding
it gingerly. It was written on peach-colored linen paper,
her writing flowing like water across the page. Her
words, however, were sharply rebuking.

> *Darling Lucy, really dear, I deserve more of your*
> *affection than these little notes you insist on sending*
> *as if I were some shopkeeper. I insist that you attend*
> *your father and me this Emberday for breakfast and*
> *I will accept no more of your paltry prevarications.*

Lucy groaned. There was no way to avoid it. She'd
managed to put her mother off for three sennights,
which was far longer than she'd ever thought she'd get
away with. But the lighter strike would begin on Pescday, which would mean that Lucy would lose most of
her excuses, a fact that her mother doubtless was well
aware of. Without the lighters, ships couldn't get their
cargoes to shore, which meant she would have precious
little to do after that. Damned strike. She rolled her
eyes, sighing heavily.

The day's discussion would no doubt center on Lucy's
marriage prospects, or lack thereof, and what could be
done to increase them. Additionally, there would be tan-
gential forays into the subjects of grandchildren, clothing, cosmetics, and hair. She could hear it now. "Lucy,
dear, you must do something with that tangle. Surely
you don't *like* looking so peculiar. It's rather hideous.
You must let my girl try her hand with you. She's a
miracle worker." And then her mother would be ringing
the bell and Lucy would find herself clenching her hands
around the arms of a chair as her mother's maid combed,

teased, ratted, braided, trimmed, oiled, ironed, and curled her hair into submission. Which would last exactly three heartbeats until she turned her head or nodded or made some other ridiculously extravagant gesture. Then her hair would spring free, stand straight out from her head, and gloat at the lesser beings who'd tried to tame it.

"I can hardly wait," Lucy muttered gloomily.

She picked up her mother's second letter, turning it between her fingers. There was no use ignoring it. Her mother would only send more, and then Emberday would be given over to an endless discussion of callous daughters wounding their mothers by their cold, unfeeling behavior. Lucy broke the seal on the letter, unfolding it and flattening it on the desk.

> *Darling Lucy, I wanted to remind you of the Summerland's Ball this Pescday. I know Caroline sent you an invitation, but since you have a lamentable habit of forgetting to open your correspondence in a timely fashion, I thought it prudent to remind you. Wear your blue silk taffeta gown with the crystal beads. I shall send a note to Blythe to get it ready in case you forget. I shall look forward to hearing all about it on Emberday.*

Lucy tossed down the letter and opened the left drawer of her desk that contained stacks of unopened envelopes. She pawed through them, finding the large cream-colored invitation bearing the Summerland's ostentatious crest in silver, red, and green foil. She pulled it out and slit it open. Dinner at nine, dancing until dawn, then a few hours' sleep before she scurried to her parents' house for breakfast. She would almost rather be dipped in *sylveth*.

She put the invitation on top of her mother's letters and pushed them to the front of the desk. She next picked up the first of the two letters lacking return addresses. The paper was heavy, expensive parchment sealed with a dollop of yellow wax that gave no clue to the sender. The round splotch contained only a plain circle impressed into it, as if from a ring. Curiously, she broke the wax and lifted the flap, unfolding the letter.

She scanned the lines. Her body clenched so tight it was hard to breathe. The paper fell onto the desk, shock making her fingers spasm. She groped after it, picking it up clumsily and reading it again.

Her gaze dropped to the cipher wrapped around her arm. She'd managed to push the thought of it to the back of her mind, behind the distracting horror of her nightmares. She traced the *sylveth* links with her forefinger. Just like Jordan, Blythe had been unable to see it. Nor had it yet begun to have any effect on Lucy. Its threat hung over her heavily. Yet astonishingly, at the moment it was not the greatest of her worries.

She reached out shaking fingers to turn up a lamp. She hardly noticed as smoke purled out the glass chimney. Even with the brighter light, the words remained obstinately the same.

There was no salutation, no signature. Only four boldly scribbled lines: *Naughty girl. You have a secret. I know what it is. What will you do to keep it?*

Lucy turned the parchment over. There was nothing to say who'd sent it. It had no postmark, which meant it had been hand delivered. What did he mean? What secret?

And then she knew.

Her eyes closed. Her fingers curled into fists. Her stomach burned.

Someone had found her out. Her ability to sense majick.

She sucked a sobbing breath. Dear Meris—no!

But then, as quick as certainty had lanced through her, doubt sealed the wound. How would anyone know? And why would anyone care? It was a peculiar ability, with little use that she could fathom. Except that it had enabled her to find her collection of true ciphers.

Realization struck a blow to her stomach, emptying

her lungs. Her collection of true ciphers. That truly was her dark secret. And if anybody discovered them . . .

The law decreed that true ciphers must be turned over to the majicars. It was a toothless law, for the most part. Anyone who found a true cipher didn't know it unless it attached, in which case he had worse problems than the law.

Lucy balled her fist, the cipher chain obstinate against the flex of her arm. It had not attached to whoever packed it in its box. It had waited for someone particular . . . for *her*. She refused to pursue the thought, fearing what it might mean. She should go see the majicars, ask them to remove it. *And likely end up a greasy black spot on the ground.* Lucy had never heard of anyone surviving an attempt to detach a true cipher. Of course few survived the playing out of the spell either.

Rumor had it that anyone desperate enough to go to Merstone Island for help never returned, not because the attempt at detaching failed, but because the majicars didn't even try. Not only did a removal usually mean the victim's horrible death, but it also meant the destruction of the cipher, making it useless for study. The majicars hungered for anything that helped them understand how Errol Cipher had accomplished his great majicks. Everything he'd done was a mystery. No one now knew how to construct the wards of the Pale, or the many other wonders he'd accomplished. He'd left behind no journals, no instruction books. So when some poor sot wearing a true cipher came begging for help, the majicars merely waited until it ran its course and then salvaged it.

Lucy not only had a true cipher wrapped around her arm; she had seven more in a secret vault drilled into the rocky bones beneath her house. All of which made her a traitor in the eyes of the law. And somebody knew it.

She picked up the second letter. Her stomach curling, she cracked the seal and unfolded the page. Again there was no salutation or signature. Just a bald beginning and abrupt ending.

Clever girl, to assemble so many treasures without getting hurt. One for each day of the sennight. Tell me, do you fondle them in the dark? Wet your thighs at the risks you take? Dangerous lovers. Are you brave or just suicidal? I wonder. I can be dangerous also. Perhaps one night you shall pet me. Or maybe I will pet you. Would you purr for me, clever kitten? I would like that. But I digress. I hope you understand me now. If you want to keep your secret, you will honor my request when it comes. Expect to hear from me soon.

Lucy read the letter half a dozen times, her stomach corkscrewing tighter and tighter. She was being blackmailed. It had to have something to do with customs. Or being a member of the royal family. It didn't matter; she couldn't—she *wouldn't*—do anything that harmed either one.

Oh, no? a niggling voice mocked. *Consider the price.*

It was steep. And it was not only she who would pay it. If she was prosecuted for being a traitor, every inspection she'd ever done, and every shipowner, captain, mate, seaman—they'd all become targets of suspicion. And her family . . . She dragged her fingernails across her scalp, pressing her skull between her palms. For more than fifty years the royal family had been in Chancery, all the Rampling wealth tied up in the lawsuit, which was why every member of the monarchy worked for a living. There was no money to keep them otherwise. The suit had been brought by those who would see the Ramplings pried off the throne, the hatred running deep in some quarters. If she was accused of being a traitor, her parents and brothers would be the first to pay. But the taint would spread quickly. Too many family members held positions of trust throughout the government and trade. Everyone would come under suspicion. All because of her. Maybe that was the point—a new way to discredit the royal family.

Lucy slouched in her chair, tipping her head back and

feeling the walls closing in on her. She drew a deep breath.
She'd always prided herself on being insignificant—a
minor royal. And yet she could single-handedly spread
an infection across the family and the crown that would
not easily be eradicated, if at all.

She picked up the two letters and read them again.
She couldn't give in, whatever he asked for. Succumbing
would only encourage him to demand more. But neither
could she let him expose her. Her gaze snagged on the
second letter with its crude insinuation. Her ears burned.
He was mocking her. She was no beauty and no prude—
she'd had her share of lovers, had grown up on the
docks, where whores plied their trade in rowboats and
alleys. Pet him indeed!

She thrust to her feet, crushing the letters in her hand.
There was one way to sour the bastard's game. He
thought he knew her. He thought she'd do anything to
protect her collection. He was wrong. Lucy looked at
the cipher on her arm. She'd turn her ciphers and herself
over to the majicars before she'd let this shag-bag twist
her around his finger.

Eventually exhaustion overtook Lucy and she crawled
into bed after having devised and dismissed a dozen
plans to deal with her blackmailer. When she woke just
before dawn, she knew that she needed advice. And
there was only one person she could trust. That is, if
Sarah didn't kill her first.

She sat up blearily, wincing at the sound of her joints
cracking as she stretched. Anyone who heard that would
think she was a hundred years old. Today, she felt like
it. With a loud sigh, she kicked off her bedclothes and
went to unbolt the door separating her apartment from
Blythe's chamber. Hardly had she slid the bolt back
when the door was flung open and her lady's maid
hurled herself into the room.

"Well, then, ye've woken, have ye? And keepin' me up
all night worryin'. Don't think I didna hear ye trampin'
about like a cat in a cage. Ye ought to be ashamed of

yerself, not a single thought to anybody's feelins but yer own."

She ratcheted out these words while straightening the bed and then attacking the fireplace. Blythe was shorter than Lucy, and much slighter, with pale brown hair and dainty hands and feet. She moved quickly and deftly, like a bird. But she was no songbird. She was a magpie, Lucy thought grumpily. Sharp, pushy, and domineering.

She swept up the ashes and poured coal in the grate with irate vigor. "Cook made a lovely dinner and ye bein' awake and didna even come out of yer hidey-hole. Poor thing was devastated."

Lucy snorted. Janet didn't care whether Lucy ate her food or not. She cooked for her husband—the butler—and their four children. Lucy was just the excuse for using better-quality ingredients. She interrupted her maid's harangue.

"As soon as possible, I will be leaving to visit Sarah at Faraday."

"Might early, isn't it? Darker than Hurn's own shadow out there."

"Sarah doesn't sleep."

"Ye might be interruptin' a private moment."

"I might."

"Ye wouldna like it if she interrupted ye with one of yer gentleman callers. Not that ye'd give her much chance. Canna remember the last time ye had a caller."

"I've been busy," Lucy said. In fact, she avoided bringing lovers home, preferring by far to keep them away from Blythe, who would report all the details back to Laura Trenton. Not that Lucy'd had time, interest, or energy for any recently. "If you're quite done with that fire, perhaps I could dress and have breakfast." She shivered in the chill and reached for her dressing robe.

Blythe sniffed, bustling around to snatch the garment. She held it for Lucy to step into, then buttoned it down the front. Lucy sighed and waited. Blythe had a very clear opinion about her job duties and Lucy was not allowed to interfere or avoid them, no matter how hard she tried.

A knock at the door signaled the arrival of breakfast. Blythe answered, taking the broad tray into the sitting room and setting it on the table beside the remnants of the previous night's snacks. Lucy sat with Blythe opposite. The other woman slapped at Lucy's hands as she would have tried to uncover the dishes.

"Stop that. Let a body do her work."

"That's not what I pay you for."

"No? I'm yer companion and lady's maid. I donna wake at this hour for my own health."

"And I have told you a hundred times to go ahead and sleep, that I could manage very well on my own."

Blythe snorted. "As if I'd go shirkin' my duties."

Lucy stirred a dollop of honey into her tea and slathered butter on her toast. "I hired you because my mother would not stop pestering me about my complete inability to care for myself, and was on the verge of hiring someone intolerable to hound me every waking moment. What I pay you for, and what you consistently refuse to do, is live your own life in my home under the guise of being my companion and lady's maid."

"What kind o'woman would I be if I took yer money without doin' a lick of work? Besides, ye need lookin' after."

"I am perfectly capable of taking care of myself."

"Yer mother donna seem to think so."

"My mother hardly thinks I can use a spoon without choking myself. If you want something to do, help Janet in the kitchen or visit the almshouses. Better yet, why don't you and James start a family—have a dozen or two. That might keep you occupied and out of my hair."

"Yer mother'd only find somebody else."

"I'll deal with that coil of *sylveth* when I come to it. If you want to be paid for doing something for me, then by all means, let it be for having children and distracting my mother."

" 'Twould certainly be less aggravatin' work," Blythe said tartly, and stood up. "Now, better be quick about things. I'll have Jamie flag a footspider afore he's off to the docks."

James was a rigger. Every ship coming into port before the Chance storms had to be stripped, its yards, masts, and cordage taken down, overhauled, and stowed until the ship was fitted out again. Like most riggers, James had been a sailor, retiring once he'd been "spliced" to Blythe. He lived in Lucy's house, performing maintenance in exchange for room and board. He was a quiet man, and patient, as he'd have to be married to Blythe. Perhaps Lucy should speak to *him* about starting a family. . . .

She daydreamed about a swarm of little Blythes carrying three-pronged spears. They surrounded their mother, poking and prodding until she tore at her hair and screamed, while Lucy sat in quiet solitude in her own quarters, untroubled by the ruckus. She smiled and drained her tea, burning her tongue on the hot liquid.

When Blythe returned, she helped Lucy wriggle into her corset. Lucy held the bedpost, bracing her legs wide, as Blythe snugged it. It was not so tight she couldn't breathe or walk briskly, but was nevertheless a nuisance. Still, it did good things for her figure, pushing up her ample breasts and thinning her waist. Next Lucy stepped into thin, close-fitting gray wool trousers and allowed Blythe to help her on with the overdress. It was made of Nardian *tetch*, a soft, durable material that did not readily show wear. Slits ran up the fronts of both thighs to her hips, allowing her free movement. Burgundy and gold embroidery circled the cuffs and square neckline in a wide band. Blythe laced it up the back. Lucy bent and slid on her midcalf boots. She put on her earrings and applied her cosmetics lightly while Blythe braided her hair, looping it up on her head in a fashionable, though sturdy, coif. It could withstand sea winds and rain.

"Ye say ye donna need me, but I'd like t'see ye manage that on your own," Blythe said smugly as she set aside the hairbrush.

Lucy examined herself in the mirror. The twilight purple of the overdress was a good color for her, making her skin look fresh instead of sallow, and complementing her fiery hair. Lucy made a face at herself and swung her blue wool cloak over her shoulders.

"I didn't say I don't need you. I said I wanted you to listen to me and stop hovering," Lucy pointed out.

She left Blythe and went into her office to retrieve the two blackmail letters from her lockbox. She slid them into a pocket inside her satchel and slung it over her shoulder beneath her cloak. She returned to her bedroom to collect her gloves, catching sight of her customs seal sitting in a small crystal bowl on her nightstand. Beside it was her pouch of seal blanks. She stopped short and stared. No—it was impossible. She went to the other side of her bed and picked her seal up, turning it over in her hand.

"What's the matter, then? Thought ye was in a hurry."

Lucy hardly heard Blythe's pointed remark. Her fingers closed around the cool metal. How could she have forgotten to lock it up? She scowled, trying to remember returning home after the salvage. It was murky. No one else could take the seal from her waist, any more than one could remove her royal necklace. She *must* have taken it off. But she'd never leave it just sitting out. It didn't matter that no one else could use it—that it was majickally keyed to respond only to her. She always, *always*, secured it under lock and key. If somehow someone got ahold of it and turned its majick—it could be used to smuggle goods.

Wordlessly, she returned to her office and locked up the seal and pouch of blanks. One little salvage and *sylveth* spawn collection, and her mind turned to bread pudding. Well, she had better pull herself together. She couldn't fight her blackmailer with soggy bread.

Chapter 7

The morning was drizzly, the air smelling of salt brine and coal smoke. The stooped footspider hauling her cart was of middling years and balding. His green and white striped uniform was grimy and damp. James handed Lucy into the cart, giving the man Sarah's address. He was stronger than he looked, and faster. He trotted off at a sharp pace.

The city was already bustling, even as the sun streaked the eastern sky orange and pink. Servants scurried along the streets carrying baskets and carts, and the farther Lucy descended from her home in Blackstone into the center of the city, the more the savory scents of cooking meats, breads, and spices filled the air. Lights winked to life in black first-floor windows, and high up in Rampling Castle, torches bobbed and weaved along the battlements as guards made their dawn rounds.

The footspider began climbing up into Salford Terrace, where Glamley Street ribboned along the top of Harbottle Hill. It was a mere stone's throw from the castle's curtain wall, and housed the finest shops in Sylmont. The storefronts gleamed with pink-veined marble, sleek alabaster, precious metals, and sparkling glass. *Sylveth* lamps glowed softly from the limbs of arching white-skinned elm trees. Majicars were required to perform three months of service to the crown each year, allowing for expensive public projects like *sylveth* streetlights. Crowding about Glamley Street on the hills north and south were the imposing residences of the wealthy and aristocratic, the roadways guarded and gated to keep the riffraff out. Below was Sherborn Park, an emerald green expanse scattered with pretty woods, gardens, and quiet pools, and crisscrossed by footways and cart paths. There was a hedge maze on the western side, where lovers often met in clandestine assignations.

The footspider jogged through the park, guided by knee-high lights set in copper stalks shaped like sea ivy. There was an arching bridge over the Chigwell River, which really wasn't much more than an exaggerated stream. The bridge emptied onto Glamley Street just a short distance from Faraday. The footspider pulled up front, panting. He bowed when Lucy dropped a silver full moon in his outstretched palm.

"Thanks be, Mistress," he said, pocketing the heavy coin and trotting away before Lucy could change her mind.

FARADAY was inlaid in small flowing brass letters in the archivolt above the polished oak doors of the shop. A pair of *sylveth* lamps inside gold bell shades lit the covered entry. The lamps were almost as expensive as the building had been, but Sarah had claimed that money was drawn to money, and no one was going to visit a shop on Glamley Street if it didn't ooze wealth and refinement. Lucy stood back from them, not entirely trusting the *sylveth* was safe.

Before she could ring the bell, one of the doors swung open to reveal Sarah's butler, dressed in dark blue livery. He ushered her up the stairs, opening the doors of the sitting room and announcing her.

The room was decorated in shades of windstone green and rose pink, with delicate furniture made of ivory-colored wood. Sarah sat on the chaise with a stack of papers, sipping a cup of steaming tea. She was an exotically stunning woman, with ash blond hair, snapping black eyes, and olive-toned skin. She was several inches taller than Lucy, svelte, with full breasts and a narrow waist that had little need of a corset. Her long fall of hair was woven with silver and brilliant blue crystal beads that matched her necklace and bracelets.

"You look appalling," she said, setting aside her papers. "Like you've not been to bed in days. Please tell me a man's the cause of it, not one of your dull books or, worse, work."

Lucy's lips twisted humorlessly. One of the things she liked best about Sarah was her unrelenting honesty. Not that she wasn't capable of tactful deception—she was a businesswoman after all, and no one stroked bureaucrats and temperamental customers like she did. Part of her early education in Esengaile, though she'd never confided exactly what the nature of that education had been.

"Oh, I think it's safe to say a man's at the heart of it."

Sarah's brows arched. "Is that so? And you running out in the chill morning to tell me about it?" She *tsk*ed. "I'm going to have to teach you a few things about the care and feeding of lovers. But I suppose it's too late now. No doubt he's gone off in a fit of pique that his charms could not chain you longer to your bed. Though perhaps that will work in your favor—he'll be despondent at your aloofness and grovel for your attention. Men can be so predictable. But do sit down and tell me all about it."

It wasn't so easy a tale to begin. And Sarah wasn't going to like hearing it. Especially the danger Lucy had put both her and Faraday in. Lucy rubbed her hand over her mouth, feeling the heavy cipher cold beneath her sleeve.

"What have you got to drink?"

"I take it you're not asking for a cup of tea," Sarah said drily, and went to the sideboard. She chose a short, bulbous decanter from the dozen collected there, and poured a glass of celery-colored liquid. She handed it to Lucy. "That should cure what ails you."

"What is it?"

"It's Shepet. From Esengaile."

Lucy swirled it. "I've never heard of it."

"That is because it is considered the exclusive drink

of the Drailie, and therefore highly illegal to export from Esengaile."

"Is it?" Lucy lowered the glass without sipping.

Sarah laughed out loud, shaking her head. "Oh, gods of the air, your expression is priceless. Think about it. We are partners in Faraday. You don't think I'd knowingly involve you with smuggling? I know what it would do to your career. And to me, for that matter. I'd be summarily expelled from Crosspointe, thank you very much. So put your mind at ease. While Shepet is illegal to *export* from Esengaile, it is quite legal to *import* it into Crosspointe. A few cases make their way over the Inland Sea each year and I make it a point to lay in a supply. Try it."

Lucy lifted the glass and tasted the liquor. Tart sweetness spread across her tongue, numbing her throat as it trickled down into her stomach. A tingling pleasure unraveled along her nerves. Her legs went soft and she wobbled. A feeling of euphoria spread through her, and she felt a sudden welling of strength and power. Like she was invincible.

Sarah poured herself a glass, returning to her seat and tucking her legs under her. She motioned Lucy to sit opposite.

"Well then? It must be quite a tale for you to be drinking this early in the day. I'm on the edge of my seat. Tell me your darkest, most delicious secrets."

Lucy looked down into her Shepet, then gulped it all before raising her eyes. "I am being blackmailed."

Sarah unfolded her legs and straightened, her eyes narrowing to slits. "Blackmailed? About what? By whom? Explain."

Lucy fumbled in her satchel and handed Sarah the letters. The other woman scanned them, frowning. She looked back up at Lucy.

"Secret? Treasures? What's he talking about?"

Lucy turned the glass in her fingers. "All my life I've been able to sense majick. Doesn't matter how small. I know where it is and how strong the spell."

A sudden chill filled the room. Sarah folded her arms, sitting back. Her face was ominously expressionless. "You can sense majick," she repeated. "And for this you're being blackmailed."

"Yes. No. In part."

"And the other part are these treasures?"

"Yes."

"They must be illegal, these treasures of yours. Else you could not be blackmailed. And you questioned my ethics with the Shepet."

Lucy licked her lips, hearing the murderous edge of Sarah's fury beneath the calmness of her tone. "That's the sum of it."

"What are they?"

Lucy didn't let herself look away. "True ciphers."

Sarah blanched. "You have unexpected depths. And perilous hobbies."

"Mind if I have another drink?" Lucy didn't wait for an answer, pouring herself another glass. She held the decanter up in silent offering.

"Yes, please. The occasion definitely warrants it."

Lucy filled Sarah's glass and returned to her seat.

"So I expect you're telling me all this for a reason."

"I need help. I can't let this overflow onto my family, onto you."

"What do you want me to do?"

"I have to get rid of my collection. Before he asks for whatever it is he wants. If I do his favor, I'll be in his power. And if I don't, he'll expose me. Either way, it will be a disaster. If I get rid of them, I get rid of him."

Sarah's gaze could have cut rocks. Gone was the svelte hostess who'd greeted Lucy's arrival with warmth. In her place was the dragon—all teeth and claws, with a pitiless glint in her eye. This was the Sarah who'd fled Esengaile half-naked and pursued by killers, crossing half a world without money, without food, without shoes. She'd sold herself into indentured servitude for the chance to come to Sylmont. Six years later, she'd clawed her way to freedom and success. And in those six years . . . There was a lot Lucy didn't know about what Sarah had done, what had been done to her, in those years. But one thing she did know—Sarah would kill before she'd allow anyone to steal the home and safety she'd achieved. Even Lucy. Maybe especially Lucy.

"Seems easy enough. Drop them in the harbor."

Lucy rolled her eyes, slapping her forehead with the flat of her hand. "Now, why didn't I think of that? Just walk down to the water and toss them in. Splish-splash." She dusted her hands together. "Easy as buckling my shoes. How stupid of me not to think of it."

"My, my. This is all so unexpected. Since I clearly don't have a full grasp of the situation, why don't you enlighten me? And while you're at it, explain how you expect me to help with your little crisis." Sarah's voice had grown even more frigid, if that was possible.

Lucy grimaced. "Point taken. Let me be more clear. There are seven ciphers. Five are small—an earring, a pipe, a candlestick, a knife, and a pewter mug. The last two are a rather large chair and a flying jib. The second weighs near two hundred pounds. Neither can be easily moved or dropped unnoticed into the harbor.

"My blackmailer must know this—he knows how many I have." She bunched her fist. "How can he possibly have found out? I brought them home one by one. Each was hidden or boxed. The company who dug the vault doesn't know what it was for. I only open it to put acquisitions inside and it's sealed only to me." Lucy's voice rose. She stopped, her lips pinching together, her fingers flexing. She wanted to hit something. She drew a breath, trying to ease the tightness in her chest. Succumbing to panic and fury wasn't going to help.

A moment later she began again, her voice lower, tightly reined.

"This bastard must have people watching me, probably for a long time. If I tried to dispose of the ciphers in the harbor, he'd stop me, one way or another, even if I could toss in the chair and the jib. No, I've got to get rid of them without him discovering what I'm up to."

Lucy sat forward, snaring Sarah's dark gaze.

"Look, I know I'm an ass. I know the danger I've put you and Faraday in, the danger to my family, to customs, to everyone who knows me or who's even met me. It's unforgivable and I don't expect you to try. But the only way to save yourself and Faraday is to help me. And quickly. I don't think I have much time before he makes his demands. If I comply, the result will be the same—he'll have hard evidence that I have broken the law. He'll have me on the rack forever, and that means he'll have all of you too—guilt by association. If we get rid of the ciphers, all of you will be all right."

"Laudable, I'm sure," Sarah drawled, swallowing her Shepet and setting the glass aside with a hard click. Suddenly she shot to her feet, standing over Lucy with her hands akimbo. "By the gods of the air, what could have possessed you? I would have thought you'd have a lot more sense. I *did* think you had more sense."

She abruptly paced away to the other side of the room. Her cheeks flagged red as she spun around and marched back to stand over Lucy. "Is that it? Is that all you're hiding?"

Lucy's eyes dropped and Sarah made a guttural sound deep in her throat.

"Gora!" she swore in her native tongue. "You are really getting on my wick! I swear on Braken's buggered ass that I will slit your throat if you don't come all the way clean!"

Lucy licked her lips. "During yesterday's salvage, I came across another true cipher."

"Another? Just lying about like shit in a chicken yard. Wait—you've got eight of them? What have you been gabbling on about seven for?" Sarah's voice had dropped into utter calm. It was a bad sign. Her threat about slitting Lucy's throat was not entirely an idle one. She was more than capable of it, and it wouldn't be the first time she'd killed. Or even the second.

"Because I don't have the eighth. It has me."

It took a moment for understanding to register. Sarah's eyes widened, her face turning chalky. "It has—? *Gora*," she murmured. "But—you seem—are you all right?"

"A poetic sort of justice, isn't it? So far it doesn't seem to have had any ill effect on me. But then Errol Cipher was a bastard; he liked to torment his victims, let them anticipate what was coming. I expect one of these days my skin will slough off or I'll turn into a spider or have the sudden urge to walk off the top of a mountain." She shrugged. "There's nothing I can do about that."

Inside, there was a part of Lucy that quailed into a quivering ball at what the cipher was going to do to her. But there was another part of her, one that was almost feral in its strength and fury. And that part of her wasn't going to be bullied. She wasn't going to let a nameless, faceless stranger push her around, not the four-centuries-dead Errol Cipher, not the blackmailer. For a moment she was nine years old again, trapped against a stack of shipping crates. She remembered the man's face, its thin, cruel lines, the twisting sneer, the diamond glitter in his sleepy eyes. And his touch. His finger on her face. Iron cold and intimate.

The bottom fell out of her stomach. Could it be? After all these years? She'd exposed her secret talent to him— had he been stalking her since? Lying in wait until he could use her?

Her flesh crawled. A suffocating feeling of helpless desperation swamped her.

Suddenly the cipher on her arm flared with heat. Fire seared up over her shoulder and down to her feet. Lucy convulsed. An agonized animal sound erupted from her lips. She convulsed again and slid to the floor. Her arms and legs jerked and twitched.

Then as quickly as it had begun, the rolling waves of lava abruptly ceased. Lucy slumped, pressing her face against her knees and taking harsh, gasping breaths.

"Lucy? Are you all right? What's happening?"

"Errol Cipher," Lucy rasped, and began coughing.

Sarah rubbed circles in her back, then went to the sideboard and splashed water into a glass. Lucy took it with a shaking hand, the cool liquid soothing her throat. Sarah helped Lucy back up onto the chaise.

"It appears I'm running out of time," Lucy said when she'd regained control of herself. Her skin felt scalded. But if nothing else, the cipher's attack had broken the shackles of her childhood panic. She was grateful for that. Purpose filled her veins. She had to get rid of her collection before either the cipher or the blackmailer destroyed her. She couldn't let her stupidity hurt anybody else.

They spent the morning arguing plans. Nothing seemed feasible. Lucy didn't want to let anyone else take the chance of handling the ciphers. But she was watched.

"It's too risky for you to try dumping the small ones into the harbor," Sarah insisted after Lucy had come back around to it for the third time. "Whoever he has spying on you could be in your home, could be at work, could be the baker or the milliner—anyone. You'd never know if someone had seen you. The next thing you'd know, the majicars and the guard would be arresting you. And even if you weren't caught, that still leaves the last two. I don't suppose they can be burned or chopped to bits to make things easier, can they?"

Lucy shook her head. "Errol Cipher spelled his toys to last. Even things that shouldn't last more than a few days—like flowers or food. There's even a story of a dog that he ciphered. It's supposedly still alive today, barking ceaselessly, stopping only to eat or drink. It never sleeps. Once it attached to an entire family. Until the last of their bloodline is gone, it won't die. Can you imagine?"

"I knew there was a reason I don't like dogs," Sarah said. "But that leaves us no closer to getting rid of your ciphers. I don't suppose you have any secret passages?"

"Not a one."

"We have to disguise them. Make them look like something else, something that doesn't look out of place."

"Like what?"

Sarah was pacing around the room, her brow furrowed. The remains of a late breakfast lay on the table. Lucy was surprised she'd been able to eat. By all rights, she ought to be so tied up in knots that she couldn't swallow a grain of rice. Yet she'd gulped her meal like a stevedore.

Suddenly Sarah whirled.

"Burn your house down."

"What?"

"Burn it down. The house collapses; the ciphers are buried. Easy. If you empty the vault first, even if he digs, he won't be able to find them easily."

Lucy bit down on her objection. It wasn't a bad idea. Except—burn her house down?

"Can we keep that as a last resort?"

Sarah shrugged and went back to pacing. A few minutes later, Lucy had an idea.

"Chance," she breathed, sitting up straight. "That's it! The Harvest of Chayos."

"You want to give your ciphers to Chayos? Not a bad idea, really, but she might have something to say if any of her Delats succumb to them."

"Not if it wasn't one of her carts that picked up the offerings."

"It could work. The carts are big enough, and the city will be mobbed with them for sennights. If we dressed our collectors up as Delats, no one would think it odd."

"Everybody gives to Chayos during the Harvest. Even the Braken-blind sailors who blame Chayos for Hurn and Meris. They don't want to chance her turning her face away and having the wood in their ships fail. I would be just doing as expected, what I do every year. The main question is, can I stall him until the Harvest begins? Decay is sennights away."

"You can always burn your house down."

"Or break a leg."

"Or have yourself kidnapped—hold yourself for ransom, maybe even torture yourself. A public scandal. No one could blame you for not cooperating during something like that."

"I expect the blackmailer might."

"Then burn down the house. Or break a leg. I know some people who would be happy to help with that."

"I thought you'd offer to swing the hammer yourself."

"Oh, I'll be right there."

"I didn't think revenge was your style."

"You should know better than that."

And despite Sarah's bantering tone, Lucy could hear the banked core of fury inside it. Sarah was helping her, but her friend had not yet forgiven her.

Chapter 8

In the night, another gale blew in. Lucy woke to the sounds of the shutters rattling wrathfully. The rain pounded like stampeding horses on the roof tiles. She groaned, pulling her pillow over her head. The weather should not be so violent so soon. There were still more than seven sennights until Chance. Which meant it was going to be a bad season. She pitied the sailors out on the Inland Sea, and sent a prayer to Meris to keep them safe.

With Blythe's peppery companionship, Lucy quickly ate her breakfast. She couldn't help yawning, her jaw cracking. She'd fallen asleep only after hours of tossing and turning. And when she finally did drift off, the stranger from her childhood stalked her through a shadowy dream city crawling with *sylveth* spawn. She woke just as the stranger reached for her throat, spines erupting from his eyes.

Though she wasn't hungry, Lucy forced down her toast and bacon so that her stomach wouldn't growl embarrassingly later. Afterward, Blythe pinned up her hair and helped Lucy dress in a corset, stockings, trousers, chemise, and undertunic. Lucy donned her saffron customs surcoat that made her look sallow and sick. Not that the tight brackets around her nose and mouth and the dark circles under her eyes helped any. She collected her seal and satchel, donning her cloak, gloves, and thick-soled boots.

"Donna be forgettin' the ball tonight. I'll have yer bath ready when ye get home. Donna dawdle," Blythe said, shaking her finger at Lucy. "Yer mother sent a message that Jack will collect ye at eight. Ye donna want to keep yer brother waitin'."

"I will come home promptly at sundown," Lucy promised, feeling slightly less annoyed with the prospect of the ball. She'd not had occasion to see her younger brother for two sennights, and hadn't anticipated seeing him for at least two months more. He was a journeyman shipbuilder with Wright and Rossum out on the south claw. As ships piled into the harbor looking for safety from the coming Chance storms, the dockyards would overflow with ships getting refitted and repaired. Jack would be working every waking moment. Sundown laws didn't apply to shipbuilders. Lucy wondered how he'd managed to get away for the night. She had a dark suspicion that her mother had had something to do with it—her mother and the Summerland's ball, and Lucy's criminal lack of a husband.

Downstairs, James had a footspider waiting. Lucy brushed the water from the seat and climbed beneath the canopy, pulling the oilskin apron over her lap. He set off at a stumbling trot, his head bent into the whipping rain.

The customs docks were a complex system of warehouses and docks where ships could be inspected, their cargoes off-loaded and certified, their passengers interviewed, and their documents evaluated. The footspider dropped Lucy at the base of the pier leading out to the wet docks. Revenue cutters lined the pier like suckling puppies, bobbing on the waves. The wind pushed at Lucy, making it difficult to catch her breath. She hunched over and struggled forward. Spume geysered on either side, dousing her in a frigid, salty shower.

She showed her badge to the charcoal-clad Hornets at the door. Inside, she went first to the expansive mudroom, where she sloughed her dripping cloak and exchanged her boots for one of the dry pairs lining the back of her small closet. She toweled her face and arms dry and dabbed futilely at her hair before dropping the towel in the hamper. She glanced in the mirror. Her kohl had not run. A small grace. Her plump cheeks were scarlet, clashing with her auburn hair. She stabbed her fingers at the loosened tendrils to tuck them back in. They sprang free, ignoring her muttered invectives. At last she gave up, hearing the toll of the sunrise bell. Alistair would be spawning kittens. As far as he was concerned, anyone who wasn't in the customs chambers precisely as the bell started tolling was late.

She collected her satchel and jogged up the circular staircase. Ahead of her ran three others, all wearing the same saffron surcoat. At the third landing, the group crossed a long gallery, dodging around the hodgepodge collection of couches, chairs, and tables that stuffed the waiting area. On the other side was a pair of plain double doors opening into a large rotunda.

At the center of the room was a corralled area full of padded benches. Surrounding it was a series of angular stalls containing tables and stacking bins made of wire and wood. Ringing the walls were large, pie-shaped cubicles, each containing a half-dozen desks littered with papers and ledgers, and tall shelves overflowing with more books and papers jumbled with a varied assortment of objects. The walls rose high into a curved plaster ceiling that was painted blue with patterns in cream, white, gold, and pink. Recessed *sylveth* lights gave the impression of a sunny day, despite the bleak cacophony of the storm outside.

On the opposite wall of the customs roundhouse was a balcony made of scrolled iron. Beneath, a corridor led into the warren of offices occupied by the customs commissioners. Lucy blew out a breath, seeing that Alistair had not yet taken his place at the railing.

She followed the three other inspectors down a narrow walkway to join the milling crowd filling the bull pen. Lucy nodded and gave quick greetings to those around her, but was cut off by Alistair's arrival. He was trailed by two master clerks wearing saffron oversleeves pulled up over their arms to protect their coats. They each carried ledgers that they set on pedestals on either end of the balcony. The sunrise bell ceased its tolling and Alistair lifted his hands to silence the chattering of the gathered inspectors.

"Good morning," he called.

Instantly there was a swell of laughter. Someone made a sound like the howl of the wind, and someone else said loudly, "A good morning if you breathe water!"

Alistair chopped his hand in the air, his mouth pulling inward in a sour pucker. Lucy grinned. He was a man of order and precision. He didn't like anyone upsetting his schedule, even by a few grains of the glass.

"The lighter strike will begin at sundown. We need to make as much use of them as we can today to off-load cargoes. Starting Moonday, we will begin processing ships according to a priority of perishables and foodstuffs, then Crosspointe ships, then all others. Shipowners may choose to hire gangs to replace the lighters, but of course that will require crossing the strike lines, and they will be responsible for any charges stemming from such chaos."

At the word *chaos*, Alistair gave a fastidious shudder. Not for the first time did Lucy wonder about his home. Did he keep his children locked in a bare basement where they could not put grubby finger smudges on his banisters, cups, and mirrors? And how had he ever managed to get his wife with child? There was a certain messiness to the matter that made Lucy wonder how Alistair could possibly keep a stiff rod in the face of such disorder.

She chortled, covering the sound with a cough. Next to her, Stuart Kimple patted her back forcefully. Lucy straightened, waving him off. He bent close.

"Trying to picture the old man havin' a bite of giblet pie?"

Lucy snorted and began to cough again. Stuart thumped her again until she caught her breath.

"Thought so. Hard to imagine it being possible. Still,

he's got five sniveling brats bouncing around the house, and anytime I've seen the missus, she's grinning ear to ear. Old man must let loose his anchor sometime."

Lucy shushed him and turned back to Alistair, who was glaring down at her from his perch. She schooled her features, nodding at him to continue.

"Without the lighters to transfer cargoes to the warehouses, we will have to do most of our inspections aboard ship. This of course will take much longer and be more costly. You will need to be very careful to document your time thoroughly. And do not allow yourself to be rushed. Shipowners will be understandably anxious, as will everyone else downstream. However, it can't be helped. You have a duty to Crosspointe and the crown, and you must fulfill it to the best of your ability. You will be assigned two extra Hornets as well as extra stevedores, box knockers, and clerks. Teams will be stationed here and along the dirtside docks only.

"Collect your documentation and vouchers from my clerks. You may select your extra team members in the south gallery. Be quick, now. Daylight is burning. Miss Trenton, please join me in my office."

Lucy frowned. She didn't want to get the bilge of the extra team members. She sighed. Hopefully Hig would be down there taking charge.

"Hear you took the helm on the salvage," Stuart said as the assembled inspectors milled.

"That's right," Lucy said tersely. The horrors of that night were still too fresh for casual chatter. She didn't know if she'd ever want to talk about it. At least not in the bright light of day without a drink in her hand. And not to someone like Stuart.

"Took one on the bows myself, few years back," Stuart said softly, surprising her. "Knucklebone weir. Not as big as this last one. Storm wasn't as rough either. Thank the gods. Two ships lost. The *Koro* out of Orsage and the *Swift*, one of ours. *Sylveth* tide came right behind." Stuart paused over the memory, his expression suddenly sober. "It was an ugly day," he said at last.

The look Lucy exchanged with him was full of bleak understanding and sympathy. She wondered if the nightmares still pursued him in the night. She thought they probably did.

"They're going to be asking questions. Routine debriefing. Stirs things up, though. Don't let it rattle you. Later, if you want to talk—I'll stand you to a bottle."

Lucy nodded, grateful. Stuart winked and waved, following the other inspectors out of the roundhouse. She had forgotten about the debriefing. The customs official in charge of the initial salvage was required to make a report, verbally and in writing. Lucy made a face. She should have been working on that. No doubt Alistair thought she had it ready. His sense of order was about to suffer a blow. Besides, she'd had other things to worry about. Not that she was going to tell him about any of that.

She wound through the narrow passages until she arrived at the lobby of Alistair's offices. One of his clerks and four scribes were scratching away with their pens. The clerk nodded to Lucy.

"Follow me," she said, guiding Lucy through several more rooms to Alistair's private office. The clerk knocked with ink-stained fingers. The door was swung open, and Lucy stepped inside. Her guide did not enter with her, but pulled the door shut and disappeared.

Lucy was surprised to see that Alistair was not alone. Aside from his senior clerk, who'd opened the door, there were three other people present. They looked at Lucy as if she'd interrupted a heated conversation.

"Ah, Miss Trenton. We've been expecting you."

Alistair was sitting bolt upright in his chair, his pale fingers tapping a staccato pattern on the chestnut wood. His iron gray hair looked as if he'd been running his fingers through it. His mouth was puckered in tight disapproval and his deep-set eyes glittered with anger. Whether it was aimed at her or not, Lucy didn't know. She hesitated, glancing around at the other visitors.

On her left, standing with her back to the bookshelves,

was a round-faced woman. She was shorter than Lucy, with close-cropped, muddy brown hair. Her cheeks were red and her chest rapidly rose and fell, as if she were out of breath. Sitting on the chaise was another woman. She was older than the first, her dyed hair an impossible shade of yellow. She wore it piled up on her head, her high-collared dress lending a severity to her doughy features. Her mouth was set in a hard line, her blue eyes bugging slightly from her head.

The last of Alistair's guests was a ridiculous little man standing by the window. His legs were spraddled wide, his brown eyes stormy. His frothy cravat squeezed his neck like a noose. He wore a brocade frock coat over an embroidered vest. His pocket-watch chain strained across his bulging belly. Blousy pantaloons enveloped his thighs, and his thick calves were sausaged in white stockings. He perched precariously on fashionable high-heeled silver-buckled shoes. He looked like a gaudy rooster on stilts.

"I mean to get to the bottom of this mess, Crummel," he said in a high-pitched voice to Alistair, ignoring Lucy entirely. "I want the truth. Don't care how high I have to go. George Gintley is a friend of mine. Don't think he'll protect you while you cover up for thieves!"

His voice grew louder as he spoke, scraping Lucy's skin like a serrated knife. What was he nattering on about—thieves?

"Please calm yourself, Mr. Higgelsham. Shouting does no good. Now, Miss Trenton, if you will come sit, we will begin."

Alistair gestured at a high-backed chair sitting at the end of his desk and facing outward toward the room. The senior clerk sat ready behind the chair with a lap desk across his knees. Lucy frowned. This looked a whole lot more like a trial than a debriefing. She stepped slowly forward until she was standing beside the chair. She glanced down at Alistair and then back at the three visitors. She did not sit down. A dull ache was beginning at the back of her head. She winced as dull needles prodded the constant *sylveth* ache that lived in her back and legs. One of them wore a cipher. A weak one. Probably designed to hide a sagging jowl or to freshen breath. Combined with the majick cobwebbing Alistair's office—mostly from locks on ledgers, drawers, and cabinets—Lucy felt queasy.

"Miss Trenton, allow me to introduce Lady Warrinton, Mrs. Pladis, and Mr. Higgelsham. They are the owners of the *Sweet Song*—the third of the ships that wrecked Merisnight."

Lucy nodded, her breath catching hard in her chest. The night of the salvage she'd not known the names of the ships, but she knew them all now: *Hero's Revenge*, *Windswift*, *Sweet Song*, the *Vacubyr* out of Kalibri, and the *Dreshel Panir* out of Reshnival. She'd never forget the names of those ships.

"They have requested to be present at your debriefing, and Lord Gintley has agreed." Alistair's gaze swept over his three guests. "So long as they do not disrupt the proceedings."

He waited until each of the three reluctantly agreed.

"Very good. Be seated, Miss Trenton."

Lucy did as she was told. The three shipowners stared at her like rats eyeing a hunk of cheese. Lucy drew a heavy breath. This was going to be bad. And worst of all, it was going to keep a full team off inspection, which would make Alistair very short-tempered. With the lighters about to strike, customs could ill afford the waste of time and staff.

"Start with your account of the salvage, from the moment you opened the sheds."

"That's it? She'll lie. You've got to *make* her tell the truth," Higgelsham said, his chest puffing.

Before Lucy could retort, Alistair responded. "And how do you suppose I do that?"

"Majick. They've gotta have some spell that'll force a person to speak the truth."

Alistair shook his head. "Such spells are quite unreliable, so much so that the crown does not allow them in any government operation whatsoever. They are quite simple to fool. Now, please sit down. Miss Trenton, if you are ready?"

Lucy was anything but. She was holding in her fury by just her fingertips. But she had little choice. She told the story succinctly and without any embellishment. She focused on the process of collection, documentation, and storage. She'd hardly explained about leaving Rebecca Rae in charge when Alistair interrupted her.

"You left one of the harbormaster's clerks to oversee the first shed while you opened a second?"

"I did. She's a bonded master clerk and the *Windswift* was about to run up on the weir. No customs teams had yet arrived and I believed we'd lose cargo if I didn't get a second shed ready in time." She didn't try to defend herself any more than that. She felt the eyes of the three shipowners like those of dogs waiting for table scraps to fall on the floor. She wasn't sure what they were accusing her of, but she wasn't going to apologize for running the salvage the best way she knew how with the resources she'd had.

"I see." Alistair wrote something down, the *scritch*ing of the pen loud in the silence. He laid the pen aside. "Continue, please."

She stumbled over the description of body collection. She wondered what had happened to the knacker who lost his arm and the woman they'd had to put in the majicar's crate. She swallowed, wishing for something to drink, but refused to ask, knowing her fuming audience would take it as weakness. She finished with Henry's arrival.

Without waiting for any invitation from Alistair, the short-haired, round-faced Lady Warrinton hammered out a question. "Marten Thorpe? Isn't he Edgar Thorpe's brother?"

"Yes, and a gambler too, or so I've heard," said Mrs. Pladis with a sniff, dabbing her nose with a handkerchief.

"And you let him just walk into the salvage sheds?"

Lucy bridled. "Captain Thorpe and Captain Truehelm

are commissioned officers of the merchant navy. I was glad to have their aid. It proved invaluable, and saved the life of at least one knacker." All of which was true, no matter if she also thought Marten Thorpe was a contemptible gambler, not to mention insufferably rude.

"Then how do you account for the missing cargo?" demanded Lady Warrinton, thrusting forward until she stood over Lucy, her chest rising and falling like bellows.

Lucy glanced at Alistair. "Missing cargo?"

"Mrs. Pladis, Mr. Higgelsham, and Lady Warrinton are concerned that some of their cargo may have been stolen from the salvage sheds."

"That's—" Lucy caught herself and began again, less heatedly. "Why do they think so? The sheds were sealed by the majicar after each was filled. No one could break in." Unless the thieves had a stronger majicar. But that wasn't what these three were suggesting. They thought her team, or she, had filched goods before the sheds were sealed. Lucy's jaw hardened, her teeth grinding together. Never in her career had she even bent the customs law, much less broken it. Who were these people to accuse her?

"Several valuable pieces of merchandise from the ship have been offered for sale in the black trades," Alistair explained.

Lucy sat silent, waiting for more. When nothing was forthcoming, she looked at the shipowners in perplexity. "What makes you think they even came through my sheds? What about those on the south claw? Have the records been reviewed?"

Alistair shook his head. "They have been sent out for independent evaluation."

"And what if they weren't recorded? What if her people pocketed them before recording them in the ledgers?" Mrs. Pladis spoke slowly, her head tilting back so that she could stare down her nose at Lucy. "Royal blood won't protect you. No one is above the law." The last was said with a sneer.

"I have no need of protection from the law. There's

no proof your missing goods were ever turned in. What if someone smuggled them past the cordon?" Lucy snapped back. "You've no evidence to make these slanderous accusations, and I will not sit here and listen any longer. I have work to do."

She stood, the chair rocking back with the force of her movement. She strode to the door. Fury boiled inside her.

"Miss Trenton. You have not been dismissed." Alistair's voice was cold.

Lucy stopped, her hands curling into fists as she jerked around. Her face burned with anger and the humiliation of being chastised in front of these people.

"Please sit so that we may continue." He gestured at the chair she'd vacated. His clerk had straightened it again.

Lucy glared, unmoving. "I have stated the facts. There is nothing more to be said."

"You are mistaken. Sit."

Lucy returned to the chair, walking gracelessly. Her stomach churned with the force of her anger. She felt hot. She laced her hands tightly in her lap and fixed her stare on a painting of a summer garden on the opposite wall.

"Thank you. Now, as I said, Mrs. Pladis, Mr. Higgelsham, and Lady Warrinton have some concern that goods from their ship were smuggled out of the customs sheds. You've described the events of the night. I would like to hear your evaluation of the personnel, particularly the clerks borrowed from the harbormaster. I would like to hear their names and duties in the salvage."

Mechanically, Lucy replied. She spoke in short, monotone sentences. Alistair pressed her for details and she told what she knew, still in that same uninflected voice.

"Now, do you remember anything out of the ordinary—a variance from proper procedure perhaps, or someone out of place?"

Other than leaving Rebecca Rae in charge while she opened the second shed? "No."

"Did you notice any salvagers sneaking into the sheds or out?"

"No."

"Did you notice anyone attempting to gain access to the sealed sheds?"

"No."

The questions continued, often repeating themselves, often asking what she'd already answered in her description of the salvage. Lucy felt her anger increase with every question, aware of the condemning stares from the three shipowners. The subject returned to Jordan and Marten.

"Were you aware of Marten Thorpe's reputation as a gambler?"

"Yes."

The three shipowners squirmed and made noises of triumph and disbelief, as if she'd admitted to a terrible crime.

"And yet you allowed him inside the shed? Allowed him to participate in the body collection?"

"Yes."

"Why would you permit that rather than having him escorted out?"

"I am not aware that Captain Thorpe has ever been convicted of a crime. He does, however, have a reputation for being an able captain and he has experience with salvage and body collection. I thought his service was a valuable resource."

"How long did he have access to the sheds?"

Lucy couldn't remember. At the time it seemed like hours.

"I don't recall. Perhaps a glass, maybe two."

There were outraged gasps from Higgelsham and Mrs. Pladis.

"Was he ever left alone?"

"No."

"Who accompanied him?"

"Captain Truehelm or myself."

"And did you see any evidence that he took something from the sheds?"

"No. Or I would have had him arrested."

There were now sounds of disbelief from the three shipowners. Lucy unlocked her gaze from the painting and stared at each of them in turn. Lady Warrinton's eyebrows were arched so high they nearly disappeared into her hairline. Higgelsham muttered, and Mrs. Pladis tapped her long, scarlet fingernails on the arm of the chaise, her eyes hooded as she considered Lucy.

"Is it possible you did not notice him taking something? A bundle, perhaps the size of a loaf of bread? He could have used majick to conceal it."

Lucy scowled. Anything was possible. Still, she hated to give these people the satisfaction of saying so. And Marten had not used majick. That was one thing she knew for sure—though she could not believably say so. He *had* worn a cloak and she'd been very tired, her brain fogged by the horrors of the body collection. . . . It *was* possible he'd slipped something beneath. . . . "I do not think so," she said finally.

"How can you be sure?" demanded Mrs. Pladis.

Lucy looked at the woman, but did not answer. She was responsible only for Alistair's questions.

"Miss Trenton? Did you hear?" Alistair asked.

"Yes."

"What is your answer?"

"I am not certain. I said that I did not think so."

"Aha!" exclaimed Higgelsham.

Lucy ignored him. "I cannot imagine why Captain Thorpe would risk his commission, reputation, or prison for such a dangerous theft. I don't know what could be valuable enough to induce him to take such a chance."

"No? What about blood oak the size of my arm? Would that be a great enough prize?" Lady Warrinton bent forward, her jaw quivering with her intensity.

Lucy's mouth fell open, the air draining from her lungs in a gust. Blood oak? Gods! It had to be worth all the cargo sitting at anchor in the harbor this very moment.

"Well, I think we've gathered as much information as Miss Trenton has to give us today. I will expect your written report on my desk first thing on Moonday. You may go now and join your team. Here is your assignment."

Alistair handed Lucy a folder. His face was unreadable.

"Mr. Crummel! I protest—!"

"Mr. Higgelsham, at this point, there is no evidence that the blood oak was ever turned over to us as salvage. The records are being evaluated, and Miss Trenton's account offers no suggestion of anything untoward. I will review her report and proceed from there."

"But she could be in on it! She and that Thorpe— they're probably working together. I won't stand for it! I want them both arrested!"

Lucy's left hand was on the door handle. She felt herself turn to ice, felt the cipher on her arm turn fiery hot. Rage blurred her vision. She clenched her hand. A sudden surge and heat. She twisted, wanting nothing more than to get out of the room before she clouted Higgelsham across the face. The door swung forcefully open, crashing against the wall. Lucy stared down at her hand. The bronze handle remained clutched between her fingers. It glowed red, the stem that had attached it to the door soft and twisted. Shock made her go cold; instinct urged her to move. She flung herself out, still clutching the cooling metal handle in her hand.

She fairly ran through the corridors back to the empty roundhouse. She banged into a table in the outer gallery and yelped. The sound seemed to echo and brought her to her senses. She took hold of herself and forced herself to walk decorously down the stairs.

There were people in the foyer now, entering and leaving with quick, busy steps. Lucy turned under the stairs toward the south gallery and bumped hard into someone. She stepped back, already apologizing, only to look up and meet the amused brown eyes of Marten Thorpe.

Lucy's apology faded in midsentence. "What are you doing here?"

"My, but you're testy in the morning, aren't you?"

"I'm busy."

Lucy went to brush past him. He caught her arm.

"My apologies, Miss Trenton. I did not mean to offend."

"I doubt you can help it. But it is unimportant. Please excuse me. I am late."

She glanced pointedly at his hand on her arm. He did not let go.

"This will only take a moment. I thought you might like to know that the knacker—Joe Priddle—is alive. The healers say except for the loss of his arm, he has suffered no ill effects from the *sylveth* creature."

Lucy looked up. "Thank you. I am glad to know it. It is kind of you to come and tell me."

There was the sound of feet on the stairs and raised voices. Lucy stiffened, recognizing Higgelsham's high-pitched accents. Marten followed her gaze as the three shipowners stepped off the stairs into the lobby. They stopped in midstride, gaping.

"Cobbler's balls," she swore softly, yanking out of Marten's grip and stomping away. Her hand tightened on the bronze handle, feeling it heat in her hand. She caught a savage breath when in the gloom of the passage, she saw the cipher glow beneath her sleeve.

Chapter 9

There was a light burning by the front door, but otherwise the whitewashed brick house appeared deserted. It was a narrow, cramped place, dwarfed between two grand residences. Sparkling lights lit their windows and gardens with fairy brilliance, dispelling some of the gloom surrounding their shabby neighbor, badly in need of a new roof, masonry repairs, paint, and a gardener. It was much like a poor, frumpy relative from the country keeping company with its fashionable and wealthy betters. However, it was affordable and had a genteel address, which was all that mattered in society. Or near enough.

Marten turned the corner. The wind picked at his hair and cloak, sending a chill up his back. Urgency prodded at him. He didn't have a lot of time, especially after the debacle this morning with Lucy. He scowled. He couldn't seem to stop provoking her. Truth be told, he liked her sharp tongue. But making her angry wasn't getting him anywhere. He had to do better.

Standing in the shadow of the wall, Marten scanned the street. Nothing seemed out of place. The ordinary business of the evening was well under way. Richly dressed visitors arrived and departed from the front doors in carriages and handcarts, while servants carrying baskets and bags scurried along to the back doors. Strains of music floated from various houses and created an annoying dissonance like a mob of children loose in a conservatory.

Marten rubbed at the bristles along his jaw and glanced up at the bruised sunset. He was going to be late. Damn Lucy and damn himself for spending the rest of the day in a back-alley dice game. Edgar was going be very put out, and Marten could ill afford to offend his elder brother. Especially after Lucy had brushed him aside like so much dirt off her hem.

Her fury this morning had been palpable. Who were the three who'd followed her down the stairs? Their appearance had been enough to send Lucy running, and she wasn't one to back down from a fight. He'd learned that much about her. So what made her run?

He shrugged. It didn't matter. He only needed her not to run away from him. Marten smiled his anticipation. He liked a challenge, and this game was turning out to be far more interesting than he'd expected.

His attention caught on a flicker of movement. He stared, trying to bore through the gloom. A rumpled young maid emerged from the shadows, smoothing her clothing as she hurried back to her post. Seconds later, a liveried footman strutted back along the wall. Marten grinned, savoring the feel of his stomach unclenching, of his pulse slowing, as he felt the danger pass. It was the thrill of danger—of balancing on the edge of winning big and losing everything.

Buoyed by the rush of exhilaration, he stepped onto the street. He walked purposefully, his skin tight and prickling. A clatter on the other side of a wall made him start. He shook himself and continued on. He was a ship's captain, for Braken's sake. He'd sat in a crow's nest during the worst storms the Inland Sea had to throw at him. He'd stared down the throat of a Koreion. What were bullyboys after that? What's the worst they could do? Kill him? Break his bones? Cut off a finger? He swallowed convulsively. A hand? Marten walked faster, pushing through his creaking front gate and letting it snick closed.

He jogged up his front steps and rapped sharply on the door. It was unlatched and swung open almost immediately. Good man, Baskin. Marten slipped inside, feeling no little relief as the door shut firmly behind him. He turned the lock.

"I am late, Baskin," Marten called as he headed for the stairs. "We have to hurry. My brother will froth at the mouth if I ruin the dinner."

A light bloomed as a lamp was kindled. "Well then. Don't want to hold ye up. Give us our money and ye can be on yer way."

Marten stopped and turned, his mouth dry. A wiry man with straight brown hair sat in a chair in the center of the front salon. He was framed by four hulking bullyboys who smelled of sweat and gin. His eyes glittered as Marten came to stand in front of him.

"Neckbitt. Making house calls now?"

The other man smiled, a yellow, bucktoothed smile. "Figured it was only fittin', seein' as how ye haven't been by in a while. Figured a toff like yerself mighta got so busy ye fergot the money ye owes me."

"As it happens, I haven't forgotten. I don't have the funds at the moment," Marten said coolly, his stomach tightening. There wasn't a lot of point to lying.

"That so? Well, that ain't such good news." Neckbitt's glittering stare hardened. "Might be you'll be ruinin' that dinner after all. Seems ye need motivatin' to pay yer debts. Boys?"

They didn't leave any marks on his face. Two held Marten by the arms while the other two pummeled his chest and gut until he slumped to the floor. He couldn't breathe. He gasped, head reeling. Blood and vomit blended on his tongue. His body shrieked with pain. The animal part of him howled for him to *run*! Run away! But he could only lie curled up helpless at their feet, his arms clasped around his stomach. He watched a booted foot draw back to kick him.

"I'll have it!" he ground through clenched teeth.

"Hold," Neckbitt said. He squatted down, gripping Marten's chin.

"Ye'll have it, will ye? And when might that be?"

"In a few sennights. I'll have it."

"I've heard promises like that afore. Mostly anchorless. Where ye gettin' the blunt?"

"My brother. I'm—I'm doing a job for him. When it's done, I'll have what I owe you."

"Must be quite a job." Neckbitt considered him a moment longer and then stood, straddling Marten and wedging his head between his filthy boots. "Three sennights. And fifty percent extra fer interest, trouble, an' insult. Mind yer not late. Or trust me, ye'll live to regret it."

With that they left. Marten listened as they clomped across the floor and the door shut with a bang. He staggered to his feet, weaving drunkenly. His stomach heaved and he vomited into a wastebasket, pressing his hands against his agonized ribs. He lurched into the foyer and found Baskin in the closet beneath the stairs. The valet's face was bruised beneath the gag that had been knotted around his head and he'd been tied hands and feet with strips of a curtain. Marten freed him. Baskin bounded to his feet, cursing. He was a small, bandy-legged man with close-cropped gray hair and deeply tanned skin. His hands were rough and scarred with years of working as a stevedore.

Marten leaned heavily against the doorjamb. "Stop. I take it your pride is hurt worse than anything else. Good enough. I'm late and I cannot beg off. If Lucy Trenton doesn't come around, I'll need to be in my brother's good graces. Or Neckbitt will cut off my balls and feed them to me." Marten shuddered. He wouldn't put it past the moneylender.

"You're a damned fool if you think that brother of yours will bail you out of this mess," Baskin said harshly, reaching out to help Marten up the stairs.

"Maybe so. But it's the only hedge I've got."

"Better bring that miss to heel, then."

Marten thought of Lucy's expression when he'd first bumped into her that morning. She'd looked like a spider had just crawled into her drawers.

"I'll get her. But it doesn't hurt to hedge the bet. Now help me get cleaned up. You'll have to bind my ribs. No time to track down Keros." He was an unregistered majicar, one that Marten used on shipboard to keep his crew healthy. The cost and risk were more than made up for by the efficiency that came from having a healthy crew complement. And Keros liked the freedom from the demands that came with being a registered majicar.

"Just as you say, Cap'n. But if I was you, I'd be looking for a place to hole up till after Chance and then I'd set sail for the freelands. Neckbitt ain't gonna stop hunting you. And he ain't the only one you owe. Them others'll be right behind."

"They won't have to. They're all going to get their money. I'm not going to let Lucy Trenton hole my ship."

"A moment, Marten, if you please."

The command in Edgar's cultured voice was impossible to ignore. Marten halted and schooled his features into a mask of curious pleasantry. He turned to face his elder brother, his bruised muscles and broken ribs flaming. He breathed shallowly, ruthlessly ignoring the pain.

Edgar Thorpe, Third Commissioner of the Merchants Advisory Council and eminent tradesman, shared the same broad shoulders, prominent nose, and whiskey brown eyes as his younger brother. There the resemblance ended. He stood half a head shorter than Marten, with balding, dirty-blond hair. His closely trimmed beard couldn't entirely disguise his loose jowls or the pocks from an illness he'd suffered as a child. But he was dressed impeccably and expensively in sharp contrast with Marten's shabby sea captain's uniform. It was the best suit of clothes Marten owned, and the heavy wool coat hid the bindings around his chest. He looked well in it, he knew. He was lean and tan, his hair streaked gold from the sun. But while he had good looks and charm, Edgar had the gilding of money. A lot of money. And when he commanded, men obeyed. Including Marten. Especially Marten.

"I do not want to keep you from your guests. Edira wouldn't soon forgive me for ruining the first course," Marten said, referring to his brother's tyrannical cook. Once when he'd been less than punctual, she'd salted his meat to the point of inedibility.

"We shall be brief," Edgar assured him, motioning Marten into a salon. His guests went eagerly ahead into the dining room, their moods made merry by aged whiskey and fine wine.

Marten sighed quietly and did as told. He'd managed to arrive a narrow ten minutes before the meal, in time to drink a glass of whiskey and pour a second. He glanced around the room, wishing for the drink he'd set aside on the way in to dinner. Beeswax candles burned in cut-crystal chandeliers, and the honeywood paneling was carved in linenfolds and polished to a high sheen. He could smell the scents of roasted meat and vegetables drifting in from the kitchen and his stomach growled, reminding him he hadn't eaten since his breakfast porridge. He grimaced and went to stand beside the fire. Edgar shut the glass doors and joined Marten.

"Let's be swift. Have you anything to report?"

Marten's lips tightened. "I wasn't aware a report was required. I believe the terms were that I have until the Pale begins to shift. Yes?"

Edgar nodded with an ironic smile. "Unless this is the year they fail."

Marten rolled his eyes. "Every year those rumors chew through Crosspointe like rats in a hold of grain and still the wards have never failed. But then again, if they should choose this year to do so, the bet would be moot. None of us would likely survive to collect."

"Very pragmatic," Edgar said. "You win either way. If you call getting caught out in the Chance storms winning."

"I'd be free of those damned creditor duns at any rate."

"You really ought to stop gambling. It will be the ruin of you."

Marten eyed Edgar in disbelief. "That's rich, coming from you."

"Come now, brother. I'm a businessman. I merely provide the service. You need not partake. And as your brother, I recommend that you don't. You're teetering on the edge of losing everything, of going to the blocks. I don't think you'd like wearing the iron collar."

"I won't be when I win our little wager." Marten's jaw knotted. He would not let himself fall so low as to become an indentured servant—he might as well be a slave. He'd jump off his own ship into a current of *sylveth* first.

"Ah, yes. I ask again, how is that coming?"

Marten grimaced. "She's running ahead of me. But I'll get along her broadside and career her. I'll have her tipped on her side in no time," he said, slipping into sailing slang.

Edgar lifted his brow. "Oh?"

Marten smiled and winked broadly with a confidence he promised himself was deserved. "Even the most iron-hard women can be softened in the bedroom. All a man needs is a firm hand on the wheel and a gentle touch. I have had some success in the arena."

"I hope so. For your sake. You are, as the saying goes, under poles and at sea."

Marten raised his brows at Edgar's concern. "I should think you'd be more worried that I might succeed. It is quite a sum you'll be paying me."

Edgar clapped his hand on Marten's shoulder and laughed. Marten caught his breath as pain sliced through him. His brother didn't notice.

"That's why I run the house; I win either way. Though in all truth I have much more to lose if you fail than if you win. I hope most heartily that you do not disappoint."

*   *   *

The meal was superb. The steaks were thick and suc-culent, the ham juicy, the sauces rich, the wines crisp and fulsome. If it hadn't been for the pain in his chest and the nagging problem of Lucy, Marten would have enjoyed himself thoroughly. His straitened circumstances had reduced him to simple meals of casseroles accompa-nied by hard, brown bread and sour ale. But that would soon be over, he promised himself. He'd win his bet, pay off his debts, and live more frugally. Edgar was cor rect. He needed to give up gambling. Before he was thrown in prison, or worse. And in that moment, for just a moment, Marten truly believed he would.

A sudden rumble of agitated voices at the other end of the table distracted him. He looked up, his fork caught halfway to his mouth.

"Oh, dear," the matron beside him muttered in her trembly voice. "Such abominable manners. In my day, they'd know better than to be so disagreeable at dinner. . . ."

Marten muttered something vaguely amenable, trying to hear the blossoming argument.

"I say, that Patmore chap is an ape-drunk liar. The wards have never failed and they never will. What's he about, claiming they will? The Sennet ought to have him up on charges. And that rag he works for, the *Sentinel*. It's fraud. They're a menace, I tell you!"

This was from a rotund little man with a bald pate and a florid complexion—Minister Credelsham. A com-patriot of Edgar's from the Merchants Advisory Council.

"Come now, Charles. You ring a fine peal, but really, how do we know he's wrong?"

"I didn't say he's wrong, Venner," Credelsham inter-jected. "I said he's lying."

"The *Sylmont Sentinel* stands behind him. I know Jon-athon Greyson personally. He's a fine, honorable man. He wouldn't publish anything he didn't have some proof for." Venner was a lanky man with thinning brown hair and a long, hooked nose. His knobby fingers were stiff and swollen with rheumatism.

"It's a bag of moonshine," a younger woman drawled. "Why should the Sennet bother to refute such dribble?"

"Because they can't," said another man with shaggy brown hair. Nicholas Weverton was heir to a massive shipping fortune. One of the founding families of Crosspointe, the Wevertons built the first docks and warehouses in the harbor. The whelp was sharp, a true shark among minnows. He'd already taken the helm of the family business and was well on his way to doubling or tripling the Weverton fortune. Even Edgar could learn a thing or two from him.

"I think we can all agree that the majicars have little idea how the Pale works," Weverton added. "Given such a fact, how would they know if it were failing?"

"Surely if there is a problem, His Majesty would do something to protect us," said a timid woman.

Edgar snorted and set his wine aside with an audible click. "His Majesty is an incompetent fool and if you're depending on him to fix the wards, you'd be well off to buy a warm cloak for the storms."

Marten studied his brother over the rim of his glass. It wasn't at all like Edgar to express his opinions so adamantly, and never at dinner. He tended to vigorously quash any conversation that might sour the food.

"Besides," said Credelsham, "he's quite tied up with the Chancery suit. Damned good thing, too. Royalty finally doing some actual work to support themselves. Leeches, all of them."

"Maybe we'll have the Ramplings off the throne yet," Weverton said quietly, swirling his wine in his glass and sniffing it.

Marten couldn't tell by his uninflected tone if it was intended to be a joke or not, but it was met with a startled silence, quickly broken by Edgar's jovial tones.

"Now, Nicholas, I must ask you not to be treasonous at the table. It will curdle the cream and upset the ladies," he said, taking his wife's hand gently and folding a kiss inside her palm. "Shall we speak of something more pleasant?"

"I'd have thought that it *was* a pleasant topic in this house," Weverton said, quirking his brows, his expression provoking.

Marten leaned back, rolling the stem of his wineglass back and forth between his fingers and watching his brother's face between slitted eyes. Edgar didn't like to be baited, in his own home and in front of his wife especially. Weverton was powerful enough not to fear Edgar, but he ought to. There was nothing Edgar wouldn't do, no limit he wouldn't break, to preserve his honor or to get revenge. None at all. He could turn savage in the space between breaths. But his expression remained congenial, though there was a slight tension to his jaw that Marten thought foreboded ill.

"I am more interested in that blood oak find," Edgar said. "Didn't I read about that in this evening's edition of the paper? A ship found a chunk?"

"And promptly lost it when it broke up on the knucklebone weir," Weverton added.

There was an explosive babble of voices as everyone joined the speculation. Marten said nothing, envy making it hard to breathe. Blood oak was essential to creating larger majicks, and it was more scarce than anything else in the world. The majicars had for years bemoaned the fact that they had an insufficient supply—hardly any—and no one knew where the trees grew. Bits of it washed up on shore, or, as in this case, were found floating in the shipping lanes. Sailors earned a cut of the profit that came from a blood oak discovery. What Marten could have done with such a prize! He swallowed, the want so severe that he thought he might suffocate in it.

"Word is that someone has got ahold of it and is selling it on the black trades. His Majesty is quite up in arms over it," Weverton said. "He's claimed it for the crown, citing eminent domain."

"Whatever for?' asked Venner.

Edgar set his knife and fork down, wiping his mouth with his napkin. "He plans to have the majicars use the blood oak to fashion a protective Pale for a new port on the Root, and to establish a caravan road leading into Glacerie and out into the freelands."

He glanced at Weverton, but the other man seemed startled by the information.

"But how? Isn't that impossible?" The timid woman spoke again, looking pleadingly around the table, her cheeks flushing.

"Of course it is," Weverton said in his desultory way. "The majicars can't fix the Pale we have. How would they create another?"

"As you say, sheer folly," Edgar said.

"But why? Why another port?" asked the man with rheumatoid hands. "Everything comes through Crosspointe. We have room enough to expand the port and we already have wards. Why go to such an expense?"

"His Majesty claims it will protect us from the Jutras Empire," Edgar said.

"Building a port on the Verge will protect us from Jutras?" Credelsham asked.

"Of course not," Edgar said, his genial mask slipping. His smile faded and his hand fisted on the table. "Rampling believes that building stronger trade with the freelands will strengthen them against invasion and keep the Inland Sea free of a Jutras stranglehold. But the only thing that will stop the Jutras is extermination. We ought to be using the blood oak to develop defenses and weapons. The freelands would pay a pretty penny for them and it would preserve our trading base. Even if the majicars could create a new Pale, which they can't. His Majesty is a fool." He rapped on the table with his knuckles to emphasize each of the last words.

Silence dropped like a shroud. Edgar's guests appeared thoughtful, worried, and no little bit admiring. Nicholas Weverton was watching Edgar appraisingly. The moment passed and the conversation turned into speculation about who had the blood oak. Marten let the voices fade, drinking down his wine and gesturing for more, trying to numb the increasing pain in his chest.

The course was cleared away and the next brought. Servants poured fresh wine and Marten found himself idly watching Edgar's young bride. His third. They'd been married less than a year. Cecy was a pretty thing, diminutive and quiet, with raven hair and fine bones. She had skin the color of cream and the texture of silk. She bent toward her husband like a flower to the sun, entirely enthralled. Edgar seemed helpless to stop touching her. He kept reaching over to brush his knuckles over her cheek or lightly grasp her hand and kiss her fingers. Pregnancy made her seem even more fragile and it was clear by Edgar's constraint that he feared hurting her.

Unaccountably, Lucy's face floated across Marten's mind's eye. She was appealing, with auburn hair, pale blue eyes, and red, plump lips. He gave a minute shake of his head. She was pretty enough, but she was also driven. He preferred his women more passionate and outspoken than Cecy, and more self-indulgent than Lucy. She probably wore a corset in her bath.

A footman entered and handed Edgar a note. He excused himself and withdrew. Cecy watched after him, looking flustered. She was only a shadow of Edgar; she had no ability to entertain the guests. A few moments later, the footman returned and approached Marten.

"Captain Thorpe, sir. The master asks you to join him," he said, bowing.

Curious, Marten rose stiffly, excusing himself from the table. Edgar was in the small salon, leaning on the mantel, turning a parchment absently between his fingers. Beside his elbow was a packet of papers tied with a yellow ribbon.

"Is something wrong?"

Edgar turned around, giving his brother a measuring look. "You're a bit stiff."

Marten winced. He should have known he couldn't fool Edgar. "Aye, so I am."

"Your gambling is going to be the death of you."

"It might well be."

"I always figured you'd die at sea. A proud, brave death." Edgar shook his head. "How deep are you?"

"Nothing to worry about. Winning this bet will take care of the worst of it."

"So much? And if you don't win?"

"I will." Marten hoped he sounded more confident than he felt.

Edgar sighed, looking down at the fire. "I may have raised you, but I am not your father. I cannot force you to stop gambling. Nor can I protect you from the consequences. I can't and I won't. I'll regret what happens, but you are a man and free to choose your own path, no matter how stupid it is." He paused, then turned back to Marten.

"I have here some information concerning Miss Trenton. It should help you. But it has its cost. The thing is, as you've correctly pointed out, I made a bet against you. And I've taken other markers on your failure. I cannot help you without undermining the trust of my other clients and compromising my own reputation. Wouldn't you agree?"

Marten nodded slowly, frowning, his mind racing with sudden eagerness. "What do you have in mind?"

"Double the bet. That should settle any ruffled feathers."

A hot shiver of fear and anticipation ran down Marten's spine. It would be almost enough to get him entirely out of debt. He didn't think. "Yes."

Edgar's brows flicked up. "Be sure, Marten. You will certainly be donning an iron collar if you lose. I love you, but I will not save you."

Edgar couldn't say it more clearly. Fear twisted in Marten's gut. He ignored it. "I'm in."

"Very well. I will make your excuses to my other guests. You're welcome to stay and peruse the materials. There is an invitation to the Summerland's ball this evening. Miss Trenton will be in attendance. When you are ready, I've put a carriage at your disposal." He went to the door, pausing just inside. "Good luck, brother. And good hunting."

Marten's hand shook as he scooped up the packet and parchment and retreated to an armchair.

A half glass later, he wrapped them up again, his heart thumping. It was a thorough accounting of Lucy's habits, her routines, her favorite haunts, her favorite foods, her friends, even her latest clothing purchases. There was no portion of her life that wasn't dissected and exposed. Marten tucked the packet inside his breast pocket, smiling. Time to go to the Summerland's. This time, Lucy would not put him off.

Chapter 10

The day improved only slightly after the inquisition in Alistair's office. Hig had recruited the necessary extra team members, bringing the complement up to thirty, including the majicar, with whom Lucy had not worked before.

The *Reval's Hunt* had been in port for nearly a sennight. None of the crew had been permitted to disembark and they were fuming. Lucy was glad of the two burly Hornets that accompanied her as she inspected the sailors' personal belongings. Of the twenty-two-member company, she found five who were smuggling items in hidden pockets in their duffels and clothing. It was past the eleventh glass before Lucy finished with the crew and began the ship inspection. The rest of the day was spent running up and down ladders as the box knockers opened up casks and crates on deck and in the hold, making use of any available space to conduct inspections, while the stevedores loaded what they could into lighterboats, which were rowed to the customs warehouses on the dirtside docks. Those goods would be inspected later. But despite the frantic pace Lucy set, only a small portion of cargo had been off-loaded when the sundown horn sounded.

Lucy took refuge in the work, banishing the incidents of the morning to the back of her mind. But she couldn't help wondering how Alistair would account for his missing door handle. She dreaded Moonday, when she'd have

to turn her report in and find out. Then again, there was
always a chance the cipher would kill her before then.
The thought was almost comforting.

At sundown, she left Hornets guarding the ship from
entry or exit and returned home. She went directly to
her office to lock up her seal and the inspections paperwork for the *Reval's Hunt*. She stopped cold, the
day's correspondence taunting her from the middle of
her desk. Almost violently, she dug through the stack.
She found the letter she feared near the top, with the
same bold, black script, the same unrevealing seal.

Her chest constricting, Lucy broke the seal and unfolded the parchment.

> *What did Sarah say when you visited her yesterday?
> Did she cut your anchor chain and set you adrift?
> Maybe not. You spent so much time together. But
> then she prefers women. Perhaps you do as well?
> Did you pass the morning sipping each other's
> cream? How I'd like to have a taste. But I digress,
> my little eel. Have you realized yet you are well and
> truly netted? There's no escape. My instructions will
> arrive soon. I suggest you obey them. I imagine
> your family would suffer dreadfully.*

As before, there was no signature.

Lucy read the missive three times, a bitter taste filling
her mouth. His lewd insinuations only inflamed her
loathing. But she didn't dare indulge herself; she had to
put a good face on the evening. She wasn't going to give
the blackmailing bastard the satisfaction of seeing her
squirm. She put the letter in the office vault with the
first two and went to bathe, finding herself mordantly
hoping the cipher on her arm would kill her soon and
put her out of her misery.

It took all her concentration and a quarter of a decanter of brandy to put aside her black mood and welcome her brother Jack with a semblance of cheerfulness.
He hugged her, standing back to admire her. Lucy found

herself blushing as his brows rose. It was a beautiful gown, made of sapphire silk taffeta. Her breasts were pushed up and nearly out of the neckline. A gossamer net covered her exposed flesh, lending a false air of primness to the otherwise outrageous décolletage.

"Trying to catch a cold?" Jack asked. His face was ruddy and freckled. He had ginger hair, with a goatee and mustache. He wore a fashionably cut cashmere suit with a long coat and polished boots. His waistcoat and turned-back cuffs were finely embroidered with gold thread. Lucy didn't have to examine it to know that their mother had done the work herself. She was the most sought-after embroiderer in Sylmont, reserving her talents for members of the royal family.

"To catch a husband, actually," Lucy said sardonically, turning in a circle. "What do you think—will I have men crawling after me with rings?" She fluttered her lashes and breathed deeply so that her breasts rose and fell.

"Until you open your mouth, maybe," he said, offering Lucy his arm. "Mother's idea?"

"Who else?"

At the Summerland's, Jack danced twice with her before abandoning her to her fate.

"I am under orders to find a wife as well," he explained, uncowed by Lucy's withering look. "I should mingle."

"And taste?" Sarah asked archly as she joined them.

"Oh, most definitely," Jack said with a wink. He glanced at the crush of bodies filling the ballroom. "Such a lovely banquet, too." With that, he disappeared.

"You're looking peevish tonight."

Lucy glanced sidelong at Sarah. "Am I?"

Sarah brushed a strand of white hair away from her cheek. "Mmmhmm. You look like you want to bite someone."

"Maybe I do," Lucy said darkly, taking a glass of bubbling pink wine from a servant.

She looked around at the crush of people, most of

whom she either didn't know or didn't want to know. Her eyes were gritty and her back and feet hurt from standing most of the day. Worse was the constant brush of majick, like the scrape of needles against the underside of her skin. It made her shiver with pain and sent a hot thrill down her nerves at the same time. Too many people with too many ciphers.

"I heard from my friend again."

"Oh?"

"Yes. He mentioned you. Apparently he has some idea that we are lovers."

"Ah. He doesn't know you very well, does he?"

"On the contrary. If anything, he knows me too well."

"Do you think he's here?" Sarah asked, turning to survey the crowd.

Lucy snarled. "Him or a minion. Coward."

"Thinking twice about a nice warm fire, are you?"

"Time is fleeting. More so than you think." Lucy hesitated, not wanting to mention the incident with the door handle. But she'd already kept too much from Sarah. "If anything happens to me, you'll see the fire's lit, won't you?"

Sarah stilled, then slowly lifted her wineglass and drank. She lowered it, tapping a polished red fingernail against the glass.

"If anything happens . . . ," she repeated. "But something has, hasn't it?"

"During my debriefing about the salvage this morning—after I was accused of stealing the blood oak find—something happened to the door handle of Alistair's office. Seemed to melt right off. Disappeared."

"Did you see who was responsible?"

Lucy shrugged. "Couldn't see much. I was going through the door at the time."

"Ah." Sarah tapped louder. "A rough day, then."

Lucy smiled crookedly. "I admit, I'd rather be in bed."

Sarah raised her dark brows. "Oh, really? With whom?"

Lucy choked on her wine, snorting pink bubbles through her nose. "Very funny."

"Perhaps you'd like that one?" Sarah pointed to a paunchy man with sagging yellow skin. Stretched over his belly was a garish green and purple striped coat piped in gold. He wore a black wig and rings on every finger. "Quite a catch. It's a wonder he can move with all that metal hanging off him. Of course, I should think you'd want him to be able to move. In bed, I mean. So let's see. Oh, yes. Over there, just coming in. He'd do nicely. Quick romp under the covers and off he goes across the sea. No messy scenes. Gossip says he's quite a good lover, and you, my dear, could use a really good lover."

"Him? Marten Thorpe? You must be joking."

"Marten, is it? You're acquainted with him?"

"He's—" Lucy paused, looking for words. "He helped with the salvage the other night. And he came by the customs docks this morning."

"And that means what?"

"He's just . . . irritating."

"And apparently interested."

"No. He helped with the salvage because of Jordan, and this morning's meeting was mere courtesy. Believe me when I say that he is anything *but* interested. Which is fine by me."

"Too bad. He's quite handsome. If you go in for that sort of thing." Sarah's gaze followed a petite chestnut-haired woman weaving gracefully in and out of the dance.

"So he is."

"Shame. I bet your mother would like him," Sarah said with a perfectly straight face.

Lucy couldn't help it. She barked with laughter. The people around her stared curiously. At last she gained control of herself, wiping the tears from the corners of her eyes.

"I'd trade a case of Shepet to see you introduce him as your future husband."

"Mother would faint. Father would not forgive me. At any rate, as I said, he's not interested."

"You *are* of royal blood. . . . Maybe you can catch him that way?"

Lucy gave her a withering look, reaching up self-consciously to make sure the necklace with the royal-crest pendant was tucked well out of sight. "A lot of us are royal. We're rather like locusts. It isn't the temptation you seem to think it is. And I don't need to *catch* anyone, thank you very much. Have you been conniving with Mother as well?"

Sarah smiled. "If he had any taste All right, I'll leave it alone," she said as Lucy drew a breath. "Have you heard about the strike?"

"The lighters. Strike begins at midnight. And I can tell you, it's going to be a mess."

Sarah made a face. "I was talking about the stevedores."

"What?"

"There's word that the stevedores will join the strike in support of the lighters."

"It's all just one damned thing after another." Then Lucy smiled maliciously. "Alistair is going to have convulsions." Another thought struck her. "Maybe this will interfere with my new friend's timetable. This will draw out my inspection of the *Reval's Hunt* for at least a few days."

"If they don't settle the strike. Given the timing, chances are good they will or there will be riots."

"I can hope, can't I? What makes you think the stevedores are going out too?"

Sarah smiled smugly. "I've got my sources. They aren't often wrong."

And they weren't. At Faraday, Sarah heard a lot of gossip from well-placed sources in the government and Merchant Ministry. If Sarah said it, then probably it was true.

"What about your family? Have they got cargoes coming in?"

Lucy shrugged. "Doesn't everybody?" She groaned. "This sennight is going to be dreadful. Everyone's going to want their ships inspected yesterday." She yawned. "I really need to go home and get some sleep."

Sarah chuckled. "If you'd stop being such a silent partner in Faraday, you could sleep late whenever you wanted."

Lucy smiled without answering. One day she would take a more active role in running Faraday, but for now, she liked being a customs inspector. She loved the work, loved the thrill of finding smuggled or counterfeit goods, loved the respect the position earned her. She thought of the three shipowners who'd accused her of theft and smuggling. Who were they to accuse her? But the truth burned: She *was* corrupt. She'd broken the law when she'd hidden away the true ciphers. She remembered what she'd said to Marten Thorpe: *I have a deep respect for the law. But you flaunt it.* Bitter irony welled up inside her. She was no better than he.

"Why don't you go home?" Sarah said, interrupting Lucy's self-castigation. "This ball is a bore. There's no reason to stay."

"Mother thinks differently. According to her, I am an elderly twenty-seven years old and about to get shoved to the back of the shelf, where I will soon be covered in dust and spiderwebs. If I don't net a man soon, I never will. I will have to give her a full report of the ball tomorrow."

Sarah tried to suppress her smile and failed. "If she wasn't an invalid, you'd really be in trouble."

"She was content to ignore me until Stephen had his first child. Now she insists that Jack and I must be conscripted into blissfully happy marriages. She is determined that we will comply as quickly as possible, and—"

"And so she commanded you both to the Summerland's to choose the man and woman who will make all your dreams come true. Not to mention provide her with more chubby-cheeked grandchildren."

"In so many words, yes."

Sarah surveyed the crowd, smirking. "Well then. Since the handsome captain is not to your taste, which choice morsel do you want?"

Lucy shook her head and exchanged her empty glass for a full one. "I don't believe I am quite the catch Mother seems to think I am."

"I don't know. I've always thought you were a catch," Sarah said, winking.

Lucy felt herself blush and looked away. Sarah laughed softly.

"I'll not be trying my wiles on you, sweetheart. But don't go thinking you aren't some man's dream. Because you are lovely, and smart, and oh, my, what a mouth."

"A smart mouth, I think is what you mean."

"Exactly so. Who wants a simpering doll when he can have you?"

"Good evening, Miss Nettles. I was hoping you would be in attendance. You are looking more lovely than ever. Would you give me the honor of the next dance?"

Sarah's admirer was tall with dark, curly hair cropped close to his head. He was dressed in the latest fashion, his face painted more expertly than Lucy's. He wore a weak cipher. Lucy wondered what it was for. Some sort of protection? A charm to make him captivating or to keep his clothes from wrinkling? Or something more sinister? Her eyes narrowed suspiciously as he bent over Sarah's hand and kissed it. He didn't let go as he straightened.

"Minister Brackelar. You flatter me," Sarah said, dropping her eyelids so he wouldn't see the mockery in her expression.

"Not at all. You are absolutely the most divine creature in the room. Ask any man here."

Lucy couldn't help herself. She snickered, covering her mouth with her hand and looking wide-eyed and innocent when the minister at last deigned to notice her.

"Pardon my manners, Minister Brackelar," Sarah said, as if she were the one who'd ignored Lucy. "Let me introduce my good friend, Miss Lucy Trenton."

The appellation of *good friend* made his indifferent expression shift to calculation. He took her hand and kissed it. The annoying prod of the cipher grew sharper. Lucy's gaze snagged on his left cuff link. That was it.

"Your servant, Miss Trenton."

"I am pleased to make your acquaintance," Lucy said thinly, pulling her hand away.

"I don't want to be a cad and leave you at loose ends, Miss Trenton. But would you consent to my borrowing Miss Nettles for this waltz?" he asked as the first strains began.

"If Miss Nettles wishes."

"Shall we?" He held his arm out, never once considering Sarah might not so wish.

Lucy made a face at Sarah, who rested her fingers gingerly on his arm. The couple disappeared into the glittering horde, leaving Lucy alone. She sighed, suddenly feeling dizzy from the heat of so many bodies crammed together and the heavy mix of perfumes. She drained her wine, then wished she hadn't as her head spun faster. She wanted a glass of water and a breath of fresh air. She scanned the hall, locating a set of doors opening into the garden. She edged her way through the crowd toward them.

There was a cool edge to the night that felt delicious after the smothering heat inside. The storm had blown over, leaving the stars sparkling. Lucy breathed deeply, or as deeply as she could, squeezed by her corset. She wandered up the crushed-stone path away from the party, following the merry sound of tinkling water until she came to a small cloister surrounded by skeletal orange trees grown over with jasmine and climbing roses. Within was a circular patio that contained a fountain. It depicted a voluptuously nude woman passionately entwined with an equally nude, muscular young man. Water spangled from the bower into which they retreated, and tinkled into the basin below, where three other nymphs watched longingly. Colored-glass lamps set in nooks within lit the sculpture with soft rainbow light.

Her feet and head aching, Lucy sat down on a bench, feeling a certain sympathy for the watching nymphs and wishing again for water to drink.

"Good evening."

Lucy started and twisted around. The man stood in the shadows of the path.

"Who is it?" Lucy asked, knowing already.

Marten Thorpe paced into the light, casting a swift glance at the fountain before fixing his gaze on Lucy. He moved stiffly, his expression rigid with discomfort.

"I hope I am not disturbing you. It was a bit close inside."

Lucy's brow crimped. He'd arrived only a half glass ago. But he didn't look well. Perhaps he was ill.

"Not at all," Lucy said, folding her hands primly and watching him as he prowled aimlessly around the fountain. She was suddenly certain he'd come out here looking for her. As he had come to see her at the customs docks this morning. But why?

"What do you want?"

He stopped dead. "I beg your pardon?"

"You followed me, this morning and now. You don't have a high opinion of me, so it cannot be because of my scintillating company." She paused. "It's the strike, isn't it? You've got cargo you want to off-load and you want me to expedite the customs inspection."

He began shaking his head before she was halfway through. "The *Ravenstrike* is already headed to dry dock."

Lucy crossed her arms. "So what do you want? You *did* follow me out here."

Marten's expression was rueful. "I did."

"Why?"

"You certainly don't waste words, do you? All right. I wanted to be alone with you."

Lucy only stared. He shook his head and started to chuckle, then caught his breath, pressing a hand underneath his heart.

"What's wrong?"

He gave her a wry look. "Call it a difference of opinion."

"You were in a fight?"

"In a manner of speaking."

"You did not come away the winner."

His expression was pained. "Is it so obvious?"

Lucy was reluctantly impressed that he didn't prevaricate. It said something about his character. "It's interesting that you don't have bruises on your face," she observed.

"Is it?"

He flushed and glanced away, fingering the hilt of his belt knife. Lucy merely watched, torn between amusement and curiosity. Thus far in their acquaintance, he'd appeared completely in control of himself. Now he seemed nervous.

"Why did you want to be alone with me?"

He paced around the fountain, examining the lovers and the watchers. Lucy felt her cheeks heat as she realized just how intimate a sculpture it was.

"It was a bet," he declared abruptly, still not looking at her.

"A bet?" Lucy couldn't help the antipathy in her voice.

"That I could charm you. That I could convince you to come to dinner with me, be seen on my arm. You, who are notoriously careful in your associations."

The way he said *careful* was clearly no compliment. Lucy bristled.

"Convince me? What, by insulting me at every opportunity?"

He shrugged as he turned to face her, his expression unrepentant. "It was a losing bet. As soon as I met you, I knew you wouldn't be taken in by flattery. You are known not to suffer fools willingly, and even your arm injury didn't fog the opinion you'd formed of me." His lips tightened in a humorless smile. "I believe you called me corrupt and cancerous."

It was Lucy's turn to look away. She'd had no business accusing him, not when she was just as guilty of breaking the law. Worse, she pretended to be scrupulously honest. He did not.

"You're right, of course. I have bad habits. Dangerous ones," he continued, rubbing his palm over his ribs meaningfully and wincing.

"Why are you telling me this?" Her voice was sharper than she intended, though whether her anger was directed at him or herself, she wasn't sure.

He rubbed the back of his neck. "I have come to the conclusion that I must concede the bet. I do not think I shall win you over."

Lucy's brow furrowed. "You followed me out here to say you couldn't win this bet that I didn't even know about?"

His reaction surprised her. He flushed, eyes dropping. He muttered something.

"What did you say?"

He looked up, his gaze skewering her with startling intensity. "It was—" He stopped. Abruptly he bowed. "Your pardon, Miss Trenton. I should not have imposed on you," he said crisply, and retreated.

Unthinking, Lucy leaped to her feet and blocked him. "That's all you have to say?"

"I have inflicted myself upon you long enough," he said, staring over her head.

"I think that should be my decision," she said frostily, annoyed with the way he towered over her. Behemoth. "Why did you follow me out here if you've given up your bet?"

He licked his lips, looking up at the new moon, like a shard of ice in the sky. "It seems that I have a penchant for pain. As bizarre as it sounds, I have an unremitting desire to suffer the knife edge of your tongue, more so than I already have."

He glanced down at her, his gaze volcanic. Lucy could only stare incredulously. His words seemed at odds with the suppressed fury that radiated from him.

"You—" She stepped back, scowling. "Have you been at the bottle?"

"Not nearly enough, apparently."

Silence fell between them. Lucy scrambled to make sense of what he was saying. Unbelievable as it seemed, she was beginning to understand that he *was*, in fact, interested in her, though she'd denied the possibility to Sarah. Unexpected eagerness rushed through her. He had wit enough, and he was handsome. He wasn't the husband that her mother thought she ought to be looking for, but then, Lucy wasn't interested in a husband. She wanted distraction. She wanted to forget about herself, about the cipher on her arm and the melted door handle, about the accusations of theft, and most especially, she wanted to forget about her blackmailer. Marten had an ability to charm, when he wanted. And she was feeling in the mood to be charmed.

She tilted her head, looking defiantly up at him. "So what exactly do you want?"

His nostrils flared. "I want . . . I thought . . . privately, out of sight, you might . . ." He broke off with a sound of frustration. "It's pure foolishness. I'm bilged on my own anchor."

Lucy ignored the last. "Might what?"

The muscles in his jaw flexed with the force of his leashed emotions. "I had hoped you might wish to keelhaul me again in that splendid way you do. I've enjoyed it so."

"Is that all? Very well. Come join me."

Lucy returned to her seat on the bench. She hardly knew what she was doing. Flirtation was not like her. But for the moment, she didn't care. The cipher weighed cold and hard on her arm. Her blackmailer could be watching from the bushes even now. She had little to lose, and wanted to touch a bit of fire before her end came. She was filled with recklessness, uncaring of any consequences. The feeling was heady and thrilling.

Behind her there was a long silence, and then the scuff of Marten's feet on the walk. He came to stand in front of her. His face was hidden in shadow.

"What now?"

"You have the rakish reputation. You tell me."

"Perhaps you'd like to stroll around the gardens and remark on the weather," he said mockingly.

"How dull. Is that what you would normally do when beginning a female . . . friendship?"

He shook his head with rueful disbelief. "You are direct, aren't you?"

"I can manage tact, on special occasions and with my mother," she replied as she stood. "But the moment doesn't really call for it, does it? Given who you are and the circumstances. And I believe you did say you *wanted* to suffer the knife edge of my tongue, did you not?"

"Indeed."

Without warning, he grasped her arms and pulled her close. She looked up at him in surprise, anticipation coiling tightly inside her. He brushed a finger down her cheek, his expression considering.

"To be frank, what I really wanted was a *taste* of your tongue."

He bent, sliding his hands around to cup the nape of her neck. He kissed her slowly, his tongue sliding gently between her lips. For a moment, Lucy stood rigidly, and then she returned the kiss. Heat unraveled along her nerves and knotted delightfully in her stomach. He pulled away, his fingers rubbing slow circles on her shoulders, his breath tickling her lips.

"That was frank," he said huskily. "Let me be more so. I want you."

Before she could answer, he kissed her again, his mouth more demanding. Lucy responded eagerly, her blood pounding. Her hands crept up to his shoulders to steady herself. His arms wrapped around her, pulling her close against him.

The sound of approaching voices made him pull away. He was breathing hard, Lucy noticed wonderingly. She was finding it difficult to catch her own breath. She licked her lips, tasting a hint of whiskey. Marten turned his head as the voices sounded louder. He stepped back.

"I don't want to leave you, but I should not like to

be seen with you. Given the idiot wager I made. Will you let me see you again?"

Lucy nodded before she considered. She didn't want to think reasonably about it. And if she stopped to think at all, she'd probably refuse.

"When?"

"With the strike, I shall be very busy," she said slowly.

"You must eat. And tomorrow is not a workday. Have dinner with me."

"I will be visiting my family. I won't return until late."

"I am entirely at your disposal. Shall I call for you at nine?"

She nodded. "I will look forward to it."

The voices were just on the other side of the trees now. Marten reached for her hand and kissed it, rubbing her palm with his thumb.

"Until tomorrow." And then he was striding away.

Marten's ribs were screaming, but he didn't care. It had been a stroke of genius to offer Lucy the half truth of the bet. It would give him a legitimate excuse to keep their activities private. He'd be in her house tomorrow. From there—he needed only to get ahold of her customs seal and imprint the blank inspection disks Edgar had given him. Then he would have the money he needed to pay off Neckbitt and his other creditors.

"You're not leaving already?"

Marten grinned and reached out to shake the hand of Cyril Brackenridge. They'd known each other since they were children. He was as tall as Marten, with a slight frame and a wide smile. He was dressed quite finely in a dark green frock coat over a long charcoal vest.

"You're cutting quite a dashing figure tonight," Marten said.

"Making a peacock out of myself to attract the women. Should have gone to the sea like you. Women like a man in uniform. Come, don't leave before we have a drink and a cigar."

Marten readily agreed and they went to a smoking

salon, where men of every stripe had taken refuge. Cyril offered Marten a cigar and took two brandies from the footman.

"Here, now," he said, handing Marten a snifter and guiding him to a pair of chairs. "Tell me what you're doing here at this horrendous crush. Which beauty is your prey this time and why are you conceding the field so early?"

"Who said I'm conceding?"

"Oho! Tell me."

"It isn't seemly for a gentleman to discuss his conquests." The brandy was very fine and dulled the pain of Marten's chest a little.

Cyril laughed and took a pull on his cigar, blowing the smoke out in a blue cloud. "You're quite right, of course." He sobered, bending forward and speaking in a hushed voice. "I can't help but notice you are in pain. Are you well?"

Marten shrugged, his face heating. "I'm still breathing."

"It's none of my business, man, but I hate to see you in such straits. What can I do?"

"Not a thing, my friend," Marten said jovially. "I've got myself in a bit of a hole, but I'll have it turned around in a couple of sennights."

"You're certain? I could spot you. . . ."

But Marten only shook his head, clamping down tightly on the feral thing inside him that leaped at the money like a dog after a juicy bone. He'd gotten himself into this mess, and he would get himself out. But he couldn't help but wonder whether he'd have such noble self-control if his assault on Lucy's defenses had not gone quite so well. He shoved the thought away. Of course he would, he assured himself. Of course he would.

He didn't leave the Summerland's for another hour and a half. He was very glad to have Edgar's coach at his disposal and rode away in a happy fog, marred only by the disgust he felt for having accepted the small pouch of coins that Cyril had thrust upon him as he left.

"I'll pay it back," he promised in the darkness of the coach. That and the rest of the money he owed. All he needed was Lucy and her customs seal.

Chapter 11

It seemed that Lucy had hardly fallen asleep before Blythe was shaking her awake. A repulsively cheery Jack was waiting to escort her to their parents'. She clambered inside the hack, falling asleep on her brother's shoulder. He elbowed her awake three-quarters of a glass later as they pulled up. Their parents' manor house sat on a bluff overlooking the river in the formerly fashionable neighborhood of Cranford. Behind it, the foothills rose in verdant swells, fading to blue mountains behind. The view of the harbor was magnificent.

Lucy let Jack help her down. She resisted the urge to rub her eyes, well aware that her mother would chide her for smearing her cosmetics. Jack was whistling a merry tune.

"You know that's bad luck, don't you?" Lucy said.

"On board ship. But luckily we are safe on firm ground."

"You don't have to sound so happy about being here. Or have you good news for Mother? A bride to announce, perhaps?"

Jack shuddered in mock horror. "Hurn forbid. But rest assured that Mother's attention will be entirely on you, my aged sister. After all, I have many good years in which to produce offspring, but you—well, being a woman, and a ripe one at that, you're running out of fertile years. In no time at all you'll be a dried-up husk with no value whatsoever except for your wit, wisdom, and charm. And what use is all that without a drooling, squirming, howling child in tow? Mother will hardly realize I am here, with you in her sights."

He grinned, gesturing for Lucy to precede him as the door was swung open by a footman.

"You're no help at all," she said, removing her cloak.

"Self-preservation, dear sister. I am young, but not stupid. I have dutifully attended the Summerland's ball and simply could not find a suitable woman. They were all simpering idiots or worse, too light in their skirts. There was not one that I could introduce to Mother."

Lucy snorted. "And you think she will accept that?"

"If I promise to diligently keep looking. And if I point out that you didn't dance even once except with me, nor did I see you speaking with a single eligible gentleman."

"You didn't see me at all. You vanished, no doubt with one of your light-skirted ladies."

He shrugged. "Mother will believe me, and besides, am I wrong?"

Lucy thought of Marten and their encounter in the garden. "No, I didn't manage to speak to a single eligible gentleman," she confirmed.

"Then Mother will have all the truth she is prepared to hear," he said smugly, tucking her hand in the crook of his arm and following the footman into the morning room.

"Maybe Stephen and Caroline have arrived with the baby, and Mother will be so occupied she'll forget about me."

But in fact, Lucy's elder brother and his wife had sent a note saying that mother and baby were ill and could not attend. Lucy's father and her brother Robert had been called to the warehouse in the night and would return when they could. Robert's wife was at home, too pregnant to ride in a jolty hack up to Cranford and back. Which allowed Laura Trenton to focus entirely on the problem of her one and only daughter.

Jack and Lucy found their mother sitting before the fire stitching a flourishing pattern on the sleeve of a dress. She smiled when she saw her two youngest children, resting her work in her lap, but did not waste words on a greeting.

"There you are. Sit and tell me about the Summerland's ball. What did you wear, Lucy?"

Laura Trenton fixed her needle-sharp gaze on her daughter. Like Lucy, she was plump, with pale blue eyes. Her skin was pale and clear, with few wrinkles. Her cosmetics were expertly applied, and her hair was dyed a youthful strawberry blond. Her royal necklace was displayed prominently on the outside of her bodice. Her full skirts hid her wasted legs, paralyzed in a fall when Jack was only a few months old.

"I wore my sapphire taffeta." As if her mother hadn't directed Blythe to put Lucy into it.

"Good. You look quite well in it. And did you enjoy yourself?"

"Indeed. The evening was more entertaining than I expected."

Her mother's interest sharpened. "Oh? Did you meet someone, then?"

Lucy hesitated. She shouldn't say anything about Marten. But the same heady recklessness that had seized her when she'd met him in the garden sang through her again. Surreptitiously she closed her right hand around her left arm, feeling the cipher beneath her sleeve. Was that the culprit? Was it driving her against common sense? Even so, she couldn't stop the words.

"Actually, I did. A very handsome man. Well connected, also. Captain Marten Thorpe."

"What? You didn't. When?"

Lucy smiled sweetly at Jack's astonishment. "Shortly after you abandoned me for the card room. He and I are dining together this evening."

Her mother straightened, her hands closing around the arms of her chair. "I forbid it. Do you know the man's reputation? He is a gambler and a rogue—he either wants to ruin you or steal your money. You cannot possibly be involved with him!"

"Ruin me? Is that even possible?" Lucy cringed from the irony. The answer was yes, but not in the way her mother meant. And it wasn't Marten who had in mind to ruin her.

"I won't have you making a spectacle of yourself. You're a Rampling. Do not forget it."

"I doubt I could," Lucy said, rubbing the pendant hidden under her clothes. "But even so, I don't expect to make a spectacle of myself. Marten Thorpe is merely an agreeable companion."

"Nonsense. He is a rogue. You mustn't have anything to do with him. And that brother of his—he's done nothing but undermine William's rule, accusing him of corruption and saying the merchants could run Crosspointe better. It's all treason. And they say he murdered his first wife. Monstrous! Stay away from that family, Lucy. I forbid you to see this man."

"Mother, *they* say a lot of things that aren't really true. What about the things *they* say about Cousin William? Besides, I am dining with Marten, not his brother."

"Absolutely not. He is not right for you and you may not see him. Now," Lucy's mother said in a bright voice, folding her embroidery and setting it aside, "tell me your news, Jack."

Lucy sat silently as Jack told stories about his work and the people he'd encountered. Her mother had made up her mind and expected that Lucy would accept her decree. Ordinarily, she would, having no real interest in Marten Thorpe. But then, ordinarily she wouldn't have bothered with him in the first place. She'd have let him walk away in the garden, if not chased him away. But things had changed. More than her mother could possibly understand. Even if she outwitted her blackmailer, there was no way to save herself from the cipher. The knowledge filled her with a growing wildness, her habitual prudence and caution having washed away like it had never been. She wanted . . . to feel, taste, touch, smell, and hear everything she'd never had the courage

to experience before. And she was going to start with
Marten.

Jack continued to talk, covering Lucy's silence. But
when carriage wheels clattered in the drive, their mother
dispatched him to greet their father and elder brother.

"Tell them to wash and change quickly," she ordered.
"And tell Soames we'll dine in half a glass."

Lucy waited expectantly as the door closed. It was
clear her mother had more to say, and she wanted to do
so in private.

"I want you to promise me not to see Marten
Thorpe."

Lucy answered simply and baldly. "No."

Her mother's mouth dropped open and then clamped
shut. She began to speak and then caught herself, her
eyes narrowing. "What's wrong?"

The change of subject took Lucy by surprise. "What
do you mean?"

Her mother frowned, bending forward and scrutinizing
Lucy as if trying to see inside her daughter. Her fingers
tapped the arms of her chair. "Something has happened.
You aren't yourself. You'd never entertain the notion of
this man otherwise. What is it?"

Lucy shook her head. "Sorry, Mother. This is something I have to take care of alone."

"No, you don't. Whatever it is, we can help. And if
we can't, then Cousin William will certainly be able to
do something."

"No. Not with this." She spoke adamantly, then hesitated. If the blackmailer exposed her, her family would
have no warning. Unless she said something.

Lucy stood, pacing across the room and back. She felt
ambivalent about confessing her stupidity to her mother.
It surprised her. She ought to feel more embarrassed,
making every attempt to conceal what she'd done. But
her pride seemed to have vanished, leaving behind brash
stoicism and heedless bravura. She halted.

"All right. The truth is that I am in trouble and plenty

of it. There's not a thing you or anyone else can do to help," she said bluntly. "Better that the family is as far from my mess as possible. Especially Cousin William. If I'm lucky, I'm the only one who'll pay the price."

Her mother blanched. "Dear Chayos, you're frightening me. It simply cannot be that bad. Now, sit down and tell me about it and we'll see what can't be done." Her mother sucked in a horrified breath, her eyes widening. "You're not pregnant?"

Lucy's sudden bark of laughter tore at her throat. "No."

When she said nothing else, her mother prodded her. "Breakfast will be on the table in a few minutes. Do you want to discuss this in front of your father and brothers?"

"I don't really want to discuss it in front of you, Mother."

"Lucy! Don't be insolent. I am not going to let this go. If I have to, I'll follow you home. Your dinner with Captain Thorpe will be all the more cozy for my presence."

Her mother's chin jutted. She had that obstinate, predatory look, like she'd rather die a painful death than lose this argument. Which she probably would. Lucy shrugged. This wasn't an argument she needed to win.

"All right. Remember when I was a little girl and I told you I could sense majick?"

"Of course. You were lonely and wanting attention. Stephen and Robert didn't have time to play with you, and everybody else was cooing over how cute Jack was and then I had my accident. You told stories so that we'd pay more attention to you. Our fault, really, for not trying harder with you. But you grew out of it. What does that have to do with anything?"

"Actually, I didn't grow out of it. I just stopped telling you about it when I was nine and a man who was wearing ciphers nearly killed me when I told him I could see them."

Her mother's cheeks turned the color of milk. Her

mouth opened and closed, but no words issued forth. Lucy almost laughed.

"I decided that since my talent only seemed to get me in trouble, I should stop mentioning it. It wasn't good for much, anyhow. But as it turns out, it's helped me find a number of true ciphers. I've taken up collecting them, you see. I keep them in a vault cut into the rock beneath my house."

"You didn't . . . can't!" Her mother's hands crept up to cover her mouth.

Lucy continued on. "The problem is that someone else discovered my secret and I'm being blackmailed. He will expose me if I don't do as he asks. Well, actually, that's *a* problem, but not really *the* problem. On the night of the salvage, I sensed another true cipher. I couldn't resist; I had to find it. Unfortunately, this time my luck ran out and it attached. It's begun to work on me and I don't think I have a lot of time left. So you see, there's nothing to be done. I've worked out a way to frustrate my blackmailer, but if it doesn't work, you need to be prepared for suspicion. You should warn Cousin William. I cannot. I am constantly watched."

Her mother sat rigid, her face turned to gray stone. She hardly seemed to breathe. Lucy watched her, waiting. She should have felt a certain triumph for disconcerting her imperturbable mother, or guilt for causing her such shock and pain. But she felt neither. Since she'd woken that morning, she'd felt removed from herself, from all the fear and worry she knew she ought to be feeling. It couldn't last. Soon her emotions would overwhelm her and she'd turn into a gibbering idiot. But for the moment, she was depending on that distance to get through the morning.

Suddenly there was a knock at the door and a footman announced breakfast.

"Give us a moment," Lucy said. When the door closed again, she turned back to her mother. "Will you be all right? Do you want me to explain it all to Father, Jack, and Robert?"

"Explain?" Her mother's voice was strangled. She paused, her mouth crimping. Lucy watched with something akin to wonder as her mother visibly pulled herself together. Her expression smoothed. She pinched her cheeks until they were pink and then folded her hands loosely in her lap. Only her eyes remained turbulent, with a hollow, haunted look. As she met her daughter's gaze, Lucy felt the first crack in the inner shielding that kept her safe from her own emotions.

"There shall be no mention of this during breakfast. When we are done, we will retire to privacy and discuss the matter further," her mother announced in a brittle voice that firmed as she spoke. "Call the footman to carry me in, please."

Lucy's father and brothers were waiting in the dining room, deeply involved in a discussion about the missing blood oak and Cousin William's unexpected plans for a new port on the Root. Her mother let the conversation go on, despite her usual rule against political or work-related conversation at the table. When Lucy's father eyed her with quizzical surprise, she waved her hand.

"Go on, then, get it out of your system."

Lucy ate and listened, adding nothing to the discussion.

"Everybody knows the majicars are incapable of creating a new Pale. What is Cousin William thinking?" demanded Robert on the opposite side of the table. His curly black hair was slicked back and clubbed tightly at the nape of his neck. He resembled their father, with blunt features, a wide mouth, and tea-colored eyes. He was clean-shaven with broad shoulders and a paunchy waist. His meaty hands were scarred from years of working in a warehouse.

"The Jutras are trying to strangle us—they've swallowed nearly every country east of here. If they surround us, they'll own us," their father said.

"We have ships and majicars. We'll fight. A port on the Root does nothing for us."

"They have majicars of their own," said Jack around

a mouthful of bread. "And besides, we'd need an army. They won't be stupid enough to march down to the shores so that we can use our ships against them. They'll just sit beyond the Verge and blockade every port. It'll be a siege. They'll just wait for us to starve, or ambush us when we come looking for a fight. A port on the Root gives us a safe base and it will help the freelands maintain their economies and finance defenses. Cousin William will be able to organize an alliance of the freelands against the Jutras."

"Pie in the sky," Robert said scornfully. "And a waste of blood oak. Better for the majicars to use it to create weaponry. We could sell it to the freelanders, which would accomplish the same things and not cost us a million drals.

"And what if the majicars waste all that blood oak and still can't make a new Pale? Then we'll be without a new port, and without a source of power for weapons. It's too valuable to take chances with. This is the largest find of blood oak in more than twenty years!" Robert thumped his fist on the table, then glanced at their frowning mother, ducking his head.

"I think we've said enough on the subject," said their father. "Cousin William is a careful man and will not begin this project without some assurance of success. Now, Lucy, tell us about the wrecks—did you have any part in the salvage?"

She flicked a glance at her mother, whose gaze hardened with warning. Lucy didn't need it. It was one thing to announce her problems to her mother, another thing entirely to speak of them in front of the servants.

"I happened to be the senior on-site," she said. "I took the van on the salvage."

Then followed a barrage of questions from her brothers and father. Most of it concerned the logistics of the salvage and the ships, but there were two that hit Lucy hard, sending cobweb cracks across her emotional shields.

"Did you see any of the collection?" Jack asked eagerly.

"Yes," she said tersely.

"What happened? What was the *sylveth* spawn like?" He sounded like a young boy looking for a scary bedtime story.

Lucy rested her hands on the table, staring down at her plate as she sought a reply. At last she looked up. "We didn't have a majicar. Ours went to help with the cordon and the rest couldn't get across the strait. We put one knacker in a box—she'd been infected. We cut another man's arm off there on the ground. As for the *sylveth* spawn? They were out of a madman's nightmares. I hope we caught them all."

She stopped abruptly, picking up her teacup in a trembling hand. She drank blindly.

A turgid silence fell, broken by the scrape of silverware and the clink of porcelain. At last her father broke it. He clearly was looking for a safer topic. And found another nettle patch.

"What did you hear about the blood oak? Any scuttlebutt at customs about who might have it or how it slipped through the cordon?"

Lucy pushed her plate away. "Yes, I've heard a rumor."

"And?" prompted Robert, uncowed by Lucy's withering look.

"Jack, you were telling me quite a funny story about bringing a ship into dry dock. Please tell it again for Robert and Thomas."

Jack obliged their mother with a sidelong look at Lucy. Before long, the moment was forgotten as everyone began chuckling. Lucy pasted a smile on her face, but felt the tension inside her rising. She was like a trapped animal, wanting nothing more than to retreat to the safety of her burrow. Except there was no place safe for her anymore. She thought of Marten and wild desire surged inside her. He was like the promise of a drug—something to make her forget for a little while. With him she wouldn't have to worry about questions or even being polite. With him she could let go a little. Stop trying to hold herself together.

It took all her willpower not to stand and walk out right then and there. But there was one more ordeal to come. If only she could keep herself from shattering before then.

Jack kept everyone laughing until breakfast ended. Back in the morning salon, Lucy retreated to the window while her mother dismissed the servants.

"Lucy has news you need to hear," her mother announced when everyone had settled. The strain had returned to her voice.

Lucy obeyed the implicit command and told her story again. She ignored the exclamations from her brothers and father, pushing on to the end. "And to answer your question, Father, the shipowners have accused me of stealing the blood oak. There is an investigation under way."

If she expected a reaction, she was disappointed. Her father and brothers stared in blank shock, like wooden dolls.

"What have you done?" Robert muttered at last.

"Are you all right?"

Jack came to stand beside her, his hands stretched out but not touching, as if he might break her, as if he might be contaminated by her. Her mouth stretched in a tight smile and she stepped back, resting her hand against the window. She shivered. She felt cold and realized that it was creeping up her left arm from the cipher. She swallowed and stared in horror at the rime of frost spreading across the glass. She pulled her hand away, aching pain leaching through her flesh to her bones.

"I have to leave," she said, fleeing toward the door.

"No—we have to figure out what to do." Her mother was frantic. "Thomas, stop her."

"I cannot stay." Lucy held up her hand. Sparkling flakes of ice drifted to the floor and crusted on her sleeve.

Her family gaped. Panic rushed through Lucy as the rug under her feet crunched with cold. She grasped the door handle and then jerked back. A slab of ice a finger-width thick glazed the doorway and crept outward over the paintings on the wall and up to the ceiling. Her father pulled her mother nearer the fire as her brothers leaped to help him. Lucy remained standing, ice sluicing from her like water out a broken dam.

She couldn't hear anything but the pounding of her own heart. She saw her father's lips moving, but was deaf to the words. She glanced down at her arm. Light glowed beneath her sleeve and shone out the cuff over her hand. Pain wrapped her in a cocoon of thorns. It was hard to breathe. Suddenly she knew this was the end: She was going to die. Fury shook her. She would not kill her family too.

She lumbered across the room, her steps slow and graceless. Her fingers fumbled around a small marble-topped table. She picked it up, determined to break through the chessboard glass doors and make an escape for herself. She turned, swinging the table with all her might. Glass shattered and a number of wooden cross-frames splintered. She swung again and again. Each time, more of the wooden window scaffolding broke away. She tossed the table away, pulling at the wreckage until there was a hole large enough for her to squeeze through. Without a backward look, she grasped the edges of the door and pulled herself out. Her dress caught and she jerked free. Deep cuts laced her palms and fingers, the blood hardening into ice.

Frost formed on the grass as she stumbled out onto the lawn, heading for the pebbled driveway. She lurched along, following the scrolling curve of the drive. The house had disappeared from sight when Lucy realized that she no longer felt the searing cold. Blood ran from between her tightly fisted fingers. She stopped, bending and retching violently. When she was done, a wave of dizziness struck her. She swayed, sinking to the ground.

"Lucy?"

She looked up. Her father and Jack had followed her. They stood twenty feet away, hands outstretched as if in supplication.

"It's passed," she said hoarsely. "I have to go home."

Home. To what? She was dangerous. She shouldn't bring her danger back to Blythe and James and everybody else. She'd have to go somewhere else. Regretfully, she thought of Marten. He didn't deserve this either. She was a pariah.

"Jack, get a hack. Quickly!" her father ordered.

Her brother dashed off. As he passed by Lucy, he paused and put a hand on her shoulder. She nearly sobbed at his gentle, blameless touch.

"What am I going to do? Where can I go? I can't take this home. I should go to Merstone—but I can't! I have to get rid of the ciphers first."

Her father edged forward, kneeling down before her. He gently gripped her shoulders, pulling her against his chest and pressing his chin against her head. He stroked her hair. She could no longer hold back her tears, sobbing her remorse and fear.

"Sh, sh, sh—sweetheart. It's going to be all right. We'll take you home and send everyone away. There are maji cars in the family—did you forget? They'll help. It might take a few days. You must calm yourself. You must think rationally if you are to get through this."

His voice was soothing, as if talking to a frightened animal. As her jagged crying subsided, he pushed her up, wrapping his handkerchief around one of her hands. He pulled off his cravat and wrapped the other. The crunch of wheels on the driveway warned them that Jack had found a hack. It rolled around the curve, Jack standing on the footrail. He hopped down and came to help Lucy.

"Go fetch your sister's cloak and a blanket," their father said, waving him off, and then guided her to the door of the carriage. He helped her inside and settled beside her on the seat. She sat rigidly. Jack quickly reappeared and clambered inside. Their father put her cloak around her and tucked her beneath the blanket.

Jack knocked on the roof of the carriage and it jolted to life. Lucy closed her eyes, snuggling against her father's chest. She felt her fragile control melting. Quivers radiated from deep inside her. She began to tremble, and then quake. He pulled her more tightly against him, closing both arms around her. At last the tremors subsided. Lucy slumped against her father's warmth, sniffling and wiping the tears from her cheeks. The pain from her hands began to burrow through her daze. She held them up. The white handkerchief and cravat were blotched crimson and she couldn't seem to uncurl her fingers.

"Here, this might help."

Jack unstoppered a bottle of brandy and held it for her to drink. She took a healthy swallow, feeling the alcohol burn down into her stomach. She drank more and nodded to Jack to pass the bottle to her father.

"So, don't we have egg on our faces," Jack said drily. "All those years telling you to stop making up stories about sensing majick, and you were telling the truth all along."

"Which makes this whole mess my fault," her father said heavily, rubbing his hand in a circle on her back. "If we'd believed you . . ."

The resentful child hiding inside Lucy crowed vindication. Yes! Yes! It was all their fault! They should have believed her; they should have listened. But the adult Lucy knew better. She shook her head.

"When has anyone been able to stop me from doing what I want to do? I knew what going after true ciphers meant and I went after them anyway. You ought to be blaming me for tangling you in this mess. I thought I could get rid of them by faking a Chayos Harvest collection. But I don't think I'm going to have enough time before . . ." She drew a breath.

"I'll send word to Hedrenion. He'll think of something. It may be a few days." Her father paused. "Can you hold on?"

"I'll do my best. Can I keep that bottle of brandy?"

The two men chuckled, as she meant them to.

"You should try to stay calm. The . . . attack . . . started when you told us your story. It may be that it responds to your emotions. They may have nothing to do with one another, but it couldn't hurt you to keep your composure. Call it a precaution."

"I'll do what I can." Which meant not looking at her mail, not having nightmares about *sylveth* spawn, not thinking about the cipher or the blood oak, and . . . she couldn't see Marten. Not that she wouldn't have canceled their appointment anyhow. Lucy sighed. She had those new books. She'd spend tonight and tomorrow curled up by the fire reading. After that, she'd have work to lose herself in.

"Just ask Cousin Hedrenion to hurry," she said, thinking of the salvage report she had yet to write for Alistair.

When they arrived at her home, she was startled to realize the sun had set. Where had the day gone? She allowed her father and brother to help her out of the carriage, but then waved them away when they would have accompanied her inside.

"Go home. I'll be fine."

They both began to argue, but Lucy refused to listen.

"I'll be all right. I just want to be alone. Blythe will send Janet and her family away and bandage my hands and then I'm going to get into bed. The best that you can do for me is to just, please, get word to Hedrenion tonight."

They hugged her and departed and she went inside, hiding her hands inside her cloak. She trotted upstairs and went straight to her bedroom. She caught a glimpse of herself in the mirror. Her cheeks were smeared with dried blood from where she'd wiped away her tears. Her dress was torn and stained with crimson and her eyes were swollen. Her hair was wild, like it had been picked at by a swarm of crows. She looked, in a word, dreadful.

And worse, she couldn't do anything to repair the damage without Blythe's help. She sighed and rang the bell.

When her maid entered, Lucy was sitting on the bed, her cloak wrapped tightly around herself. She'd wiped away the stains on her face with water from the basin on her washstand. Blythe stopped short, eyeing Lucy's disarray with surprise. Lucy didn't wait for her to speak.

"I'm in trouble, Blythe. And I need your help. But before that, I need your word that you won't say anything about it to anyone. Not even James. If you can't promise, just go. My mother will take you in and help you find another place."

The diminutive maid jerked back, her cheeks flushing and her nostrils flaring.

"I never! What kind of woman do ye think I be? Scurryin' off in times o'trouble. We be family and family donna abandon each other."

"I need your word."

"Ye have it. Now, tell me what's goin' on."

Slowly Lucy dropped her cloak. Blythe gasped as she saw the bloodstained rags swaddling Lucy's hands.

"Mother Chayos! What have ye done?"

Lucy hesitated. How much to tell? "I've been tangled by a cipher. A true cipher."

Her maid blanched and then collected herself. She stirred up the fire and set a copper kettle on to boil. Lucy explained what had happened as the other woman busied herself with removing the makeshift bandages and cleaning away the dried blood.

"Ye ought t'see a healer," she said, examining the deep cuts.

"Father sent for Cousin Hedrenion. He's not a healer, but he'll be able to do something. I want you to send Janet and Rupert and the children to my mother. As soon as you help me with my hands, you and James should go too."

Blythe sniffed. "I'll not be agoin' off and leavin' ye. James neither. So ye can just forget about that. I'll see t'Janet and Rupert. Now, what're ye plannin' to do about the gentleman—Captain Thorpe?"

"When he gets here, tell him I'm indisposed and send him away."

"He already be here. In yer sitting room. Been coolin' his heels a half a glass already."

Lucy tilted her head back and closed her eyes, breathing slowly. Her heart had begun to race. With fear or something else, she didn't know. She sighed and sat up. She could send Blythe to say she was sick. She looked down at her hands, covered now in new bandages made from strips of a sheet. Or she could tell him herself. She smiled, that feeling of recklessness rising intoxicatingly inside.

"Help me dress."

Chapter 12

Marten wandered around the sitting room, picking things up and putting them down again. He was unpardonably early. But he'd been driven to Lucy's door by the persistent fear that she would change her mind, and the tantalizing promise of winning this bet.

The room was comfortable, with thick rugs and cozy furniture. Lucy didn't seem to like a lot of ornament, and had limited her decorating to a few paintings, several small statues, a blown-glass vase of dried flowers, and a handful of miniatures. The shelves lining the walls were crammed with books. Marten ran his fingers along the spines, reading the titles. Philosophy, art, history, fiction, poetry. Marten pulled a volume down and flipped through it. He read a couple of pages, jerking around in startlement when the door opened.

Lucy was shockingly pale. Her eyes were sunken and she walked jerkily. She wore a severe dark blue dress with a high collar and long sleeves. Her hair was caught loosely behind her head and hung down her back in a brilliant curly fall.

"Captain Thorpe. I had not expected you so soon."

Marten's stomach curled at the distance in her voice. She went to stand before the fire, her hands clasped behind her back. Her coldness was palpable. She had every appearance of despising him. His mouth went dry. What had happened since last night?

"I apologize for inconveniencing you. I hoped you

might be available sooner than planned and did not mind waiting if not. But . . . you look terrible."

"Goodness, such flattery. You'll turn my head."

"I thought it was to be truth between us."

Her brows flicked up. "Then I don't suppose I should expect a wondrous eulogy cataloging the virtues of my face, eyes, lips, or general beauty, should I?"

"I didn't think you were the sort to want such empty compliments," he said carefully. He couldn't gauge her mood.

"Empty, yes," she murmured.

She stared a moment, as if her mind had fled far away. Marten shifted. Something was terribly off. Something writhed behind her eyes and she held her body tightly, as if she might shatter. Or explode. Suddenly she tipped her head back. Her eyes glittered.

"I am not well. I will be indisposed this evening. You can find your own way out, yes?"

With that, she began to retreat. Instinctively, Marten leaped to intercept her. He couldn't let her leave. Not when he was so close—

"Just like that? Don't I deserve some sort of explanation? Or did I disappoint you with too much unvarnished truth?"

She glared a moment, the look in her eyes feral and rabid. He recoiled. She was changed and he didn't know how or why. He felt as if he were caught in an erratic current and surrounded by knucklebones. Before he could think of anything to say to defuse the moment, she returned to the fire, her back straight, her hands hidden in her full skirts.

"It's cold, tonight."

Marten frowned at her abrupt shift. Had she been at the bottle? "It is," he agreed, following behind her cautiously. "Would you like me to stir the fire?"

"No. It wouldn't do much good."

There was an odd inflection in her voice that struck Marten with foreboding.

"You're in a fey mood."

"Am I?"

"You don't seem like yourself."

"And of course you know me well enough to say so."

He crossed his arms and leaned back on his heels. This was a chancy tack to take, but at least she was responding. "I think I do."

"As it happens, I believe you might be right. I don't think I am myself. I wonder who I am." This last was said more to herself than to him. Then she caught him off guard, her gaze locking with his. "Who do *you* think I am?"

It was a test. He could feel it. Everything hinged on his answer. With anyone else he'd have responded flirtatiously. But he'd sabotaged the possibility of deflecting her mood that way. Which left him with . . . truth. But what truth?

"You look—like a ship caught against a lee shore— between the wind and the rocks. You're angry. And . . ."

"And?" she prompted, still shackling him tight with her stare.

He felt like she was peeling away his skin, looking deep inside. His breath hooked in his throat. What did she see? Her expression told him nothing.

"And you look like someone's cut your stays and left your sails to shred apart in a gale. You look like you'd like to kill him. Like you might, if you're given the chance."

He wasn't sure where the words came from. Something about her reminded him of his own face in the mirror. That haunted look. That sense of being just ahead of certain doom and wanting to strike out at the ones who were pushing him off the plank. He couldn't put his finger on what made him think that, but as he spoke the words, he knew their truth. Saw the confirmation in the stillness that swept her.

"Well," she said, "the reality of my day is this."

She lifted her hands from her skirts. His mouth fell open. They were wrapped in bandages, the white cloth soaked with blood. The wounds had to be horrendous.

"Braken's cods." He reached out, but halted in mid-air. She didn't seem to require or want comfort.

"I *did* say I was indisposed."

"What happened?"

She lowered her arms. "I cut myself on some glass."

"You—" He swallowed his irritation. "You did a bit more than that, I'd say."

"I suppose."

"You aren't going to tell me what happened, are you?"

She shook her head. "No."

He looked away, chewing his lips. He wanted to shake the answers out of her. And more, the blood on her hands was making his stomach churn. He wasn't given to a weak constitution; he'd seen more than his share of injuries onboard his ship. But on her . . .

"You need to have those looked at. Call a healer." His uneasiness made it a terse command rather than the tender suggestion of a caring acquaintance.

"No. It's not a good idea at the moment."

"Why?" The urge to shake her was growing stronger.

"Let's just say that I can't afford it and leave it at that."

He did not think she meant money. "Your hands will be ruined."

She looked at them again. "I won't have to write that report," she murmured. "Alistair will be put out."

"You're coming with me," he said suddenly. He yanked the bellpull sharply. The maid sprang into the room as if she'd been listening on the other side of the door.

"Get more bandages. And Miss Trenton's cloak. Send for a hack."

The maid vanished before Lucy could call her back.

"I cannot go out," she said. "Where are we going?"

"You showed me one of your secrets. I'm going to show you one of mine. And you're coming if I have to toss you over my shoulder."

He took the bandages from the maid and rewrapped

Lucy's hands himself. She trembled with pain, her cheeks gray beneath her tan. He tried to be gentle, but couldn't help swearing a blue streak when he'd unwound the drenched dressings and saw the damage. The flesh gaped, exposing bone and severed tendons. It looked like she'd been juggling a dozen very sharp swords—badly. He didn't bother pressing her for explanations; she wasn't going to answer.

When he'd rewrapped her hands, he draped her cloak about her shoulders and fastened it, pulling up her hood. Wordlessly, he pushed her out the door, following her down the stairs and into the waiting hack. He called out the address to the driver and stepped in, settling closely beside her. When he realized she was shaking, he put his arm around her.

"You've lost a fair amount of blood. It's making you feel cold."

"It is."

She sounded amused. Marten's annoyance flared.

"One day you'll tell me what's going on, won't you?"

"One day, yes."

But again that thread of amusement knotted around her voice, as if she knew a joke he did not. Marten scowled.

"Where are we going?"

It was his turn to be evasive. "You'll see. You'll have to walk some. We can't go directly there."

"That's probably better," she said cryptically.

"By the gods, I could use a drink," he muttered, running his fingers through his hair. This night had been supposed to get him out of trouble. But he had an unpleasant feeling that he was sinking into a quagmire that had no bottom. He should have walked away. Left her and her bloody hands and suffered the consequences. But the memory of Edgar's voice haunted him: *Be sure, Marten. You will certainly be donning an iron collar if you lose. I will not save you.* And his own adamant, *Yes.* He *had* to win this bet.

The hack dropped them in the Riddles, the old part

of the city that lay between Cranford and Tideswell. Part of the original settlement of Sylmont, it was constructed haphazardly, with narrow streets that wound about like tangled string and ended nowhere. The founders hadn't realized that no one would follow them over the black waters of the Inland Sea. They hadn't realized that no one *could*. So they'd built the town to defeat an invading army. As today it still defeated tax assessors, surveyors, and bill collectors. The crown ignored the place. It was too expensive and offered too little return for the effort.

The Riddles sprawled like a bloated corpse. It was governed by gangs and those who set themselves up as monarchs over a postage stamp of land, and those who cared to hire one of the private regulator companies to protect their interests. Edgar was one. He ran an expensive and fashionable bagnio in the Riddles, well-known in Sylmont and even across the Inland Sea. Here the wealthy came to take baths, eat and drink delicacies from every corner of the world, and have a bit of sexual sport—no appetite was too exotic for Edgar's customers. And when they were tired of that, they could indulge in an expansive menu of gambling—the true lure of the bagnio.

People could lose themselves in the Riddles, accidentally and on purpose. One of those people was the man Marten had come to find for the second time that day. Keros.

He lifted Lucy down from the hack and paid the driver.

"D'ya want I should wait?"

"No. We'll find our own way."

"Suit yerself." The hack shook his reins and snapped his whip. The mules clopped away.

Lucy stood beside Marten, her shoulders hunched as she huddled into herself. Her shaking was becoming more pronounced.

"Can you walk?"

She nodded. He tucked her arm through his.

"Lean on me as you need."

The streets were filthy and smelled like a midden. A stinking brown stream wound down the middle of the road, wending between piles of rubbish and the occasional half-eaten animal body. There were few noises but for the occasional burst of shouting or laughter. Rats watched the two, their eyes glinting eerily. Marten hurried Lucy along, glad of the weight of his sword on his hip and his dagger in his belt.

They walked downhill and then back up, zigzagging between buildings. She glanced behind on occasion as if someone was watching her. Marten wasn't about to lead anyone else to Keros, and so led her a mazy route. But her breathing soon turned ragged and her steps faltered.

"Nearly there."

They finally approached a tall, nondescript brick building. The windows were shuttered or gaped blankly open. Piles of refuse surrounded the place like a stinking moat. Marten pushed Lucy behind him as a beggar lunged out of the darkness. He shoved the bent old man aside and thrust open the door. It was made of splintering boards held together by scraps of wood tacked on crosswise. Inside it was heavy oak and bound in iron.

Marten swung the door shut with a thump. They stood in a small entryway. The floor was polished; the walls were painted with dramatic murals of the sea and forest, both populated by a varied host of fanciful creatures. A ship's lamp hung against the wall, providing a welcoming light. The air was far warmer than outside and carried a hint of cinnamon.

"In there," he said, pointing Lucy down a corridor into the back of the house.

She stepped forward and then sank to the floor. Marten caught her. Her head fell back on his shoulder, her eyes closed. Her lips had lost all color and she hardly seemed to be breathing. Muttering a string of oaths, Marten marched down the hallway and through the empty dining room. He kicked open the swinging door that led into the kitchen. Inside, Keros was chopping vegetables. He halted as Marten burst through the door.

"Didn't expect to see you so soon. Who's that?"

"The most annoying woman you ever want to meet. Look at her, will you?"

"Put her there," Keros said, nodding at the long table against the wall.

"She's cut her hands," Marten said without inflection.

Keros unwrapped the bandages, and lifted his brow at Marten. "What happened?"

"She cut them on some glass is all she said. Can you heal her?"

"Aye, aye, Cap'n."

"Will she be all right?"

Keros gave a small shrug. "As I can make her."

"But?"

"It won't do any good if she cuts herself again."

The majicar set to work. He heated a pot of water with a muttered word and cleaned Lucy's hands. He left the kitchen and returned minutes later with a small bag. Lucy had begun to wake and was struggling against Marten's grip. Keros unstoppered a cut-crystal vial no bigger than his pinky finger and tipped a drop onto her tongue. She slumped, falling instantly asleep.

From beneath his shirt, he pulled a long chain. At the end was an odd-shaped *illidre*. It looked like a blob of glass that had been squeezed by a fist. A closer look showed that the color moved inside the glass like opalescent mist stirred by invisible breath. Where he'd come by it, Marten didn't know. It wasn't like any other he'd seen majicars carry. But then Keros wasn't registered. And you didn't just walk into the local market to buy an *illidre*. But it worked, and that was all that mattered.

The majicar bent over Lucy, holding his *illidre* in one hand. The other grasped hers. He muttered some words and there was a flash of light and a pulse in the air that pushed Marten back a step. Moments later there was another flash, another pulse. The air went hot and his hair stood on end. Keros straightened, tucking his *illidre* back inside his shirt and raking his hand through his hair. It puffed around his head in a curly mass. He pulled a blanket from a chair and spread it over Lucy.

"She'll sleep a bit longer. There'll be scars, but her hands'll shape up fine. Now—are you going to tell me which way the wind's blowing? This have anything to do with the healing I did on you this morning?"

There was a cultured lilt to his voice that wasn't obscured by the way he ran his words together, and which belied his rough clothing. Keros rarely talked about his past, but Marten was certain he'd been born to wealth. He carried himself with a grace and ease that Marten had seen only in those who knew they were superior. His brown eyes were clear and incisive, his expression inevitably cynical and mocking. They were friends, in a way. An unregistered majicar, Keros worked aboard the *Ravenstrike* as Marten's steward. The crew knew what he was and were intensely loyal to him. His presence onboard meant fewer of them died, and they'd kill the man who lost them their healer. They kept his secret even from the Pilots, no easy task in the cramped quarters of a ship, especially when a storm struck and the injuries piled up. He'd saved Marten's hide more than once, and he didn't make judgments.

"Not really. And yes."

"The truth is a complicated thing," Keros observed, pouring two glasses of whiskey and passing one to Marten. "Anything else I can do?"

Marten hesitated. "The drug you gave her to sleep. I could use that."

Keros didn't ask questions, handing over the vial. "A drop is good for a half a glass or so. Down the bottle and there'll be no waking up."

"I'll remember."

"Do try not to end up on Chayos's altar, would you? I've gotten used to the *Ravenstrike*."

"It's the iron necklace I'm running from," Marten said, draining his glass.

Keros poured him another. "Pardon me for saying so, but is digging the hole deeper the brightest idea?" He gestured at Lucy, who was starting to wake up.

"Chance favors the bold."

"Chance is a fickle bitch. But may she spread her legs for you." The majicar lifted his glass in a salute and drank. He set the glass down as Lucy sat up awkwardly.

"Careful, now."

She started, glancing from Keros to Marten and then around the unfamiliar kitchen. "I seem to have lost a bit of time," she said, looking down at her hands. She turned them over and back, examining the no-longer-damaged flesh.

Marten watched her, wondering what her reaction would be. Wonder? Pleasure? Fear? But she remained impassive, looking back at Keros, who was pouring himself another drink.

"I have you to thank?"

"Aye."

She swung down off the table, flexing her fingers. "Then thank you. Not to be overly vulgar, but I expect I owe you some money. How much?"

Keros rubbed a hand over his mouth, then shook his head. "You can owe me."

She tipped her head. "Better bet might be to take money now."

"I don't gamble." The majicar flicked a glance at Marten. "Not like some. I can help you now, and one of these days I might need something that you might have to give. Let's leave it at that."

"Don't say I didn't warn you."

He shrugged diffidently. "Chance favors the bold, or so I've heard."

"Chance . . ." She grinned. "Chance is a sword without a handle." She lifted her hands.

Keros smiled. "So it is. I'd better take you somewhere you can hail a hack. The Riddles isn't the place for an evening stroll."

"We made it here all right."

"Chance," was Keros's only response.

Marten and Lucy followed him along a twisting route. They cut across alleys and what passed for streets, through tumbled buildings and tunnels, around islands of debris, and across creeks of putrid runoff. It was clear Lucy was entirely lost. Marten wasn't sure where they were until they stepped out of what appeared at first to be a dead-end alley into a dramatically different part of the Riddles. The street was cobbled; the buildings were painted and neat. There was greenery in the window boxes, and the sidewalks were swept clean. Pairs of Howlers were stationed every fifty paces or so. They wore dark blue uniforms with high collars, long coats, and polished knee-high black boots. Lucy gazed about wonderingly.

"Welcome to Ashford Avenue, where the fashionable set come for adventure. My brother has a very successful bagnio up there." Marten pointed up the street. "Sweet Dreams. Very exclusive."

"Howlers keep the peace. Paid for out of private monies—same money that pays for the upkeep of the street," Keros said contemptuously. "You'll get a hack here."

He took one of Lucy's hands, kissing it. "Find a handle for your sword. I'd like to collect my debt someday. And you, Cap'n. May Chance scream joy for you."

Marten shook his hand. "Once again, thank you for your help."

Keros bent close so that only Marten could hear. "Try not to hurt her. I think I like her."

"So do I." Marten was surprised to realize that it was true.

Lucy sat close to Marten in the hack. She opened and closed her fingers, hardly able to believe that they were healed. Relief made her throat ache. She clenched her hands on her cloak, feeling the stiffness of dried blood. Her bandages had not been able to contain the bleeding on their journey to the Riddles. She sighed, closing her eyes. Her head swam and her mouth felt cottony. Still, a strange energy sang through her. She wanted to dance, to run.

"Are you well?" Marten's voice was deep and gentle. Like he was afraid she was going to fall apart. Or maybe he was afraid she was going to explode.

"I am hungry."

He chuckled. "As am I. What do you propose?"

"A private meal. At my home?" Her voice inflected upward in question.

"I would like that."

The energy rushing through her ran brighter and higher.

At home, Lucy reassured Blythe and asked for a meal, remembering only then that she'd had Blythe send her cook away. Except Janet had also refused to leave, ordering Rupert to take their children to her sister in Blacksea. Lucy excused herself from Marten, retreating to wash her face and hands and reapply her cosmetics. She looked at herself in the mirror, smoothing her hands over her skirt. Somehow she thought she should look different—like the attack of the cipher and the healing of her hands should have marked her in some way. But she was disappointingly the same. She pulled back her sleeve to look at the cipher. Neither had it changed. She hid it again and rejoined Marten in the sitting room.

The meal consisted of soup, cheese, cold meats, herbed bread, and wine. Lucy ate ravenously while Marten told ship stories about terrible storms and a plague of rats. One sailor's wife had slipped a cat aboard to help with the problem, which resulted in a near mutiny and an attempt to throw the husband overboard. Cats on ships were unlucky. And on the Inland Sea, no one tempted Chance.

Lucy laughed, ruthlessly setting aside the day's events and the threats of her cipher and blackmailer. Instead she focused on the moment, regaling Marten with tales of ingenious smugglers and insufferable shipowners, and of playing with Jordan on the docks as children.

"He has four sisters and a younger brother. The girls wanted me to play frilly games with them. I have three brothers. I don't know how to play frilly. Jordan's brother, Geoffrey, was something of a black sheep and so Jordan and I became fast friends when I was eleven. We ran wild until I apprenticed to customs and he took a berth on one of his father's ships."

"He's a good captain. Few years and he'll be running the Truehelm fleet."

Companionable silence fell between them as they continued eating. She looked up to find him watching her speculatively over the rim of his glass. His eyelids were hooded. It was hard to know what he was thinking.

"You still look hungry," she said.

"I am."

A thrill rippled deliciously over her skin at the smoky desire coloring his voice.

"There's plenty to eat. Don't stop on my account."

Thoughtfully he set down his glass and stood, coming around the table to pull her to her feet. He bent, his breath whispering over her lips. "I am hungry on your account."

Then he kissed her, his mouth moving slowly. His tongue slipped between her lips. He slid his arms around her, stroking her back and hips with growing insistence. Lucy kissed him back, her own hands urgent against him. She let herself vanish in the pleasure of his touch, forgetting her troubles for the night.

Chapter 13

Marten woke slowly. He stretched and yawned, blinking in the gloom. This was not his bedroom. He turned his head. Lucy was gone. He sat up, the blankets bunching at his bare waist. Goose pimples washed over him and he swung out of bed, wrapping his hips with a sheet. The fire had long since gone out and the door to the sitting room was ajar. He grimaced. The night's play had been delightfully erotic. Lucy had astonished him. She'd not played coy or shy, but had leaped into the experience with pleasing abandon. He'd enjoyed himself thoroughly, and finally fallen hard asleep, replete. Apparently she had not been equally satisfied.

Tightening the sheet around himself, he went up the steps into the sitting room. The crumbs of their meal remained on the table. Bright sunlight flared around the edges of the curtains. The room was deserted. On the opposite wall a gold streak marked the bottom of a door in the gloom. Marten padded across and pushed it open a crack.

Lucy sat at her desk chewing on the end of a pen and frowning over a lengthy document. Numerous papers littered her desktop and her fingers were ink stained. Her curly auburn hair was loose, cascading down over the back of her chair. Marten smiled, the memory of the night before kindling his desire. Then he saw something else and his heart caught in his throat. In her left hand,

Lucy toyed with her customs seal, weaving the chain in and out between her fingers.

Instantly a plan bloomed in Marten's head. Quietly he withdrew, hope making it hard to breathe.

He fairly dashed back to the bedroom, stubbing his toes on the threshold. Biting back his pain, he rang for Lucy's maid. She arrived within a few minutes, eyeing his sheet-wrapped form with clear disapproval. Marten ignored her censure and asked for breakfast. Her lips pinched and she left, muttering loudly. Next he fumbled in his coat pocket for the vial Keros had given him and the five blank disks that needed Lucy's customs imprint to win him his bet.

When the maid returned a half a glass later, Marten was nearly shaking. He shooed her away, setting the loaded tray on the table in the corner of the bedroom. He poured a cup of tea and tipped in two drops from the vial Keros had given him. He carried the cup back to Lucy's office, taking a steadying breath before knuckling the door lightly.

"Good morning," he said, handing her the steaming drink. He sat on the edge of the desk and flipped up one of the papers. "Should I be distressed that you abandoned me so quickly for a cold chair, parchment, and ink?"

Lucy sat back with a groan, sipping the fragrant tea. "Did you sleep well?"

"I would have slept better if the bed hadn't turned cold."

She smiled, pushing her hair back over her shoulder, rubbing at her neck. Marten watched her, trying to soften the intensity of his stare. He didn't want to alarm her. His gaze slipped to the seal lying on top of the closely scribed papers. She sipped again. How long before she lost consciousness? Another sip.

"There's eggs and bacon, if you'd like. Though I could make a meal of you," he said suggestively, running a finger down the neckline of her dressing gown. She was naked beneath and he felt a rush of desire, remembering the night's sport.

She opened her mouth to answer and then her eyes rolled up in her head and she slumped. Marten caught the tea before it spilled. He took the cup and poured it into a potted plant. His pulse racing, he laid the five seal blanks out in a row on top of her desk. He grasped her hand and wrapped her limp fingers around the barrel of the seal. Holding tightly, he carefully set the end on the first blank. A green light flashed. The blank now contained a shimmering green image. It was shaped like a crescent moon inside a triangle, surrounded by a thin black ring.

Marten squeezed his eyes shut, relief flooding through him. Then quickly, before Lucy could wake, he impressed the other four seals. When he was done, he returned to the bedroom to hide his spoils away before fetching Lucy. He put her back into bed, snuggling in with her, exultation making him giddy. He tried to imagine Edgar's face when he saw the seals. By the end of the sennight, Marten would have the blunt to pay most of his debts. Neckbitt be damned!

A few hours later, Marten had returned home to bathe and change his clothes, and was on his way back to Ashford Avenue and Sweet Dreams and Edgar. He fingered the seals in his pocket, tapping his toes and wishing to go faster. He'd left Lucy in the midafternoon. She had clearly begun to find his company grating—as if she was finding it difficult to maintain a facade of pleasantry. He wondered again what had happened to her yesterday. He recalled the wounds on her hands. Someone had gone after her. His jaw hardened. As soon as he was free of Edgar, he'd look into it. He didn't like to see women treated that way, and . . . he felt an unusual possessiveness about Lucy. There was far more grit to her than he'd imagined and he liked her for it. Besides, she was a good friend of Jordan's.

He frowned, still fingering the seals. He planned to see her again—she'd agreed to have dinner with him again in two nights. He spread the disks on the palm of his hand. They glimmered with green fire in the gloom of the hack. A sliver of guilt pricked his mood. They were merely proof of his having done what he'd said he'd do. No one was going to use them; Lucy wouldn't suffer for this. His hand closed and he slid them back into his pocket, beginning to hum a merry tune.

The hack rolled up in front of Sweet Dreams and let him out. Marten paid the driver, tipping him extravagantly before turning to enter the bagnio.

It was an ornate red stone building with deep-set pointed windows, rounded turrets on the corners, and dozens of chimney pots. The outer facade was decorated with fantastical animals and foliage carved in white marble. The bagnio towered over the street, engulfing more than four city blocks. The second and third stories contained opulent suites and rooms, with the top floor devoted to servants' quarters and storerooms. The first floor contained the public baths, kitchens, and private dining rooms. The first underground level held gaming rooms and Edgar's offices. The entire building was girdled by a wide grassy band interspersed with graceful elms and beeches, all lacking leaves in preparation for winter. In the center courtyard was a spacious garden that offered secluded nooks and roomy common areas.

Marten entered under the wide arcade that tunneled through to the garden courtyard. Two Howlers stood stiffly erect on either side of the wrought iron gates. The walkway was lit by hundreds of *sylveth* lights that sparkled like fairy stars, their reflections gleaming in the white marble floor. A dark walnut wainscoting skirted the lower half of the walls. Inserted periodically along the walls were niches containing erotic statuary. Midway along there was a wide space containing a splashing fountain in the design of three Koreions devouring a ship. Bracketing it were two broad doors inlaid with green windstone. Boys in scarlet tailcoats, trousers, and gloves waited to greet arriving guests.

He entered the bagnio through the right-hand door. A pair of young girls dressed identically to their counterparts outside greeted him. He waved away their solicitations and went through a concealed door into the serving passage, making his way down to the basement level, letting himself out in the lobby outside Edgar's private quarters. There were no guards. The door, a simple, unprepossessing slab of satiny wood, was majicked against entry. Only Edgar could open it when it was locked. Which it was not now.

Marten pushed inside, finding himself inside a spacious reception area, with tall ceilings and soft light. Despite the lack of windows from being underground, the room felt airy and free. A fire crackled in the hearth, with chairs and settees clustered in cozy groups. The room was decorated in shades of emerald, brown, and gold with tapestries depicting bloody battles from centuries ago before Crosspointe had been founded. Weaponry and armor from all over the world adorned the walls, and above the fireplace was a long shield, pointed on the bottom and quartered with emerald and gold panels. Embossed in the center was a fanciful device in stark black in the shape of a sharp-toothed wolf's skull with a sword caught in its teeth. The shield was Edgar's nonetoo subtle proclamation of his ambition.

Marten crossed the room, stopping before a desk at the other end. A clerk sat behind it. He hadn't seen this one before. She was young, wearing a journeyman's pin in her rounded collar. Typical for Edgar. She was quite beautiful, with clear skin, blue eyes, and honey-colored hair. She glanced up from her work, her painted lips luscious red.

"May I help you?"

"I am here to see my brother," Marten said, smiling flirtatiously.

"Oh! Yes, sir. Won't you sit while I let him know you are here?"

He nodded and watched her disappear through a green baize door hidden behind a curtained nook left of her desk. She was gone only a minute or two and then returned.

"Mr. Thorpe would be pleased if you stepped in," she announced, motioning him toward the heavy main door right of her desk. It had already swung open. Waiting inside was a footman.

"The master is in the library, sir," the footman said.

Edgar was sitting in a cushioned chair, sipping tea while reading the newspaper. He set his cup aside on the end table. His eyes were bloodshot, as if he'd not slept. He was wearing a long black jacket with a fur collar over a white shirt unbuttoned to his waist. His chest hair was a thick pelt running down to his waistband, the blond well threaded with gray. At Marten's entrance, he looked up.

"Good morning, Marten. I had not expected to see you so soon. Dare I hope that you've had success in your endeavor and you're here to collect your winnings?" He spoke lightly, without any real expectation of it being true.

Marten grinned, fishing the seals out of his pocket and holding them out in the flat of his hand. Much as he wanted to prevaricate, to draw out the suspense, even more he wanted to see Edgar's reaction. He was gratified by his brother's sudden shift from indolence to attention. Edgar moistened his lips, reaching out for the seals.

"Let me see them."

Marten's hand closed at an unexpected wash of unease. Edgar raised his brows.

"Change your mind? Do you have a sudden yen to wear the iron collar?"

"You aren't planning to *use* these, are you?"

Edgar sat forward. "What are you accusing me of, little brother?"

Marten felt his color rising and bit the inside of his cheek. His brother was older than he by fifteen years. They shared a father, but Edgar's mother had killed herself when he was eleven years old and within a few months, their father had found a new bride, one with apple cheeks and dewy eyes. She died in a fall down the stairs when Marten was barely walking. Shortly after, their father had put the two boys in the charge of a cousin and took the helm of a ship. A few years later his ship disappeared and he'd never been heard from again.

Edgar had stepped into the role of father to Marten, teaching him how to behave like a gentleman, how to live in the world, and much more. He'd been stern and demanding, his praise hard earned and all the more valued for it. Marten had admired him all his life. Now he withered before the question, feeling a schoolboy urge to scuff his feet and look away.

"I'd hate to be responsible for her ruin, is all. It wouldn't be honorable."

Edgar laughed gently. "Isn't it late to be considering honor? You've totted up a substantial gambling debt, and you've stolen the imprint of Miss Trenton's seal. Surely if honor was a concern, you'd never have taken this bet, or else defaulted on it to save her. But here you are, aren't you?"

Despite the mild tone, the words cut deeply, if only because they were true. Marten flushed.

"Does that mean you do have plans for these?" he pushed. He might not have any honor to speak of, but he didn't want to be responsible for Lucy getting hurt. He thought of her shredded hands. He didn't doubt she'd be far more angry about the damage to her reputation if it should get out she'd allowed stamped seals to be stolen.

"You've come to care for her, haven't you?" Edgar shook his head. "I can't say I'm not glad of it, if only because it means you might at last learn a very important lesson. It could be the making of you."

Marten's hand clamped tighter around the disks, foreboding knotting his entrails. "What lesson?"

"That gambling will destroy you, and if not you, then the people you care most about."

Marten's mouth tasted of wormwood. "You are going to use them." It wasn't a question.

"What I am going to do with them is none of your business. What you should be concerned about is whether you want to wear the iron collar or whether you want to give those seals to me and pay off the knee breakers."

Edgar held out his hand again, his voice both unrelenting and sympathetic. "Make your choice, Marten. And learn from it. You don't ever want to sit down to a game table again, no matter the temptation. If you must be tempted, run the house as I do. It's far less chancy."

There was no choice. He *could not* wear the collar. Slowly Marten dropped the disks onto his brother's palm. It would be well. They were just five seals. What real harm could they do?

Edgar stood, coming around to put his arm around Marten's shoulder.

"Come on. This is cause for celebration. You'll have to tell me the entire story of your astonishing conquest over dinner. I'm buying. Though perhaps you should. You owe me one or two meals."

To Marten's surprise, Edgar didn't lead him back into the dining room in which he usually entertained, but opened a cleverly disguised door in a corner of the library. It led into a private office, where they paused while Edgar locked up the seals. Marten watched with a chill of trepidation. He suppressed it, thinking of Neckbitt and all that he owed.

He followed Edgar into a plush sitting room. His brother rang for dinner and it was brought by two dark-skinned servingmen. Marten could only stare. They were Jutras. And Edgar called his gambling foolish. This . . . this was both treasonous and suicidal.

The two men were small, topping up at Marten's shoulder. Their black hair was short, only two inches long, and oiled. They wore loose white trousers and shirts and went barefoot. Their fingernails were long and cut in points and both had yellow eyes. Around their necks were iron collars. Welts, both fresh and scarred, layered their exposed skin, and Marten didn't doubt the clothing hid more. His gorge rose involuntarily. What had the men done to deserve such treatment? But they were Jutras. They were capable of anything.

They set the food out on the lace tablecloth in an almost stealthy way before retreating to kneel against the wall in silence. Marten didn't move to sit, staring at the mute figures.

"Braken's cods, what are you doing with them, Edgar?"

Edgar's lips curved. "One of my ships netted them when theirs went down in a misguided attempt to venture into the Inland Sea without a Pilot. They make good houseboys . . . if you treat them just right."

The smug malice in his voice made Marten's skin prickle. He knew Edgar was capable of brutal violence, of maiming women and servants and ordering men killed. It was the nature of his business, of his ambition. But his hatred of the Jutras was deeper and blacker than the Inland Sea. Marten's eyes ran over the whip scars; he could almost feel sorry for the men. Except the Jutras did far worse to captives. Their bloody butchery was the stuff of nightmares.

"If someone should find out . . . you'd be thrown in irons, everything you own stripped from you. They might even toss you out on the Bramble. What if these men are spies? The vanguard of an invasion?"

Edgar sat down, picking up his silverware and polishing it on his napkin before serving himself. "They are entirely under my control. You may trust in that. I've made a study of these two—it's wise to understand the enemy. The Inland Sea is our realm, but we must be vigilant. The Jutras are like rats in the grain. They will find a way to overrun us if we do not exterminate them first, or bring them to heel in our service. The king has no stomach for making war; he endangers us all by his weakness and shortsightedness—what of this idiot scheme to build a port at the Root? But so help me, brother, I'll see Crosspointe safe if I have to spill every last drop of Jutras and Rampling blood.''

Marten swallowed, taken aback at his brother's quiet ferocity. "Still," he said, sitting so that he could see both kneeling men, "it's dangerous to keep them."

"Risk is necessary when the stakes are high. You know this. Which brings me to Miss Trenton. I confess to being pleasantly surprised at your success. Why don't you tell me how you managed to pull off your victory and with such a virago?''

The idea of discussing Lucy made Marten's stomach turn. He wasn't ready to think about it, much less tell Edgar. "It isn't enough to know that I succeeded?''

"Don't play coy. You played her masterfully. Crow your triumph. I promise to be suitably impressed.''

"You'll have to be impressed with the results. The story is not worth telling.''

Edgar stared speculatively, holding his fork and knife above his plate. At last he shrugged and began eating. "Suit yourself.''

Silence fell between them. It wore on Marten until he couldn't stand it.

"I drugged her," he blurted at last. "There was no other way.''

"And she didn't realize?''

Marten flushed, giving a lopsided grin. "I . . . distracted . . . her.''

"Ah." Edgar ate silently a few minutes. "I'm glad you enjoyed yourself, but take my advice, Marten—she was just a bet. Don't get involved with her. It won't end well.''

"What do you mean?" Marten couldn't help the harshness in his voice.

"Events are under way. Maybe if you hadn't decided to give me the seals . . . but you did. The current has us now and we must ride it to the end.''

"I don't understand. What are you saying?''

Edgar sat back in his chair, giving Marten a stern look.

"I'm saying that with this win you've cleared most of your debts. You're more free than you've been for a very long time. Don't sacrifice that freedom for Lucy Trenton. She isn't worth it. The war is beginning and there will be casualties. She's going to be one of them. Steer a wide course, for your own sake."

Marten could only stare. Words failed him. What had he done? He wanted to ask questions, but Edgar's expression was closed. He'd said all he was going to say. But Marten couldn't leave it at that. His mind raced, and he struck on an idea—he'd come at it from another direction. He went back to eating, casually turning the discussion to the salvage and the missing blood oak.

"Any word of who has it?" Marten asked.

"Nothing's turned up yet. The Crown Shields have taken over the investigation with the aid of the majicars. His Majesty is very motivated, as you might imagine. The majicars no less so. With Chance looming, the wood will be trapped here until the first ships can sail out again. It may give them the time they need to locate it before it vanishes altogether. I imagine if they don't, the customs inspections after Chance will be stringent, indeed."

"And then when they find it, there will be a new port at the Root," Marten said, watching Edgar from beneath his brows.

"Not if I can help it. Rampling is a leech. Worse. He's a fool. We've been cursed by his rule for two decades. We can't let it go on any longer."

"I'm not sure what you can do about it. He's a hale man," Marten said lightly.

"Hale men have been known to have accidents. Or fall sick."

Marten sucked in a soft breath. "All that would mean is a new Rampling on the throne," he said slowly, beginning to understand the extent of his brother's ambition. Edgar's next words confirmed his conclusion.

"That's the crux of the problem, isn't it? They breed like rats, the Ramplings. As for the people—they're

Pale-blasted, mindless fools. They'd elect a whore in Sweet Dreams, so long as she had a drop of legitimate royal blood. There must be three thousand or more heirs listed on the Wall, and hardly a single one capable of ruling. The people shouldn't be allowed to make such decisions. They are sheep. They need to be told what to do and made to do it. As for the Rampling line, it needs to be eradicated—root, stem, and flower."

"What are you suggesting?"

Edgar looked at Marten measuringly. At last he answered. "There's a sea change coming. Where do you stand, little brother? For Crosspointe? Or for yourself?"

Marten shifted uneasily. "You're the politician, not me. I'm a ship's captain. That's all I am. I have no interest in intrigues. Whether there is a port at the Root or no, I will still have a ship and the Inland Sea."

Edgar opened his mouth to speak, then visibly reined himself in and smiled thinly. "You'll never change, will you? Predictable as the moon." He shook his head, getting to his feet. "Never mind. You're right. You'd be an abysmal politician. It is enough that you are the best captain on the Inland Sea; you help make me rich. So come, it's time to collect your winnings. But first, let me pour you a drink. We need a toast."

He went to the sideboard and poured them both a healthy glass of Kalibrian whiskey and handed one to Marten. "To success: May we both get everything we deserve."

"To success." Marten rolled the dark flavor on his tongue. "That's good."

"It is one of my favorites," Edgar agreed, pouring out more.

Silence drifted between them again and Marten scrambled for something to say. At last he settled on the only safe subject he could think of.

"The strike going to be a problem for you? Now the stevedores have joined in?"

"We're mostly unloaded and in for refitting. Except

the *Firedance*. We'll want her to run prisoners out to the Bramble before Chance."

Marten nodded. Edgar held a long-standing yearly contract to transport condemned prisoners to the Bramble. The *Firedance* was fast and maneuverable. Even with bad weather and unexpected obstacles, she could make the run to the Bramble and back before the Chance storms hit. He shook his head, his mouth tasting sour. Poor bastards. He wouldn't wish that kind of fate on anyone.

"What's the matter? Don't tell me you pity those fools? They knew what they were doing—they knew the consequences. They can't complain when the law gives them what it promised. And you must certainly agree that we cannot afford to feed useless people during Chance, not when we have such limited supplies. Think of the cost. This is much more efficient, and it allows the gods to decide their fate. Not everyone dies or become *sylveth* spawn. There is hope for survival. If they should have been wrongly found guilty."

"That's a bag of moonshine. No one who's gone to the Bramble has ever returned. At least, not in any form that anyone recognizes," Marten retorted.

"It gives the bastards a chance they wouldn't have against an executioner, now, doesn't it? Every one of us who breaks the law knows the potential cost. If you don't like it, you stay out of the shadows. Or don't get caught. That's all there is to it."

He set his glass down with a clink. "Nobody on the Bramble ship is ever innocent, Marten. Not in any sense of the word. Don't lose sleep for them. I certainly won't. Now come with me and we'll fetch your winnings."

Marten began to follow him, then glanced at the two Jutras still kneeling against the wall. "You're going to just leave them here?"

"They can do no harm, nor can they escape. They may look free, but they are bound in majick so tight they are lucky they can breathe."

With that, Edgar led the way back out of his private demesnes and into the warren of gaming parlors.

Marten's feet slowed as he felt the lure of the cards and dice. "Where are we going? I don't want to play."

"It's where the vault is. For the size of your winnings, I don't have enough on hand in my office." He grinned and clapped Marten on the shoulder. "I was not expecting you to deliver so promptly. You have certainly surprised me. I'd given you poor odds."

His brother's proud reply warmed Marten's chest and he followed obediently. Edgar led him through several of the game rooms, where well-dressed men and women played avidly, never looking up from the tables. Cigar smoke drifted through the air in blue clouds, and servants offered trays of alcohol and food. Whores in elegant clothing snuggled up to players, fondling and whispering. Edgar stopped every few feet to respond to greetings, while Marten fidgeted. He knew few of the people here, preferring the parts of the gambling den that catered to less polished clients.

It took far longer than Marten would have liked to wend their way to the counting room. There Edgar took him into one of the private rooms. Marten waited impatiently for his brother to return. When at last he did, he carried a fat pouch. But it was not nearly big enough, nor heavy enough.

Marten lifted his brows in consternation. "What's this?"

Edgar tossed the purse onto the table. "Call it a sign of appreciation. I am quite pleased with the money you've made me in this endeavor. Buy your friends a round or two. Play the tables. Lose it all. Or then again, maybe you'll add to your winnings. It's all on me."

He couldn't help himself. Marten reached out and took the gambling chits. He rose with a sardonic grin. "Glad to oblige."

He lost track of the hours. He gambled, bought drinks, smoked cigars, made toasts, and gambled more. When he lost, he remembered his resolution to stop, to steer clear of gambling. The shame of his weakness made his stomach burn, even as he remained doggedly at the tables. He couldn't just leave. He should win back his losses, walk away completely in the clear.

As the night passed, he grew befuddled with drink, ignoring his growing guilt and shrinking winnings. There was a truly golden moment when he found himself in the happy position of repaying Cyril Brackenridge the money he'd borrowed only two days before. Cyril clapped him heartily on the shoulder.

"Apparently you had little need of my help. Care to tell the story?"

"A fortunate wager," was Marten's only reply.

He stayed until after dawn the next morning. He ate a hearty breakfast in the dining room with Cyril and two other cohorts, and left midmorning with his winnings. Edgar had once again left his coach for Marten's use, but did not come to see his brother off. It was just as well. Fat as the money bags were that he carried, his debt had bloomed again in the night's play. He'd quickly run through Edgar's reward chits and begun running up his tab again. He had enough to pay Neckbitt and to satisfy several other creditors, but he was deep back into Edgar again.

"You're a damned fool," he told himself, slumping on the seat, smelling the sour stink of smoke, sweat, and whiskey emanating from himself. "A damned fool."

Chapter 14

Lucy finished her report for Alistair shortly after Marten's departure and then followed her father's advice to keep calm by reading the new novel by Veprey. But she soon found that she couldn't remember anything she read and set the book aside. Her mind was besieged by the looming threat of the blackmailer and the terrifying attack of the cipher the previous day. If she hadn't broken out the doors and escaped, she didn't know what would have happened. She might have killed her family. The thought made her legs rubbery and she sank to the floor, arms wrapping her stomach as she rocked back and forth weeping silent tears of guilt and horror.

She didn't know how long she stayed thus, but eventually she rose, so drained she could hardly feel anything as she rinsed her face in the washbasin. Trying to focus on something more pleasant, she found her mind settling on Marten. Her face softened, her lips curving. He was a passionate, generous lover and he seemed to find as much pleasure in her as she had in him. A gambler and a rogue he might be, but he had his merits. She'd even agreed to dine with him two nights hence—if the cipher hadn't destroyed her yet.

The day passed slowly. Lucy couldn't seem to settle, but paced and sat down, then quickly thrust to her feet again. She flexed her fingers, hardly able to believe she wasn't crippled. It was all she could do to resist the urge to descend into the cellar and open up the stone vault holding her cipher collection; it wouldn't accomplish anything. The majick radiating from the seven was already excruciating. What she'd been thinking to want to add to them, she didn't know. Or rather, she hadn't been thinking at all. She'd just *wanted*, like an animal, without any reason at all.

Blythe brought in dinner promptly at half past six. Lucy eyed the spread askance.

"Do you think I'm going to waste away to nothing?"

"Donna be thinkin' it was me. Janet is worried about ye, not eatin' all day. Ye might at least pretend."

Lucy sighed. "I'll do my best."

Blythe sniffed and turned to leave. She paused, looking over her shoulder.

"Almost forgot. Ye have two letters there. Messengers brought 'em just as we was comin' up."

Lucy stiffened, the breath gusting out of her. She nodded frozen acknowledgment and went to latch the door behind Blythe. Slowly she returned to the table, finding the two letters lying on top of her napkin. The first was from Sarah, with *Faraday* printed in elegant script in the left corner. Lucy took a careful breath and shoved it aside with her finger. The second was heavy parchment with her name and address scrawled in the bold, black writing of her blackmailer.

She stared at it, considering tossing it into the fire unread. Her jaw tightened and she picked it up, breaking the familiar round wax seal and unfolding the parchment.

Did you and Miss Neilles put your pretty heads together? Have you devised a plan to thwart me? Maybe a bribe? But what do you have that I could possibly want? Not money. You don't have nearly enough. Perhaps a tumble between the sheets? But no. Tempting as the notion is, there's no time. I have a task for you. You have until tomorrow to complete it, or you will find your secrets exposed on the front page of the evening Sentinel. *You will*

*be arrested before dinner. Think of how it will re-
flect on customs, on your friends, on your family,
on the king.*

*There's a crate in warehouse P38. Deliver it to
my representative at the second glass after midday
tomorrow. Hockings pier, slip 47. The inventory
code is DHFH489AR.*

Lucy read the letter three times. Impotent fury choked
her. She clutched the back of a chair, her knuckles turning white as she fought it down. Beneath her left hand,
the brocade upholstery heated. Smoke curled up from
between her fingers and the fabric charred. Lucy told
herself to breathe, counting each breath. Ten, twenty,
sixty, one hundred. She concentrated on the lift and fall
of her ribs and the thud of her heart. Slowly she brought
herself under control. When she had herself in hand, she
reached for Sarah's letter. Better to know the worst. But
there was little to learn: *Come to me Moonday. As soon
as you can.* Sarah had not signed it.

For several minutes Lucy stared at the opposite wall,
seeing nothing. What could she do? There was nowhere
to run and no time left to get rid of the ciphers. She
had a desperate idea of burning down the house. It was
tempting but would only stave off the inevitable; her
blackmailer would certainly insist that the rubble be
sifted through. The ciphers were spelled against destruction and sooner or later they would be found. And there
was the danger of burning out her neighbors. She
couldn't do that. On the other hand, neither could she
steal the crate and turn it over to him. But—

She stood straight. What if she turned the tables? The
crate might give her a clue to the identity of the blackmailer. Maybe she could hold it hostage until she could
get rid of the ciphers. It was the only road open to her.

With that decision made, she folded the letters and
sat, forcing herself to eat. She'd need her strength. Besides, she didn't want to offend Janet or suffer a scolding
from Blythe by sending back the meal untouched. She

had too many enemies at the moment to start a war at home.

The next day was bleak and windy. Dark clouds scudded across the sky and the ink black waves frothed in the harbor. Lucy called a footspider and was on her way to customs well before dawn. The trouble was making a hole in her workday to go fetch the blackmailer's crate without someone noticing her absence. Concentrating on planning kept her tension and anxiety from consuming her.

There was no one in the darkened rotunda when she arrived. Lucy crossed through the corral of benches in the center and below the balcony into the warren of offices. A few yawning clerks were wandering blearily in. She marched past, ignoring them. Once again she found herself in the lobby outside Alistair's office. It was only dimly lit, and no one had yet arrived. Lucy hesitated, fingering the buckles on her satchel. She could leave the report on the desk. His clerks would deliver it when they arrived and she'd avoid any questions about the door handle.

Before she could make up her mind, the decision was taken from her. Alistair himself walked in. His iron gray hair was windblown and his lips pinched together when he saw her.

"I have my report," Lucy said defensively.

"Ah. Bring it, then."

He pushed past and keyed open the door of his office with his seal. Lucy followed. The memory of the last time she'd been there clung clammily to her skin. She raised her chin. She'd done nothing wrong. At least, she'd not done what they'd accused her of. A niggling inner voice condemned her: *But you're about to.* She gritted her teeth rebelliously. Alistair set his satchel down and turned to look at her.

"There's going to be a formal hearing," he said without preamble. "There have been some inconsistencies in the audit—the teams worked all sennight-end," he said, seeing her surprise. "The same crisis protocols apply as during the salvage—blood oak of that size cannot just go missing on our watch. Lady Warrinton, Mrs. Pladis, and Mr. Higgelsham have powerful friends who are demanding satisfaction. You are relieved from duty as of now until the hearing is complete and you are absolved. Someone else will be assigned to oversee your team. Should you be found innocent of wrongdoing, you will be paid for the time off. If you are found guilty, you will be arrested and held for trial. Do you understand?"

She didn't. She stared, unable to breathe. She was suspended? She'd done everything right on the salvage! "What inconsistencies?" she managed at last, her throat feeling as if she were being strangled by a wire. Her arm began to warm and she forced herself to relax her body.

"I am not permitted to say," Alistair replied. His expression was remote, his eyes hooded.

"You think I'm guilty."

"I think—it doesn't matter what I think."

"It does to me."

"You've always done a model job. I've never had a complaint."

"But it appears you do now." Lucy fumbled in her satchel for her report and handed it to him. "I'm sure you have work to do. You will let me know when I should be at the hearing, won't you?"

She didn't wait for a reply, but swung around toward the door. Alistair's voice stopped her halfway there.

"I suggest you engage a barrister. This is likely to get very ugly." His voice had softened into something resembling sympathy.

"I won't need one," Lucy said shortly. A prickly feeling circled her wrist under the cipher. It felt like a bracelet of pulsing needles. Her legs twitched with the sharpening pain.

"You will." Alistair came to stand in front of her, his forehead deeply creased. "Don't misunderstand your danger. It doesn't matter if you've done anything wrong or not. You'll need someone to protect you."

Lucy's lips pulled into a thin smile. "Isn't that what you are supposed to do? But don't put yourself out. I'll take care of myself. If that's all?" She strode out before he could ask her to turn in her seal or mention the melted door handle. She fled as fast as she dared, her stomach knotting as she listened for the sounds of pursuit. She broke into a trot as she crossed back out through the rotunda, down the stairs, and outside.

She threaded her way in the murky morning light along the maze of customs docks and warehouses that stretched for nearly half a league. The wet docks extended into the harbor like a floating village. Customs teams were already boarding the ships that filled every slip. It was lucky the lighters and stevedores had struck; otherwise the place would be bustling. She hoped that it was a sign her luck was changing for the better.

Warehouse P38 was located on the southern end of the network of customs buildings. It was set back from the shore in a sprawling complex of warehouses. The wind whistled around the walls like angry ghosts haunting a dead town. Lucy glanced about as she approached the double doors of P38. The complex was deserted—no witnesses to see what she was about to do.

She keyed the lock with her seal and pushed inside. The interior was dark and dusty. She sneezed, reaching for the jutting round knob just inside the door that would activate the lights. They burst brightly alive as her fingers stroked the surface. Lucy couldn't help glancing over her shoulder—what if someone saw? But there were no windows and the door was tightly shut.

Not wasting any time, she went to the inspector's desk. It was set up on a small dais above the sorting stations. It was shaped like a half-moon, with a thin layer of dust coating it. Behind was a wall of empty shelves and bins. Lucy brushed clean the small brass ring pressed into the wood above the middle drawer. She touched her seal to the circle and instantly it flickered to life, showing her own green and black signature imprint. She pulled open a side drawer and pulled out the stack of papers inside.

It was an inventory list. She flicked the pages, searching the closely written columns for DHFH489AR. The code told her the general vicinity of the crate, but this would give her better information. At last she found the entry. The *DH* stood for *Delia's Heart*, the name of the ship. It was a tramper, carrying cargoes for at least thirty investors. The listed owner of the crate was Bernwick Corporation. Lucy rolled her eyes. That didn't help much—Bernwick was a loose conglomeration of dozens of investors. It would be almost impossible to pick any single one out as her blackmailer. But at least it was a start. Her father might know something about them. The *FH* stood for "forehold." Customs divided the hold into six imaginary divisions, with the forehold being at the bow. The number 489 told her where exactly the crate was located in the warehouse, and the last two letters were the initials of the clerk who'd checked it in.

Lucy returned the list to the desk and withdrew a map from the top middle drawer, unfolding it and smoothing it out over the desktop. She ran her finger over the tiny notations until she found slot 489. With a quick nod, she refolded the parchment and put it away, relocking the desk. Her imprint faded, but it wasn't gone. Alistair's seal could read every opening and closing of the desk back to its creation. No, when they figured out something was missing, they'd know quickly who'd taken it. Guilt sluiced through Lucy as she thought of the taint that would attach to her family, to the king. The newspapers and opposition to the monarchy would make a great deal out of her crimes. Still, it was better than being caught with true ciphers. And with any luck, she'd be able to return the goods before anyone ever knew she'd taken them. With the lighters and stevedores striking, it might be days or weeks before anyone inspected P38.

Nervous anxiety goaded her into jogging the length of the warehouse. She counted the rows and turned up an aisle. It was crooked, narrowing and widening unevenly, as if the inventory had been stacked too quickly and without care. The shadows in the aisle only increased her nervousness. A sudden gust of wind made the roof rattle and she jumped. The prickling on her wrist had subsided as she walked the length of the quay. But now it returned, the pain intensifying as her heart beat wildly. She forced herself to take deep breaths, trying to contain her escalating apprehension. But to little avail. Her legs quaked with the fear of getting caught.

"And they think you stole the blood oak. As if you could manage it without fainting dead away," she said aloud, and then wished she hadn't. Her voice only made her more aware that she shouldn't be here.

She ignored the pain of the cipher, which had now begun to glow a dull white. The light fell over her hand and gave relief to the gloom. Taking advantage of it, she held her arm out as she read the inventory tags. At last she found what she was looking for. It was smaller than she expected, about the size of a boxed chess set, and wedged on its side between two larger boxes. Lucy pulled it free, turning it in her hands. It was simply joined, with a swirled device carved into the mahogany top. It was sealed by majick. She could feel the tingle in her fingers. It couldn't be a very powerful spell, however. It felt muted—just as the majick had the night of the salvage. And ever since.

She frowned and then glanced down at the cipher that continued to glow a milky color. Was it doing that to her? Suppressing her sensitivity to majick? It was a miracle, something she wished for all her life. But instead of making her feel better, the notion made her more jittery.

She tucked her prize under her arm and marched back out to the front doors. She pushed outside, locking the doors behind her and pulling her cloak close, hiding the box beneath its folds. She considered where she could go that was safe and where no one would expect her. The only solution was to choose a random spot. Well aware that someone could be following her, she turned deeper among the warehouses, winding haphazardly between them. She changed directions often, keeping to the shadows. She had no particular destination. But at last when she went around a corner, she found a bolt-hole. She keyed open a narrow side door in a large warehouse and slipped inside. She leaned back against the door, breathing rapidly. Outside the wind howled. If there were footsteps, she didn't hear them.

Her cipher still glowed. She used it to guide herself to the inspection station, where she set down the box. She examined it, turning it over. She doubted she could just break it apart. The majick locking it would likely also protect it from damage. But she had to try.

Lucy picked it up overhead and slammed it against the floor. It bounced and tumbled on end. The sound was like a thundercrack in the dark warehouse. She winced, hunching down into herself and looking furtively about. There was no answering alarm, only the wind. Lucy picked up the box and examined it. As expected, not even a scratch. She dashed it against the floor again, then stamped her heel down onto the wide, flat top. No effect. She tried again, this time jumping onto it with all her weight. Still nothing.

She set it on the desk, panting with her exertions. Her chest ached and her heart pounded. From fear, from failure—she didn't care to consider the cause. The glow of the cipher flared. If this had been an inspection, she'd have had a majicar open it. If he couldn't, she'd have it sent to the central customs office. The owner would be notified to appear and open the box, and would be charged an extra fee for the trouble. But this was not an inspection, she didn't have a majicar, and she *had* to open it.

Furiously she slapped her left hand down on the box and flung it away. As she did, a feeling shuddered through her, like a thick thread ran down her arms and legs and was given a sharp jerk. A loud *crack!* shattered the air and a burst like a great gust of wind blew Lucy backward a dozen feet. She landed hard on her back, her head snapping against the floor.

Lucy blinked her eyes. Her head hurt. Her back ached. It was dark as night. Where was she? She turned her head and realized she was lying on a stone floor. She sat up stiffly, gasping as pain drilled down her spine and spread out along her ribs. She braced her hands on either side of her, waiting for the feeling to pass. With clumsy fingers, she explored her head. A painful bump protruded from the back of her skull. She winced as she touched it. Frowning, she struggled through the fog in her mind to remember what happened. The box. She'd thrown it. And *something* had happened. Majick. The cipher.

She glanced down at her arm. The white light that had lit the way inside the warehouse was gone. Now the cipher glimmered a dull dishwater gray. She clambered slowly to her feet, using its dim light to guide her to the customs inspector's desk. She inched around to the shelves behind and went to the end where a tall cabinet stood locked. She used her seal to open it, fumbling for a lantern and striker from those lining the third shelf. They were used by clerks to illuminate the deeply shadowed recesses of stacked cargoes.

It took twelve frustrating attempts before she lit the wick. It flared to golden life, seeming to warm the air. Lucy picked up the lantern and swung about slowly. She held it high, searching for the box. She found it where it had crashed into a tall stack of barrels. It lay tilted on its side, the lid open. A charred mark on the top obliterated the carving. She eyed it wonderingly, glancing down at the dull gray glow emanating from beneath her left sleeve. The cipher had broken the locking spell.

Gingerly, Lucy picked the box up. She carried it to one of the sorting tables, setting the lamp close. With shaking fingers, she pushed open the lid. Inside was a tray of jewels, ranging in size from robins' eggs to hens' eggs, and held in place by silver brackets. Some were faceted, others smoothly rounded, and none worth less than a hundred dralions.

Lucy frowned at them. Despite their tremendous value, she hadn't been expecting anything so . . . prosaic. She picked a purple dawnstar from its nest and turned it over. It appeared to be flawless. She fitted it back under its brackets and selected a black stone with silver sparkles inside like the night sky—Braken's heart. It was very rare. She'd seen only one other before, and that on the chest of the king. Still . . . all of this for gems? None were illegal. The tariffs would be expensive, but certainly anyone who had the money to purchase these could also afford to pay the taxes.

Unless the blackmailer didn't own them. Perhaps he'd stolen them. Or more likely, Lucy had just stolen them for him. But even that didn't seem right. Not when he'd had her watched for so long. Not with what he was holding over her head. He'd not waste such a powerful trump card on smuggling jewels, not when he could use it for something far greater.

There had to be more to it.

She put the Braken's heart back into its nest and began examining the rest of the box. She took a thin knife from her satchel and dug under the silk liner in the lid and then under the jewels. Nothing. She turned up the wick in the lantern and explored the outside of the box. Excitement made her catch her breath. There was a fine crack along the bottom that she hadn't noticed before. It was too straight to be caused by the explosive opening of the box.

She inserted the tip of her knife into the seam and pried it open. The wood splintered and a panel popped open, exposing a shallow pocket about a hand's width wide and two long. Inside were folded parchments. Lucy pulled them out and then dropped them, shaking her fingers. They were majicked. And they stung. She reached for them again, ignoring the itching pain running up her fingers. She unfolded the first one. It looked like an official document, but she couldn't read it. It was written in another language. She bent close. She knew the basics of a dozen languages—she'd had to learn in order to do her work. But this—it was tantalizingly familiar, though she could read none of it.

Her gaze traveled slowly down to the bottom. There

was an enormous splotch of purple wax that had been impressed with a seal. She frowned at it. And then she knew. Her heart spasmed and it was hard to breathe. It was Jutras. She quickly unfolded the other two parchments. They were identical to the first. A contract, she realized. They had each been signed, and there was a space at the bottom for another signature and seal.

Someone in Crosspointe was consorting with the Jutras.

A frisson of fear shivered through her as she sank down onto the edge of the table, the air going out of her. "Braken's cods," she whispered. "What's going on?"

Who in Crosspointe would have anything to do with the Jutras? They were evil—Lucy could think of no other word for them. They spread through the eastern lands around the Inland Sea like an unending tide of ravenous *sylveth* spawn. They absorbed the people they conquered, turning them into warriors and slaves. It wasn't fight or die, but fight or see your families slaughtered and eaten like cattle. Lucy shivered. The Jutras atrocities and their rapacious devotion to the spread of their empire was unrelenting. They sought to bring every living creature under their domain—any that refused were murdered. As they engulfed more countries, their hunger only grew, and with it, the size of their army. Crosspointe's only defense from invasion was the Inland Sea. The Jutras couldn't cross—they had no Pilots, thank the gods. But perhaps they had another way, with the aid of a traitor.

Lucy made a sound of horror. She had to do something.

She stared at the parchments, her mind tangling in itself. Her first instinct was to take the documents to the king. Each member of the royal family could show his or her necklace and gain instant access to the king's presence. But what would happen then? Certainly William would believe her. But in recent years there had been growing discontent with his rule. The Chancery suit

further undermined his authority. It had made the entire
royal family look like profligates—leeches on society—
as no doubt was the intention. No, William might believe
her, but everybody else would point the finger at her,
accused as she was of stealing the blood oak. And certainly the blackmailer would do as promised and she'd
be in the night's papers, her collection of true ciphers
exposed. It would only confirm she was a traitor. They'd
say the contract was her doing, that bringing it forward
was just a devious plot to deflect the blame from herself
onto some made-up scapegoat. If William decided to believe her, he would be castigated, perhaps even accused
of being part of the plot.

She rubbed her forehead, feeling the beginnings of a
headache. Just the threat of the Jutras gaining any sort
of foothold in Crosspointe would cause riots. It was easy
enough to ignore the threat when the Inland Sea prevented the Jutras from ever setting foot on Crosspointe
soil, but if that protection was threatened—

Lucy swallowed, breathing slowly, trying to think. The
smartest thing to do would be to learn what the contract
said and whom it was meant for. Then she could present
the evidence to William. If she had proof, it wouldn't
matter who she was. She licked her lips. If the cipher
on her arm didn't kill her first. She shook her head resolutely. No. She wouldn't let it.

As if she could stop it.

A chill swept down her legs as she refolded the parchments with slow precise care. There was more going on
here than she'd dreamed. This wasn't just about her—it
really wasn't about her at all. She was a means to undermine King William, and perhaps open the shores to a
Jutras invasion. She snarled in the gloom. Not if she
could damned well help it!

She looked at the ruined box. She couldn't put the
parchments back inside. Nor could she take them home
or anywhere else the blackmailer might expect. She had
to hide them.

She thought for a moment. And then she had it. Quickly

she removed the jewels from their nests and put them in her satchel. She sealed the box in an empty crate and put it under a stack of empty bins and cartons. No one would look there for it soon and when someone found it, it would be hard to connect it to her without something to identify where it came from. She put the lantern away. With quick, jerky movements, she pulled off her cloak, removing her bright saffron customs surcoat and wadding it up in a ball. She shoved it behind a set of shelves before donning her cloak again and slipping outside.

The wind had increased, and now it smelled of dampness, as if rain would be following soon. Lucy hunched into her cloak, pulling her hood up over her hair, and angled back toward the docks. At the end of the complex she crossed an alley into another running behind a row of houses and shops. At the far end was a small building standing by itself. It was made of dark gray slate with white windows. Lucy went up to the cellar doors. She grasped the handles and felt a tingle in her palm as the locking spell released. She levered open one side and clambered onto the steps. As she descended, the wind snatched the door, heaving it upward. Lucy grappled it, her feet lifting into the air. Then the wind let go suddenly and the door dropped with a crash.

Lucy clutched the handle, scrabbling to find a foothold in the darkness. At last she balanced on a step and eased downward, holding her hands out in front of her, banging her knee against the corner of a table. She swore softly and vehemently, but didn't stop. On the other side of the cellar was a blank wall made of brick. She felt her way down to the corner of the wall and reached her fingers up over her head. At last she found what she was looking for: three small depressions in the mortar between two bricks. She held her fingers there for a moment. A tingle and the sound of a muted *snick* marked the opening of a hidden door. She pushed it open and a *sylveth* light sprang to life in welcome.

She stood in a small, square room. The walls were

lined with roughly constructed shelves holding a myriad of ship equipment, tools, blankets, clothing, boots, oilskins, rope, buckets, grease pencils, and paintbrushes. A stack of chests and ditty boxes filled the bottom shelves. There were a dozen mismatched oars leaning in one corner, and bolts of sailcloth in another. On the wall in between was an iron door.

The room smelled musty and briny, though it was as dry as toast. Lucy glanced up sharply as the ceiling creaked beneath the weight of someone walking across the upstairs floor. The house was a flophouse for those members of the royal family who worked on the water and who needed temporary quarters. It wasn't well-known outside of those who had cause to use it and only those who wore the necklace could open the locks and enter. Lucy had slept here on occasion, when she was too tired to go home between shifts.

The storage room she was standing in wasn't meant to be kept secret from anyone. It had been hidden entirely by accident. At some point, workmen had been hired to rebrick the walls in the cellar and had covered the doorway. The discovery wasn't made until the mortar had hardened. By then, it was too much trouble to remove the bricks and instead the door had been majicked to open when someone pressed the proper indentations. The door on the opposite wall led to a tunnel below the quay that emptied out onto a narrow wooden dock. During high tide, the dock was calf-deep in water. But for those staying at Crossley House, it meant a handy and free place to tie up a dinghy.

Lucy crossed the room and was about to go through the iron door when the stack of oilskins caught her attention. She fumbled in her satchel for her knife and sawed off a sleeve of one of the overcoats. She pulled out the Jutras contracts and slid them quickly inside, the sting of their majick making her teeth itch. She was about to fold them up, then hesitated. Slowly she withdrew one of them. If she was caught with it, they'd put her on the Bramble ship without stopping to ask questions. But if she wanted to find out what it said, she had to find someone who could translate it. Which meant keeping a copy with her.

Not giving herself time for second thoughts, she thrust it into her satchel. She quickly finished folding the ends of the sleeve tightly around the remaining copies to keep out the damp and opened the door. Darkness filled the tunnel like night. Just inside was a bucket of sand containing a handful of upended candles. Above it was a shelf holding a striker. She lit a candle and hurried out into the gloom, closing the door firmly behind her.

The passageway was low and she was forced to duck as the floor rose slightly and then evened out. She could hear the sounds of the wind rushing and waves washing against the shore. She crossed under the quay, coming to the top of a short stairway cut out of the rock. The steps were slippery with moss and damp. She eased down carefully and then took a sharp turn to the right, arriving on a wooden pier nestled in a natural alcove. It was unoccupied. The tide was coming in and waves slapped at the footings. The wind scooped into the rocky recess like cold, digging fingers. Lucy shivered, dropping her extinguished candle in the waiting bucket. She glanced about furtively, making sure that no one could see her.

The narrow dock was bracketed on either side by towering outcroppings that protruded ten feet or more into the water. Above, the heavy wooden beams of the quay provided a roof. On the left, the customs docks stretched out in the harbor. Lucy could see inspection teams swarming the decks of the ships that rocked and bobbed on the choppy waves. On the right, the expansive commercial docks owned by the Weverton family began. There was less activity there, as most of those ships waited for inspection. With the strike, there were no stevedores or lighters crisscrossing the waters, no cranes of netted cargo swinging back and forth, and no gangs of boisterous truckers waiting to haul the goods away. But rather than tranquil, the quiet seemed tense, explosive. Like a thunderstorm building. Lucy could almost feel the commerce in Sylmont grinding to a halt. If it didn't resolve soon, there might be riots as mercantile shelves emptied and didn't refill. During Chance, Crosspointe was entirely cut off by the storms. If there was a food shortage, it would get very ugly.

But the lack of traffic was good for her today. She retreated to the back of the alcove, where a rusting ladder clung to the rock. It led up to a narrow pocket below the quay. A person could worm his way beneath to an opening near one of the support pilings. It was designed as an escape hatch in case someone got caught in a storm surge or a spring tide.

Lucy slung the long strap of her satchel over her chest and mounted the ladder, the oilskin packet clutched in her hand. She paused at the top, searching. A number of deep cracks ran through the stone. She stretched far to the left. Here the shadows disguised the wall—the sun never shone here. She pushed the packet deep inside one of the cracks until she couldn't see it. It should be safe enough. It was unlikely the Chance storms would drive the waves high enough to wash it out. She gave a mental shrug. It would have to do. She didn't have any other ideas.

She climbed up over the top of the ladder and worked her way toward the misty light falling down through the opening up to the quay. She hoisted herself slowly up out of the hole, keeping herself hidden behind the piling. She peered out in both directions, her stomach clenching. She saw no one. Had she outstripped the blackmailer's spies?

At that moment the wind gusted and the pewter skies opened up. Rain sizzled across the water. The leading edge fell over Lucy and in moments she was drenched. She stared a moment in annoyed surprise. Her cloak was majicked against weather. All the same, it was soaking up the wet like a sponge. She shook her head. The explosive breaking of the spell on the box must have destroyed the cloak's protective spell as well. She gritted her teeth. The spell had cost three Hurn's eyes. Half as much as she made in a month. Not that she was in danger of getting paid anytime soon. She gusted a sigh and struggled to her feet, making a dash for shelter. She instinctively turned away from the customs docks and headed into Tideswell.

She'd not gone more than thirty feet when deafening alarm sirens shredded the air.

Lucy halted midstride, spinning around, eyes darting as she searched for pursuers. There was no one. She shook herself. Sirens weren't used for chasing down errant customs agents. Not even one who had an illegal hoard of true ciphers and had just become a thief. They were for emergencies—fires or . . .

Cold realization seeped down inside her. Her body went taut with disbelief. She was too late.

Invasion.

Chapter 15

The sirens shrieked like tearing metal. They erupted from stations all around the harbor, winding together in a skein of warning and distress. The air reverberated with the sound. The vibration sank inside Lucy and she shuddered. Then she began to run. Back toward customs.

People boiled out onto the quay from either side. They carried barrel staves, knives, cudgels, loggerheads, boat hooks—whatever weapons came to hand. Many were striking lighters and stevedores. Their faces were white with disbelief and fear. They surged past the customs docks to the Tideswell platform. It was a wide space at the center of the quay. It was surrounded by statuary and stone benches and at the top sprouted the Maida Vale. The broad avenue skirted around the Riddles, meandering up through Cranford, Cheapside, Blackstone, and Salford Terrace, ending at the castle gates. The platform also gave an unimpeded view of the harbor's mouth.

Lucy squirmed through the mass of bodies. The cipher on her arm had begun to warm again, and when she pressed against a fat man dressed in a mate's uniform, he recoiled as if jabbed. By the time he whirled about, Lucy had pushed around a trio of gray-haired women in hobnailed boots carrying the heavy awls used in sail making. She wrapped her left arm in the damp folds of her cloak and held it against her stomach. With any luck it wouldn't burst into flame.

Her heart felt like it was rattling against her ribs as she squeezed to the edge of the platform, leaning back against the thrust of the crowd so that she wouldn't get pushed into the water. She held her hand over her eyes against the wind-driven rain, squinting through the murky fog and wet.

For a while, there was nothing. Then slowly a shape emerged. A ship, but with an unfamiliar shape. It was stubby and sat high in the water. It was painted black with a yellow bowsprit and thick yellow stripes down its length. Most of its triangular black and red striped sails flapped uselessly, shredded by gale winds. The yardarms twisted and swung, the foremast listing drunkenly to the side, held in place by tangled rigging. The main course and the main topsails were still intact, keeping the crippled ship moving. Lucy shook her head, refusing to believe what she was seeing.

"Jutras."

The word was echoed all around her, accompanied by various gestures to deflect evil. Followers of Chayos bunched the fingers of their right hands into their left palms and sharply flicked away invisible dirt. Those who held to Braken stroked a splayed right palm across their eyes. Meris's adherents balled their left hands into fists and blew across the tops of their knuckles. The follows of Hurn stroked the index and middle fingers of their left hands over their eyes and pointed the fingers at the invader. But nothing made the Jutras ship disappear. Limping ahead of the driving wind, it sidled closer to the platform.

Sailors in ragged clothing scurried over the decks, crawling on the tangled rigging and trying to furl the sails, even as others cranked the capstan to drop the anchor and slow the ship. She could hear the bellows of the captain or mate calling rapid orders in Jutras. But the rigging was a mess. The main course twisted, one end flapping free. The main top braces swung and jerked as the men fought to bring the sail under control. Loose lines snaked through the air, flogging the seamen unmercifully. When the sail refused to give, they hacked it down. The heavy canvas crumpled and swept across the deck and over the rail. It rammed a seaman, sending him careening overboard. He bobbed in the water, arms flailing, his screams lost in the sounds of the siren, wind, and waves. There were shouts from the massed crowd as the Jutras sailor disappeared beneath the prow of the ship, though whether in sympathy or righteous anger, Lucy couldn't be sure. A moment later the anchor dropped at last and the ship jerked sharply, pulling ponderously around only a few dozen yards from the platform.

The sirens continued to scream. A wedge of armored Hornets pushed through the crowd, prodding people back. Lucy sank back into the throng, sifting back through the tense bodies until she stood behind the crowd, pressed up against the wall of a teahouse. She was soaking wet, but she didn't feel the cold. She didn't feel anything. A Jutras warship in Blackwater Bay. It wasn't possible. The Jutras couldn't cross the Inland Sea. They had no Pilots to navigate them through the ever-shifting currents and underwater landscape, the *sylveth* tides, and the knucklebone weirs. And yet—here one was.

She thought of the contract she'd found in the blackmailer's box. Her anger swelled, clawing like a cat. Someone from Crosspointe had helped them. Which meant— Was this ship the first of an armada? Were the Jutras about to overrun Crosspointe?

Fear sizzled up her back. Crosspointe had no army, only the majicars. But the Jutras had majicars of their own. If they had found a way to bring their army across the sea, Crosspointe would most certainly fall.

The realization jolted Lucy into action. She shoved through the crowds descending the Maida Vale and headed for Faraday. Sarah would know someone who could read the contract. If not, Lucy would take it to Cousin William and pray it wasn't too late.

There were no footspiders to be found and Lucy was soon breathless. Her head ached from her fall in the warehouse and her legs burned with the effort of climbing up into Salford Terrace. She was hungry and her mouth was sticky and dry. Her sodden cloak dragged at her. She stopped to rest in the lee of a building, bracing herself against the wall. She could no longer see the harbor, but the emergency sirens continued to wail. People milled in the street asking questions, their fear palpable.

She had just crossed into Sherborn Park when the sirens ceased. Lucy staggered. The silence smothered her. She spun around. The harbor was hidden by low clouds and thundering rain. She swiped at her eyes. Still nothing. But it was a hopeful sign.

It was midafternoon before she arrived at Faraday. She went around to the servants' entrance and pulled the bell. A scrubbing boy answered and stared at Lucy in bug-eyed startlement. She could imagine what she looked like. She didn't bother explaining herself, but thrust past and down the short flight of steps to a wide corridor of unfinished stone. She marched down to the kitchen and went inside, basking in the heat of the oven.

"What's this? Who do ye think ye are, sneakin' in here makin' a mess all over my floor?"

Lucy turned slowly, lifting off her hood. Sarah's cook was brandishing a long metal spoon in one hand, the other braced on her hip. Her round face was screwed tight with anger, her skin flushed and damp from the heat of the kitchen. When she saw who Lucy was, she relaxed slightly, but didn't lower the spoon. She'd heard the sirens too.

"I apologize, Matilda. But in all frankness, I'd rather track my mess through your kitchen than Sarah's parlor. The consequences are less dire."

"Mebbe so," Matilda said, lowering the spoon at last. "Boy, take Miss Trenton's cloak and wring it out in the washroom. Hang it by the fire, and mind ye, spread it out so it dries. I'll fetch ye something to dry yerself with," she said to Lucy, and bustled away.

The towels she brought didn't really help. Lucy was soaked to her skin. She tried to wring out the hem of her tunic, but water continued to run down her legs in streams. She removed her boots and socks, which Matilda had a scullery girl whisk away to put by the fire with her cloak.

"What ye need is a hot bath and dry clothes."

"I need a lot more than that," Lucy said sardonically, glad that the weather spell on her satchel had survived. "Better send word up to Sarah that I'm here."

The footman returned with a blanket and orders to escort Lucy upstairs. She wrapped herself up, trying hard not to drip on the plush rugs lining the hallways. Sarah opened the door and drew Lucy inside, ordering hot water for a bath.

She turned to Lucy, her arms crossed over her breasts. "You're a sight. Does this have anything to do with the sirens?"

"Not a footspider to hire between here and the docks," Lucy agreed, going behind the dressing screen and peeling off her clothing. She dropped them on top of the blanket, her skin pimpling and her teeth beginning to chatter.

Sarah passed her a dressing gown. Lucy pulled it on, putting her seal in the pocket. "The big news is that a crippled Jutras warship is sitting at anchor in Blackwater Bay." She couldn't help her snort of amusement. Maybe she wouldn't be on the front page of the evening's newspaper, after all.

She came out from behind the screen to find Sarah staring, her face blank.

"What—*that* makes you speechless? Not me having a collection of illegal ciphers? Astonishing. Maybe you should pour yourself a drink to steady your nerves. And me too, while you're at it. There's more."

"Steady my nerves? I'll have you know my nerves are

stone. I was under the impression the Jutras couldn't cross the Inland Sea," Sarah retorted, taking a decanter from a sideboard and pouring each of them a healthy snifter of brandy. She handed one to Lucy. "But this may warm the ice in your belly."

"I doubt it." Lucy took it anyway and gulped half the liquid. It went down like water. Almost immediately she felt dizzy. She hadn't eaten since breakfast.

There was a knock at the door and Sarah let in a short parade of footmen carrying copper urns of hot water. They poured them into the bathtub before the hearth and left. Lucy didn't wait for Sarah's invitation to step into the scalding water. She sank down up to her neck.

"Meris, but that feels good." She worked her fingers into her draggled hair, pulling out the pins and letting the wet mass fall behind her, outside of the tub. The fire would dry it soon enough.

Sarah sat in a low chair, sipping her brandy, her eyes turning to slits. "Now that you're comfortable, why don't you tell me what's going on?"

Lucy began with the Summerland's ball—was it only three nights ago? It seemed so much longer. She ignored Sarah's smirk when she described her meeting with Marten in the garden. In a matter-of-fact voice she described the events of Emberday, first the attack of the cipher and then the healing with Marten's unregistered majicar.

"He must be a decent majicar if you felt up to romping in bed all night with the handsome sea captain," Sarah observed.

Lucy held up her hands, turning pruny from the soak in the tub. Pink scars made elaborate geometric patterns across her skin. "I still have the use of them."

"Lucky," Sarah said.

"Maybe it's fate. Maybe I'm meant to end up on the Bramble."

"The Bramble? More likely you'll end up in a bonfire of your own making."

"Better than at the mercy of the Jutras. It may be they are about to invade."

Sarah sat up. "What are you talking about?"

"I went to work this morning and was suspended pending a hearing—they seem to think I stole the blood oak. After, I broke into a warehouse and retrieved a box—the blackmailer told me exactly where to find it. I opened it"—Lucy rubbed her fingers over the back of her head, wincing at the ache that spread over her skull at the light pressure—"rather unexpectedly and explosively. In it were a number of very valuable jewels. And this." She stood abruptly and stepped out of the tub, pulling the dressing gown back on. The linen clung clammily to her skin. She opened her satchel and retrieved the Jutras contract, handing it to Sarah. "I don't suppose you can read it?"

The other woman unfolded it, scanning it slowly and lifting her eyes to meet Lucy's expectant gaze. "It's Jutras. That's an imperial seal."

Lucy nodded. "Someone is dealing with the Jutras. And now they've sailed into Blackwater Bay and dropped anchor. The ship's in bad shape—it was storm chewed for sure. But nonetheless, it is here, and this document may be the reason why. Can you make anything out of it at all?"

Sarah shook her head. "A few words. Nothing of any sense. So this is what your blackmailer has been about. What are you going to do?"

"I was to turn it over to someone at the docks two glasses ago. The arrival of the Jutras ship made that impossible, even if I were inclined. The blackmailer promised to expose me in the evening edition of the paper if I didn't follow his orders. He may do that. But on the other hand, if he thinks I went ahead and retrieved his merchandise, he may want to try to negotiate with me first. Not that I intend to go home and wait for him or the Crown Shields. I need a place to hide until I can find someone to translate this. Do you know anyone who can read Jutras?"

Sarah's answer came much slower than Lucy hoped. "Maybe. I'll have to ask around. It'll take a day or two."

Lucy refused to let her disappointment show. "I shall just have to be patient, then."

"Not one of your strongest qualities."

"Perhaps I shall improve with practice."

Sarah smiled. "I doubt it. What will you do now?"

"Buying the evening paper seems like a good idea. And then I'll go underground. I don't have to turn up for work until the hearing. Unless the Crown Shields come looking for me, no one will miss me."

"Except Blythe, who will call out a pack of Corbies to find you."

"I'll send word to her. And to my father," Lucy said, remembering Hedrenion. Her stomach chose that moment to growl loudly. She winced.

"In the meantime, why don't I have Matilda send up some dinner and have a footman fetch the paper?"

"If you don't, I will."

After Sarah had called a servant, she turned back to Lucy with a sly look.

"Let's find you something to wear and you can tell me more about your adventures with Captain Thorpe."

"And aside from a bedsheet, what in your closet do you think might fit me?" Lucy asked, eyeing Sarah's lithe figure.

The other woman was not given the opportunity to answer. A sudden pounding thundered at the front door. Sarah went to the window overlooking the street and peered out. "Crown Shields. Apparently your blackmailer is true to his word."

"And they say such men can't be trusted. Couldn't he have waited until after dinner?" Lucy kept her voice light, even as panic thrilled through her. The cipher shot needles into her arm in response. She clutched it against her waist, trying to breathe slowly.

"You can't be here. Grab your things."

Lucy scooped up her sopping garments from behind the screen and followed Sarah into the bedchamber. It was richly decorated, with heavy, ornate furniture. Her four-poster bed sat high up on a pedestal. It was swathed with gauzy green draperies like a fairy bower. Sarah climbed up on top and reached down between the mattress and the headboard. She jumped down and pushed against the bed. It pivoted, the headboard pulling away from the wall. Beneath it was a square hole with iron rungs fixed to one side.

"You can hide down there until they leave. They won't find it."

"And if they don't leave?" Lucy asked.

"Then follow it out. Now hurry!"

Lucy climbed up beside Sarah and dropped her clothes down the shaft. They landed seconds later with a plopping sound. She dangled her satchel over and let it go before sitting on the edge and swinging her legs over to get a foothold. She paused.

"What about you?"

"I'll be fine. They'll do their search and be gone. It may take a while. Make yourself comfortable down there. You'll want this." She grabbed a thick blanket from the end of the bed and handed it to Lucy. "Now get down there and be quiet. Sooner they're gone, the sooner you'll get to eat. There are candles and things at the foot of the ladder."

Lucy still hesitated. "Maybe you should come down here too."

"I've nothing to worry about from the Crown Shields and I'm not letting them chase me out of my home and business," Sarah declared. "Now go. Get some rest if you can. I had a client bring in a load of stuff to pawn. I need you to have a look at it. I can't say for certain, but I think it might be salvage. Most of the ship marks were removed, but you can still make out some of them. One is the *Kalibri*, another the *Sweet Song*." She hesitated. "Your seal is on those crates."

"What? That can't be. I didn't put my seal on any of the salvage. It hasn't been inspected yet."

"Maybe they are from inspections you did on the ships some time ago?"

But Lucy was already shaking her head. "I've never

been assigned those ships before. The *Kalibri* was only commissioned this year."

The sounds of shouting came from belowstairs. Sarah's lips tightened.

"I'd better go. We'll sort it out later. I've put everything in the vault. It's not going anywhere. Keep quiet. I'll be back for you as soon as I can."

There was nothing left for Lucy to do but comply. Slowly she climbed down, a lump in her throat that she couldn't swallow. Above her, the bed swung firmly shut. But the cipher on her arm flared bright and hot. Her hands began to blister on the rungs as they grew fiery. She dropped the blanket and clambered quickly the rest of the way down. Heat streaked through her. Her skin felt scorched. Sweat trickled down her forehead, over her ribs, and down her flanks. She wanted to tear off the dressing gown. Her hair steamed and smelled like wet dog.

Lucy paced back and forth, bare feet slapping the smooth stone, shaking her arms, and breathing deeply. Sarah would be fine. She'd escaped from Esengaile and the men sent to murder her and she'd survived the iron collar. She'd lived years on the edge of a knife. She could take care of herself. Lucy repeated the reassurance under her breath in a constant litany. She could hear nothing but her own breathing and the swish of cloth as she moved. At last she stopped, holding her breath. Nothing. The stone walls allowed no sounds to permeate.

She returned to pacing. Her hunger made her dizzy and her legs and feet were stiff from the walk from the harbor. She found candles by the light of the cipher and lit one. She picked up her wet clothes and wrung them out, hanging them on the ladder to dry. She wrapped herself in the blanket and settled on the floor to wait.

Her thoughts tangled together as she ricocheted from concern for Sarah to worry for Blythe and James, to prayers that her family had warned Cousin William, to fears of the Jutras. And how had her seals ended up on salvage cargo in Faraday? Her mind gnawed itself as she tried to make sense of it all. At some point she fell asleep, the brandy she'd gulped on an empty stomach combining with her overwrought emotions and physical exhaustion to overwhelm her.

She woke in the dark. The candle had burned out and her cipher no longer glowed. She lay on her side, her back against the wall. She sat up, grimacing at the ache in her neck, shoulder, and hip from lying on the cold hard floor. She rubbed her hands over her face, scrubbing at the crusted drool on her cheek, and pulling a stray hair out of her mouth. Slowly she stood and felt her way across the narrow space to the bin of candles. She lit one, feeling a rush of relief as the flickering flame pushed back the darkness.

How long had she been asleep? She touched her clothes hanging on the ladder and felt an unpleasant jolt of surprise. They were nearly dry. She glanced upward, but the bed remained securely in place. A wash of anxiety woke her cipher. It cast a yellow nimbus around her wrist. She licked her lips, feeling a sudden desperate thirst, followed almost instantly by cramping hunger. She shivered, becoming aware of her nakedness beneath her dressing gown. It made her feel vulnerable.

Quickly she grabbed her clothing and dressed again, shivering as the damp cloth sheathed her skin. She had no socks or boots. They were drying by the fire with her cloak. Lucy swore softly. Her cipher brightened. She broke off, taking several deep breaths. The light of the cipher only increased. She couldn't fool it into thinking she was calmer than she was.

Well, she wasn't going to sit here getting more desperate and angry until the thing cooked her in her own juices. She grabbed her satchel and slung it over her shoulder. Grasping the rungs of the ladder, she climbed up to the top. After searching, she found a small lever hidden flush in the wall. She pried it up with her forefinger and pulled it back. Above her, a crack appeared. Lucy climbed closer, pressing her ear as close as she could. She heard nothing. Cautiously she reached up and pushed the bed wider until there was room to climb through. The room was a mess. The bedclothes were piled on the floor, the furniture turned topsy-turvy. Drawers from the dresser were upside down and the tapestries had been pulled awry. The mirror above the vanity was spiderwebbed with cracks.

Fear balled in Lucy's stomach. She climbed up out of the hole and pulled the bed so the opening could not be seen. She listened, but still there were no sounds. Slowly she picked her way across the bedchamber into the sitting room. Her bare feet squelched in the soaked rug. The bathtub was tipped on its side, the water making pools on the floor. The screen had been smashed and lay in splinters. The drapes hung in tatters, revealing the darkness outside. Lucy went to the window, careful to keep to the side so no one would see her. Crown Shields milled in the street, guarding Faraday. There was no sign of Sarah.

Lucy retreated to the hallway, inching along, listening for guards. The silence was chilling. Every room she passed was torn apart. As her tension increased, the cipher began to glow like a small sun. Lucy snatched a cloth from a hall table and used it to muffle the light.

She eased out onto the landing above the entry. It was in shambles, but deserted. Lucy heard footsteps and voices outside the door. It rattled and opened. She didn't wait but scurried back up the hallway, ducking into a service passage. She trotted the length of the house and pattered down the stairs toward the kitchen and servants' quarters. Every room was ransacked, and there was no sign of anyone.

In the kitchen, Lucy found a loaf of bread and a length of sausage on the floor underneath a broken stool. She bolted it ravenously while she searched for her cloak and boots. They were nowhere to be found. Instead she scavenged a pair of stiff heavy-soled shoes from the mudroom. They were too large, but she stuffed the toes with cleaning rags. She foraged for a cloak in one of the footmen's quarters. It was made of heavy black wool and spotted with moth holes. The hem was dirty and it smelled of mildew. But it was better than nothing.

She returned to the kitchen looking for something to drink. She found a barrel of water in the buttery. She dipped a tin cup full and drank deeply.

Her excursion had taken only ten minutes. With the exterior of the house guarded, her best escape route was the passage beneath Sarah's bed. Lucy returned up the stairs, setting her feet carefully. She froze when a step squeaked. When nothing happened, she inched upward, easing out onto the landing. She could hear a rumble of voices and then from the other end of the hallway a female Crown Shield stepped out of Sarah's room.

For a moment Lucy stared, unable to move. Then pain speared up her arm from the cipher. She turned and flung herself back down the stairs, three steps at a time. The woman shouted. Lucy raced out to the back entrance where she'd entered earlier in the day. She tripped and scrabbled up the steps using her hands. She fumbled with the latch and yanked the door open, every moment expecting hands to grab her. She didn't look back but bolted through the alley, where the two Crown Shields standing guard jerked about in surprise.

Lucy ground to a panting halt and then the shouts from inside spurred her to escape. Rain pelted her, hard as unripe olives. The two guards facing her lowered their pikes, weaving them in front of her.

"Stop and stand! You're under arrest in the name of the crown."

Lucy heard, rather than saw, the guards coming through the door behind her. She had no more time. She lunged sideways, ducking under a pike. It sliced through her cloak and dug agonizingly into her back. She screamed and yanked to free herself, tears blinding her. Suddenly more pikes appeared as guards boiled out of Faraday and came running around from the front. In seconds she was surrounded.

She turned around in a circle, crouching. The rational part of her mind, which knew she could not possibly get away from twelve Crown Shields pointing pikes at her, evaporated. In its place something wild and desperate clawed to life. Her ears filled with a roaring sound. She saw their lips moving, but the noise in her ears deafened her. Then one of them feinted with his pike, jabbing her left bicep. Lucy screeched and pulled back, clapping her right hand to the wound, glowering at the offending guard. He only laughed and prodded his pike toward her again.

The wound was deep into Lucy's muscle. The pain was terrible, forcing a cascade of whimpers from her; she couldn't stop herself, despite the malicious humor coloring the expressions of her captors. Her arm dangled against her side. Lucy cowered back, then jumped forward as the points of three pikes bit into her buttocks and thighs. The guards' laughter cut through her pain. Rage unfurled inside her like a volcanic flower. At that moment, the blood from her arm trickled down over the cipher.

The jolt of majick from it was like touching the sun. Lucy screamed as flames engulfed her. She dropped to the ground, twisting and rolling. She couldn't escape it. It was too much. She screamed, hammering her fists against the paving stones. There was nothing else she could do. She was trapped. She couldn't run, couldn't hide. She needed release. Over and over she pounded the ground.

She came back to herself abruptly, the majick draining out of her like swamping waves escaping out the scuppers of a ship. She was on her hands and knees, her head hanging as if her neck were broken, spittle dripping from her lips. Her ribs pumped as she panted deeply. She knuckled her eyes, trying to clear the gray film swathing them. Pain made her yank her hands down. She spread her fingers in dull surprise, turning them over. They were red and blistered like they'd been inside an oven. Her knuckles were shredded and swollen and her right pinky finger stuck out at an odd angle. She couldn't move it.

Lucy raised her head, turning to look around herself. Rain stung her face and raw hands.

Twelve charred lumps lay in a crumpled circle around her. The wind whipped the smell of cooking flesh and burnt hair. Lucy began to retch, coughing and gasping. Feeling too helpless on the ground, she climbed to her feet, weaving back and forth, unable to rip her eyes away from the grisly remains of the guards.

Urgency prodded at her. She should run. She should hide. She didn't move. Slowly she became aware of another sound. She lifted her gaze. Shock shuddered through her like a blow. The street was on fire. The paving stones were burning, as were the buildings— buildings made of *stone*. The flames clung to the rock, feeding on it like wood. They rose high in the air, fanned by the charging winds. The roadway was molten orange. Lucy stared as a wall melted and collapsed inward. It wasn't possible. She turned around. All the length of the alley as far as she could see was a wall of flames. Except Faraday and the island of ground she stood on.

Lucy covered her mouth with a swollen, raw hand. "Oh, sweet Meris, no!" she whispered. The cipher had done this. *She* had done this. A majickal conflagration.

Panic surged through her and with it the primitive need to escape. She darted back into Faraday, the only route open to her. She ran back through the house to Sarah's bedchamber. She pushed the bed aside, climbing onto the ladder, hardly aware of the pain of the pike wounds or her hands. She shut the door and began to climb down, but her burned and broken hands could not hold. She fell to the bottom of the shaft, head bouncing against the floor, her breath bursting from her lungs.

She lay there gasping, her head spinning, pain clamping her skull. Tears ran down her temples and dampened her hair. What had she done? What had happened to Sarah?

At last she clambered to her feet, tottering. She had to get away. She forced herself forward, limping through the tunnel, her mangled hands outstretched in the darkness. The cipher's glow was gone and her hands were too burned and broken to manage a striker. Her head spun and she could hardly think. All she knew was an animal desperation to escape, to find a place to lick her wounds. And in Crosspointe, there was only one place she could go. The Riddles.

Chapter 16

The escape tunnel emptied out under a bridge on the Westenra Canal. Lucy tugged at the bolts securing the metal grate covering the tunnel. Silent tears ran down her face as pieces of flesh sloughed away. Her fingers grew slippery with blood and moisture from burst blisters. She gritted her teeth, finally wrenching the last bolt free. She kicked the grate and it fell open with a loud clang. She waited. When no one cried an alarm, she stumbled out.

She slid down the bank on her side, clutching her hands against her chest. The wind whistled beneath the bridge and blew whitecapped waves on the canal, and the rain continued its scouring fall. Blurry crescents obscured the edges of her vision and chills vibrated deep in her chest. She stumbled along the edge of the canal, slipping and sliding on the muddy ground. The bank rose steeply beside her. She took it at an angle, her feet skidding on the wet grass. She lost her balance, sliding down to catch herself on her ravaged hands. She cried out, black mist shrouding her mind. The wind shredded the sound. She lay still until the dizziness passed and the pain subsided. *Escape.* She had to find a place to hide.

Slowly she sat up. Her borrowed cloak dragged on her, its wet length an anchor. But she didn't dare abandon it. She couldn't get all the way to the Riddles without something to cover her bloody clothes and mangled hands. Crawling on elbows and knees, she lurched up onto the narrow frontage road that followed the canal's winding path.

Back toward Faraday she could see the glow of the flames. They licked the night, undaunted by the rain. The fire was bigger than she thought possible and spreading quickly. She sucked in a breath. It could destroy half the city. If it reached the docks . . . She bit her lips, struggling to her feet. There was nothing she could do to stop it. And there was still the Jutras threat. And finding Sarah.

Fire bells rang and water carts pulled by mule teams clattered by, followed by volunteers carrying buckets. Lucy huddled inside her cloak, her feet dragging. Her hands felt like they were being chewed in a meat grinder. Cold made her bones ache. Her heart beat sluggish and heavy and she felt clumsy and nauseous. The only thing she knew was that she had to keep moving, keep putting one foot in front of the other.

A few hours after dawn she crossed into Blackstone. She was so near home. . . . Like a fish on a line, she couldn't resist the pull of it, of refuge. She shuffled along, the rain becoming heavier as the wind eased. She circled around to the southern side of her neighborhood and crossed through a small park at the end of her narrow street. She hid inside a cluster of leafless lilac bushes, barely keeping herself from bolting home, diving into bed, pulling the covers over her head, and pretending the previous day had never happened. The rain thinned for a moment, and Lucy strained to see up the street. If she could only warn Blythe and James before—

She never finished the thought. The telltale scarlet-lined cloaks of the Crown Shields flashed through the curtain of rain. There were half a dozen in front of the house. Doubtless there were more inside, searching through her things like they had done at Faraday. The idea made her grit her teeth, but then she chided herself. She'd killed men; she'd stolen cargo out of a warehouse;

she'd hoarded true ciphers—she had no right to resentment. Sarah and Blythe and everyone else were the only ones entitled to that.

Lucy chewed her upper lip, her chin trembling. Because of her stupidity and greed, her friends were going to prison. But they weren't guilty of anything. They would be questioned and released in short order, she told herself. She didn't believe it. How could they prove they *hadn't* helped her? They were guilty by association.

She couldn't keep her stomach down and retched violently into the gray thicket of lilac bushes. The only thing that came up was bitter bile. The taste burned her mouth and nose and her chest ached with the violence of the expulsion. She wiped her lips with the back of her arm, taking satisfaction in the pain that lanced through her from the pike wounds. She deserved it. She cast one last look up the street and then backed away.

The rain broke by midmorning, though the sky remained cloudy. The streets soon became crowded. People were tense, talking in hushed, angry voices about the Jutras. Word of the fire was beginning to spread and fear began to take root. Was the city about to burn? Were the Jutras behind it?

Lucy was finding it harder to keep herself going. Exhaustion and weakness tangled her feet and her vision had gone blurry. Her stomach cramped with hunger and her mouth was parched. Though she had money in her satchel, she couldn't open it. Her hands were curled into swollen claws. Her peeling skin was black and yellow and the flesh below oozed with pus. When she thought she'd pass out, she took refuge in a gazebo in a rose garden. Burlap packed with straw had been wrapped around the skeletal canes to protect them for the winter and there was little chance that any gardeners would be working and discover her. She collapsed on the plank floor, huddling into herself. She quickly fell into restless unconsciousness.

She started awake when a squad of Hornets trooped past. She shrank down. Her teeth chattered loudly and she couldn't stop them. More passed, as well as groups of Howlers, Corbies, and even Eyes. It was like a stirred wasp nest. Lucy put the edge of her cloak between her teeth to silence them, pretending to be invisible. She remained so throughout the rest of the afternoon, her mind moving hazily over the events of the last days, but she couldn't fasten on to anything. Every memory was slippery, squirming away as soon as she grasped at it. Soon she sank into confusion and again fell asleep.

Night found her shambling through the crowded, constricted neighborhoods of Cheapside. It was grimier here, with dirt streets and few sidewalks. The once-trim houses were run-down, with peeling paint and leaking roofs. Buildings leaned against one another like drunken sailors and the windows lacked glass. Lucy's boots and the hem of her cloak were soon caked with mud. Mindlessly she slogged on, dragging her feet, unable to lift them over puddles or debris, stopping every few dozen feet to rest.

It took her most of the night to reach the leading edge of the Riddles. She stumbled across the Maida Vale and slipped inside the tumbled maze with a feeling of release. Sobs clawed up her throat. She bit them back. The Crown Shields might not be searching for her here, but there were other dangers in the Riddles.

She swayed, gathering herself. In her long walk, she'd arrived at a plan for what she'd do when she arrived. If she wanted to find the traitor, she needed healing. She needed Keros. And here, where majick was more sparse than in the rest of Sylmont, her talent would guide the way.

She braced herself against a wall, avoiding the vomit and piss staining its length. Closing her eyes, she opened her senses, feeling the draw of majick from a constellation of sources. Even here in the Riddles, majick glimmered from every corner. For conveniences. For safety. For power. One source felt immense, like the moon pulling the waves. She ignored it. The majick of Keros's house had been smaller, elegant even. She scowled, sorting through the glittering shards until she found the one that *felt* like his house. She began to walk. But she was nearly out of strength. She could hardly see, hunching over like an ancient crone. But she kept on, winding a snarled path. The Riddles had been built nonsensically to confuse invaders. Streets often went nowhere. Tunnels ended in walls. There were few straight lines anywhere and the blocks were haphazardly shaped and sized. Several times she found herself in a dead end, having to retrace her steps until she could follow the thin call of majick again.

Someone spoke. She hardly heard it. It was taking all she had left to keep herself from collapsing. A hand on her arm, tugging on her cloak. Shouts. She stopped, forcing herself to hear.

"Didn'ya hear me, old woman? Twitch me yer cloak and what else ye got. Ye'll not be needin' it so long. Knackers can't be far behind ye."

Lucy turned her head ponderously, peering out from beneath the folds of her hood. The gangly youngster was hardly more than a boy. Behind him stood two skinny girls in garish dresses. The boy's cheeks were covered in downy whiskers, patchy around his mouth, and he was dressed in a fine waistcoat that hung to his thighs, the armholes dropping to his waist. Beneath were expensive trousers, now ragged and holed, tied with a rope around his waist. His feet were bare and he held a handful of her cloak in one fist, the other cocked threateningly back.

"Are ye maggoty? Give it to me!"

He yanked hard and Lucy stumbled into him. Unthinking, she grappled his hand when he shoved at her, seizing it in her bloody, charred left claw.

"Don't touch me." It was little more than a whisper. But her fear and fury merged and the cipher on her arm flared. Searing cold poured through her hand into him.

He screamed and struggled. Lucy let go almost immediately, the agony from her hand swallowing her in a scarlet tide. The boy turned and ran, followed by the girls. Lucy stood wavering, waves of pain and confounded power rolling through her. She whimpered and cried, snot running down over her lips and chin. Her bladder loosened and hot urine ran down her legs. She knew she could not let herself fall. She'd never get up. With her remaining strength, she pulled together all the shattered bits of herself she could find and told herself to *move*.

At last her legs and feet obeyed. The hot wetness dampening her legs soon turned cold, the stink twining with the rotting smells of the streets. But Lucy hardly noticed. Every scrap of concentration she had was going into taking the next step.

She didn't know how much time had passed before she found herself outside Keros's house. It looked the same. Refuse was piled against the walls and Lucy started when a lump twitched and rolled, a roaring snore emitting from it. It was only a beggar woman, wrapped in rags and curled up in a nest of paper, dead leaves, and rotting burlap. Lucy edged past her.

The door had no knob, no handle. Lucy stared in consternation. Marten had opened the door. *Majick*. The word trailed through her mind like mist. Of course. Only friends of Keros could so easily gain entrance. Lucy leaned her forehead against the rough wood, taking a deep breath. She lifted her foot and kicked. The resulting thud was dull and hardly broke the silence of the dawn. She kicked again. And again. She continued as long as she was able and then exhaustion and pain overwhelmed her. She sank down, her legs jackknifed against her chest, her back against the door. She laid her head on her knees, her hands lying helpless on the ground on either side. If he wasn't home, if he wouldn't answer, then she would wait.

Once again she lost track of time. It might have been an hour later or a hundred when she felt a hand on her shoulder and a baritone voice spoke to her.

"Come on, then. You can't lay about here. Move along, old mother."

Lucy lifted her head, raising a ruined hand to push back her hood. Keros was bent over her. The shock on his face was palpable.

"Not so old," she croaked. "Can I come in?"

She stared at him, willing him to let her in. His face was haggard with dark circles beneath his eyes. He hadn't shaved in several days, and his curly hair flopped greasily over his forehead, veiling his eyes. At last he nodded, hooking his hands under her arms to help her up.

"Come on."

Every muscle in Lucy's body screamed protest as she stood. Her hands brushed something and barbed agony burrowed down her nerves. Keros opened the door, motioning her to precede him.

"How did you find me?" he asked, removing his cloak and hanging it on a peg. His voice was hard and suspicious.

"I have a knack." Her voice cracked and she coughed.

He scowled. "What do you want?"

Slowly Lucy lifted her hands out from beneath her cloak. "Help."

"Braken's cods," he muttered. "What in the depths happened to you?"

"I . . . had an accident."

His brows rose. "An accident. Like the other night."

"Exactly." The word was slurred. "I can pay you this time. I have very valuable gemstones."

"Why aren't you seeing a Merstone majicar? One with a proper *illidre* and guild-sanctioned?"

"Several reasons. I should probably tell you the jewels are stolen."

Keros grinned, a lopsided, boyish expression that gave Lucy hope.

"And that's not the worst of it," she added, compelled to warn him.

His look weighed her. "Come on, then. Let's have a look."

He led her into the kitchen, motioning her over to the table against the wall. She staggered after.

He helped her off with her cloak. "By the gods, you smell. You need to burn your clothes."

"They're all I own."

Keros glanced at her sharply, clearly wanting to press her for more information, but he held himself in check. Instead he helped her up onto the table.

"It's not comfortable, but I'm not putting you in my bed. I don't need lice."

"You're a majicar. Can't you just—" She waved a hand in the air, and then sucked in a pained breath.

"I heal. I don't clean," he replied haughtily.

"Yes. I don't steal either."

Keros didn't answer, but took a cushion from a kitchen chair and put it down for a pillow. He went to a cupboard and took down a tin of tea and spooned some in a cup. He lifted a kettle from the cold hearth and murmured something, touching a finger to the copper. When he poured the water out, it steamed. He stirred in a dollop of honey.

"Stay here. I'll be right back."

He returned quickly carrying a leather case. The tea was wonderfully fragrant, smelling of bergamot and *chikri*, a mellow yellow tea from Glacerie. Keros unlatched his case and withdrew a green cut-crystal vial the size of his pinky finger. He pulled the stopper and dripped five drops into the cup.

"What's that?"

"It'll make you sleep. This healing wouldn't be easy under normal circumstances, but so soon after the last . . . it will go better if you're unconscious."

He held the cup to her lips. "Drink up."

Lucy stared down at it, a sluggish memory stirring in the back of her mind. Marten, her office, a cup of tea, waking up in bed with him making love to her . . .

"Come on, then. Or do you like suffering?"

She swallowed the hot liquid. It tasted delicious and

spread fingers of warmth through her. She finished it and looked at the majicar.

"What now?" She didn't hear the answer. A wave of black heaviness swamped her and she slumped senseless.

She slowly came back to herself. It felt like she'd been floating and now was sinking back down into her body. She blinked, her eyes gritty. Above her head was an unfamiliar beamed roof. She turned her head, smelling roasting chicken and vegetables. Her mouth watered painfully. She recognized the kitchen now, the polished wood floor, the parchment-colored walls with a black-and-white tile mosaic in a liquid pattern.

"Keros?"

Her voice caught and she began to cough. She sat up. Keros appeared by her side, patting her back.

"Easy, now. Here's some water."

He handed her a mug and she drank greedily. Suddenly she stopped, staring at her hands. They were pink and pale, like they had never seen sun. The calluses were gone and so were the glass scars. But they were whole. Likewise, the pike wounds were gone. She met Keros's gaze, her throat knotting.

"It appears I owe you thanks again," she said thickly.

"And some valuable stolen jewels. Come on, you've been asleep since yesterday morning. You need food. Careful of those hands. They're delicate. It'll be a few days before you can use them much. You'll want some gloves to protect them."

He steadied her as she slid to her feet.

"Easy, now," he said. Then his lip curled. "You still stink. I'm not about to try to eat with that stench. Let's get you upstairs."

He stopped at the counter and sliced off a hunk of bread, spreading it lavishly with butter before handing it to her. "That should tide you over."

Lucy gobbled the bread as she followed Keros up the back stairs to a small bedroom. It was spare, with plain furniture and white linens. A serviceable pair of brown

woolen trousers, stockings, and a buff-colored shirt and
tunic were laid out on the bed. Beside them were a
towel, a washcloth, and soap. Coal was piled in the grate
and a hip bath sat before the hearth.

Keros used his majick to light the fire and heat the
water so that steam curled from its surface. He retreated
to the door.

"Take your time. And put your clothes in the chamber
pot. Or better yet, put them on the fire and burn them."

Lucy was more than happy to peel off her filthy clothing, wrinkling her nose at the sharp odor of urine on
her trousers. She dropped them in the fire, preferring
the smell of charred cloth.

She washed quickly, marveling at her hands. But soon
anxiety descended. She'd been asleep a day, Keros had
said. And it had taken her two nights and a day to cross
Sylmont. What had happened to Sarah and Blythe and
James? Were they safe? Were they free? Was the fire
still raging? What about the Jutras?

She washed her hair as best she could, but it was so
tangled that the comb on the night table did little good.
Impatient for food and news, she abandoned the project
and dressed hurriedly. She rolled up the trousers so they
didn't drag. As soon as she was ready, she returned to
the kitchen. Keros greeted her and served her a bowl of
chicken and stewed vegetables with bread and butter.
She ate ravenously. When her stomach felt swollen and
she could eat no more, she pushed her bowl away and
sipped her tea, eyeing Keros through the steam. He'd
been watching her as she ate, and now leaned forward,
bracing his elbows on the table.

"You had three broken fingers and six shattered
knuckles, and your skin was all but burnt away. I scraped
away the damaged tissue and then healed you. Then I
found some stab wounds on your legs, back, and arms,
which I assumed you also wanted healed. I have to warn
you—anything like that happens again soon, and you'll
lose your hands. I don't think even a guild majicar would
be able to help you."

"I'll keep that in mind."

"You really have to be careful," he insisted.

"I didn't really plan to cut my hands or burn and mangle them," she said.

"It just happened, is that it?"

She lifted a shoulder in a half shrug. "Yes."

He squeezed his eyes shut, visibly reining in his frustration. He opened them again, glaring. "Perhaps you ought to try less hazardous pursuits."

"Clever idea. Wish I'd thought of it."

"What happened?"

Lucy looked away, swallowing. "Let's just say I've had better days."

Keros was silent, his brown eyes boring into hers as if he could force her to tell him what had happened. But she only returned the look obdurately. He sighed and changed the subject.

"What will you do now?"

Lucy set her cup down with a soft click. "I have some business to take care of before . . ." *Before the cipher burned her to ash.* "Anyway, the sooner I can take care of it, the better."

"I guess so."

Keros reached down onto the chair beside him and picked up a stack of newspapers and set them on the table before her.

"Makes for interesting reading. Not that you can believe everything they write. They get so much wrong. Still, it's quite riveting." He stood. "I've got an errand to run. I'll be back soon. Try not to undo all my hard work while I'm gone." He gestured meaningfully at her hands. "You're likely to get tired again soon. Don't fight it. You need the sleep to finish the healing. You know where the bedroom is. More comfortable than the table."

Lucy's hands settled lightly on top of the papers. She wanted to snatch them up, but waited as Keros cleared the dishes and set them by the sink. There was a pump next to it to draw water. Lucy was surprised to see such a convenience in a house in the Riddles. But then, Keros wasn't poor. He, like her, was merely hiding.

When he'd gone, she snatched up the first paper. It was the evening edition from Moonday, when she'd broken into the warehouse and stolen the jewels. The headlines were focused on the arrival of the Jutras ship. But low on the page was a story about her, just as the blackmailer promised. It reported her collection of true ciphers and speculated on her involvement with the salvage and theft of the blood oak. There was a hint that she had been hiding majickal abilities and that because she was a member of the royal family, her crimes were all the more heinous, even treasonous, and that they'd been deliberately overlooked by the crown. This was all based on the word of an anonymous "highly respected citizen."

She tossed the paper aside and grabbed up the second. This time, her name dominated the headlines. She was an unregistered majicar. She'd started a majickal fire in Salford Terrace and it raged unchecked, burning everything in its path. It even burned stone to ash. It was confirmed that she had a collection of seven true ciphers hidden in her house, and that the king himself was being questioned regarding her majickal abilities, as were her father and two of her brothers.

Lucy's head rocked back. She drew a shaky breath, her chin starting to crumple. Her father being questioned. And her brothers—which ones? The paper didn't say if they'd been arrested, only questioned. She soothed herself with that knowledge. Surely if they'd been taken into custody, the paper would have trumpeted it.

Another story just below the first reported that she was being investigated for smuggling. Her seal had been found on salvage items that had gone missing from the salvage sheds. They were found in the vault of Faraday, which had mysteriously been spared from the terrible fire. Her partner, Sarah Nettles, and employees were being held for questioning.

Lucy stared unseeing as the words ran together. It wasn't

possible. She never let her seal out of her sight except when she locked it in her vault at night. And no one else could use it. She hadn't touched any of that cargo. Not a single crate or barrel. How was this possible?

A worm of memory wriggled deep in her mind. She caught at it. The report for Alistair Sylday morning. Marten bringing a cup of tea. *Should I be distressed that you abandoned me so quickly for a cold chair, parchment, and ink?* She'd been in the middle of reading over her report. She had her seal out of the vault, reviewing the document before she signed it. Marten sitting on the edge of the desk watching her. Like he was waiting for something.

Lucy rubbed her hands up over her head, pressing her temples between her palms. The next thing she remembered was waking in bed with Marten kissing her, his hands on her breasts, his leg between her thighs as he pressed himself urgently against her. She didn't remember leaving her office and returning to bed. Later when he was gone, she found her report and the seal on her desk. She thought again of the drops Keros had put in her tea. And she knew. She *knew*.

Marten had drugged her and when she was asleep he'd put her seal in her unconscious hand and stamped who knew how many seal blanks. When he was through, he'd carried her to bed and made love to her.

Lucy almost didn't make it to the sink. She retched, feeling the already strained muscles in her chest and ribs wrenching with the violence of it.

It was several hours before Keros returned. Lucy was sitting in the same chair as when he'd left, the papers spread out before her. He came in carrying a canvas bag slung over his shoulder. Lucy looked up as he entered.

"You gave Marten some of those drops, didn't you? And he drugged me."

He put the bag on the counter and leaned back against it, his dark gaze unreadable. "I gave him some drops, yes."

She nodded, her lips tightening. She'd hoped he would tell her no. Not that she would have believed him. She slid her hand across the table. When she withdrew it, the purple dawnstar and silver-flecked Braken's heart remained. She stood, feeling feeble and old.

"That should cover what I owe you for the two healings and the clothes."

She didn't look at him as she headed for the doorway, her satchel in her hand.

"The doors are warded."

Lucy halted, a slow burn firing in her stomach. Deliberately she turned.

"I thought you said you didn't want me wrecking my hands again. Because if I have to, I'll tear a hole in your wall. But trust me on this—I won't have to."

His jaw went slack a moment. "Are the papers correct, then? You're a majicar."

She shook her head. "No."

"Then go ahead and try."

Lucy's chin lifted. "All right."

She turned again and walked down the hallway, taking her cloak from a peg. It had been cleaned. Keros followed her, standing close, his nostrils flaring like those of a hound sniffing after a fox.

"You may want to stand back," she said, reaching for the door.

He grabbed her arm. "Don't. Rest here a day or two. Until your hands finish healing."

She turned. "Why?"

"Can't we say I don't want to see my work go to waste, and leave it at that?"

"Marten drugged and framed me for smuggling, and you helped him. Why should I trust you?"

"I didn't know what he wanted with the drug when I gave it to him. And I did heal you. You need a safe place to recuperate. I won't tell anyone you're here. I owe you that much."

Lucy hesitated. He sounded sincere. And she had nowhere else to go. "All right."

"Good. Then go upstairs and sleep while I cook." He took her cloak.

She obeyed, fatigue wrapping her like a shroud. She trudged back to the kitchen and went to the stairs, stopping on the first step.

"You won't tell anyone I'm here?"

He shook his head. "No."

"Marten?" she pushed.

"He'll not hear it from me."

She nodded and began up the stairs.

"Lucy. I've known Marten a long time. He's got his flaws. Some more serious than others. But he has only ever hurt himself. This . . ." He shook his head, frowning. "This is difficult to believe."

"People change. Most everyone I know wouldn't believe that I'd ever break into a customs warehouse and steal something, much less—" She bit off the rest, taking a breath. She smiled grimly, motioning toward the table with her chin. "You should be careful where you sell those jewels."

With that, she went upstairs.

Chapter 17

Marten burst through the doors of the morning salon where Edgar was eating breakfast with Cecy. Marten flung the papers he was holding down on the table in front of his brother.

"What in the holy black depths have you done?" he demanded.

Edgar's welcoming expression faded, turning icy. He set aside the letter he was reading and stood, bending to take his wife's hand and kiss it.

"Your pardon, Cecy. I'm sure Marten doesn't mean to distress you. We shall step out for a few moments and I'll rejoin you as soon as may be."

He gathered up the papers that his brother had thrown down and stalked out.

Marten followed, seething with guilt, fury, and dread. The stories flooding the *Sentinel* had accused Lucy of outrageous, impossible things, but one struck him to the core—her seals found on smuggled goods. Seals that he'd stolen and given to Edgar. It was a Bramble offense. He'd tried to find her, to apologize, to explain, to confess—he didn't know. But she'd been suspended from her job and her house had been seized by the Crown Shields. Her friends and servants had been arrested and she had disappeared. Now there was bounty on her head. And he was responsible. He and Edgar.

Inside his office, Edgar slammed the door and

rounded his desk, shoving his chair aside violently before turning on Marten.

"What do you mean barging into my home and addressing me like a common servant? You had best remember your place and your manners. Cecilia cannot take your brutish behavior in her delicate condition."

"Brutish? *Me?* You goat-cracking bastard. She'll be sent to the Bramble. She never stole anything from the salvage, never smuggled anything. How could you do this?"

"Me? You stole her seals. She'd never be in this predicament if it weren't for you. Not that she's innocent. She may not have smuggled, but she apparently kept a hoard of true ciphers and set that fire in Salford Terrace. And don't affect to be surprised. I told you she would be a casualty and I tell you again to give her a wide berth. She's going to the Bramble and with luck, she won't be the only Rampling on the ship." He paused, saying slowly, "I'm very fond of you and I'd regret it if you found yourself sharing passage with her on the *Firedance*."

"Wide berth? Brother, I intend to find her and crawl on my knees begging forgiveness. And after that, I'll go to the lord chancellor and confess everything." He hadn't thought of it until that moment, but the words felt right, like he meant them.

Edgar sighed, righting his chair and sitting. He rubbed a hand over his brow. "Don't be a fool, Marten. Nothing you can do or say will save her now. All that will happen is that you will embarrass yourself and me, and you will likely be found guilty of conspiring with her. Your name has already come up in the salvage investigation—your tarnished reputation precedes you. If you tangle yourself in this anchor chain, you will certainly find yourself pulled under."

"When I am responsible for her ruin? What kind of man do you think I am?"

Marten cringed from the scornful look Edgar gave him.

"I think you know the answer to that, much as I wish I could believe differently. Besides, she deserves what she gets for allowing you to succeed."

Marten recoiled. He held himself rigid and still, speaking quietly. "You may be right. I may be the worst sort of man, but I won't let this stand."

"I'm afraid I can't let you interfere, brother."

"There's nothing you can do, short of cutting the tongue out of my head or murdering me."

Edgar raised his brows. "Shall I tell you what I can do?"

He pulled open a desk drawer and removed a leather folder. "Do you know what these are? They are your markers. All of them. You owe *me* money, of course. The other night at Sweet Dreams you ran up quite a tab. I knew you would, given the slightest encouragement. You're into me for nearly five drals. I have also bought markers from several others you owe, though you are to be commended for paying most of your creditors off with your winnings from the Lucy Trenton bet. What's left amounts to nearly three more drals. Altogether that's more than you are worth, I believe."

Edgar lowered the pages, his eyes glittering. "I can call your debts in right this moment. If you cannot pay, I can have you sold into servitude. How do you think you'd do in an iron collar? Think about it, Marten—at least fifteen years of your life. Presupposing you didn't dig the hole deeper for yourself in the meantime; you and I both know you cannot resist the lure of the tables. You'd lose your legal voice. Nothing you could say would be heard by anyone who matters. So think carefully about speaking out. I should not like you to act hastily."

Marten's hands clenched. The kindness in Edgar's tone did nothing to change the threat. A threat that he believed with all his heart. His brother didn't make idle threats. Marten growled helplessly, the sound tearing at his throat. Edgar had his balls in a vise.

"Stop this. What good can come of sending her off to

the Bramble? She's just a damned customs inspector,"
he pleaded.

"She's far more than that. And with her help, Crosspointe may be saved. Sacrificing her is nothing compared
to that. Now, I'd like to get back to Cecy. And Marten,
if you ever cause such a scene again in front of my wife,
I'll call your markers and send you to work in the coal
mines. You'll never see the light of day again."

Marten allowed himself to be escorted outside, striding jerkily down the sidewalk. Guilt and rage choked
him. Despite Edgar's threatening advice, he had to find
Lucy. Somehow, he had to make this right for her. How
could anyone believe such lies? A secret majicar like
Keros? The idea was laughable. Even more so was the
notion that she could possibly have a collection of true
ciphers. Lucy would not bend the law, much less break
it.

He clenched his jaw, coming to the bottom of the hill.
Ahead of him a half league across Salford Terrace near
the royal castle was a swollen column of oily smoke. A
fringe of orange showed beneath, even so far away. The
wind pushed it north and east toward the harbor and
the shipyards. Marten sucked his teeth. Lucy could never
be responsible for this. He didn't know her very well,
but he knew that much.

He had to find her. But where would she have gone?
Her home was seized, her family arrested. He didn't
know her friends. Except . . . Jordan.

He began to run.

Marten had never been to Jordan's home. Usually
they encountered each other at Sweet Dreams, where
Jordan liked to visit the baths and enjoy the attentions
of a long-legged whore or two. Occasionally they met in
society. It took Marten longer than he liked to get the
address from the merchant marine guildhall. He was
startled to learn that Jordan lived in Cheapside near the
river. He'd have guessed Salford Terrace or Blackstone
at the least. But his flat was unprepossessing, upstairs of

a bakery in the middle of a long row, the buildings built up against one another, sharing common walls.

Marten rang the bell and waited, shuffling his feet. He couldn't lose the memory of Lucy soft and warm beneath him, her eyes shining with passion, her mouth biting and tasting. And her hair—it had been an astounding surprise. Her red curls had hung like a silky waterfall to her waist. He felt himself growing hard and slammed his fist against the wall. The pain returned him to reality. He was a fool. He'd betrayed her. She wasn't going to be interested in bedding him again. The knowledge only made his mood worse.

He rang the bell again, yanking hard on the pull. The door jerked open at last and Jordan stood inside. He wore buff-colored trousers with boots and a white shirt hanging open. His hair was loose around his face and he hadn't shaved. His neck and chest were dappled with reddish blue love bites and scratches.

"Marten. What brings you here?"

"I need your help. Can I come in?"

Jordan hesitated. "Very well."

Marten followed his friend up the narrow stairs to a utilitarian flat. The floors were bare; the furniture was solid and lacking ornament. The light was bleary through the rippled windowpanes. Jordan motioned for Marten to sit and closed the pocket doors that led deeper into the flat. Marten heard women's voices, one low and husky, the other sweet and melodic. The sound of their conversation was cut off abruptly as the doors drew shut.

"My apologies. I didn't mean to interrupt your sport," he said, lifting his hand to his forehead in a mock salute.

Jordan shrugged unrepentantly, glancing down at the marks on his chest. "Exuberant, aren't they? But no need for concern. I needed a rest anyhow."

Marten forced a smile, catching sight of the newspapers scattered over a low table. He could see this morning's headline: ROYAL TREASON: LUCY TRENTON'S BETRAYAL. He bit the inside of his cheek, tasting blood.

"I expected something different," he said, his gaze

sweeping the room, unwilling to broach the subject of Lucy now that he was here.

"Oh? Gold furniture and *sylveth* chandeliers?" Jordan dropped into a stuffed chair, slouching down and negligently kicking out his feet before him.

"Something like that."

"This suits me well enough. I don't need a lot of fancy feathers. And I don't ask my family to visit."

Jordan's expression was stiff, warning Marten off the subject. The Truehelms were a very old, very wealthy family, with several estates across Crosspointe. Jordan's father was the lord chancellor, and one of his sisters was First Sept of the Metals Guild, his brother a Pilot. He captained one of his family's ships, but rarely spoke of them. There was clearly something amiss there, but Marten had always respected the other man's privacy and didn't pry.

"What is it? Moneylender trouble?" Jordan asked, watching Marten toy with the buttons on his turned-back cuffs.

Marten answered slowly. It grated that Jordan assumed his gambling was the heart of the matter. Was he so predictable? But of course he was. Edgar had wagered on it. For a moment he remembered the way Cyril Brackenridge had pressed money on him at the Summerland's ball. He was pathetic. The knowledge was bitter. He wished desperately for a drink, but Jordan hadn't offered. Sudden realization rocked him. Jordan hadn't offered because he was not welcome here. He was to be held at arm's length. He was a liability—sooner or later, he would betray his friends for money. He could read the truth in the guarded watchfulness in Jordan's demeanor. And worst of all, he was about to confirm that dismal opinion.

At that moment, Marten knew he'd never place another bet again. He saw the contempt in Edgar's eyes mirrored in Jordan's expression. He felt himself shrinking with humiliation. He wanted to scurry away with his tail between his legs. He caught himself up short. He couldn't let Lucy go to the Bramble for his deceit. Honor meant telling the truth and accepting the consequences. He had to take what he deserved. If he wanted respect, he had to earn it. Starting now.

He lifted his gaze, meeting Jordan's eyes levelly. "You know I was caught up against a lee shore with a gale blowing me in. Edgar gave me a way out. A substantial wager. Enough to get me almost entirely out of debt. I had to take it. I didn't think I had a choice." He paused, disgusted at himself. He'd had a choice. He could have been a man and not dragged an innocent woman into his mess. He raked his fingers through his hair, pulling the tie at the back of his head free. His hair fell around his face. He pushed it back, bracing himself for Jordan's anger.

"I won it. Did exactly what Edgar asked."

"And you felt the need to rush over and tell me about it?" Jordan's expression had turned sour and his upper lip curled with repugnance.

Marten thrust himself to his feet, pacing. He averted his face.

"You know, I always thought my gambling was only about me—that no one else got hurt if I was arrested, or if the moneylenders came after me. If I lost, it was my bones that got broken, my ass that was going to the Bramble."

"Stupid. I take it you've learned different?"

Marten nodded. "And I need your help to set it right. Doesn't matter what happens to me. I deserve whatever I get."

"Commendable, I'm sure," Jordan said coldly.

Marten acknowledged the disapproval, one side of his mouth curling upward. "I know I'm a bastard."

Jordan didn't dispute the point. "Why don't you tell me what you want?"

Marten drew a deep breath and blew it out, speaking quickly. "I stole stamped seals from Lucy Trenton. Edgar's using them to frame her for smuggling. When I confronted him, he threatened to call in my markers and put the iron collar around my neck. Then anything I say will be discounted out of hand. I've got to put a stop to this before he can silence me."

Jordan sat forward, his face hardening, white lines bracketing his mouth. His fingers curled around the arm of his chair, biting deep into the leather.

"You framed her?"

"Edgar did."

Slowly Jordan stood, his hands clenching, the muscles in his jaw working. "But you stole stamped inspections tags from her and gave them to your cocksucking brother."

Marten nodded.

Jordan moved faster than Marten would have thought possible. He grasped Marten by the collar and slammed him against the wall. Jordan pulled back his fist and smashed it into Marten's face, pummeling his face and chest. Marten didn't fight back, warding off the blows as best he could with his arms. Something inside him welcomed the punishing fists, welcomed the pain. He *deserved* this.

Jordan lowered his hands and slugged Marten twice more in the pit of his stomach. Marten doubled over, sobbing for breath. His left eye was nearly swollen shut and his right eye was blurry. Blood trickled down his right cheek from where the heavy signet ring on Jordan's left hand had ripped his skin. His lips were split and the metallic taste of blood filled his mouth. He slowly came erect, steeling himself for Jordan's next attack. But the other man had withdrawn and stood with his arms folded over his chest, as if to keep himself reined in. His hands were swollen; the skin across his knuckles had split and bled spiderweb patterns down his fingers.

"I ought to kill you."

"I wouldn't stop you." Marten's lips were too swollen to form the words properly.

"What's your brother about, going after Lucy? What does it get him?"

Marten shook his head, leaning back against the wall for balance when dizziness assaulted him. "I've thought about it. He hates the royal family. He discredits them this way. But there has to be more to it. The papers are calling her an unregistered majicar and accusing her of starting the fire in Salford Terrace. They say she killed a bunch of Crown Shields and that she hoarded illegal ciphers. It doesn't make any sense. What could he possibly gain by all that? Who'd believe it?"

"Everybody who doesn't know her," Jordan said shortly. "They've pulled in her family and a number of her friends. Could one of them be the target?"

"Or the king."

"What do you want me to do?"

"Your family has hands in almost as many pots as Edgar. Find out what he's up to. If I can get around in front of him, maybe I can force him to back down on Lucy."

Jordan nodded. "It'll take a day or so."

"Do you . . . do you know anywhere she might have gone? I don't know her haunts."

"No. I've looked a few places, but nothing. She won't be sitting idle. She'll be going after the truth herself. She's tenacious. She'll find it."

"We have to get there first. Edgar is too dangerous."

Jordan smiled thinly. "You saw her, that night of the retrieval. She held *sylveth* spawn in her hands and didn't flinch. She helped cut off a man's arm and then went back out to fight off the spawn. If there's one thing that's true about Lucy, she doesn't back down and she doesn't give up. She's going to find out who did this to her, and she's going to go after him."

Marten swallowed. If she was reading the papers, she must already have worked out that he was part of it. An odd pain began in his chest that had nothing to do with the blows Jordan had dealt him.

"Then we have to hurry. Edgar will kill her if she interferes with him. With all those stories in the paper, no one would blame him. He'd be a hero."

"There's only one place people go to hide in Sylmont. The Riddles. Start there."

"The Riddles?" Would she go to Keros? Marten dismissed the idea. Even if she wanted to find him, she couldn't. And why would she trust the majicar? Especially if she'd figured out Marten had stolen her seals.

"There's something else you ought to know," he told Jordan. "I went to visit her on Embernight. We were to have dinner. But when I got there, she'd been attacked. Her hands were shredded to the bone, tendons sliced through—someone had been at her with a knife."

"What?"

"She said she cut herself on some glass. She wouldn't tell me what really happened and she wouldn't go to a healer. I ended up taking her to a friend of mine for a healing. An unregistered majicar."

He lifted his brow at Jordan, waiting for accusations or recriminations for yet another illegal transgression. But Jordan only scowled broodingly, rubbing a hand over his cheek and jaw.

"He healed her?"

"Aye. It was a close thing, though. I don't think it was Edgar—it wouldn't make sense if he was planning this other. I think she has another enemy out there."

"Then you'd better hurry and find her. I'll send word when I've learned anything."

He spoke with a finality that Marten recognized as dismissal. He straightened, stepping away from the wall. Jordan followed him to the top of the stairs, watching impassively as Marten lurched down to the door.

"Marten. Just so you know. You and I are done. When this is over, if you're still alive and she's not, I'll plant you in the ground." He turned and disappeared without waiting for an answer.

Marten put his hand on the door, wiping the blood from his cheek with his sleeve. "If I'm still alive and she's not, I'll dig the hole myself," he murmured.

Chapter 18

It was Emberday again. Lucy had slept most of the past two days, waking only to bolt food like a starving dog and scour the papers. It astonished her that she was being talked about more than the Jutras were. The news about them was oddly muted and without any of the sensationalism that colored the revelations about her.

According to the *Sentinel*, the Jutras ship was no threat to Crosspointe—at least not now. It had been attempting to cross the Inland Sea when it was caught in a storm. Only incredible luck brought it safely into Blackwater Bay. The sea-battered Jutras had been easily captured and now were being held in Blackstone. Their makeshift prison was a manor with bars on the windows surrounded by a high wall and guarded by Crown Shields and majicars. The question now was what to do with them. Numerous letters and editorials argued the point, from sending them to the Bramble to torturing them for information about invasion plans for Crosspointe.

The explanation was all quite rational and comforting, making the arrival of the Jutras seem anomalous and insignificant. And maybe it was. Maybe it was a coincidence that they had arrived on the same day she'd discovered the treasonous contracts. But everything inside Lucy screamed *Danger!* There was terrible trouble brewing, and she could do little to stop it, not with the papers calling her a renegade majicar and a traitor. Not with a fire she'd started obliterating Salford Terrace. Not after she'd supposedly stolen the greatest blood oak find in centuries. The public had already convicted her. No one would trust anything she had to say—she wasn't even sure Cousin William would. Not that she thought she'd be allowed to see him, even with the royal necklace. She was too dangerous.

She read the gleefully condemning stories in bleak silence. Everything inside her ached to answer, to revolt, to somehow turn everything around. But she was paralyzed. The words surrounded her, washing over her like an inexorable tide, heavy and deadly. How could any one woman push back such a sea?

She did not speak to Keros. He cooked for her, heated her bathwater, and poured her tea and brandy. So far he'd been as good as his word and had not betrayed her to anyone. But she dared not trust him. She kept herself tightly bottled, aware that he watched her obliquely as if she were some sort of wild animal—like she might turn rabid and attack. Even alone in her room, she neither cried nor ranted against her fate. Emotions did no good. She needed to be dispassionate. She needed to think and reason. She needed to make a plan.

Thankfully the cipher remained quiescent on her arm. Its disks had turned gray and lifeless again. Lucy wondered if it had burned itself out in starting the fire. It was a majickal blaze, impossible to stop with mere water. Even the majicars fighting it were having little impact. The fire continued to eat through houses and businesses, coming ever closer to the shipyards and harbor. It seemed impossible to Lucy that she could be responsible for the devastation. She dared not think about it, about the lives lost or the cost. If she did, she'd sink in a bog of despair.

But on the third day of her stay with Keros, she could no longer sit idle. She woke refreshed, the fatigue of her healing vanished. She dressed and went downstairs. Purpose lent energy to her steps. Today while the cipher remained silent, she had to start fighting back. And the place to start was with Marten Thorpe.

"You're talking today?" Keros asked when she greeted

him. "I thought maybe my healing had withered your tongue." Once again he was in the kitchen cooking. It seemed to be his haven.

"I didn't have anything to say."

"And now you do."

"I have questions."

"Do you?" He motioned her to the table, where he set bowls of porridge, a pitcher of cream, brown sugar, and stewed blueberries. "Sit down."

Lucy did as told, spooning sugar and blueberries onto her porridge and drizzling a healthy serving of cream on it. Her stomach cramped in anticipation and she ate fully half of it before she could slow down enough to talk.

"Where can I find Marten?" she asked suddenly.

Keros sat back, his brows lowering as he considered Lucy. "Is that wise? He's betrayed you once. Surely he'd not hesitate to turn you over to the Crown Shields. There's quite a reward."

"You didn't seem to think he'd hurt me," Lucy pointed out.

"I said I find it hard to believe. But you do think so. And the reward is a tempting prize for a man like him."

Lucy shrugged. "I need answers."

"Very well. If I were looking for him, I'd go to Sweet Dreams, his brother's bagnio. He's a regular patron, and you wouldn't have to leave the Riddles. If you go wandering about in the rest of the city, they'll catch you. I shouldn't like to see that happen."

"Why not?"

He scratched his head consideringly. He wasn't handsome, Lucy decided, watching him intently. His nose was long, his lips thin, his jaw rounded. His curly hair hung to his shoulders in a careless mop. But his eyes were riveting. They were deep-set and roiling with suppressed emotions—almost haunted. They made her want to trust him. She looked away, gritting her teeth. She didn't dare.

He leaned forward, laying his hand on top of hers, waiting until she looked up again. "I won't betray you."

Lucy was still, caught again by that haunted look and

the taut pull of his voice. She licked her lips and nodded. He sat back, returning to his breakfast. For a few minutes, the only noise in the kitchen was the scrape of spoons and the crackle of the kitchen fire.

"Do you know anyone who can read Jutras?" Lucy asked, abruptly making the choice to believe him. She needed help, and she was running out of time.

His attention sharpened. "Careful how you go. A question like that might make me think the papers hold more truth than I gave them credit for."

"I'm not a traitor," Lucy snapped.

He cocked his head. "Then why would you need someone to read Jutras?"

The implication was clear. Even communicating with the Jutras was treason. And now a warship had sailed into the harbor. Was she conspiring with those aboard, sending secret messages perhaps? Lucy chewed the inside of her lower lip. How much to tell him? Finally she reached down to her satchel beside her chair and opened it, pulling out the contract. She slid it across the table.

"Because I need to know what that says."

Keros unfolded it. "What is it?"

"It looks like a contract."

"For what?"

"Did I mention that I need someone to translate it?"

He acknowledged her dig with a quirk of his lips, passing the parchment back.

"I don't know anyone. Marten may be your best bet. Or another sea captain. Those who often sail east would have reason to pick up the language."

Lucy clenched her teeth. Marten again. If she went to another captain and was caught, that person could be accused of conspiring with her. She couldn't do that to anyone else. Enough of her friends and family were already caught in that trap.

"Do you mind if I ask where you came by that document?"

"I stole it."

"Who from?"

"I don't know. That's what I need to find out."

Keros tapped the table with his fingers. "You have the most vexingly cryptic way of answering the most straightforward questions. How can you not know who you stole it from?"

"The name on the lading was Bernwick Corporation, but I'm not sure that they had anything to do with it. The contract was hidden in a false bottom."

"What makes you think it wasn't Bernwick? Couldn't they have tried to smuggle it?"

Lucy nodded. "Of course. But—" She did *not* want to tell him about her blackmailer. "I have reason to believe it was someone else. The same someone who's been feeding the newspapers their stories."

Now it was Keros's turn to be silent. Lucy finished her breakfast and sipped her tea, lost in thought.

"May I ask *you* a question now?"

"You can ask."

His mouth quirked again. "Did you start the fire?"

Lucy hesitated. Then nodded. "Sort of."

Surprise made his mouth fall open. He collected himself. "How? *Are* you a majicar?"

A sudden recklessness seized her, and the urge to set the record straight about the fire. She was so tired of false accusations.

"I've been attached by a true cipher. When I was cornered by the Crown Shields, it . . . exploded."

"You've . . . that explains a lot."

"Does it?"

"That's why they're having so much trouble putting it out. It's Errol Cipher's majick. By the gods. We are in trouble. And it explains your hands. Both times."

Lucy made a small shrug of agreement.

"May I see it?"

"No. I appear to be the only one who can."

She pushed up her sleeve, exposing the cipher on her arm. He stared.

"Where is it?"

"See what I mean?" She pulled her sleeve back down.

"But you can see it."

"Oh yes. What fun would it be for Errol Cipher if his victims couldn't see what was coming?"

She rubbed her hands over her face, dragging her fingers through her hair, yanking with annoyance at the tangles. She hadn't combed it in days. Nor did she intend to.

"Do you have a pair of shears?"

"Certainly."

He left and returned a few minutes later with a long pair of cloth scissors. He handed them to her. Lucy took them and, grasping a hank of her hair, cut through it. Keros watched silently as she clipped it all off, leaving the ends hanging ragged around her shoulders.

"Charming. You'll turn heads."

"Do you think you can do better?" Lucy held out the shears. "Be my guest."

He came around to stand behind her and began trimming the edges. When he was done, her haircut was more even, though it still resembled a raspberry bush. Lucy didn't look at it. Her hair had been her vanity. Now it was a rat's nest. She pulled the tangles out with her fingers and braided her hair in a fishtail braid down the back of her head. She tied it with a short length of brown ribbon that Keros handed her.

He helped her sweep up the lengths of fallen hair and tossed them into the fire.

She wrinkled her nose. "Quite a stench."

"It's safer," was his only explanation. He opened a window, waving a towel to push the smell out.

"Wouldn't majick be easier? For a lot of things?"

He cast a sidelong look at her. "No."

"Why not?"

He sighed as if at a tired question. "First, it could interfere with the majick of the house. It could disrupt the wards and some of the conveniences. It takes planning to avoid that."

"But you healed me without planning. Twice."

"And it played havoc, I can tell you."

He shut the window and Lucy gathered up her satchel.
"Where are you going?"
"Sweet Dreams. To find Marten."
Keros nodded. "I'll show you the way."

Two days later and Marten still had not appeared, and
Lucy was growing angry. Her mood was not improved
by the freezing rain that had begun earlier in the day.
It glazed the cobbles and the bare trees in a slippery
cocoon. Lucy watched the entrance of Sweet Dreams
from where she crouched beneath a low stairwell in the
alley opposite. Two mourning doves had taken refuge in
the same space, cooing unhappily. Ice formed around
Lucy's feet and stiffened her cloak like wood. But she
was not cold. Resentment danced in her blood like open
flames. Marten should be here. He was a man interested
only in pleasures of the body and the tables. A man
who'd tricked her. Who'd played her like a maestro.
   It made her sick to think of her eager response to his
confession at the Summerland's ball. He'd lured her by
pretending he was torn between his interest in her and
his desire to be honorable. The bait had been flattering
and Lucy went after it like a starving rat. She'd been
such a credulous fool. He'd told her he couldn't be
trusted. Why hadn't she believed *that*?
   And now, when he ought to be sticking to his usual
foul habits, he'd become elusive. She ground her teeth.
How much longer could she wait for him? She reached
up and snugged her hood more closely around her head.
If he didn't show tomorrow, she'd go hunt for him.
   She was still watching when a carriage rolled up just
before the seventh glass. *Sylveth* lamps lit the entrance
of the building brightly so that Lucy had no trouble
seeing. Two men alighted. She didn't recognize the first.
He was a stocky man, balding, with rich clothing and
high-heeled shoes. He wore a heavy chain around his
neck that glittered with precious stones, and he carried
himself with an arrogance that came from money and
power. The man with him—

Lucy gasped, her hands leaping to press the sound back into her mouth. The man with him was the stranger of her childhood. She couldn't breathe. She huddled into herself, frozen still, as if that could protect her.

He'd aged, of course. It had been nearly twenty years since he'd held her by the neck and tried to choke her. His dark hair was streaked with gray, and it was receding. His face was sharper. He remained slender, his clothing the height of fashion. Though he was smiling, the expression was thin and cruel. He was listening to his companion with desultory interest, swinging a knob-headed cane as his trunks were unloaded.

The carriage rolled away and the two men went inside. Lucy slumped, her heart pounding so hard that she thought it must tear through her chest. She pressed her fist against her throat. She could almost feel his hand sliding slowly around her neck, his fingers biting into her flesh. What was he doing here? It wasn't coincidence, any more than the arrival of the Jutras ship.

She crawled out of her hidey-hole, feeling like a crone. She turned and staggered blindly back toward Keros's house. He had to be her blackmailer—she'd revealed her ability that day. He'd probably been spying on her ever since. Somehow—but *how*?—he'd puzzled out that she was collecting true ciphers. It gave him the leverage he needed to blackmail her.

Every thought of Marten evaporated as she began to run through the night. All that remained was her memory of being trapped against a stack of crates fighting off the stranger, and an unrelenting compulsion to get inside Sweet Dreams and find out who he was and what he was planning, before the Jutras attacked and overran Crosspointe. She shuddered. She'd rather her family ended on the Bramble than in the hands of the Jutras.

As she ran, serpentlike heat uncoiled up her arm and burrowed through her body as the cipher woke again.

Chapter 19

It had been three and a half days and there was still no word from Jordan. Marten had been scouring the Riddles in search of Lucy, his hood pulled low so that no one would see his face and wonder at his two black eyes, puffed-up jaw, and swollen lips. The Riddles was a frustrating place, with streets that went nowhere, bridges between buildings, doors that covered walls, and walkways that went through buildings and ended up belowground. It was easy to get lost once he left the small zone he'd become acquainted with. He'd been to see Keros once, but the majicar had not been home and the wards had not let him pass inside the house to wait. Not that Keros would be all that sympathetic once he knew what his friend had done. He didn't mind Marten's vices, but he had a strict sense of right and wrong. And while it wasn't always so easy to predict where the line was, Marten didn't doubt that he'd crossed it.

His search had proved fruitless, despite questioning everyone he came across and offers of coins to loosen their tongues. Last night, he didn't find his way out until close to dawn. His change purse was missing, the strings hanging free from his belt. His watch had been stolen and he'd nearly been dragged by the hair into the hovel of a lice-ridden whore. After a bath to scrub away any new creepy-crawly friends he might have gained from the encounter, followed by four hours of sleep to shave the edge off his exhaustion, he was ready to go again.

Except that he should have heard from Jordan by
now. Marten paced the foyer of his house, Baskin watching from the doorway into the front salon.

"Why hasn't he sent word? Surely he'd have discovered something by now. His father's the cracking lord
chancellor."

"Mebbe took longer than he thought," Baskin
suggested.

"Still, he'd tell me." But would he? Jordan might be
inclined to let Marten stew in his own juices. "We're
going over there. Get my cutlass."

There was no answer at Jordan's home. Marten
yanked the bellpull fiercely and then pounded on the
door. Nothing. The shutters were closed, the place looking abandoned. A slatternly woman pushed open the
bakery door downstairs of Jordan's flat to stare at him
suspiciously. Her hair and apron were liberally dusted
with flour and her nose was red. She swiped an arm
across it and sniffed thickly.

Marten motioned for Baskin to follow and walked to
the end of the row, going around to the alley behind
Jordan's flat. He tried the back door, but it was locked.
He stepped back, surveying the upstairs.

"There's a window open left of the balcony."

"Aye, Cap'n, so there is."

"Can you get up there?"

"If'n I can climb to th' top o' th' main in a gale blow,
I can get up there."

Baskin handed his cloak to Marten and scurried up
the wall like a spider, finding hand- and toeholds in the
half-timbering. He clambered over the balcony rail and
leaped to the ledge of the window, pulling himself
through the opening. Moments later he thumped down
the stairs to unlock the back door. His seamed face
was grave.

"It's ugly, Cap'n. Master Truehelm's been killed."

Marten froze for an instant, then dashed up the stairs
three at a time. At the top, he slowed, crossing the landing into the dining room. Beyond was the salon. Here

the furniture was tossed about like thrown dice. There was shattered crockery on the floor and smears of blood on the walls. The pocket doors leading into the sitting room where Marten and Jordan had talked days before hung drunkenly.

Marten followed the trail of blood and destruction into a short corridor on the other side. The first room was an office. It was empty and untouched, as was the bedroom next to it. At the end was a last room and this was where he found Jordan. He lay spread-eagled on the bed, his hands and feet tied to the posts. He was naked to the waist. His face and chest had been battered and his wrists and ankles were raw from where he'd struggled against the ropes. His throat had been slashed and blood stained the sheets and congealed on the floor. His skin was gray and his eyes stared blankly above sunken cheeks.

Marten could only stare. Who had done this? Why? He started when Baskin came up beside him.

"What do ye want to be doin' with 'im, then?"

"Do with him?" Marten repeated stupidly.

"Ye gonna call the law?"

Before he could speak, another voice answered.

"I think not."

Marten turned around. Edgar stood in the doorway looking severe. Behind him were four meaty men.

"You see, someone might suspect you of committing the murder," Edgar explained softly. "There are witnesses who will say they saw you come in, and that you were covered in blood when you left—"

He abruptly flung his arm up, tossing the contents of a crockery jar at Marten. The liquid was thick and sticky and cold. It spattered his face and chest. Marten looked down and saw that it was blood. He raised his head, mouth slack with disbelief.

"What is this?"

"Isn't it obvious? It's Master Truehelm's blood. You came here and attacked him, wanting revenge for beating you so badly."

"You killed Jordan?" Marten asked in disbelief.

"No, Marten. This is your doing. I may have been the weapon, but you wielded it. You didn't think I wouldn't have you watched, did you? Because of you and your obsession with Lucy Trenton, young Captain Truehelm started asking questions in inconvenient places. These matters are too delicate and too important for me to allow anyone to upset them. I told you there would be casualties." Edgar glanced at Jordan's body. "He'd be alive now if you hadn't ignored my advice. And now you must pay a price as well.

"I would prefer not to have to turn you over to the Crown Shields and have you tried for murder. But it will be your choice. You can step up in front of the lord chancellor and explain how you murdered his son, or you can don the iron collar. Your markers have been called, your properties seized, and you have been found in arrears. If you cannot produce the funds owed immediately, then you will be sent to the auction block. I will purchase your contract; you need have no fear of being sent to haul slops on a back-island pig farm. If you behave, I will even allow you to go to sea from time to time.

"But, Marten, understand this. If you step even slightly out of the bounds I set for you, I shall not hesitate to turn you and your bloody clothing over to the Crown Shields. It is your decision. The Bramble or the iron collar."

"You cocksucking son of a whore," Marten swore. "I'll not let you get away with this. Jordan was my *friend*."

"And I am your brother. I am trying to help you. Consider your choice well. Do you want to see what becomes of you during the full fury of the Chance storms?"

Marten didn't answer. He couldn't. He was trapped and he knew it. The Bramble was certain death. Or worse. If he submitted to the collar, he might still find an opportunity to help Lucy. He hung his head, his mouth twisting.

"I'll do it." The words caught jaggedly in his throat. He swallowed, the tendons in his neck straining.

Edgar nodded, unsmiling. "Good. We'll go to Chancery now and you can surrender yourself."

"What about Baskin?"

"You can keep him. Have him fetch your things. You'll spend the night in Fargate. I'm sorry for that, but the law requires it. Don't worry. Serving me won't be terribly onerous; it may even be an improvement on your standard of living."

Marten burned with humiliation as he slowly stripped down to his smallclothes and re-dressed himself with clothing that Edgar had brought with him. They were his own, filched from his house. His lips compressed tightly. Not his house anymore. He had nothing. Less than nothing. He dressed quickly, stamping into his boots and buckling on his sword.

"Put those bloody things back in the duffel. I'll hold them as collateral against your good behavior. Better wash your face. We don't want to raise suspicion."

Marten did as told, moving arthritically. Every muscle was coiled tight, but he dared not do anything. When he'd cleaned away the spatters of blood to Edgar's satisfaction, his brother gestured toward the door.

"Come on, then. No sense wasting time."

Edgar put a warm hand on Marten's shoulder and squeezed sympathetically. Marten's shoulder twitched, but he did not shake him off. He must play this part if he hoped to help Lucy.

"We can't just leave him here like this," Marten rasped, looking down at Jordan's body.

"We must. He'll be found soon enough. Let us go quickly now. We haven't much time."

Edgar's affable manner grated on Marten like metal filings. But he could do nothing. He nodded, shame turning his blood cold. Bracketed by the four men, Marten followed Edgar down the back stairs, Baskin trailing behind. At the end of the alley, another of Edgar's men waited with a hack.

The journey to Jabry Inn seemed to take only a few grains. Contrary to its name, it was neither an inn nor a single building. It was a sprawling network that included schools, dormitories, dining rooms, teahouses, law chambers, offices, courtrooms, stationers, and a hostelry. The High Court of Chancery convened here, in an imposing two-story building located at the center of the sprawl. There were also two grassy parks and a formal garden hiding within the expanse known as Jabry Inn. Here was the financial heart of Crosspointe, where laws were made and disputes resolved.

The hack pulled up outside a smaller square building with a domed roof and spires on each corner. The wind had picked up and clouds scudded across the sky. The temperature was dropping, promising more freezing rain, or possibly snow. Edgar left three of the bullyboys outside and led the way up to the bronze doors. Carved in the archivolt were the words LET ALL WHO COME HERE BLESS THE GODS THAT YE MAY SERVE AND BE FORGIVEN OF YOUR DEBTS. Marten swallowed hard and went inside. His legs felt clumsy and numb, and he stumbled over the threshold. Every part of him wanted to turn and run. He forced himself to walk forward, his steps slow and halting.

Inside was a small vestibule with red tiled floors and plaster walls painted with yellow and white stripes and hung with paintings of ships. It contained a desk and a clerk. The woman wore a dark brown robe with belled sleeves over her dress. A pin at her throat showed she was an articled clerk of Chancery law. She looked up as Edgar approached.

"Master Wedling, if you please. He is expecting me. I am Edgar Thorpe."

"Yes, sir. If you will wait just a moment?"

She stood, tucking her hands into her sleeves, and withdrew. A few moments later she reappeared.

"Master Wedling will see you. If you would step this way."

They walked down a short hallway and through a bull

pen of copyist desks arranged in long lines, down another hallway, and into a spacious office. The walls were entirely covered in bookshelves holding massive leather-bound volumes printed with gilt lettering on the spines. There was a small sitting area with comfortable couches and, at the other end, an ornate desk with brass fittings and several straight-backed chairs opposite it. A balding blond man sat behind the desk. He was examining a document, a book open beside him.

Edgar ordered the two bullyboys to remain in the hallway and motioned Marten inside. Master Wedling stood. He wore the dark green robes of the senior Chancery officials. The cuffs of his sleeves hung nearly to the floor and were embroidered heavily with yellow thread, as were the edges of his robe. A gold chain of office lay along his collar. The pendant was enameled with Cross-pointe's thirty-two-rayed compass rose in black with a set of *sylveth* scales inlaid in the center.

"Commissioner Thorpe, I am pleased to see you again. And this is your brother?"

"This is Marten. Is everything in order, Master Wedling? I'm afraid I have a pressing engagement. But I'd like to see my brother settled before I go."

"Certainly, Commissioner. Please sit. I must read through the documentation and have Captain Thorpe sign. As soon as he does, we can apply the collar and have him taken to his cell. We can publish the announcement in the morning's *Sentinel*, and put him on the block by noon on Hurnday."

"That's the soonest? I had hoped for tomorrow."

"Yes, sir. It is the law."

"Then it will have to do."

He might as well be a ham that a butcher and a housewife were haggling over. Marten's gorge rose.

Edgar and the Chancery master sat. Neither suggested that Marten should follow suit and he had no inclination to do so. Instead he stood rigidly as Master Wedling ran down the list of his debts. The list was tediously complete. Edgar had purchased all his markers, from the baker and grocer to the cobbler and the chandler. There was no direct reference to his gambling losses, which were vaguely cataloged as unpaid services.

"Do you agree that this is an accurate and complete inventory of your debts, Captain Thorpe?"

"Yes," Marten said, his teeth clicking together.

"And can you remit them at this time?"

"No."

"Very well. You will be sold at auction into indentured service until such a time as you expiate your obligation. Your total monies owed amounts to nine dralions, two Hurn's eyes, six glyphs, two crescents, and four coppers. The sale of your house and belongings, the value of which Commissioner Thorpe has provided me, reduces the total by seven and a half dralions. The standard contract pays you one and a half Hurn's eyes per annum, plus room and board, one set of clothing, and one pair of boots per year. You are also entitled to one half day free per sennight, and one dram of grog per sennight. Other expenses that your employer suffers on your behalf will extend the life of this contract, so long as the cost is documented and presented to this office within two years of the calendar year in which they were incurred. The extension of the contract will be calculated according to the going rate for indentured servitude during the year the documented costs are reported.

"Additionally, you will be required to pay the costs of your confinement here and for the auction, as well as for filing the papers. This amounts to . . ." He scratched some figures on a paper, rubbing one finger down a column of numbers on another page and scratching again. He set his quill aside. "The Chancery costs amount to five crescents and six coppers. This will be added to your total debts, making it one dralion, seven Hurn's eyes, six glyphs, and eight crescents. At a rate of one and a half Hurn's eyes per annum, your term of service will be . . ." He paused again to calculate. "Eleven years and eight months. Does this sound satisfactory to you, Captain Thorpe?"

Marten's throat worked, but he could say nothing. He could earn the same in a single season at sea. But Edgar wasn't going to give him the opportunity. Instead he was going to spend nearly twelve years in the collar! He couldn't do it. He shook his head adamantly.

"Be advised, Captain Thorpe, that you are not required to sign the contract. However, it substantially increases the Chancery costs if you do not. The matter will require secondary interviews and a more extended stay. The delay would at least triple your costs, if not more, adding months to your term of service."

Marten closed his eyes. He couldn't do it. And yet—Edgar had his balls in a vise. There was nothing he could do. If he turned recalcitrant now, he'd only hurt himself. His stomach churning, he nodded.

"Very good. Then I will have you sign here. Also, it appears that you have suffered recent injuries. Please document those on this page. Your new employer will pay for reasonable medical expenses incurred while performing any assigned duties. However, he will not be responsible for injuries sustained prior to taking possession of you, nor shall the office of the lord chancellor. These expenses must be borne by you and will add to your service contract."

Marten's hand shook as he signed the proffered documents. When he had, Master Wedling went to a wall vault, withdrawing an iron collar. It looked like two half circles hooked together by a hinge. There was a loop on one side, as if to allow a chain to be attached. He set one curve of the cold metal around the back of Marten's neck. It was all he could do to stand still. The Chancery official pushed the other half of the circle under Marten's chin until the collar closed. He went rigid, his head feeling swollen and hot. It was hard to breathe. Hard to swallow. He thrust his arms out, snarling.

"Easy, now. It's a shock at first, but you get used to it. Give me a moment and it will be all over," Master Wedling said.

Marten forced himself to stand still, every muscle

quaking with the effort. Sweat dribbled down his ribs and his cock curled up between his legs.

"By your debts you are bound to serve so that you are not a burden to your family or society. Serve well. Your employer deserves all your skills, your mind, and your talents. Give your best to him and you shall know you are a man," Master Wedling intoned. And then he muttered something under his breath. Suddenly the collar heated and just as quickly turned icy cold against Marten's skin.

The Chancery official stepped back. "Done! All right, then, everything's in order. I'll send the notice to the paper tonight and on Hurnday at noon, Captain Thorpe will stand at auction."

"Excellent," Edgar said, rubbing his hands together. "Then I shall leave my brother in your capable hands. Good night, Marten. I shall see you the day after tomorrow." He put his arm around Marten, pulling him close and speaking low in his ear so that Master Wedling could not hear. "Take this time to think about your new situation. So long as you behave, I will be a fair master. But impose on my good nature again, and I won't hesitate to chain you like a dog."

He put his finger through the metal loop on the iron collar and gave a gentle jerk to reinforce his point. The edges of the collar bit into Marten's neck and he grunted.

"Think hard, Marten," Edgar advised, standing back. He glanced at Master Wedling, whose back was turned, obliviously sorting the paperwork at his desk. Edgar's gaze was bleak as he reached out to grip Marten's cods, twisting viciously. Marten gasped, his gorge rising and filling his mouth with bile. Gray film clouded the edges of his vision.

"I love you, little brother. But never forget I have your balls in my hand, quite literally. If you so much as think about crossing me again, I'll lay you out and cut them off myself."

Chapter 20

It was well past midnight. Lucy sat at Keros's kitchen table, her leg propped on a chair, waiting for the majicar to return home. She'd slipped on the ice in her frantic flight from Sweet Dreams. Her ankle throbbed heavily, so swollen that she'd been unable to remove her boot. She'd been sitting there for hours, her mind tangled in the memory of the stranger, of his hands on her throat, of the meaty smell of his breath. He was her blackmailer; she was certain of it. It was too coincidental to see him at Sweet Dreams and right now. Had he been on his way to meet Marten? She shivered, feeling time draining away. But she had the contract—could they proceed with their plot without it? Of course they could. The Jutras were in Crosspointe. Whatever the plan was, it was well begun. To hope to stop them, she had to get inside Sweet Dreams. But how?

She was still brooding over the question when Keros wandered in, smelling of ale, smoke, and a faint odor of bloodweed.

"Good night! Why are you still awake?"

"I seem to have hurt myself." Lucy looked meaningfully at her leg, her mouth bending stiffly around the words.

Keros probed gently with his fingers. She yelped and slapped at him.

"Stop that! And don't you dare ask if it hurts."

He shook his head. "At least it's your ankle this time.

Good of you to heed my advice and avoid damaging your hands."

"Wasn't it? And I still have stones to pay you with."

He came and knelt down beside her. "I'm going to have to cut off the boot."

"You smell like bloodweed." Her lip curled and she leaned away.

He lifted the front of his shirt and sniffed. "So I do."

"You don't smoke it. Your tongue doesn't show it. I'd have noticed. Unless you've just begun. Which would be stupid. How stupid are you?"

"I'm hiding a fugitive who began a majickal fire that's burned a third of Salford Terrace, who illegally hoarded true ciphers, and who has been accused of smuggling and stealing blood oak. And, not to forget the minor details, has been attached by a true cipher and could annihilate me at any moment, even if she didn't want to, though I think just at the moment she might like it very much. Stupid doesn't begin to describe what I am. Now hold still."

He cut away her boot, trying not to jerk her ankle. Lucy wrapped her fingers around the arm of her chair, her knuckles turning white, her body going clammy.

"How are you doing? That cipher isn't about to start fires in my hair or some such, is it?" Though his tone was cheerful, Keros's skin was pale, strands of his curly dark hair clinging to the sweat dampening his forehead and cheeks.

Lucy glanced down. The *sylveth* disks pulsed white and faded to gray. The pulsing continued, slow and steady, like a heartbeat. Her arm tingled, but nothing seemed imminent.

"It's fine for now."

"For now," Keros repeated with a wince. "All right, this next bit is going to hurt some. I can't help but move your foot as we remove the boot, and I've cut it away as far as I can."

"And you can't use majick."

"I'm saving my strength, don't you know. Besides, the pain might remind you to take better care of yourself. Though you do seem to be something of a masochist. Come on, then, ready?" He spoke lightly, but Lucy could hear the worry beneath.

"Do your worst," Lucy said, holding her breath.

"That comes later," he said, and then slid the boot free.

Lucy grunted and squeezed her eyes shut. The throbbing in her ankle turned vicious. She moaned softly.

Keros cut her sock open and peeled it away. Her skin was the color of sun-ripened plums. The majicar stroked his fingers over her swollen flesh, probing gently and muttering.

"It's probably broken. What did you do?"

"I ran. I fell. I ran some more."

"You really ought to try to be more careful."

"Yes, I should," Lucy said feelingly, referring to far more than walking on the ice.

Keros sat back on his heels and scratched his bristled jaw as he looked at her. "This would go easier if I gave you some drops to make you sleep."

Lucy was shaking her head before he finished. "No."

"Didn't think so. All right. Relax if you can. Whatever you do, don't move. And do *try* to keep your cipher from getting too excited, won't you?" His voice was brittle. Still he didn't hesitate.

Lucy sat back in her chair, gripping the arms again and taking a deep breath.

"Ready? Here we go."

His hand trembled as he pulled his lumpy *illidre* out. Holding it one hand, he put the other over her ankle. Lucy twitched and caught herself.

The feeling that penetrated her ankle was neither heat nor cold. It sizzled, uncoiling in looping strands of power, wrapping around her pain, and collapsing it like ash. It sank into her bone, winding around and tightening, creating strength. Lucy had a sense of when the bone healed—a fitting together, a sense of wholeness. Then she felt a movement in her swollen flesh, like a sponge squeezing dry.

Without warning, the cipher roared to life. Heat blasted her and she felt incandescent. She convulsed, kicking and flailing. Her head snapped forward and back, her back arching so that she balanced on her heels and her neck. Both chairs burst into flame. Fire licked her, gentle and searing. Keros grabbed her around the waist and flung her to the floor. She landed hard on her side, the air bursting from her lungs.

"Lucy! Can you stop it? Try to stop it!"

She heard his voice from far away. Her veins flowed with liquid glass. She felt the majick surging in her as it had in the alley behind Faraday. She clutched at it; she couldn't let it get loose again. She'd rather die first. But she couldn't stop it.

The majick filled her like a dam. The pain was beyond bearing. Lucy wept, her moans soon turning to shrieks. She pushed up on her hands and knees, trying to get out, to run away. But her muscles collapsed. She wrapped her arms around herself, pressing her face against her thighs. She rocked back and forth, needing movement, but the pressure only increased. Her skin felt like it was splitting. Lucy howled, the action giving her some release.

She didn't know when the majick stopped flowing into her. Slowly she came aware that the pain and pressure weren't getting worse anymore and the fire had ceased to burn. But she was full of majick and unable to release it. She was stranded on an island of pain with no escape.

"Lucy?"

Keros's rasping voice was close to her ear.

"Can you hear me?"

Lucy's only response was a wordless moan.

"Listen to me. When majicars are initiated into the guild, they undergo a rite of passage. They touch raw *sylveth*. It fills them with an overwhelming majick and either they control it, they die, or they become spawn.

I think the cipher is doing something like that to you. You *can* control the majick."

Lucy made another inarticulate moan. Keros seemed to understand the question. *How?*

"It's different for everybody. My majick comes to me like a wind. I imagine a sail harnessing its power. For some it's like fire, others like a puzzle, and who knows what else? You have to envision what would contain the essence of your power and bring it into being inside you. Like water in a jar, or fire in an oven. Don't try to empty it or to put it out. It might kill you."

Lucy clutched at Keros's words, trying to make sense of them. Her mind was fragmented, shattered by the tidal wave of pain. She felt raw, like she'd been turned inside out, every nerve ripped from her flesh, every bone broken. She felt the power churning inside her. It was like a Koreion—a great sea worm—its spines ripping bloody gobbets of her loose, slashing away at her flesh with its saw-toothed talons, as it sought a way free.

In the corner of her mind, she laughed at the irony. The essence of this power was a beast that ruled the Inland Sea, destroying ships and swimming in *sylveth* without harm. Couldn't it have been a mouse or a kitten?

She convulsed again, muscles shuddering violently. The Koreion of majick was growing again. Soon it would rip her apart. She had to find a way to control it. But how? And then she realized. Not control, contain. One didn't harness the wind, nor had Keros tried. There was no chaining it, no bringing it to heal with a whip and a stout stick. She must tame it. Befriend it.

She didn't have much time. The sinews of her body were pulling taut, attenuating with the pressure. There was a cracking sound and fire ignited in all her joints. Her mind splintered apart. She grasped at the pieces, trying to focus. It was like fighting a rip current. The pain dragged at her, pulling her down, pulling her apart. She struggled against it, gathering her scattered senses, piecing her sanity back into a fragile semblance of wholeness. It was decrepit and missing pieces, but it would have to do. She set to work, following instinct and hope.

She began by calling up an image of herself in her mind. Carrot-headed, plump, snub-nosed, and freckled. The edges of the vision were misty, but it was recognizable enough. Next she thought of the power within her, the Koreion wrapping her in its strangle grip. Her imaginary self stood inside the heavy coil of its body, wedged between the mesh of spines that porcupined down its entire length.

She hesitated, uncertain of what she ought to do next. Should she talk to it? She had no words. They skittered senselessly across the surface of her mind, spinning away into nothingness. She lifted her imaginary hands and laid them on the body of the beast. Its skin twitched, soft as cashmere. Lucy was astonished. She'd not expected anything so wonderful.

The skin beneath her hand rippled with muscle and suddenly the Koreion's head reared up above her. It dripped with soft, waving protrusions. Fine, needle-sharp teeth densely crowded its long, pointed snout, the slitted nostrils fluttering open and closed. Lucy could see her reflection in its enormous lidless eyes, like shining black mirrors, wider around than she could reach, and slashed with silver in the shape of a scythe moon. A single pair of limbs protruded from its powerful shoulders. They were tipped with four-fingered claws; the talons of each were as long as Lucy's legs and were serrated. In between they were webbed.

Confronted by the enormous beast, Lucy's hard-held focus began to unravel. Befriend this? The idea was absurd. The best she could do was offer herself as a meal—not even that. A snack. She waited for it to strike, for a wickedly clawed foot to rip her open from stem to stern, for the spined coils to crush her. But nothing happened. The mounting majick halted as the beast scrutinized her.

Except for in works of art, Lucy had never seen a Koreion before. Odd that she'd choose such a creature to represent the cipher's majick. Or maybe not. It was a creature of *sylveth* and it was perhaps the most frightening animal she could imagine. But it was not real, she told herself. It was only a figment of her imagination. A way to think about it so that she could control it. As if a Koreion could be controlled.

Whimsically, she held out her hand, startled when the sea dragon stretched out its head, touching her fingers. Its muzzle was covered in feathery scales that tickled, even in this place that was no place. Its tongue slid out its mouth. It was brilliant blue and vee shaped, with a white stripe up the center. The tip widened into a slightly cup-shaped oval. Its paper-thin surface was covered with fine, wire-sharp bristles and silvery veins. The sea dragon brushed its tongue over her hand. Fire erupted where it touched. Lucy jerked back, turning her hand over. The skin was scored by dozens of fine cuts that bled freely.

The Koreion stretched out its head again. Its breath washed over her wounded hand. Coolness smothered the heat. The blood stopped flowing. White scars like embroidery floss remained.

"Thank you," imaginary Lucy said.

It whuffled her fingers again. A sudden sense of wellbeing surged through her. The pain of the cipher's power eased suddenly. She moaned her relief, feeling the majick settling down inside her, like churned sand sifting to the bottom of the sea. It was still there, heavy and waiting, but no longer threatening. For now.

She slowly became aware of Keros urgently calling her name. She relaxed her concentration, allowing the images of herself and the Koreion to fade into shadow. Drawing a deep breath, she opened her eyes.

They didn't open.

Terror ripped through her. She groped at her face, digging at her eyes. There was no blindfold, nothing at all to prevent her from opening them. Except that she couldn't. Her stomach heaved violently and bitter vomit erupted from her nose and mouth. She choked and gagged, feeling Keros's hands grip her arms. She clawed at him, fighting him off with savage, inarticulate snarls.

Suddenly the Koreion was there in the darkness behind her eyelids, rising up as if from the black waters of the Inland Sea. Its face filled her mindscape, so close she could taste its breath, like brine and wind. Lucy cringed from it. She had no control of this thing. It was inside her, but separate. Alien.

Its maw opened slowly, widening until she could see nothing else but its V-shaped tongue and the silvery blue walls of its mouth. Its fanglike teeth gleamed as if lit by a white light. Lucy gasped, her chest and throat clamping tight. Her heart rattled against her breastbone as the beast drew closer. Then suddenly it lunged at her. It snatched her into its mouth, flicking her into its throat with its tongue.

It swallowed her.

Crushing force enveloped Lucy. She screamed and thrashed, closed inside the silvery blue cocoon of the beast's gullet. Everything she touched felt like razors sleeved in hot silk. Then the cocoon began to shrink, closing hard around her. It pressed suffocatingly against her, the pain of it beyond anything she'd ever experienced. Deeper and deeper it sliced, until she felt like she'd been chopped into a thousand pieces, every drop of her blood squeezed out. She prayed for oblivion, for release.

Then the pain was gone. It vanished like it had never been. Instead a feeling of well-being and comfort seeped through her, dulling the sharp edges of remembered agony. She panted, her heart still pounding as if it would tear through the walls of her chest.

"Lucy! Lucy!" Keros sounded frantic.

She opened her eyes. She *opened her eyes*. Relief made her giddy. She took a slow shaky breath. "Do you have to be so loud?"

Keros snorted. "I suppose that answers my question. Come on, let me help you up."

Lucy let him take her hand. Part of her was astonished and grateful that he was willing to touch her after the cipher's attack.

Acrid smoke filled her nose and she coughed. Panic surged up inside her again as she remembered the chairs catching fire. She lurched about, clutching Keros's arm. "Fire!"

"Easy, now. It wasn't like Salford Terrace. I've put it out. Though it appears I need some more furniture."

He pushed the smoldering chairs out into the mud-room next to the kitchen and brought two more from the sitting room, pointing imperiously to her to sit in one. She wiped her mouth with the back of her arm as he opened the windows before returning to the table and sitting down opposite to her. Lucy was still reeling, and her gaze lingered on the black scars marring the wood floor.

"How are you?"

She turned her attention to her injured ankle. The bruising had vanished and with it the swelling. She rotated it, feeling no pain.

"You healed me," she said, knowing it wasn't the answer he was looking for.

"Seems so."

"Why did the cipher do that? This time and before?"

"I don't know what happened in Salford Terrace. But this time, my healing might have triggered a defensive spell. It might have thought I was trying to tamper with it, so it decided to finish you off before I might free you."

"*It thought*. Lovely. It has a mind of its own."

Keros shrugged. "In a manner of speaking."

"Then why didn't it do it the first time you healed me? Or even the second?" She dragged her fingers roughly through her hair. "Gods, I'm making a ridiculous habit of it."

"I don't know why it didn't flare up. You'd have to ask Errol Cipher about that. It's complex majick, and what he did . . . who knows how it works?"

"At least it's decided to let me live for now," she said darkly, the memory of pain etched indelibly on her bones.

Do you mind if I ask how you controlled it?"

"I—" Lucy hesitated, the moment stretching.

"Never mind. It's not really my business," Keros said, going to grab a broom to sweep up the debris from the burnt chairs.

"No, it's not that," she said quickly. "It's just—"

He waited. But when she couldn't find the words again, Keros's mouth twisted into a bitter smile.

"Don't worry about it. You've said it often enough. You've no reason to trust me."

His expression was an odd mix of resentment, uncertainty, and . . . hurt. She looked at him, astonished. He *cared*. When had that happened? She'd thought his aid stemmed from his guilt over giving Marten the drops. She'd been grateful for the help, no matter the reason, but knowing he felt something more for her struck her to the soul. She grabbed his arm.

"It's true; I don't have any reason to trust you, except that you've been faithful to your word all week. So stop being an ass and sit down," she snapped. "Do try not to interrupt."

Keros gave her a startled look and acquiesced, sprawling in his chair with a bemused smirk.

Lucy chewed the inside of her cheek. How to explain to him when it didn't make any sense to her? She made a frustrated sound, wishing for a glass of Sarah's Shepet. Keros seemed to read her mind, fetching a decanter of brandy and pouring out a healthy dose for each of them. Lucy nodded thanks, cupping the glass in both hands and gulping the liquid, appreciating the rush of heat in her belly. She set the glass down and he refilled it.

"At first I thought I sort of made friends with it," she said at last, swirling the golden liquid pensively.

"Made friends with it?"

Lucy grinned. "Yes."

"But?"

Her smile faded. "I thought it worked. But when I pulled away it . . . swallowed me."

He frowned. "What do you mean? What swallowed you?"

"You said to picture the power as something. So I did. It was a Koreion."

His face went slack, his brows shooting up. "Couldn't you have picked something a little more innocuous, like a mouse—or, by the depths, knucklebones?"

"That's just it. I'm not sure *I* did the picking. I think it did."

"The cipher?"

She shrugged. "Or the majick."

"Oh."

"Oh? That's the best you can do? You're the majicar. What does it mean that it swallowed me?"

"You're hulled?"

"Are you asking me or telling me?"

Keros stood, coming around to put his hands on her shoulders, his fingers rubbing in gentle, soothing circles. Lucy leaned her head back against his stomach, marveling again that he was willing to touch her despite the threat of the cipher.

"It didn't kill you. That's all that matters. Now, are you hungry?"

"Enough to eat my boots."

"I think I can manage something better than boots. But one day you ought to learn something about cooking," he said as he went to the stove, where an orange pot sat.

"I suspect either the cipher will have me or the Bramble will, long before I need to cook."

"You could get very hungry in the meantime."

"You mean if you decide to stop taking pity on me?"

"Indeed."

"I have the jewels. They ought to buy me a dinner or two."

"Yes, your stolen booty. Likely the bulletins have gone out on them. You'd doubtless be arrested the moment you walked into a pawnshop."

"Terribly formal, pawnshops, aren't they? I ought to be able to find someone less rigorous in their standards. I won't get as much from a fencing cully, but certainly enough to eat for a sennight or two."

"Or the cully will steal the gems, cut your throat, call the guard, and get the bounty. I don't know if the Crown Shields will care if you're dead."

"You're a very cynical man."

"And you should learn to cook."

"I expect I'll be able to filch something from the kitchens at Sweet Dreams," Lucy said offhandedly, tracing the grain of the kitchen table with her forefinger.

Keros stopped in the middle of ladling lamb and rice stew into a bowl. "You'll what?"

"Filch something from—"

"I heard you. I thought perhaps my brain had melted out my ears and I was hallucinating. It appears that yours has done the melting. Exactly how do you plan to gain access to Sweet Dreams? And why would you even want to?"

Lucy let go of her droll manner. In perfect seriousness, she said, "I have reason to believe that I might find some answers inside. I'm hoping you'll help me get in."

Keros gave her a hard stare and returned to serving the stew. He brought it to the table with a crock of butter and some crusty bread. She watched his shuttered face as she ate. She should tell him about her talent, about the stranger, about her blackmailer. He should know everything before he went any further with this. She finished her stew, pushing the bowl away and picking up a slice of bread. She tore it between her fingers, nudging the crumbs into designs.

"I've been able to sense the presence of majick since I was child. That's how I found your house without Marten. That's how I found the ciphers. . . ."

She told him everything, feeling a certain relief in sharing it. He listened without Sarah's anger, without her family's horror, without any reaction at all.

"So that's why I want to get inside Sweet Dreams. Will you help me?"

She'd find a way inside the bagnio one way or another, but it would help considerably if Keros would use his majick to disguise her entrance. She'd dye her hair and dress as a maid. Her hands were callused and rough from her customs work. No one would ever suspect her. There was likely an army of maids working in the bagnio. She'd blend right in with their ranks.

"Braken's cods. A knack for sensing majick. If the Sennet knew . . ." He shook his head. "This is a foolish idea. Dangerous. What if they catch you? They'll surely kill you."

"If they catch me. But I don't matter. Crosspointe does, and my family. Besides, the cipher is bound to get me anyhow."

He was unconvinced. "There's also Edgar Thorpe. He is no one to cross. If he finds out that you're there—it'll get very ugly. His business is none too legal and if anyone recognizes you, they'll call the Crown Shields. He'll rip your heart out with his bare hands for bringing such a threat to his doorstep."

"Two shoots from the same seed," Lucy said caustically.

Keros shook his head. "No. Marten used you abominably, and the next time I see him, I plan to put a curse on his cock. Weeping sores that won't heal, and no possibility of enjoying a woman for at least a decade. But he's a kitten compared to his brother. Trust me when I tell you that chancing Edgar's ire is a mistake. He'll not hesitate to destroy you. Viciously. And the people he has dealings with are no better. Maybe worse. They stay under their rocks and let him do their dirty work."

Lucy reached out, taking his hands in hers. "Thank you. Your concern means a lot. I can't tell you how much. But I don't have a choice. There's no other way to find out what's going on. Anyway, I'm not after Edgar Thorpe. He'll never even know I'm there."

"If you're lucky, and so far, your luck has been damned bad." Keros stood, his body rigid. "I have to think about this. I'll talk to you tomorrow." With that, he disappeared upstairs.

Lucy watched him go. He hadn't said no. Tomorrow she would convince him to say yes.

Chapter 21

It was nearly midday when Lucy woke. She found Keros sitting at the table reading the paper. He looked up as she entered. His expression was grim. Dark moons circled his bloodshot eyes. Lucy's stomach clenched with foreboding.

"What is it?" Her throat was so tight the sound was barely a whisper.

"I'll help you."

"You will?"

"I think it's dangerous beyond reason, but yes, I will. Might not even take majick. I'll need the day to ask some questions and figure it out."

"What made you change your mind?"

He folded the paper, setting it carefully on the table. "They are sending your family, friends, and servants to trial. Even your customs team. And they mean to convict in time for this year's Bramble ship."

Lucy's knees sagged. She sat down hard on the bottom step. "No." Then just as suddenly she lunged to her feet. "I have to stop this."

Keros blocked her. "And do what?"

Lucy struggled against his grip. "I have to tell them it was me and no one else. Once I tell them the truth, they'll have to let everybody go."

But he was shaking his head. "It won't matter. You didn't do most of what they're accusing you of. But they don't care. They won't release anyone until they get the truth they're looking for. Which means telling them what you don't know—like where the blood oak is. It would be for nothing. You'll all end up on the Bramble, and Crosspointe will still be in danger from traitors and the Jutras. Right now, only you and I might be able to stop them, and I can't get access to the king. You can."

"Not now. Not under this cloud."

"Don't you think the people behind this don't know that? Don't you think that's the point? They know you stole the contract and they can't afford to let you get to the king. So they paint you with as black a brush as they can muster and when you're caught, you'll end up going straight to the Bramble with no chance to tell anyone what you know. It's a ploy. If you give yourself up, you'll be giving them exactly what they want."

"But the ship sails in less than two sennights. Keros, these are my family, my friends! I can't just let them be convicted and sent to the Bramble. You know what will happen to them when the Chance storms hit." Her eyes closed and against her mindscape she saw the *sylveth* spawn that had crawled up on the beach during the salvage. The things that had once been people. Only now they had the faces of her father, her brothers, Sarah, Blythe, and Hig. She pushed against Keros's chest. She could not let that happen.

The majicar's hands gripped tighter. "Lucy, listen to me. The only sane and reasonable thing you can do to help them is find out who's behind it all and tell the king. That will give him a legitimate reason to stop the trials. Without evidence, anything he does just looks like nepotism. He'll be castigated. There will be revolt. His enemies are just waiting for such an opportunity. His hands are tied unless you do something to help him."

She slumped. He was right. The problem was, she didn't know if she could do it, much less in time.

"What if they believe all the lies? My father, brothers, everybody. What if they think I tricked them, that I abandoned them?" She pulled away, looking up at the ceiling and drawing a shaky breath. "But I did, didn't

I? I did this to them. They ought to think the worst of me."

"You didn't do all of it. We've all made stupid mistakes."

She didn't find his words comforting. "Did your mistakes kill people?"

Keros didn't answer, his expression remote. Instead he returned to the table and picked up his cloak from the back of his chair. He slung it around his shoulders and pinned it in place, pulling on his gloves. "I'll be back. You should eat something. There's fresh eggs and cheese." He smiled thinly. "You'll have to cook for yourself."

Lucy sat at the table, unfolding the paper. Her stomach knotted as she read the headline sprawled across the top of the page: LUCY TRENTON INDICTED IN ABSENTIA—ACCOMPLICE TRIALS TO BEGIN SEADAY. In two days.

Her eyes burned hot and prickly as she scanned the article. Everyone on trial. The list of names seemed endless. No one important to her seemed overlooked. Only Jack and her mother weren't included. She prayed they'd not be caught. The charges included conspiracy and smuggling, hiding a rogue majicar, arson, destruction of property, disruption of business, murder, and theft of the blood oak. The story recounted all her apparent crimes, with the unceasing insinuation that she could not have succeeded in all this alone.

"I couldn't have accomplished all that in my lifetime," Lucy muttered.

The three owners of the *Sweet Song* had been interviewed. She could almost hear Mrs. Pladis's snide voice: "Lucy Trenton is an arrogant thief, thinking her royal blood will protect her. But she is wrong. This country will not stand for anyone flouting the laws. She's made off with the blood oak. She may as well have stolen food out of the mouths of the poor men who died bringing it home. And now when Chance is upon us and the little ones are so hungry."

The other two owners repeated the accusation, and

then the reporter, Phineas Heep, moved on to Alistair Crummel, who said that Lucy had been "unsettled during her salvage debriefing," a fact that suggested her guilt, concluded Phineas Heep.

Lucy glowered. "Because I couldn't have been righteously indignant. Oh no, it must have been my guilty conscience showing."

> An odd occurrence following the debriefing was later connected to Lucy Trenton's majickal abilities. She stormed out of Crummel's office and tore the bronze door handle away. A subtle threat against those who would bring her to justice? No one can say for certain, but clearly Miss Trenton is no innocent.

Phineas Heep then went on to interview several disgruntled captains who claimed that Lucy had blackmailed them into paying her bribes to prevent her from holding up their cargoes on false claims of smuggling.

> And it has come to light that on the morning of her suspension from her trusted position as a customs inspector, she used her seal to break into a warehouse and steal a valuable collection of jewels. The Crown Shields are investigating. In the meantime, the fire in Salford Terrace continues to rage, burning everything in its path. A cadre of majicars has slowed its pace, but cannot seem to snuff the flames. It's a fearsome sight. Stone walls and cobbles turning to ash. What kind of monster is Lucy Trenton to visit such terror on her neighbors and friends?

Lucy squeezed her eyes shut, crumpling the paper. She drew a harsh breath, not wanting to read any more. There was too much painful truth mixed in with the lies.

Coward, she jeered. *Look at what you've done. Take responsibility.*

She opened her eyes, smoothing the paper back out and reading further.

> In a related story, Minister Edgar Thorpe, a well-respected member of the Merchants Advisory Council, has come forward with disturbing allegations that Lucy Trenton gave his brother, Captain Marten Thorpe, a cipher that caused him to ruin himself with illegal gambling. Captain Thorpe has revealed that he aided Miss Trenton in smuggling the blood oak through salvage, and that she compelled him to do so with majick. Sadly, though Marten Thorpe had no choice in his actions, he must pay the price. Lord Chancellor Truehelm has forgiven his transgressions insofar as Captain Thorpe will not be sent to the Bramble. However, tomorrow he will be auctioned into indentured servitude. A steep price to pay for the bad luck to suffer Miss Trenton's notice.

Stunned, Lucy flipped pages to the notices of impending auction. She found what she was looking for halfway down in the third column. It was exactly as Phineas Heep had reported. Marten would be put up for sale to the highest bidder at noon the next day in the main market square in Blackstone. Lucy reread the notice three times and then pushed the paper away, her fingers tapping a slow cadence on the table. Marten was going on the auction block. And she was going to be there to watch.

Keros returned after sundown. Lucy heard him come in and began to prepare an omelet. She *could* cook; she just despised it. She heated butter and tossed in onions and bacon. She added eggs whipped with cream, and toasted bread on a fork over the fire.

"Smells good," Keros said as he came in. He took the toasting fork from her. "I'm impressed."

Lucy put the food on the table and they sat down to eat.

"You're quiet. I take it you read the paper?"

She nodded. Then, "I'd like you to help me with my hair."

"Shaving yourself bald, are you?"

"I want to dye it. With ink."

"It would hide the color well enough. Make you less recognizable."

"So I thought."

"I know how to get you inside."

"Do you?" Lucy looked up, her interest sharpening.

"First thing every morning and evening, there's a shift change when most of the servants who don't live in the bagnio come and go. It's orderly—you won't be able to slip in through the seams. But with my help, and Lora Clump's, you will," said Keros with satisfaction.

"Who is Lora Clump?"

"She is a scrub maid, responsible for cleaning the bathing rooms. A rather filthy, disgusting job, and one from which she is willing to take a vacation. With compensation. She's about your size and has sold me her uniform and lent me her identification tab. Handily enough, she's a dark-haired woman. Your choice of hair color should be appropriate. Not that anyone will notice. She wears a cap and maids are invisible to most people. I'll give you a glamour to disguise you to those who might know her. Can you clean?"

Lucy grinned. "I have many talents."

He returned the grin. "Aye, that you do. The only problem will come when your first shift is over. They'll start looking for you if you don't leave."

"So I have to leave. Unless I get permission to stay."

"Chancy. My glamour will fade by then."

There was a tightness to the corners of his eyes and

a tension in his jaw that revealed his concern, despite his offhand tone. He caught her looking at him and slapped his hands down on the table.

"Damn Marten! And damn me for giving him those drops."

"He's your friend. And I'm no one important. Why wouldn't you help him?"

"I'm an ass."

"True. But then so am I. I am going to watch Marten's auction."

"I thought as much. Lora's shift begins at sunset. Don't miss it or you won't get inside."

"I won't. Are you done with your dinner? Let's do my hair so we can get to bed."

"Is that an invitation to the myriad delights of your sheets?" He waggled his brows.

"Myriad delights? Painting it on a bit thick, don't you think?"

"Many women enjoy a bit of flattery."

For a moment she recalled that Embernight, standing in front of the fire across from Marten, her hands shredded. She'd accused him of being too honest, of not offering the usual flattery. *I thought it was to be truth between us.* She almost laughed at the irony.

"I've had enough of lies for the moment, thank you. And I am well aware that I am no prize. The one claim to beauty I had is gone." She stroked her hand over her shorn hair and then gave a harsh laugh "Height of vanity to be regretting my hair when everyone I know is going on trial and I'm being hunted."

"It'll grow back one day."

"Hair doesn't grow in the grave, Keros. And in my recent encounter with *sylveth* spawn, I didn't see any with a flowing mane. But enough of this. Let's get to work."

Lucy dangled her head over a basin as Keros combed the ink through her hair. He took his time. But when he was through, her hair was nearly black.

"Let's not forget your eyebrows," he said, painting

them carefully. "You should wash out the residue. You don't want any color to rub off and give you away."

"I'll do that. And thank you."

"I helped get you into this mess. It's the least I can do."

"Guilt, Keros? And here I thought you liked me."

"Guilt, yes. Certainly that. But it also happens I do like you."

Lucy only raised her brows skeptically.

"Surprised, are you? Sharp-tongued virago that you are, you should be. But you have a few good qualities too. Rabid focus on finding the truth . . . oh—I enjoy the spontaneous combustion too. Let's see, what else? You seem to appreciate my humor. I always like a good audience. And you don't insult my cooking. That wins you a few points."

"Are you through?"

Keros stood, taking Lucy by the hands and pulling her to her feet. He gazed down at her.

"I took you in because I felt guilty about assisting Marten in his theft. And I am helping you because it is the right thing to do—for you, and for Crosspointe. I may be a renegade majicar, but I am a loyal son of this country. However, with all that said, I also enjoy you. Very much. I want you to be safe, and to have the chance to grow back that lion's mane of yours."

Lucy swallowed, a hard lump lodging in her throat. In all things that counted, he'd become her friend. It was a gift. She pulled back, patting him on the cheek lightly. "That doesn't mean I'm inviting you to bed."

Keros put one hand over his heart. "I am crushed."

"You're a fool."

"Aye, that we can agree on. Now go wash your hair and get some sleep. I'll wake you early. It will take you some time to get to the main market square before Marten steps onto the block. You don't want to miss his comeuppance."

"No, I don't." But as Lucy went to bed, a nagging doubt chewed at her. Why was Marten being sold if he'd successfully stolen her seals? Surely he ought to have gained something by framing her? If not money to keep him from this predicament, then what? And why had his brother claimed she'd given Marten a cipher? Of course, such a lie saved his life, kept him from being sent to the Bramble. It made sense. But the lie also was another nail in her coffin. Was that the real intent?

The questions chased one another around her skull, keeping her awake almost until dawn. But despite her anger at Marten, somehow the thought of him wearing the iron collar did not make her as happy as she'd thought it would.

Chapter 22

Marten's cell was entirely devoid of comfort. The bed was made of rough wood slats and topped by a thin pallet of tattered sail canvas stuffed with mouldering straw. The walls and floor were unfinished stone and the only other furnishing in the narrow cubicle was a chipped chamber pot. A small grille in the door allowed his jailors to see inside, and another barred window high in the outer wall let in a thin gray light.

Marten lay on the bed staring up at the roof. The iron collar pressed hard into the back of his neck. He ignored its bite, thinking only of Jordan's battered body. He groaned, rubbing the heels of his hands against his eyes. If not for him, Jordan would be alive and Lucy— Did Lucy know? What must she think?

He dropped his hands to his sides, clenching them on the canvas pallet. Why was Edgar going after her so rabidly? All this to discredit the monarchy? It seemed like overkill. He thought of her shredded hands, how someone must have slashed at them over and over with a knife. His stomach lurched and he rolled over and retched onto the floor. When at last nothing more came up, he rolled back to the wall. His mouth tasted like a sewer. He was sure of one thing: Edgar had not cut her up. He wanted her humiliated and discredited, not mutilated. But someone did. Who? And why?

For the first time, it occurred to Marten that the reason no one had been able to find Lucy was that she was dead. And in that thought was a pain so fierce that he thought he was dying. He lay there gasping, waiting for it to recede. His mind was whirling chaos. All he knew was the bewildering pain of a loss so deep there were no words.

He came back to himself when someone slapped him hard across the face. Back and forth. The shock cut across the sucking hurt and jarred him back to awareness. One guard held him by the shoulders, while another drew back to smash him across the mouth again.

"Ye done wailin' like a sucklin' baby? 'Cause we ain't gonna listen t'yer bellyachin' no more if'n we have t'smash ye t'bits."

"What?" Marten rasped, blood dribbling from his nose down over his lips and chin. Then, "Yes" when the guard cocked back to hit him again.

"Good, then."

The guard roughly shoved him back. His ribs flared where Jordan had punched him. Marten waited until the door thumped shut before he pushed himself up to sit with his back against the wall. The depth of his reaction to the possibility of Lucy's death was appalling. And bizarre. Unless . . .

No. Absolutely not. He was not—he *could not* be—in love with the woman. He hardly knew her! And yet . . .

He rubbed his palm over his chest. It hurt, like a ragged, bleeding wound. By the gods, how had this happened? He snorted softly. Braken's curse. It wasn't enough that the sea god suffered from tormented love; he wanted to share his pain. Because even if Lucy was alive, there was no way Marten was ever going to win her over. He'd been the key to destroying her. There was no forgiving that.

He bounced his head back against the wall. He was torn between hoping she was alive and safe and fearing she'd been killed. Or worse. He could not put the image of her shredded hands out of his mind. Damn, what a fool he was!

*   *   *

On the second morning of his incarceration, Baskin arrived, sent by Edgar to make sure that Marten was presentable. The valet shaved him and helped him into a fresh set of clothing. The elbows of his shirt were wearing thin and the cuffs of his trousers were frayed.

"Should've run to Tiro Pilan when ye had the chance," Baskin muttered as Marten stamped into his boots.

"Aye, that's a fact." His voice dropped. "Is there any word on Lucy?"

"Lots o'stories in the paper," Baskin answered shortly. "Yer not goin' t'like 'em."

"I haven't liked any of it since it began. Tell me."

"It be yer brother. Says ye became a gambler on account of Miss Trenton puttin' a spell on ye. Says she forced ye to smuggle the blood oak through the salvage."

Marten swore and slammed his fist against the wall. The pain only fed his fury. If she was alive, if she was reading that bilge— "I've got to find her."

"Expect she'll be attendin' today. I would if'n I was her. Be wantin' t'see ye squirm."

Marten stared. "That's brilliant. Find her. Tell her to meet me. Gaoler's Coach. Soon as may be."

"Beggin' yer pardon, Cap'n, but ye ain't free to be makin' appointments. Not that she'll be wantin' t'talk with ye."

Master Wedling entered before Marten could answer. He was flanked by two guards. Unlike customs, Chancery employed the Blackwatch. They wore polished brown boots that rose up over the knee, and black breeches and coats over red shirts. The coats were frogged with red trim. The two guards were women, one with graying hair, the other hardly out of drawers. Both were grim-faced and unyielding.

"Good, you are ready. The wagon is outside. I just need to attach this," Master Wedling said, holding up a chain. "Turn around."

Marten shifted, his back rigid. Master Wedling fixed the chain to the loop on the collar.

"Very good, then. Come along."

Marten turned to follow, the chain snaking over his shoulder, the collar pressing against his neck. In an undertone, he said to Baskin, "You know what to do."

They led him out of the building to a platform. The breeze was sharp and the sky was overcast. The tang of acrid smoke tainted the air from the fire in Salford Terrace.

Beside the platform waited a wooden cart pulled by a white mule. The railings were low, about knee-high, allowing a good view of any occupants. They were swathed in crimson bunting with a gate on the side that lifted aside. Master Wedling led Marten on board. As the cart shifted with their weight, deep-sounding bells clanged softly. They were hung beneath the cart and on the mule's harness to call attention to its passengers as it rolled along.

"You must put this on as well," Master Wedling said, unfolding a white tabard. On the front and back was the word DEBTOR embroidered in the same glaring crimson as the bunting, and below it, a figure of a man on his knees, hands raised in supplication. Master Wedling fastened the chain to an eyebolt on the rail behind the driver and stepped back onto the platform. "Yours is the only auction today. I expect you'll fetch a pretty price. There'll be plenty wanting a pet ship's captain," he said in what seemed to be an effort at reassurance. "Well, then. Off you go."

The rail gate was dropped into place and the cart jolted to life. Marten braced himself as the chain tightened and the collar jerked against his neck. Led by four guards and trailed by four more, the cart rolled down the alley out onto the avenue, the bells ringing loudly. The street was crowded with people who pointed and yelled, laughing at his predicament. Marten burned with humiliation. He knew he looked disreputable with his black eyes and swollen lips. With the addition of the tabard, collar, and chain, he looked like a dangerous animal. He deserved this. If only for what he'd helped Edgar do to Lucy. With a snarl, he fixed his gaze on the back of the driver's head, ignoring his audience.

The drive seemed endless. The cart jerked and bounced over the uneven cobbles and occasional chuck-hole. Every jolt sent jabs of pain up through his bruised ribs, jerking the chain tight as he staggered for balance.

The main market square was not far from Jabry Inn. The cart rolled slowly up the cordoned center, stopping beside the scaffold at the far end. It stood before a squat tower made of mottled black and green stone. It had been built as a memorial to the three founders of Crosspointe—Errol Cipher, the first William Rampling, and Trevor Culpepper. Behind it in the distance rose a black column of smoke from Salford Terrace.

A guard clambered up on the cart and unchained Marten, pulling him down a set of carriage steps like a recalcitrant dog and then up onto a great block of black basalt shot through with veins of white quartz. The Chancery scales and compass were carved in relief on each of the four sides. From where he stood, Marten could see over the heads of the gathered crowd to the edges of the square. His guard, the gray-haired woman, continued to hold the chain, pulling him around in a circle to show him off like a prize cow. Marten couldn't help but resist. She yanked and the collar bit hard into his neck. He stumbled forward and the crowd cheered. She yanked again and he dug his heels in. Undaunted, she changed her angle and the collar pressed against his windpipe. He was forced to turn and stumble toward her again.

There was a brassy trill of trumpets and the crowd quieted. Behind him on the scaffold, a rich baritone voice rang out.

"Ladies and Gentlemen, lend me your attention, please. We are gathered here today to auction this man,

Captain Marten Thorpe, into indentured service for a term of eleven years and eight months. He is thirty-two years old, in good health. He is a seasoned ship's captain with current registration and documentation. He's been a captain for ten years with not a single wreck. I have his anchor sheets and logs available. Additionally, while he has some injuries, they will in no way interfere with his ability to perform his duties aboard ship. You will have half a glass to examine the documents and then we will begin. The bidding will start at one dralion, seven Hurn's eyes, six glyphs, and eight crescents."

The next half glass was interminable. The guard dragged Marten around in circles, jabbing at him to answer when potential buyers asked him questions about his experience and qualifications. He saw no sign of Lucy. Nor did he see Edgar. His bladder tightened. What if someone else purchased his contract? He hadn't considered it before, assuming his brother would make good on his word, or threat.

The horns sounded again and the guard led Marten to the front of the platform.

"Very good. Let us begin. Who will meet the starting bid?"

"So bid!"

Marten's gaze fastened on Edgar, who stood below him in the front row flanked by his bullyboys, relief making his legs rubbery. The bidding continued in rapid staccato, but he hardly heard it. He combed the crowd for a telltale sweep of red hair and a pair of brilliant blue eyes. She was there, witnessing his humiliation; he could feel it.

Marten started when the crack of the gavel ended the bidding. Edgar had won, at a cost of nearly three dralions. Far more than Marten's debt. But then, Edgar hadn't called his markers for the money, but for his silence. Money wasn't the object. Nor was it a bad investment. His wages would have cost Edgar far more over the next twelve years.

The guard pulled him back down the steps, handing over Marten's chain with very little ceremony. She peeled the tabard over his head and disappeared.

Edgar jingled the chain lightly. "Have you learned your lesson yet, brother? The house always wins."

Marten didn't answer.

"Let us be off, then. I have business to attend to."

The bullyboys crowded in around Marten as he trailed after his brother. They meandered past the merchant stalls with Edgar stopping here and there to chat with friends and business acquaintances. Marten continued to search for Lucy out the corners of his eyes to no avail. When they arrived at the carriage, Edgar motioned Marten to the rear. A new brass loop had been installed on the baggage rail.

"You'll ride behind."

Edgar handed the end of the chain to one of his bullyboys, who clipped it onto the loop, jerking Marten up onto the step as he did. He grunted. The bullyboy grinned. Another clambered up, sandwiching him between their muscular bulk. Edgar shut the door and the carriage wheels rattled over the cobbles, the horses' hooves clopping.

They were turning onto the avenue leading out into Blackstone when Marten saw Lucy at last. She'd cut her hair short and dyed it a flat blackish brown that made her look mousy. But her eyes were the same piercing blue, her jaw strong and jutting. She glared at him, rage narrowing her eyes and pulling her lips into a thin smile at his predicament. She stood at the corner beside a lamppost, only feet away from the wheels of the carriage. No one but Marten noticed her.

His heart leaped at the sight of her. Alive. By Braken, she was alive. At the moment, he didn't care that she hated him. All that mattered was she was still in this world.

He drew a breath, closing his eyes with relief. When he opened them again, she was gone. He searched the crowd, twisting and standing on tiptoe, but could find no trace of her. The carriage lurched and the chain pulled taut. He glanced down at himself and humiliation seared him. This was what she'd come today to see. Not a man, but a slave.

Unreasonable anger made his jaw tighten and sent a rush of warmth through his muscles. If he hadn't been trying to help her, he wouldn't be in this blasted situation. He wouldn't have gone to Jordan, and Edgar wouldn't have called his markers. Didn't she know how much he'd given up to save her? What right did she have to enjoy his disgrace? A small voice whispered, *Every right.* He quashed it, suddenly far too aware of the cold iron around his neck and the fact that for the next twelve years his life was no longer his own.

He drew a tight breath. He wasn't going to let Lucy be an anchor tangling him in its coils. She was a grown woman; she could damned well help herself from now on. He had his own hide to look out for.

At that moment he believed he could dismiss her from his mind and heart and forget about her.

Instead of going to Thorpe House, the carriage took them to Sweet Dreams. It pulled up to a private entrance on the side of the bagnio. A closed-in portico kept off the rain and weather and screened guests from view. As the coachmen pulled the horses to a halt, Marten was unclipped, his leash retained by one of Edgar's bully-boys.

The door leading into Sweet Dreams was made of burnished copper and engraved with a busy scene of Blackwater Bay. There was no visible means of opening it. Edgar set his hand in the middle and muttered something guttural that Marten couldn't understand. The door slid silently back into the wall.

This was a part of the bagnio that Marten didn't recognize. The entrance was a landing made of alabaster. A balustrade circled the lobed front overlooking the broad hall below. On either side of the landing, two wide staircases curved downward like great white wings.

Edgar veered down one of these. The hall at the bottom had inlaid wood floors with swirling patterns that suggested the wind surrounding an enormous compass rose. Overhead, chandeliers sparkled fire and on the walls hung rare artworks from all over the world. Plush chairs and couches lined the walls and heavy curtains hid private nooks. Everywhere there was gilding, on the groined ceiling and pilastered walls, on the fringes of the draperies and tablecloths, and on the low tables, stools, and benches. The hall glowed like dawn.

They crossed to the other side under a broad arch that led into a smaller set of sitting rooms and salons. There was also an entry leading to the bathing rooms, gambling rooms, and restaurant areas of the bagnio, and another into Edgar's private rooms, which was where they went now.

Edgar took Marten's chain, ordering his bullyboys to wait. Once inside, he shut the door and Marten realized with a chill that he could not leave these rooms without Edgar opening it up again.

"I'll show you to your quarters."

"Here?"

"I want to keep a close eye on you, and I plan to be quite busy here at Sweet Dreams. Until I'm certain you'll behave yourself, you'll live here. Your man will be at Thorpe House, so you'll have to dress and shave yourself. It will give you a chance to understand what you have lost, and what you might gain from my goodwill."

He took Marten to a small room that appeared to have recently been a storage closet. The walls were plastered and painted dull gray. There were no windows, and only an oil lamp to light the gloom. The bedstead was narrow, the mirror polished steel, the dresser plain wood. The floor was cold and bare and the sheets were coarse.

Edgar turned to Marten, speaking with a kind of unhappy reserve, as if he didn't like what he was forced to do, but was ruled by a necessity he couldn't alter. "I'll have someone show you where to empty your slops and get wash water. There is a bathing room that the servants may use and you'll dine with them as well.

"For the moment, I have no duties for you. However, that will change soon. In the meantime, you will remain here unless you are bathing, dining, or cleaning up after yourself. Every time you leave, you will be accompanied by a guard. Ring the bell when you wish to go."

He turned, then paused, looking back. "Consider where you are, Marten. Look at what's become of you. I suggest you think hard about where your best interests lie and forget about Lucy Trenton once and for all. I told you before, she is destined for the Bramble."

Chapter 23

Lucy fled the market square breathless and sick to her stomach. Watching Marten led about by a collar and chain had disgusted her. He'd been like an animal, pulled this way and that, staring balefully at the eager crowd. She wondered where he'd gotten the bruises and swelling on his face. She'd thought she would feel triumph when the gavel struck. But instead she felt hollow and unacountably angry. It had nothing to do with him, she told herself. She wouldn't like seeing anyone treated so. He deserved to be punished for what he'd done to her, but no one deserved *that*. Yet despite her repulsion, she couldn't tear herself away. She watched him until he was loaded onto the back of the carriage.

It wasn't until his gaze fastened on to her that she realized he'd been looking for her since stepping onto the block. When their eyes locked, it felt like a blow. Fury erupted in her belly and she glared back. He closed his eyes, an expression she could only interpret as relief washing over him. It was like wind on the fire of her rage.

Suddenly the cipher on her arm tingled and went cold. A rime of frost sparkled on the lamppost beside her. Panic-stricken, she bolted.

The cold followed her. She shoved through the crowd, and dashed down an alley and out onto a wide street. Footspiders trotted up and down and hacks waited outside the shops. The sidewalks were crowded with clerks, solicitors, barristers, and shoppers. Lucy ran into the street. Coach drivers yelled at her to get out of the way and one footspider swung a fist at her when she nearly tripped him. But she dared not stop. The tingling had turned painful, a bracelet of fiery needles driving into her flesh. The cipher was going to erupt again.

She found herself running toward Salford Terrace. Toward the fire she'd started outside Faraday, and the majicars who were now fighting it. Instinctively she veered off, turning down a narrow road that took her toward the harbor. But she'd hardly gone twenty steps when a mad idea made her falter. *What if . . . ?* Ice to battle fire? She glanced down. Her hand was sheathed in a glove of ice. She turned it over, making a fist. The ice cracked and flaked off. Was it possible? What if she could use the cipher's majick against itself?

She spun around and ran back the way she'd come.

Salford Terrace was a wasteland. Even the dirt of the hills smoldered. There wasn't a tree or a building left, or even any lumps of stone or wood to say there ever had been any there. There were only piles of wind-drifted ash. The only landmark Lucy recognized was the castle up on Scarbrey Hill. The fire had burned a swath that arrowed down toward the harbor. The flames were smaller now than that first night, but just as determined. Lucy could see the brilliant colors of the majicars' robes as they battled the blaze. They were close. She'd come out onto the burn less than a quarter of a league from the fire line.

Heat wrapped her feet. She looked down in surprise. The ground was still smoldering here. As she watched, flames leaped suddenly to life, licking her boots eagerly. Lucy watched them stupidly. Then understanding reached her. She jumped back. The fire followed, clinging. Her boots blackened. She curled her toes, scrambling onto the road. The flames pursued her. Where she stepped, the cobbles caught fire. In only moments the greedy flames grabbed hold of the fresh tinder. They spread quickly to the buildings on either side as Lucy watched in horror.

Her boots were burning fiercely now. Lucy kicked them off. On either side of her, flames roared. Smoke billowed from the buildings. She coughed and choked, her eyes streaming.

An intense pain streaked up her arm into her neck. She staggered and fell to her knees. Mindlessly, she slammed her hand against the ground. Fragments of ice sprayed against her face. Seconds later, a veil of ice swept over her, sealing her inside a cold cocoon. Outside Lucy could hear the roar of the flames, could smell the smoke and taste its bitterness in her throat. She had to stop it. But how to tap the power of the cipher? Keros would kill her if she mangled her hands again. She sobbed. Damn Errol Cipher anyway! She hoped to Meris he'd been reborn as a manure-eating beetle.

Her cocoon was thickening. It was a deadly shield. It would kill her if the flames didn't. She should try to get away. But she didn't move.

Instead of stopping the fire, she'd spread it. The cipher *had* to be able to turn it back around. But all she could think of was the ice and the penetrating cold. Why not? What did she have to lose? It was not hard to focus, not after her experience with the Koreion of her mind. She narrowed her concentration on the cold, waiting until she could feel it with every beat of her heart. Then she gave a great angry mental thrust. *Out!*

Nothing seemed to happen. Or did it? She shook her head, the cocoon crackling, ice shards cutting into her jaw and neck. She ignored the pain, blinking to clear her eyes. Triumph made her giddy. It *had* moved. If only just a few inches. She eyed the flames. It was going to take a whole lot more than that.

Lucy closed her eyes, drawing herself inward. For a moment she floundered, fragments of her mind scurrying away like cockroaches in the light. She pulled them back, focusing on the cipher, on that endless itch inside her that told her majick was there and where. She concentrated on it, imagining it like a reservoir of water. She felt something building, a pressure inside that swelled, pushing against her innards. She held it, instinct telling her that the more it built, the more effect it would have.

The pressure tightened, turning rock hard. Her tendons stretched and her joints cracked with the strain of containing it. Her bladder ached for release. Lucy could hold it in no longer. She reached out with mental hands and ripped apart the reservoir walls, shoving on the collected majick at the same time.

Power erupted from her in an endless tide. It hooked grapnels around her bones and through her flesh. The tug of it was agonizing. It pulled on the ethereal inner part of Lucy that made her *herself*. At first she didn't resist. The pain was too great, the drag unrelenting. But the stubborn part of her plopped down like a stubborn ox and hauled back. Why should she go? Why should she give in? The grapnels clawed harder and Lucy wrenched violently, indignant. The cipher *was not* going to beat her. Not this time. Not yet. She still had things to do.

A red haze obscured her vision, darkening to black. She shook her head to clear it, gritting her teeth against the whirling dizziness. She matched her body to her inner tug-of-war and flung herself backward, giving a great mental jerk as she did. The wicked hooks tore free, leaving Lucy flat on her back on the cobbles.

She panted, her ribs bellowing, feeling as raw as if she'd been keelhauled. She had a sense of the Koreion circling around her and then vanishing. She rolled onto her stomach and then to her knees. Her muscles shook so that she could barely hold herself erect. Her hands were so numb she couldn't feel them. But laughter bubbled inside her. She'd done it! But had she stopped the fire? She doggedly turned, her shoulders hunching as if against a blow, her fists coming up defensively.

Her jaw fell open. A sparkling fairyland of ice spread out before her as far as she could see. A glimmer of gold caught her attention. She stepped forward to examine it and slipped. She fell to one knee, her other leg stretching painfully wide. She pushed herself back up using her hands, balancing cautiously on the flats of her feet.

Her gaze snagged back on the gold, and she caught her breath at the unearthly beauty of flames dancing inside a sheath of ice. As she watched, they flickered and shrank, leaving behind a crystal sculpture the shape of fire. The ice cocoon rolled out over the blackened scar like a glass sea. It rose up over the buildings on the far side and south where the fire still raged. Had raged. Now it was dying beneath the thick glaze.

Slowly Lucy became aware of voices, of shouts and people running up beside her on the street. She backed away, slipping and sliding. The cipher warmed on her arm. No!

Again she fled. She dived into whatever opening appeared, winding through a maze of alleys and streets, running until she was breathless. She slowed down, coming aware that her feet hurt. She looked down at them. The socks had charred away up to her ankles. Her soles were bloody and the tops of her feet were blistered and red.

She glanced about. She stood on a narrow street in Blackstone outside a bakery. Across the street was a milliner's. More shops lined the road. There was no sidewalk here, but the buildings were neat and tidy. They were half-timbered, the whitewash dingy from coal smoke. Lucy limped along, aware of the suspicious looks of shopkeepers and customers alike. She hurried her pace. They'd be calling the guard soon. She looked like a thief or a vagrant, which in most people's minds were the same thing.

She crossed a street and ducked around a corner. She found a nook between two buildings near the coal-delivery chutes and wedged inside, squatting down and wrapping her cloak around to cover her feet. She couldn't get to the Riddles like this. She'd be crippled before she got halfway to Cheapside.

The familiar recklessness reared up. *Coward.* Of course she could. All she needed was a little fortitude and resolve. She looked at her bloody feet. Keros was going to be rude about this. She rolled her eyes, imagining his mockery. First the hands, then the ankle, then her feet. She was a smart girl—couldn't she figure out a way to get back that didn't involve tearing her feet to shreds? Nor did she have time to make the trek. Even with boots, her excursion to the burn had robbed her of precious time. She had to get back by the time the evening shift of maids entered Sweet Dreams. She couldn't afford to miss this chance to get inside. She wouldn't get another.

She rubbed her hands over her face, trying to think. She needed a hack. But none were going to stop for anyone looking like her. So either she needed a pair of boots, or . . .

Lucy stood and limped over to peer out onto the street. Carriages, hacks, and footspiders filled the thoroughfare. The wind was starting to bluster again and pedestrians clutched their cloaks around themselves, quickening their paces. Ash drifted in the air, spinning with grit into stinging whirlwinds. As she watched, a hack pulled up a dozen feet away and dropped off a pair of elderly women. They bustled inside the embroidery shop after telling the driver to wait, shouting at each other in tones that indicated both were hard of hearing.

"Hurry then, Aggie. Clarence'll want his tea exactly at four. Why you couldn't wait until tomorrow, I just don't know. All this way for a bit of floss. Paying for a hack from Harwich, when Clarence could have driven us over tomorrow."

"Now, Vera. I said I'd pay for the hack, so you can just stop fustering about it. I must have the periwinkle tonight if I'm going to have the waistcoat ready in time. Tomorrow is George's birthday and a poor mother I would be if I didn't have a proper gift for him."

The ladies disappeared inside. But Lucy had heard enough. Harwich. It was a small town on the south side of Blackwater Bay between Waterfoot and Skegby. It was no closer to the Riddles than she was now, but if she stowed away in the boot . . .

She eyed the hack driver, who had clambered down and was adjusting the harness on the mules. He stamped his feet and snugged his caped cloak against the wind, keeping his hood pulled forward to protect his eyes. Lucy bit the tip of her tongue. It would be safer to go left and cross the street and approach the hack from behind. But it would not take long to purchase the skein of embroidery floss. She didn't dare waste the time.

Pulling her own cloak tight around herself, Lucy stepped out onto the edge of the road, forcing herself to walk without limping. She held her shoulders erect and walked quickly back down to the cross street and turned the corner. She halted, leaning back against the wall, holding her breath. A footspider cast a tired glance at her as he jogged past. Lucy nodded to him and then inched back to peer around the corner. The hack driver continued to try to warm himself.

The boot at the back of the carriage was buckled closed, leaving a small opening at the bottom no bigger than a cat. She licked her lips. It was going to take her a little time to get inside. At that moment the elderly ladies emerged from the shop. The driver leaped to open the door and let down the step. The two old women were fussy and jabbered at him loudly as the wind caught the door and slammed it against the carriage. Lucy took advantage of the driver's distraction to make her move. She forced herself to keep to a hurried walk as she approached the hack. She dodged behind the back, watching the carriage shift as the first of the two women got inside. Quickly she worked at the buckles, freeing the first two easily. The third refused to give. She yanked on it, feeling the carriage give again and hearing the door slam shut.

The driver was climbing up onto the seat now. Lucy thrust herself under the boot flaps. She scrabbled for handholds as the hack started to move, her feet dragging over the cobbles. She grasped a metal rail and pulled herself up, kicking her feet wildly. Once inside, she pulled the flaps down, closing herself in darkness. She leaned back against the rear of the carriage, pulling her knees against her chest. Her feet throbbed and her heart thundered against her ribs. But despite her exhaustion, aches, and pains, a satisfied smile curved her lips.

She nodded off, jerking awake as they rolled over a bridge. The hollow rumble of the wheels echoed loudly. The air in the boot was stuffy and dank. Lucy eased onto her hands and knees, pushing aside the flaps to see out. They'd just crossed the river. The road was angling back toward the harbor and southern end of Tideswell. Lucy began working at the reluctant buckle. Her right thumbnail bent back halfway and she swore. She held her thumb tightly in her left hand for a moment, and then set back to work. At last she pulled the strap free. She attacked the next one and soon the opening was big enough to slip out of easily. Lucy scooted to the edge of the luggage shelf, letting her feet hang down.

The hack went around a curve and down a short hill. Lucy slid down, letting her toes drag over the cobblestones. As the road flattened out, she tensed. With a heave, she shoved herself out. She fell on her side and rolled to the edge of the road. She swiftly leaped to her feet and ran back up the hill, veering left up a dirt walkway. She hadn't gone far when she stepped on a rock and staggered to a halt.

"Crack it!"

The words rang out loudly and she bit back the rest. She hobbled in a circle, shaking her foot to ease the pain. When she could put weight on it, she began again, slower this time, picking her way more carefully, though her feet were so raw there was no way smooth enough. The path took her into the Riddles, well south and west of Keros's house. The ground became littered with discarded junk, broken bricks and stone, and piles and pools of waste. The stench was revolting, and worse was accidentally stepping in something disgustingly sticky that squelched.

A few men approached her for a quick squib against the wall, but she snarled at them, shouting invectives and waving her fists like a madwoman. There were more-willing women in the Riddles and the men retreated to go in search of them.

She still had a full glass before the shift change when she at last arrived back at Keros's house. She pushed inside, panting.

"You took your sweet time—Braken's cods! Not again! Are you absolutely incapable of going even one day without needing a healing? Just look at your feet. Where are your boots? Please tell me you did not lose a pair of perfectly good boots. And whew! What have you been rolling in? You stink!"

Lucy eyed Keros darkly. "I need a bath, not a healing. And yes, I lost my boots. They were on fire."

"On fire?"

"Did you think flames that turn stone to ash would be stopped by leather?" Not that she hadn't thought just that, but she didn't say it.

"You went to the burn? Whatever for? What about Marten's auction?"

Lucy took off her cloak, ignoring the last question. She still hadn't decided how she felt about Marten being sold into indentured servitude, and she didn't like that she should pity him.

"I didn't mean to go to the burn. It just sort of happened."

"How?"

"Oh, please. The cipher, what else?"

He shook his head, rubbing his hand over his eyes. "The gods must hate me. And you." He paused, his eyes narrowing. "Let's go upstairs. You can tell me all about it while you bathe."

Lucy lifted her brows at him, but didn't object. The notion of a bath was far too tempting. He sighed in exasperation as she shambled across the floor, leaving a trail of blood and other, less pleasant detritus. He muttered something uncomplimentary and swept her up in his arms. He carried her up the narrow stairway to her room, dropping her unceremoniously onto the bed.

He filled and heated the tub.

"All right, get in." He folded his arms, watching her.

"My, such chivalry. You're not even going to turn your back?"

"And miss seeing all the damage you've done to yourself? I don't trust you. You'll hide things."

"Whatever fills your sails," Lucy said. The ever-present recklessness was growing stronger. She felt daring and wild. She stripped off her clothing, refusing to let herself feel embarrassed. She smiled when she looked up and found that his face was flushed.

"You can always look at the wall."

"This view is very nice," he drawled. "At least I know what Marten sees in you."

Lucy looked down at herself, wrinkling her nose. "He likes shrewish fat women, then?"

"Your fat is in all the right places."

"I think your taste might be suspect. When was the last time you had a woman in your bed?" she retorted. She didn't wait for his sardonic answer, but stepped into the tub, sucking a pained breath when the warm water hit her cuts and burns.

"Are you all right?"

"Not really. But I'll live."

"I could try to heal you, but . . ."

Lucy shuddered, remembering what had happened when he'd healed her ankle. "I think I'll try it the old-fashioned way this time: I don't feel like talking to my cipher again."

"Perhaps you are right. You have been hard on the furnishings."

He watched her scrub her hair and duck under the water. He fetched an ewer of water and finished rinsing the soap from her hair, and then took up the sponge and scrubbed her back. She leaned forward with a pleased groan.

"Are you going to tell me what happened?"

"Marten's brother bought his service contract."

"That's odd."

"Is it?"

"Why didn't he lend Marten the money rather then send him to the block?"

Lucy frowned. "In the paper his brother said I gave Marten a cipher that made him gamble, and that I used majick to force him to help smuggle the blood oak across the cordon during the salvage. But I didn't have anything to do with either. Why would Marten tell his brother I did?"

"Maybe he didn't."

"But then—why would Marten's brother want to frame me?" Lucy said slowly.

"I hate to say it again, but Marten is the one you have to talk to." He handed her the sponge and went to sit on the edge of the bed. He looked somber. "Lucy, this makes it even more dangerous for you to go into Sweet Dreams."

"I don't really have a choice, do I?"

"I suppose not. But be very careful. Please."

Her smile curved like the edge of a scythe. "Don't worry." She lifted her arm where the cipher wrapped it. "If he comes after me, I'll make sure he burns up in the inferno with me."

"That's comforting," Keros muttered. Then he changed the subject. "Why did you go to the burn?"

"Marten saw me. I ran and just ended up there."

"What happened?"

"I didn't realize the dirt was burning. I walked out onto it and my boots caught fire." She grimaced. "Then I backed up and started a whole new front to the fire."

Keros groaned. "Gods! And they'd managed to slow it down, too."

"Well . . . I might have put it out."

"What? Stop parceling it out to me in dribs and drabs and explain yourself before I drown you."

Lucy complied, telling him the entire story. He listened in silence, wrapping her in a bath sheet as she stepped out of the tub.

"That's . . . astonishing. And you think you put the entire fire out?"

"Maybe. I just don't know how long the ice will last or what trouble it will cause."

"Can't be worse than the fire."

"No?"

"You'd better get dressed or you'll be late. Your scrub-maid uniform is in the wardrobe. I'll see what I can find for your feet. When you're ready, there's soup on the stove."

He went to the door and looked back at her diffidently. "Was it what you hoped, seeing Marten chained like a Jutras slave?"

Lucy gave an infinitesimal shake of her head. "No."

Keros hesitated a moment longer. Then he nodded and went out, shutting the door quietly behind him.

Chapter 24

After six days of impersonating Lora Clump, Lucy had no better idea what the stranger of her childhood might be up to. Nor had she made progress deciphering the Jutras contract. She had, however, developed an unhappily familiar acquaintance with the variety of revolting residues that could be left behind in a bathing room. Her hands were rough and scaly from scrubbing, and her job duties left precious little time for anything else. But she was determined to change that. And her plan wasn't going to make Keros happy.

The day's headlines had cemented her decision. Exhaustion and distraction had contrived to keep her from reading the trial accounts of the past sennight. But this afternoon she'd woken eager to learn what she could about her family. She'd lumbered downstairs and found Keros gone, the papers stacked by the hearth to be burned.

She'd taken the lot to the table and poured over the stories. Shock turned her stomach inside out. She could hardly give credence to what she was reading. She clutched the edges of the paper, reading the first story again. LUCY TRENTON CONVICTED OF TREASON AND MURDER. According to Phineas Heep, the lord chancellor had ruled nearly as soon as the crown had presented its case.

"Lucy Trenton's unwillingness to come forward and

defend her innocence is damning in and of itself," declared Phineas Heep.

She has been found guilty of being an unregistered majicar, shamefully withholding her skills from the people of Crosspointe. She is responsible for setting the Salford Terrace fire, resulting in hundreds of thousands of dralions in losses to the crown, to Sylmont, and to the wretched people caught in its path, as well as the horrible deaths of at least twenty-eight innocent victims. Only the timely intervention of the Sennet has stopped the flames and saved the rest of Sylmont from certain destruction.

Additionally, Trenton has been convicted of using her position in customs to smuggle goods, robbing the crown of needed revenues, and stealing the food out of the mouths of those in desperate need. The families of the men serving aboard the ill-fated *Sweet Song* must not only suffer the dreadful loss of their husbands, brothers, and sons, but they do so without their rightful share of the blood oak find. They may look to Lucy Trenton during Chance when their children go hungry and their hearths are cold because they haven't the money to buy necessary staples.

In perhaps the most painful scene ever witnessed by this reporter, the lord chancellor ended the trial by finding Lucy Trenton guilty of murdering his own son, Captain Jordan Truehelm. As previously reported, Truehelm was found murdered Pescday. Clearly Trenton had seduced him, overcoming his superior strength with her majick, slitting his throat while he lay helpless to defend him-

self. There was not a dry eye in the court-
room as the lord chancellor pounded the final
gavel. Such are the men who make this country great. Lucy Trenton, you have much to
answer for.

Jordan dead? Lucy's head rang as if her ears had been
boxed. It wasn't possible. It had to be a mistake. Who
would do such a thing?

She read through the account again and then fumbled
through the papers until she found the report of Jordan's
death. Grief seized her heart. He'd been found in his
bed days after someone had broken in, tied his hands
and feet, beaten him, and then killed him. The rats had
been gnawing at him. His flat had been ransacked and
valuables stolen. Written in a shaky hand on his naked
chest had been a single word: *Lucy*. Her stomach felt
revolt at the news.

She vomited into a dirty pot in the sink. They'd killed
him to frame her. She was certain of it. She wrapped
her arms around herself, knotting her hands into fists.
Her legs were shaking, but she refused to give in to the
swamping sorrow and fear. She might not have murdered him, but she was responsible. If he hadn't been
her friend, if she'd stuck to the law and not made herself
and him a target, he'd still be alive.

She walked stiffly back to the table, straightening the
papers with forced precision and beginning to read
again. She was determined to learn the status of her
father, brothers, and friends. The news was equally
bleak. Lord Chancellor Truehelm was expected to rule
the next day that they had conspired with Lucy to com-
mit treason. As far as the reporter Phineas Heep was
concerned, it was a foregone conclusion.

Her stomach heaved again and she fled back to the
sink. She hung her head over it, bracing her arms against
the counter. She gasped, tears and snot running down
her face. The Reckoning was on Sylday, just three days

hence. Then all convicted prisoners would be sentenced. The day after, the Bramble ship would depart. The memory of the salvage and holding the many-eyed blob of muscular flesh as it sprouted spines and greedy tongues made her retch again.

At last she straightened, swallowing hard, wiping her face with the backs of her hands. She was responsible for this mess. She had to fix it. Purpose swept her and her jaw hardened. She'd made a new plan to find out about the stranger and the Jutras contract. Tonight she'd set it into motion.

She looked down at the cipher. The *sylveth* disks had turned an angry orange. But for once there was no heat, no cold, no tingling—no unusual sensations at all. She had a sense of it waiting. Slowly she lowered her arm. The question was, what was it waiting for?

Keros returned a glass and a half before sunset. He found her stewing over the papers, her expression grim.

"I see you've read the latest," he said cautiously, setting his bag on the counter and leaning his hip against it.

"My trial is over. I've been convicted."

"I know."

"Were you going to tell me?"

"Yes. Though with a little less melodramatic flair than Mr. Phineas Heep."

"I'm going to ask to be a live-in scrub maid at Sweet Dreams."

Keros surprised her by nodding slowly. "I thought as much."

"You aren't going to argue?"

"No."

His expression was tightly austere and Lucy wondered at it.

"How are you going to convince them to let you stay on?" he asked.

"Lora Clump's family are water rats. With the strike and Chance looming, there's no work, and so there's a crowd packing her house. Living at Sweet Dreams lends the family more space and takes a mouth away from the table. It's perfectly reasonable."

"I won't be able to renew the glamour. Once it fades, they'll know you're not Lora."

"It will last my first shift. After that, I'll keep my head down. You said it yourself—no one really looks closely at maids. There's only a few days left before Reckoning. If I haven't found the truth by then, it won't matter," she said bleakly.

If anything, his expression turned more severe. "It will," he said softly. "You still have to warn the king about the Jutras, even if you fail to save your family and friends. No matter how hard it is, you have to see this through all the way." He paused. "If you have to choose, then it's your duty to keep yourself safe and alive."

Lucy's lips crimped together. "About that. If anything happens to me, you need to go get the copies of the Jutras contract and take them to Cousin William. Tell him everything that's happened."

Keros blanched, his face turning the color of milk. "Me? Have you forgotten what I am? And anyhow, why would he allow a ruffian like me to have an audience?"

"You'll find a way."

Keros shook his head adamantly. "No."

"I'll write a letter. It will corroborate what you say."

"Good. Send it to him. Better yet, take it to him yourself."

Lucy ignored this last. "Someone might intercept it. Who knows who is involved in this or how high up it goes? I need you to take it to him. Put it in his hands." She paused. "If I can't," she added placatingly.

"It's impossible."

"Please."

Keros just shook his head again and turned away. "It's nearly sunset. It wouldn't do to be late when you're asking to stay on."

Lucy hesitated and went upstairs to put on her uniform and scribble the hasty letter. When she came downstairs, she laid it on the table between them. They ate silently, the scraping of their spoons the only sounds in the kitchen.

When he was through, Keros rose without speaking and came around to stand behind Lucy. He dipped his finger in his wine and drew a series of symbols on her forehead and neck. He then murmured a singsong chant, squeezing her shoulder and pressing down hard as he did.

The feeling of the spell was like cold oil washing down over her. It slid along her skin, wrapping her in an unpleasant shroud. Lucy felt the Koreion stir when Keros settled his hands on her shoulders. She closed her eyes, imagining herself stroking its soft, feathery muzzle. *Easy, now. He's only doing what I've asked.* The sea dragon nuzzled her and subsided. A flash of well-being suffused her and she smiled.

"What's funny?" Keros asked snappishly, starting to clear the table, carefully avoiding touching the letter.

"I am. You are. This whole mess."

"If you say so. You're wasting time, Lora Clump. It's time for you to go to work."

Lucy took a breath and nodded. "Thank you for all you've done."

Keros strode to the sink and dropped the dishes with a clatter. His back was straight and stiff. "I've done all that I'm going to. I'm not going to take the letter to the king."

"Then put it in the mail. It's the only warning Cousin William will have if things don't work out for me."

Keros laughed, a harsh, angry sound. He spun around, his eyes narrowed in unexpected fury. "If things don't work out? Don't you mean if they catch and kill you?"

"That, or if they catch me and throw me on the Bramble ship," Lucy said, her own anger blossoming. She glared back at him, her hands on her hips, her chin jutting.

After a long moment, he sighed and rubbed his hands over his face. "You're a damned fool. We both are."

"Undoubtedly. You'll send the letter?"

"And if I say no? Will that stop you?"

Lucy shook her head slowly. "No."

"Fine. I'll do it."

"Thank you. I owe you again."

The majicar shook his head. "Then pay me back by not getting caught."

Lucy's lips twisted. "I'll do my best."

In the guise of Lora Clump, Lucy awaited entrance to Sweet Dreams. She allowed the other servants to sift into line ahead of her. Tucked inside her shirtwaist was the Jutras contract. She'd left her seal with Keros, telling him to drop it into the harbor at the first opportunity. She'd given him the remaining gems she'd stolen as well. Over her shoulder she held a small bag containing a comb and her few other belongings. Unthinking, she touched her hair. It was tied in a tail at the base of her neck, the fractious curls that wouldn't cooperate pushed up under her cap.

"Come, now! Step lightly and stop yer mooning."

The underhousekeeper's shrill voice cut across Lucy's maunderings. She hunched and shuffled forward, bobbing her head respectfully.

"Yes'm. Sorry, mum. I didna mean t'dawdle," she said breathlessly.

"Yer Lora Clump, yes? Yer the last of the lot. Come on, then."

"If ye please, mum. I'd like t'ask . . . I mean, beggin' yer pardon, if it be no trouble . . ."

The underhousekeeper was a thin, sallow woman with sharp features and widely spaced buckteeth. She shook a bony finger at Lucy. "Come on, then. Spit it out. What do ye want?"

"It's just that wi' th'strike, it be so crowded at home. Wi' Chance comin' and food bein' so scarce and all, I wondered if'n I might be 'lowed t'stay on as a boarder maid. Leastwise till end o'Chance." Lucy spoke diffidently, averting her eyes and digging her toes in the gravel.

The underhousekeeper sniffed. "As it happens, it may be that ye can. We'll be filled up tighter than a Jutras slave ship and needing extra hands. I'll see if the housekeeper'll have ye. In the meantime, get to work. Time's wasting."

Lucy was assigned to a set of bathing rooms in the east wing. She collected her buckets, brushes, rags, and cleansers and wound through the maze of squat, narrow service passages. The first bathing room was filthy and smelled of incense, roast pork, garlic, and sweaty sex. Lucy rolled her eyes, then set about cleaning up.

She drained the water from the pool and scrubbed down the basin, walls, and floors. She fetched fresh towels, soaps, sponges, and wooden scrapers, piling the old ones in a cart to be washed. She rinsed down the slatted wooden benches and swept the ashes from the iron stove, refilling the kettle of water on top. Next she took store of the wines and liquors in the cabinet, noting down on a slate which needed restocking. She'd pass the list to the wine steward. She then moved to the sitting area and cleaned it, removing the stained coverings and replacing them with fresh ones. She fetched bowls of dried fruit, honey-roasted walnuts, crackers, chocolate truffles, and spiced sausage. Lastly, she refilled and lit the scented oil lamps in niches on the walls. When the room was ready, she rang the bell to notify the housekeeper.

The entire night went the same way. Sometime around the second glass, she fetched a sandwich and a mug of sour wine from the kitchens. Her hands itched and burned from the harsh cleanser and her back and shoulders ached from scouring on her hands and knees. She sat with the other girls in the small dining room, eating silently, too tired to do anything else. Several bolted their food and snored softly on folded arms. The underhousekeeper rousted them out and they returned to

work. Lucy cleaned several bathing rooms more than
once as different guests moved in and out.

Finally the end of her shift came and she put her
cleaning things away, following the other scrub maids
out to the exit. Each was checked off as she departed.
The underbutler stopped Lucy when she gave him her
name.

"Ye are to report to the housekeeper. Off ye go."

Relief uncurled in Lucy's stomach, even as her lungs
filled with lead. The glamour was fading. If the housekeeper noticed . . . She hurried, arriving outside the door
breathless. She knocked sharply. A young maid answered the door, the folds of her cap nearly hiding her
face. Lucy wished for the same concealment. She went
inside, ducking her head low.

The housekeeper sat in a wingback chair near the fire.
There was a tray on a table with her breakfast. She
sipped a cup of tea and set it aside with a click.

"I understand you wish to stay on as a boarder maid."

"Aye, mum," Lucy answered with a quick curtsy.

"The evaluations I have of your work are quite good.
I see no reason not to allow you to board. It will change
your duties, however. You'll be servicing the more discreet areas of the bagnio. You'll be expected to answer
any summons promptly, whether day or night, and you
will be released for half a day once a sennight, and a
full day once a month. You'll need to be polite and if I
find that you're gossiping, you'll be put out immediately
without references. Lettie has your room assignment.
You can begin this evening."

Dismissed, Lucy withdrew, going in search of the underhousekeeper. She found her in the kitchen eating
breakfast.

"Ye'll be rooming in with Janet and Betsey. Eat yer
breakfast and have one of the girls show you the way.
Best take a bath. Yer a might bit ripe, and ye'll be seen
by guests now. Don't want to scare any delicate gentlefolk." The underhousekeeper snorted with uncharacter-
istic humor. "Ye'll need a fresh uniform, too. The girls

will tell you where to go. Keep your room tidy. Now let me be.''

Lucy ate a bowl of porridge with bacon drippings and chopped nuts. She drank two mugs of weak tea and then followed an abigail up to the top of the bagnio. Her room was under the slanted roof and overlooked the alley behind. The room was frigid. She stirred the fire in the grate and added a small scoop of coal, not knowing what the ration might be. There were three narrow beds around the walls and a single wardrobe. The other two girls were absent, for which Lucy was grateful. She felt the majick of the glamour fading and didn't know if they'd recognize she wasn't the real Lora Clump or not.

She rinsed her face in the washbasin beneath the window and shivered. She wanted to begin exploring, but forced herself to crawl into bed. First she needed a few hours' sleep. She pulled the scratchy wool blankets around her chin, staring up at the cracked plaster ceiling. Somewhere under this same roof was the stranger from her childhood, the man who was out to destroy her and her family and friends. Somewhere under this roof were the answers she needed to save them. She had three days to pry them loose. Three days until Reckoning Day.

Chapter 25

Marten had been cooped up in his bilge-hole prison for seven days, escaping only to dine, bathe, and empty his slop jar. When he wanted to leave his room he was forced to knock, and the waiting guard followed him about like a starving dog. He'd learned to go to the kitchens and bathing room during the middle of the day, when few servants could take a respite from their duties. This meant the food was often cold and overcooked, but the opportunity to avoid an audience more than made up for it. He was painfully aware of the sidelong stares and muttered conversations speculating about his plight. He didn't blame them. It was Edgar's intent that he should be the brunt of servant gossip and feel his circumstances acutely. He maintained a stoic expression in the face of the tittle-tattle, but inside his room he paced back and forth, unable to sit. He was caught between worry for Lucy and fury at her for causing his plight. He should have let well enough alone and forgotten about her as Edgar advised.

Edgar. Marten knew his brother was capable of violence and cruelty. He'd seen it in the scars on the Jutras slaves that Edgar kept. He'd seen it in other times and places as well. But it had affected Marten little, until now. His brother had neatly cut his stays and bottled him up.

He was just about to make his midday foray to the kitchen when his door opened without warning.

"Master wants ye," the burly guard said tersely, motioning Marten out.

Marten was led to the private dining room, where Edgar was waiting. Edgar's Jutras servants knelt on the floor behind him, their heads bowed as they awaited his command. Their collars gleamed in the candlelight. For a moment Marten felt his own closing around his throat. He swallowed hard, tearing his eyes away. Edgar chuckled softly, wiping his mouth with his napkin. He leaned back in his chair, scanning his brother up down. Marten bit the inside of his cheek.

"How are you finding yourself, brother?"

Marten did not reply.

"Come, now, I am your master. You must make an effort to be obedient and respectful. I should not like to have to lesson you in proper manners."

Marten ran his tongue around the inside of his teeth, saying at last, "Certainly, Edgar. The accommodations are all that might be expected."

Edgar chuckled. "All that someone in your humble position might expect, eh? You're quite mistaken, actually. You've been treated far better than others in similar circumstances." He gestured languidly at the kneeling Jutras. "However, I have made concessions, being that you are my brother. I hope that the last sennight has not spoiled you into thinking you don't have to earn those concessions."

"Earn them?"

"Indeed. Of course, one might expect you to be sufficiently grateful that I kept you out of the hands of some vicious master who would use you mercilessly."

"Grateful you framed me for murdering Jordan," Marten couldn't help saying bitterly.

"I did warn you to behave. But that is neither here nor there. At the moment, I want to discuss you. I am a man of business, and I have a considerable investment in you. I could easily put you to work in a base occupation, but I would rather have the use of your considerable skills and experience as a sea captain."

Marten couldn't help the flood of eagerness that washed through him. To be out on the waves with the wind blowing in his face . . . the thought of it nearly made him sick with want.

"Oh?" he asked diffidently.

"Just so. But that means no more foolishness about Lucy Trenton. She's been convicted of treason."

"She's been caught?" Marten said, dread slithering into his stomach.

"Not yet. But it's only a matter of time. When she is, she'll be sent to the Bramble. No doubt of it. There's nothing you can do, brother. I advise you to look after yourself. If you cooperate, perhaps you will even win back your freedom."

"What do you have in mind?" Marten said with disgusting eagerness.

Edgar smiled again, folding his hands over his belly. "Captain Micawber has fallen ill. I want you to helm the *Firedance* when it departs on Moonday."

"The Bramble ship?"

Edgar sat forward, his calculating gaze latching tightly on to his brother. "Yes, the Bramble ship. Except that you'll not be leaving the prisoners on the Bramble. Rather you'll be sailing to Bokal-Dur."

Marten was certain he couldn't have heard right. But the two kneeling men had jerked their heads up at the name of the Jutras port city. "What?"

"You'll be sailing to Bokal-Dur. It's a kindness really. The prisoners don't have to endure the horrors of Chance, of becoming *sylveth* spawn. Instead, they have the opportunity to live out the fullness of their lives."

"As . . . Jutras slaves?"

"You certainly don't think they should be freed, do you? After all, they are criminals. Slavery is far less cruel than being exposed to the Chance storms, so you may set your mind at ease, if it should bother you at all. It's a profitable venture, one that requires keen discretion. Captain Micawber has served well, and will be missed.

I hope that you will be equally reliable. Indeed, I am counting on it."

He stared expectantly at Marten, whose mouth opened and closed as he sought an answer. Taking the prisoners to the Bramble had always seemed monstrous, if expedient. Crosspointe couldn't afford to feed useless mouths; food was far too expensive. On the Bramble, they faced a dreadful fate: being turned into *sylveth* spawn. Oh, a few might survive and remain relatively human. But most did not. The gods determined their doom. It was said that any who returned from Chance on the Bramble would have their sentences forgiven. The gods' will would be done. No one had ever returned. Nor would they, going to the Jutras slave pens. Marten wondered whether, given the choice, the prisoners would choose the Bramble or the Jutras. He knew what he would choose. And he knew what he had to choose now.

"I'll do it."

"Very good. In that case, I have a reward for you. See how agreeable I can be? How generous?"

Edgar waited, expecting a reply. Marten nodded jerkily.

"Quite," was all he could manage through the rocks clogging his throat.

"You will dine with me tonight. I'll have a new uniform brought to you; you can't be seen in those rags. You may also have your man Baskin. Do have a shave and a trim. You're looking dreadfully shaggy. I'll have someone call for you."

Marten returned to his room, his hunger forgotten. He was disgusted with himself. He dropped down onto the bed, holding his head in his hands. Captaining an illegal slave ship. This was lower than anything he'd done in his life. Except perhaps what he'd done to Lucy.

He swore, thrusting to his feet and slamming his fists against the top of the dresser. He yanked his right hand back, shaking it. The damage to his hand from punching the wall in his cell at Chancery had only begun to heal.

But he welcomed the pain. It was no more than he deserved.

Suddenly he felt the walls closing in on him. He had to get out. He banged on the door and it opened.

"I'm going to clean up," he said, and strode out, not waiting for his guard.

The servant bathing rooms were squeezed in a slot between two large pools. There was a separate one for women and for men. A long, gloomy passage divided the two, with doorways at one end accessing each and one going upstairs to the servants' quarters. The guard did not follow Marten down the hallway.

His shoulders brushed the walls as he walked and a chill prickled over his scalp. It felt like the walls were squeezing him. He hurried, his lungs constricting. This shouldn't bother him. He was at home in the close confines of a ship. Yet he couldn't seem to grapple his nerves underground in the bagnio.

He was muttering epithets as he reached for the door to the men's side. It was painted black, the women's side red. He turned the handle just as the door to the stairway opened and a scrub maid came through dressed in a drab red and cream uniform. She glanced at him in startlement. Marten froze, the breath rushing out of him.

"You!" he whispered hoarsely.

Lucy just stared, her eyes wide. Hardly thinking, Marten reached out and snatched her wrist. He opened the bathing room door, looking inside. As he'd hoped, no one was there. Quickly he drew her after him. There were shelves at the far end piled with towels, scrubbers, and soap. He dragged her along, ducking out of sight behind them.

"What in Braken's name are you doing here?" A swarm of emotions boiled up inside him. Relief, anger, fear, and something else he didn't like to think about.

Lucy yanked her arm out of his grasp, glaring balefully. "I was about to have a bath."

"Crack it! What are you doing in Sweet Dreams? Dressed as a maid?"

She bared her teeth. "I'm looking for answers. Some pox-ridden lobcock stole my seals and framed me for smuggling. You wouldn't happen to know anything about that?"

Marten flushed and looked away. His throat burned.

"Don't bother lying. I know it was you. I know about the drops you put in my tea. Though why you hung about after, I don't know. Or perhaps you were overcome by my magnificent charms," she said acidly.

"I'm sorry. I didn't think any harm would come of it. I never thought he'd do this to you." The words sounded hollow, even to him.

"Who?"

The word was sharp. Marten looked at her in surprise. She'd put so much together already.

"Edgar. My brother."

"Why? Why me? What does he get out of this?"

Marten shook his head, running his fingers through his hair. "I'm not sure. He hates the crown, and certainly he wants to discredit your family and raise public discontent with the Rampling rule. But why he's going after you so rabidly—I don't know."

She only lifted her brows in patent disbelief. He gritted his teeth. She had a right not to trust him. But then a realization struck him.

"If you're not here about Edgar, then why are you here?"

She hesitated, clearly unwilling to reveal herself to him.

He swore softly, then gripped her shoulders. "I know I used you badly. And I regret it. That's what this is about." He hooked a finger under the collar around his neck. "Edgar put it on me so that I couldn't come forward and tell the truth about what I'd done. I don't have a legal voice anymore. Let me help you. Let me try to put this right."

Lucy snorted softly, but then grudgingly spoke. "There's a man staying here. I think he's involved."

"Who is he?"

"That's what I'm trying to discover. He's wealthy. A merchant of some kind. I haven't seen him since I've been working here. I've just become a boarder maid, which should let me into places I haven't seen yet and give me more time to look for him." She paused, considering him. "Reckoning is only a few days away. My friends and family are going to be on the Bramble ship if I don't find something to say they are innocent."

Marten bit his tongue at the mention of the Bramble ship. He should tell Lucy about Edgar's scheme, that the *Firedance* was really a slave ship destined for Bokal-Dur. But it would serve no purpose. Not now. "What does he look like?"

"He's not much taller than I am, with dark hair streaked gray. It's curled and oiled. He's slender and dresses fashionably. The last time I saw him he was carrying a cane."

"Why do you think he's involved?"

Her expression tightened and her eyes went flat. "I have my reasons."

Reasons she did not want to share with him. He nodded, accepting it. He didn't have any choice.

"I haven't seen him, but I've been largely confined since my arrival."

Silence fell between them. Marten wanted to apologize again, but he doubted she would listen any better a second time. At last he settled on saying, "How can I help you?"

The look she turned on him was cutting. She wrapped her right hand around her left forearm, clutching them close against her stomach. She looked like she'd rather swallow a vat of *sylveth* than suffer his help.

"Do you read Jutras?" she asked at last, her nostrils flaring white at the effort.

Marten felt his face go slack. "Jutras?"

Her head jerked in an affirmative. "I found a document. Written in Jutras. It may tell me something."

"I know some," he said. Any ship captain who sailed east on the Inland Sea where the Jutras were swallowing up countries like a gluttonous pig had to learn enough to read the broadsides and papers and get a fix on the way the winds were blowing. The danger came from not only the Jutras but desperate people trying to escape them.

She was looking at him, her lower lip caught between her teeth as she wrestled with trusting him. At last she came to a decision.

"I have it hidden. Can we meet again?"

"I am being held in Edgar's private apartments, so I do not have freedom to wander. I think I can get away for another bath tomorrow. Or I'm allowed to go to the kitchens."

"Or maybe I can come find you," she said thoughtfully. "Surely maids must be assigned to his quarters. I might be able to learn something."

Marten shook his head adamantly, fear streaking through him at the thought of Lucy sneaking into Edgar's quarters. She'd be caught. "The doors are majicked against intruders. My door is also majicked and guarded. It would be a fool's mission," he said brusquely.

Her brows arced. "And I wouldn't want to be a Pale-blasted fool twice, now, would I?"

"I won't betray you again." Marten spoke as forcefully as he could. He wanted her, *needed her*, to believe him. The trouble was, he wasn't sure he believed it. He wanted it to be true, hoped it was, but the doubt niggled at him. His record so far was abysmal. He'd given Lucy's seals to Edgar to dig himself out of debt, and he'd agreed to helm a slave ship. The fact was, when he was up against it, he didn't know how low he'd sink to save himself. The realization made him queasy.

"Just at the moment, Marten, I can't imagine trusting you if I don't have to." She hesitated. "I am grateful that you took me to Keros and had my hands healed, and I take no pleasure in seeing you in the iron collar. I knew what sort of man you were. I called you corrupt and cancerous. Should I be surprised to find out that's who you are?"

He looked away. "You don't understand. Edgar had Jordan killed."

Her face went pale, but she didn't seem surprised at the news of Jordan's death. "Why?"

"A lesson to me. I had gone to him to get help uncovering what my brother was up to, and to help me find you."

"Jordan was killed because he was trying to help me?" Her voice was thin and anguished.

"Because of *me*," Marten said, taking her hand in his. It was trembling. "Edgar told me not to push and I did anyhow. He had Jordan killed and has created evidence to frame me if I don't cooperate with him. If I hadn't asked for Jordan's help, he'd still be alive." His lips tightened. "When I told Jordan what I did to you, he hit me. Repeatedly."

"We were good friends," she said, pulling her hand from his grasp. She wiped her eyes, blinking away tears.

"So were we. Until I told him. That was the end of it. Lucy, if he catches you, the very least my brother will do is turn you over to the Crown Shields and send you off on the Bramble ship. He's dangerous. You cannot go wandering about in his apartments. He keeps everything majicked, anyhow. There's little that you would find."

Lucy's expression was bleak. "I don't have much choice, do I? I'd better leave before someone finds me here. I need to get washed and back to work."

Marten nodded reluctantly. "I'll be here tomorrow at this same time. I don't know how long the guard will let me dawdle, or if there will be anyone else here. You might look for me in the kitchen midmorning."

He couldn't find anything else to say as he walked her back to the door. She reached out to pull it open and he put a restraining hand on her arm.

"Be careful. Please."

She looked down at his hand and then back up at him. "Don't you understand? I'm not like you. I don't care what happens to me. I only want to save my family and friends before Reckoning Day. I can't afford to be care-

ful. And another thing. I was convicted of Jordan's murder yesterday."

With that, she slipped out the door and across the
corridor to the women's bathing room, leaving Marten
feeling as if she'd punched him in the jaw.

Chapter 26

The warm water of the baths did nothing to thaw Lucy's numb arm. The cold from the cipher that had begun as soon as she'd seen Marten was unrelenting. She washed quickly and returned to her room at a trot. She pulled the Jutras contract from beneath her mattress and tucked it back in her shirtwaist. She hadn't dared leave it with her clothing in the bathing room, where someone might have found it. She shied away from thinking about her meeting with Marten. It was strange how little anger she felt for him. She wanted to believe he meant what he said, and he probably did. For now. But he followed the tide of fortune wherever it went. He was entirely unreliable.

Her stomach growled and twisted and she smothered all thoughts of him, going downstairs to eat. She sat in a corner and avoided meeting anyone's eyes, all too aware that Lora Clump might have friends among the other maids. She ate quickly before returning to the safety of her room.

She itched to go begin her search for the stranger, but knew she should wait for her summons to duty. She'd have to wait until after her shift if she wasn't going to raise suspicions. But seeing Marten had given her a jolt of hope. He could read Jutras and might be able to translate the contract. It was a step closer to the truth, to freeing her family and friends. For a moment, she found herself wondering about her mother and her brothers' wives. What had become of them? And Jack? She'd not had time to worry about them. The paper had not mentioned them and she'd assumed they'd managed to find someplace safe to hide. She bent her head, sending a prayer to Meris to keep them safe.

She was summoned by an imperious bell before the two girls she shared a room with returned. She was sent to clean in the guest rooms on the second floor. She collected her cleaning supplies and set to work. Emptying the slop jars was the worst. Her stomach revolted at the stench and she wished she hadn't eaten. She swept out the grates and rebuilt the fires, cleared dishes, dusted, and set out bowls of nuts, dried fruit, and candy, and bottles of wine. She filled the kettles for tea and ewers for washing, and straightened the rooms. Most of the guests were preparing for dinner. She scurried quietly in and out of the bedrooms and dressing rooms, averting her eyes from the half-dressed men and women.

Majick permeated Sweet Dreams like a cloud. There were charms on the floors and the walls, no doubt to deaden sound, and others on the roof and walls, probably to keep the heat in and the cold out. There were spells on the lamps and the sconces, on the chairs and the bed tables. It made Lucy feel like she was being pursued by an insistent swarm of wasps. Her ears hummed and her skin twitched. Still, it was bearable. It was the cipher, she decided. Somehow, it was insulating her talent to feel majick. *So it is good for something besides starting fires and icing up rooms,* she thought sourly. Probably the poor fool that Errol Cipher had destined his gift for had not been as grateful as she for the deadening effect.

She'd just returned from fetching one guest's forgotten shawl from the bagnio when she saw the stranger at last. She froze on the top step, her heart thumping as she watched him walk down the hallway away from her. He leaned lightly on his cane, his limp trivial. He was followed by a footman carrying several bundles. They stopped outside a door. The stranger produced a key and they went inside. Seconds later, the empty-handed footman withdrew. Lucy watched from the landing, twisting the delicate fabric of the shawl so tightly she heard threads snapping.

She pulled herself together with an effort, turning up the opposite direction at a sedate walk, hearing the footman's quick steps going down the stairs as he departed. She returned the shawl in a daze, her hands shaking. What should she do now? But she knew. No one noticed her as she gathered up her things and retreated to the service passage. Abandoning her supplies, she hurried up the passage until she passed the long stretch of blank wall that indicated where the sitting area at the top of the landing was. Lucy slowed, trailing her fingers along the wall. How far down the hallway was *his* suite of rooms?

She got her answer when an itching, gnawing sensation engulfed her fingers. She jerked her hand back, shaking her fingers. The feeling faded slowly. Nervous tension twined around her ribs, squeezing tightly. This was it. The majick emanating through the door was different from that saturating Sweet Dreams. This was sharper, hotter.

Lucy took a deep breath. Her heart fluttered with near panic. For a moment she was the nine-year-old girl trapped against a stack of crates in her father's warehouse trying to escape from the stranger clutching a hand around her throat. She tore away from the memory, panting. Bloody light flared in the gloomy corridor. She gasped and looked down at her cipher. It had turned a livid red. The numbness she'd felt with Marten turned now to something else. It wasn't heat. It was more akin to a hill of ants crawling over her skin. The feeling was not painful, but neither was it pleasant. Lucy clenched her fist, ignoring it as she resolutely opened the door.

The sitting room was empty. It smelled of *thuvalet*, a sickly sweet tobacco imported from Esengaile. There were several books open on a low table, and the fire in the grate had gone out. There were only two candles burning on the mantel. The feel of majick was stronger here, the sense of ants crawling more maddening. Lucy clutched her arm close against her side and sidled through the room, pretending to straighten and dust.

She went through the pocket doors into a small dining room. Again, it was empty; the debris of a small meal remained on the table. Lucy took a gasping breath, realizing she'd been holding it. Where was he? Had he left already in the time it had taken her to return the shawl?

Now she didn't bother to pretend to clean, but tiptoed on, peering into the small office. Empty. That left the two bedrooms and attached dressing rooms. Lucy eased down the short hallway, peeking into the first. It didn't look like anyone had used it. She went to the next room, her steps slow. She edged to the doorjamb. The dressing room was empty, but the open bedroom door cast a column of brilliant light into the room. Clothing was laid out, the wardrobes standing open. She heard movements inside the bedroom and the murmur of voices. Without pausing to let herself feel her fear, she slipped inside, ducking down behind a settee, and crawled around to hide behind the dressing table and oval mirror.

Her breathing sounded loud in the dim quiet. She covered her mouth with one hand, pressing the other over her heart to steady it. The sensation of crawling ants was becoming more unnerving. The feeling expanded up over her shoulder, filling her chest cavity. Her stomach heaved and she fought it down. She closed her eyes, reaching out to soothe the Koreion. She could feel it winding restlessly back and forth out of reach. At last she gave up, ignoring the cipher's attack as best she could.

She started and hunched down when the *sylveth* lights of the dressing room flared to brilliant life.

"If you'll just sit, sir," came a nasal voice on the other side of the dressing table.

Lucy froze as the chair was pulled out.

"You'll have to hurry, Jenson. Thorpe is rather impatient and I've no desire to antagonize him at the moment. I still need him."

"Just as you wish, sir."

Lucy heard the rattle of drawers and the thumping of brushes and combs on the top of the dressing table. Then there was silence as the valet worked. The feeling in her arm and chest spread to her other arm and down into her stomach. It was nearly unbearable. Yet she forced herself to sit quiet and still as a stump. It took nearly half a glass before the valet had finished.

"That will do, Jenson. Now bring me my coat and stick."

The valet did as ordered. The stranger rose and went to the middle of the room. Lucy inched up, peering around the corner of the dressing table. He would have been handsome, she supposed, if he did not wear an expression of arrogant scorn. His hair curled and waved in the latest fashion. He was dressed in a dark plum waistcoat with a black coat and trousers. The cuffs of his coat were turned back up to his elbows and glittered with gold and silver embroidery set with sparkling gems. The pattern on his waistcoat matched. His cravat was intricately tied in a lacy waterfall. Lucy's gaze fastened on the square gold pin on his lapel. He'd been wearing that nearly twenty years before. She had no idea what it might signify. He pulled on a pair of plum-colored gloves and took his walking cane from the mule-faced valet.

"Very good, Jenson. I shall not need you until quite late. You are dismissed."

"Yes, Master Sharpel. Thank you, sir." The valet bowed and withdrew.

Sharpel waited until the door shut. He stepped closer to the mirror, examining himself with a thoughtful eye. He smoothed one hand down over his waistcoat, then adjusted his cravat. Lucy trembled. It felt like he was looking straight at her. She dared not move. But then he returned to his bedroom. A minute later he appeared again, fastening an intricate earpiece over the lobe of his ear. It was made of gold filigree and set with tiny drops of rainbow-hued *sylveth*.

As soon as he walked into the room with it, there was a surge of majick. The squirming nest of ants inside of Lucy exploded into rampaging movement. She bit back a whimper, sagging down to the floor. The sensation eased only slightly as he left the room. Lucy heard the front door open and shut. She was going to lose him! Swiftly she crawled out of hiding and ran to the door. She opened it a crack. He'd already reached the top of the stairs. Hastily she stepped out into the corridor and trotted after him.

At the first floor, he crossed the foyer and went through a set of gilded doors guarded by two footmen. They swung them open for Sharpel to pass, bowing. Lucy waited a long minute after he had disappeared and the doors closed. Then she hurried up to the footmen.

"Beggin' yer pardons, but the master sent me t'give a message t'Master Sharpel and he's gone off and I got t'catch 'im." She tripped over the words, panting as if she'd been running. "He says it's important."

The footmen exchanged a look and then one nodded. "Be quick, then. Use the service hallway when you leave."

"Yessir," she said, bobbing a curtsy, and then scooted through before they changed their minds. She ran down the parchment-colored marble stairs, the heavy soles of her battered shoes thumping loudly. She hesitated just above the bottom, peering over the balustrade. She didn't see Sharpel. But she felt the hard edge of his ciphers prodding at her from the left-hand corridor. She descended and followed after, winding through the twisting passage, following the majickal trail like a bloodhound.

It brought her past several lounges crowded with gaming tables and players. Entertainers sang and danced and footmen carried trays of food and drink. There were smaller salons where people sat eating and drinking and laughing uproariously. *Sylveth* lights glimmered like fireflies and the air was redolent with the various perfumes worn by the guests. Lucy clung to the wall, ducking her head down and carefully avoiding the ladies and gentlemen parading majestically in their finery. They didn't deign to notice her, though a footman did, chasing her down and grabbing her by the scruff of her neck.

"What's this, then? You ain't supposed to be here."

"Master sent me w' a message and I gotta deliver it or he'll be swattin' me," Lucy whined, trying to pull out of his grasp. "Footmen at th'door said it be candy."

"They did, eh? Well, it's not. Guests don't wanna see your kind crawling about. Get off with you, but be quick about it and take the service passage back. And don't get in the way."

He shoved her and Lucy scampered away. The tang of Sharpel's majick was easy enough to follow. The squirming mass of ants inside her grew more frantic as she drew closer to him.

She came to a sitting area with arched doorways leading out to different passages. A fountain tinkled merrily in the center. She hesitated. Her quarry hadn't gone through any of the arches. Instead, the trail seemed to stop at a wall on the opposite side of the room. She scowled. He couldn't have just vanished. Not even Errol Cipher himself could have done that.

She edged around the curve of the wall. On the other side of the room, she found a cozy nook with plush couches facing a blank wall. No one sat here. A curtain of majick hung across the front of it. She felt its tingle, separate from the roiling mass of insects inside her. Her nose wrinkled as she caught a whiff of a decidedly unpleasant stench. Like carrion. A thrill of inexplicable fear unraveled along her bones. Without thinking, she began to turn away. She stopped herself with an effort, biting the inside of her cheek. What was she doing? Then she smiled tightly. Of course. The majickal curtain was designed to deflect unwanted intruders. Only people who truly wanted to cross would suffer through the strange fear and reeking odor of death.

Squaring her shoulders, she turned abruptly and thrust herself through the invisible barrier. For a moment she felt the clutch of hands clad in rotting flesh snatching at her legs. A smothering fog of death clung to her skin like a sticky shroud. She shuddered, rubbing at her arms. The feeling slowly seeped away. But the chill dread remained with her. Resolutely she shrugged it off, stepping between the two tall brocade chairs in the corner. Excitement made her breathless. There was a door secreted in the wall. The handle was cleverly hidden in the wainscoting. Lucy glanced over her shoulder to see if anyone was watching. No one was. She gripped the handle and twisted. The door opened easily. She slid inside and closed it quickly behind her.

She stood in a corridor paneled with Jasaic wood. It was a mottled mix of light on dark undulating shapes. The floor was covered with a thick brown rug with patterns of yellow woven into the edges. *Sylveth* lights glowed warmly inside frosted crystal bulbs down the center of the beamed ceiling. Paintings and sculptures were interspersed along the wall. The only sounds were the muted laughter and conversation beyond the door behind her. She was alone in the corridor.

Sharpel's majickal track pulled her to the right. She followed it. A number of passages forked away, and periodically she went by a closed door. She ignored these. The trail turned finally down an unprepossessing branch passage, dead-ending at another door. It was made of Jasaic wood with snarling gargoyle faces pushing out from its surface. Lucy hesitated outside. The feel of Sharpel's majick was strong here. She swallowed, breathing deeply to steady her fraying control. Her quarry couldn't be far.

She reached for the handle. The door cracked open without a sound. The scent of roasted meat, fresh-baked bread, and other savory dishes wafted through the slit. Lucy's stomach rumbled in response and she winced. On the other side was another sitting room. It was decorated in rich dark hues of blue and red. The floor was covered in a thickly piled rug from Normengas with its distinctive knot pattern. Over the mantel was an obsidian sculpture depicting a skeletal wolf's head biting a sword. Lining the walls were shelves containing books bound in blue and red leather, their titles printed in gilt. *Sylveth* lights in recesses around the edge of the ceiling provided light. Lucy slid inside, pulling the door shut. She started and dropped behind a chair at the sound of voices.

Her heart pounded as she waited. But no one entered. Slowly she tiptoed to the double doors on the other side of the room. She pressed her ear to the wood. There were at least two men. One had to be Sharpel. The frantic crawling sensation washing down her legs and over her scalp told her that much.

She put a daring hand on the handle, pulling the door open a bare crack. She could see a dining table covered in a lacy tablecloth, with shining silver and sparkling crystal. She stiffened in shock, her hand clenching. Marten sat with his back to her, his hair caught up high behind his head, the shorter underlayer neatly trimmed behind his ears and around the back side of his skull. He was dressed in his captain's uniform, with brilliant gold braid and crisp new fabric. His gleaming boots were new and his cutlass was fastened at his side. He lifted his glass and drank, setting it back down with a distinct *thunk!* His back was pike straight and rigid.

Lucy could not see who else was sitting at the table without opening the door wider. She didn't dare. Instead she listened.

"My brother, Marten, will be helming the Bramble ship in a few days," announced a man's gravelly voice. "I've just learned the Pilot assigned will be Idron. A good choice. He's a family man. I've asked him to step in for a visit this evening. It should be quite productive."

Lucy frowned. It was unusual for Pilots to meet with shipowners or even captains prior to a voyage. There was little point. The conditions on the sea were as changeable as a child's mood. From one moment to the next, a knucklebone weir could grow, a sandbar could lump up, or a shoal could change to deep water. It was a Pilot's special talent to sense a safe path across the sea, and the captain's talent to shift tack or catch wind according to the Pilot's directions. Every year fifty or more ships were lost to the vagaries of the sea. Which was why she couldn't resent Marten captaining the Bramble ship. He'd never had a wreck. He was one of the best captains on the sea, or the luckiest. She didn't care. He would get the ship to the Bramble safely. *And once there . . .* Bile rose in her throat. Perhaps she should wish for a less able captain, one that would wreck and kill them cleanly.

"Come, now, try this next wine. It's very fine and complements the beef well," Edgar said, and the butler poured while footmen took the serving dishes around. The meal went on for another glass and a half. Lucy stayed at the door, but heard nothing useful. She learned Sharpel made his home on an island in the Wigan Sound and that he was widely traveled. It was odd that she'd never heard of him, as long as she'd been a customs inspector. But then, he could just as easily import most of his goods through Tilman and bring them around the horn to Sylmont or port them over at Blakely. He traded in smaller, more lucrative items like art, spices, fabrics, tobacco, and precious stones. Lucy's mouth hardened, hearing the latter. It only helped confirm that he was her blackmailer.

When dinner was done, the gentlemen rose and approached the door she hid behind. Lucy scrambled into a shadowed corner behind a chaise, holding her breath. Edgar poured brandy and offered cigars. Soon the room was full of choking green *thuvalet* smoke. Edgar and Sharpel fell into a discussion of the proposed port at the Root, while Marten stood at the mantel in brooding silence.

"Rampling is a madman to think of wasting blood oak that way," Edgar declared. "We need to develop weapons to stop the Jutras. The profit would be tremendous and we wouldn't be sitting here like pigeons while the

Empire swallowed the Inland Sea and cut us off entirely."

"Mad? You give him far too much credit. I should say he's criminally stupid. Even more so for his mercy to the Jutras. He should have packed the lot off to the Bramble. Instead he wastes good food, soldiers, and maj-icar service hours. In the meantime, who knows when they'll break free and wreak havoc? And what does it take to capture a blint like that Trenton girl? He ought to be arrested for incompetence. Better, send the entire line—root, stem, and flower—to the Bramble."

At the sound of her name, Lucy jerked.

"In all honesty, I don't know how she's managed to hide this long. By all accounts, she's soft and not tremendously bright. The best that can be said about her is that she's tenacious, rather like a dog on a meaty bone. I would venture to bet that she is likely dead. Struck over the head by a footpad or, more likely, murdered by someone she's been blackmailing."

"She's not dead," Marten muttered forcefully.

"Oh?" Sharpel asked in arch surprise.

"You heard me."

"Do tell."

"She's tougher than you think. And you're right— she's tenacious. I expect she'll surprise you both. She's no traitor. She'll prove herself. Wait and see."

Lucy felt a flush of warmth at his adamant defense. But then fear turned her blood to ice at the purring threat in Sharpel's reply.

"Edgar, dear boy, I think your brother's got his cock in a knot over Miss Trenton. I do hope that won't be a problem."

"Not at all. Marten always looks after his own best interests. If he hasn't learned his lesson yet, he will tonight. I imagine that will rid him of any lingering rebelliousness."

"I could surprise you, brother," Marten growled.

"No. You are as predictable as the tides. It isn't your fault. Your mother was weak. A milk cow, really. Ring the bell and here she comes, placid and stupid. You are not to blame for your blood."

Marten lunged to his feet, kicking his chair over. Lucy held her breath.

"My mother was a sweet child that our father raped in a wine cellar when her family refused his offer," Marten said, his voice drawn tight as leather soaked in saltwater and dried in the desert sun. "She went to her wedding pregnant and terrified of her new husband. But at least she didn't slit her wrists in her bed like your whore of a mother."

"Now, brother, no need for name-calling. My mother no more killed herself than yours just tripped and fell down the stairs."

There was a moment of blistering silence.

"What do you mean?"

"Can you possibly not know? My mother was pregnant with a footman's by-blow. Father discovered it and"—Edgar snapped his fingers—"snip, he took care of the problem. He couldn't have a bastard muddying the line, and he certainly could not trust her."

Again there was silence. When Marten spoke again, his voice was strangled. He cleared his throat, speaking slowly. "What does that have to do with my mother?"

"Oh, dear. I thought you had sorted it out a long time ago."

He sounded surprised and disappointed, even rebuking. Lucy felt herself growing annoyed on Marten's behalf.

"Even then I could see what a blight Belinda's blood was on our family line. You were such a difficult child, brave as anything, but weak-willed and imprudent. You were ruled entirely by your baser passions. It's Belinda's fault; your infirmity comes from her. And now look at how you've turned out; you've ruined yourself with gambling and you're wearing an iron collar. I had to protect our name. I couldn't allow another of father's blunders to sully the Thorpe name. One was quite enough, thank you."

"You are saying . . . my mother was pregnant? And you killed her?"

"Quite so," Edgar said proudly.

There was a sudden thud of flesh on flesh. Bodies thrashed and furniture crashed against the wall. Sharpel shouted and Edgar swore. Marten said nothing. There were more sounds of fighting, the crack of wood snapping, tearing cloth, grunts, and growling. It sounded like a pack of dogs fighting. The door opened and Sharpel shouted for footmen. A heavy body crashed against the chaise Lucy was hiding behind, shoving it backward. She pressed herself into the corner. There were more thuds and then Lucy saw Marten's face. It was bloody, his mouth stretched in a rictus of rage. He picked his brother up by the front of his coat and shoved him back so that he held Edgar pressed against the wall, his arm a strangling bar on his brother's throat.

"You deserve to be flayed alive," Marten muttered.

Edgar thrashed from side to side. His cheek was split open and one eye was swollen shut. His nose was unnaturally crooked and blood ran over his lips and chin to stain his cravat. Lucy stared, trapped. She had nowhere to hide.

Edgar's head turned, avoiding the next blow. His gaze locked with hers. His mouth opened. Marten's fist connected again and Edgar's head snapped back. Just then, hands gripped Marten and dragged him away.

Turgid silence fell, broken only by the rasping breathing of the two brothers. Slowly Edgar slid down to sit panting on the chaise. He pulled his handkerchief from his pocket and dabbed his mouth. After a few moments, he stood, staggering slightly.

"It appears I must thank you, brother. For if you hadn't gone rabid, I never would have discovered Lucy Trenton, hiding right here behind the furniture." He gestured at her.

She rose defiantly, her chin jutting, even as her legs shook like plucked harp strings. Marten swore, anchored in place by two burly footmen. She looked at him. His eyes were haunted.

"Shall I call the Shields, sir?" one of the footmen holding Marten asked, glaring balefully at Lucy.

"Not just now, Whit. I'll not let the king sweep her out of sight before she answers some questions."

Lucy shivered at the brutal promise in his eyes as he spoke. And from the shadow depths of nowhere, the Koreion returned.

Chapter 27

Edgar withdrew to clean himself up, after having one of the footmen remove Marten's cutlass and setting another to guard Lucy. Sharpel lounged against the mantel, his hooded gaze fixed on her. She sat rigidly in the chair she'd been pushed into. The silence was thick. Suddenly Sharpel spoke.

"You missed your appointment."

Lucy's head jerked around. Her legs twitched in reaction to the sensation of frantic bugs crawling beneath her skin.

"So I did."

"I did tell you things would go ill if you did not cooperate," he said, absently stroking a finger over his earpiece.

"True. But then, you didn't get what you wanted, did you? So I'd call it a draw."

"It's not I who's bound for the Bramble, though I should be more afraid of Edgar, were I you."

Lucy smiled with bravura. "I'm not afraid of him. As for the Bramble, you'll find yourself there sooner or later. And I'll be waiting for you. There's not enough *sylveth* in the world to make me forget you."

Sharpel chuckled. "Such a shame. I do regret that I could not have dipped my nib in your ink. I'll bet you're a screamer. And that mouth of yours. Mmm. Hot, sweet, and sharp. Delicious. You could make a man beg. Am I right?" he asked, turning to Marten.

The footmen clutched at Marten as he growled inarticulately and lunged.

"My, high-strung, isn't he? But then, perhaps I've underestimated your charms, my dear. Have I abused you by offering too faint praise for your prowess?"

"Certainly you will never have the pleasure of knowing," Lucy returned tartly.

"How disappointing. Still, there is time before the Bramble ship departs. Perhaps Edgar might let me borrow you for a few turns of the glass."

Lucy thought of her cipher and grinned malevolently. "That would be delightful. I should enjoy being alone with you."

"Then I shall arrange it. With proper restraints, of course. I believe Edgar has just what I'll need."

He smirked at Marten's string of epithets and Lucy felt a twist of uncertainty in her gut.

"Perhaps then I can convince you to tell me where you hid my property."

Lucy's lips peeled back in a death's-head grin. "I seem to have forgotten where I put it. My memory is so fickle, you know."

"I'm sure I can help you remember," Sharpel purred.

"Do you think so? You'll have to pardon my doubts. You seem so utterly forgettable."

Sharpel crossed the room, bending over her. His breath smelled of wine. He reached out, stroking a gentle finger over her cheek and down between her breasts. Lucy cringed from his chill touch.

"I'm confident I could prod your memory."

"I should think prodding goats would be more your expertise."

Marten chortled. Sharpel ignored him, lifting his hand and brushing his thumb over Lucy's lips. She forced herself to remain still.

"Such a foul little mouth. I wonder what other sounds I can extract from it?" His hand dropped to cover her breast. He pinched her nipple, softly at first, then harder.

"Tell me, my dear, wouldn't you like me to make you scream?"

Lucy feigned a yawn, covering her mouth delicately. He continued his assault, watching her intently, his arched brows taunting.

"Get your stinking hands off her, you bung-holed bastard," Marten said in a low, harsh voice, struggling against the footman who gripped his collar.

"Take him out of here," Sharpel ordered.

The footmen dragged Marten out and Lucy was left alone with her blackmailer. He wasted no time, grabbing her hair in his fists, hooking his thumbs in her mouth, and forcing it open, thrusting his tongue inside. Lucy squirmed and kicked out, but he yanked her hair hard, shoving his knee into her stomach to immobilize her. His teeth cut her lips and tongue as he ground his mouth against hers.

At last he drew back, triumph lighting his blue eyes. "You suffer or die by my mercy. If you don't tell me what I want to know, I'll cut off your feet and your hands and rip out your tongue so that all you can do is lie there while I ride you. And when I'm done, I'll let every man who wants it have a prod at you. No one will save you; you'll be the perfect whore."

"Go hull yourself," Lucy said hoarsely, unable to keep the horror from her voice. "Besides, I'm not *your* prize, am I?

He broke into a smile and Lucy shivered at its brutality and malice.

"Don't make the same mistake that Edgar has. It suits me to let him think he is in command of this scheme, but he has no more power in this than you do. I planted these seeds before I first saw you and it is almost time for my careful husbandry to come to fruition. You cannot stop it, and though Edgar will certainly try when he finally realizes what he's become a part of, he will fail utterly. But I want that box back. And I want it now."

Lucy snarled, struggling against his grip. "Don't you mean you want the contracts? How could you betray us to the Jutras?"

If he was surprised that she knew of his real interest in the box, he didn't show it. Instead he focused on her second question. "Betray *us*? My dear girl, I *am* Jutras."

Every muscle in her body went slack, her mouth dropping open. "What?"

"You think you are safe on this island and you do nothing to understand your enemies. Such arrogance. But the Inland Sea cannot protect you forever, not even for another month."

"What do you mean? How?"

"How? By force of majick—yours and ours." He stroked his finger over the cipher on his ear.

"How can you be Jutras?"

"My parents were captured in the taking of Aderilias. But my people are neither arrogant nor stupid. We are strengthened with each country we claim. We give our captives a choice—fight and become Jutras citizens, or become slaves. My parents became *picrit*—warrior caste." He tapped his chest. "As am I. When I was born, I was given to the *vendri*, a superior *shaghi* within the *picrit*."

At Lucy's look of utter confusion, he clarified. "The *picrit vendri* are spies. My parents were *picrit daelies*, common foot soldiers."

"You're a spy for the Jutras," Lucy repeated stupidly. She couldn't get her mind around the idea. She had known someone was conspiring with the Jutras, but to have a spy living here for years, plotting. Not to mention a warship full of them in the middle of the city. "Gods help us," she whispered, beginning to comprehend that this really was an invasion.

"Do you think they will answer? These gods of yours—Chayos, Meris, Hurn, and Braken?" He looked up as if waiting. Then shook his head, bending back down so that his face was even with Lucy's.

"They do not care, I think. So I will ask one last time—where is my property?"

Lucy clenched her teeth. "Go hull yourself."

He shook his head. "It will make no difference to

what happens to Crosspointe, but I will keep my promise to you. Enjoy your hands and feet and tongue. . . ."

He bent and mauled her mouth again. Lucy gagged at the choking force of it, waiting for the cipher to erupt. But it was entirely quiescent; only the dreadful sensation of insects squirming beneath her skin remained. But that was caused by his ciphers, not hers. He lifted his head at last, letting go of her hair and wiping his mouth with a handkerchief.

"As I said, enjoy them while you still can."

Before Sharpel could say anything more, Edgar returned. He wore a different suit of clothing. His left eye was swollen purple, and his lips were pulpy. A streak of plaster on his right cheek closed the wound there, and his nose looked like a squashed sausage. When he spoke, his voice was nasal and thick.

His gaze settled on Lucy's bruised and bleeding mouth, before he gave Sharpel an amused smile.

"Marten's in a dither."

"I told you he's got his cock in a knot over her."

Edgar shrugged. "I'll cure him of that right now. Come with me."

"He's Jutras!" Lucy shouted before Sharpel could stop her.

Edgar turned around, frowning. "Who's Jutras?"

"He is. Your partner. He's plotting an invasion and using you to do it."

"Is he, now? How . . . curious." He turned to open the door.

"I have proof. A document, written in Jutras. He made me steal it from customs for him. It's here."

Lucy pulled the parchment from her shirtwaist and handed it to Edgar, looking triumphantly at Sharpel. The other man only yawned and examined a fingernail.

"Where did you get this?" Edgar demanded harshly.

"I told you—he blackmailed me into stealing it."

"Did he really? Sharpel?" Edgar said, flicking an eyebrow up. "Do you care to respond to Miss Trenton's accusation?"

"Not at all. Last-ditch effort to escape her fate, I presume. I do wonder about the document. What is it?"

"A contract. And oddly, Miss Trenton, it only confirms my worst fears about your family's rule. It's signed by the Dhucala himself and is meant for your cousin the king. It promises that Crosspointe will give Pilot compasses to the Jutras in exchange for peace. That vermin would have the run of the Inland Sea." He looked up from reading the document. "Thank you, Miss Trenton. With this I shall destroy the Ramplings once and for all."

He tucked it inside his vest coat and motioned the others to follow. Lucy wanted to throw up. What had she done?

It took both footmen to hold Marten when they emerged from the room and he saw Lucy's face. He lunged at Sharpel, swearing loudly. The other man ignored him, pushing Lucy after Edgar.

They wound through the burrow of passages, ending up at another sitting room. This one contained plain furniture and few embellishments. The floor was covered in a woven mat, and the planked walls were bare except for displays of swords and armor.

The Pilot Idron was waiting inside. He set his drink aside and rose as the small group entered. He was shorter than Lucy, with close-cropped dark hair and beard. He wore a suit made of soft green *dosken* with a cambric shirt beneath the long, draping blue robe that most Pilots affected. It was plain except for the Pilot's brooch at his throat, which matched the heavy ring on his right forefinger. But even had he been dressed as a dockhand without any of the jewelry of his position, his eyes would have given him away as a Pilot. The brown disks were fractured with jagged threads of black, crisscrossing like cracks in porcelain. A few wandered out into the whites of the eyes. He looked haughtily at Edgar, his fingers tapping in annoyance.

"Good evening, Pilot Idron," Edgar said affably, making no effort to explain the wounds on his face, or the blood trickling down Lucy's chin. "My apologies for making you wait. I'd like to introduce you to Master Merchant Sharpel. My brother and his friend are merely here to observe. Please ignore them."

"Observe what?" Idron asked, not bothering to acknowledge Sharpel.

"Let me show you. I know you'll be quite interested," Edgar said, bustling across the room and ignoring the Pilot's protests. He pressed his hand against the center of a plain panel and the wood slid silently back, revealing a room reminiscent of a theater. There were rows of yellow-covered seats set in a descending semicircle on wide stone steps. They stopped about halfway down behind a four-foot drop to the floor of what appeared to be a stage. It was painted black, as were the walls and ceiling. In the middle of the lowered stage was a large basin. It looked like an oversized teacup without a handle. The rim was three feet high and six feet across and it was covered in a black fabric.

Edgar led the way down the center aisle, stopping at the top of the steps leading down to the stage. "Pilot Idron and Master Sharpel, please sit down in the first row so that you might see. You two sit over here out of the way," he said to Marten and Lucy, pointing to the other side of the room. The footmen pushed them over there and thrust them into seats.

"I'm so sorry," Marten whispered, and earned a cuff on the side of his head.

Pilot Idron remained in the aisle while Sharpel sat down.

"Master Thorpe, I demand an explanation. You indicated in your missive that we were to discuss a matter of urgent importance to my family, did you not? I have no interest in your little theatrical productions."

"Indeed, Pilot Idron. This is very much of importance to you, as will become clear shortly. Do sit. It will not take long"

The Pilot hesitated and then complied with a loud *hmph!* and a tossing of his robes.

"Very good. We are nearly ready, then. Just one or two more details . . ."

Edgar descended to the stage, crossing to the rear and disappearing behind the curtain. He was gone several minutes and by the time he returned, Idron was boiling in his seat. But Edgar's appearance was enough to surprise everyone into silence. Lucy felt Marten tense. His brother was wearing the knacker clothing they'd worn during the *sylveth* spawn collection. He pushed a small trolley cart before him, the items on top covered by a black drape. He was followed by two more footmen, who climbed up to stand in the aisle beside the Pilot. A snake of foreboding coiled around Lucy's throat. The wriggling mass inside her scrabbled harder. He'd brought powerful majick into the room. She twitched and jerked. A low moan escaped her lips.

"And now for our final guest." Edgar turned and gestured. Two more black-clad men emerged holding the arms of a struggling young man. He was pale, with straight dark hair and wide, full lips. He was angular and clean-shaven, his nose prominent. He was probably twenty years old, Lucy guessed, holding her breath, though she wasn't entirely sure why.

Pilot Idron lunged to his feet. "Daniel! What is going on, Thorpe? I demand you release him at once."

Edgar's voice inside his mask sounded eerie. "Oh, no, Pilot Idron. We may have need of your lover's company, depending on how cooperative you prove to be. And your wife. She is dining upstairs even now with your daughter. I would despise interrupting them, but of course, business can never wait for personal pleasure."

Pilot Idron sputtered, trying to push down to the stage area. The waiting footmen grabbed his arms.

"Oh, no. It's much too dangerous down here without protective gear," Edgar admonished. "You are far too valuable to risk. Now then, you are in a hurry and so I will not delay any longer." He whisked away the black cloth covering the cart. Lucy leaned forward. There was a cage containing a glossy black rat and a small bottle of something silvery. The bottle itself was made of *sylveth*. And inside . . . The foreboding circled tighter. She wrapped her arms hard around her stomach.

"He's Pale-blasted," Marten muttered. And then, "How is it possible that he brought raw *sylveth* into Crosspointe?"

"I don't know. I don't know." Lucy reached for his hand, holding tightly, her mind revolting against what was coming next. Edgar would not be so stupid, so cruel. . . . But even as she watched, Lucy learned he would.

He lifted the gate of the cage, putting his black-gloved hand inside and grasping the rat by the scruff of the neck. Lucy heard the animal's outraged screeches as it clawed with its hind legs, its long pink tail whipping wildly. Unperturbed, Edgar removed the stopper on the small bottle, lifting it into the air.

"I know that you have all seen the effects of *sylveth*. But I'd like the memory to be fresh. Pilot Idron and Marten, do pay close attention."

Lucy's fingers tightened on Marten's. Edgar was mad.

He tipped the bottle so that a drop fell on the rat's twisting head. The transformation began instantly. A ripple passed over the animal. Suddenly its fur glittered like splinters of steel. It shrieked, a long, hideous note. Then the sound changed, turning deep and bellowing. Another ripple passed across its body, and now it doubled in size. Edgar was having difficulty holding on to it. He dropped it into the basin, standing over it to watch. Lucy could see the animal as it convulsed. Its legs lengthened and developed a dozen joints each so that they moved like tentacles. They were tipped with two-pronged claws with curving pincers that clacked noisily. The rat rose up on its spider-tentacle legs, its face squashed flat against a hard, round body. A halo of stiff bristles stood out from plate bone armor like lethal dandelion fluff. Its eyes were the size of Lucy's hands and had turned a dull orange. It turned, examining its watchers. Its lips pulled apart, revealing two rows of short jagged teeth that stretched half the length of its body. Pink seeped down the length of its spines, turning black at the roots.

Lucy swallowed, shudders racking her. The nest of burrowing insects within rioted and felt like they were digging out of her skin. She rocked forward and back, wanting to scream.

"It is quite startling, isn't it?" Edgar said, putting the stopper back on the bottle. "How fast it works. You wouldn't know it was ever a rat. Imagine what it might do to a man."

Ignoring the creature in the basin, he stepped close to Daniel, Pilot Idron's lover. He ran his fingers over the young man's face, cupping his chin in one hand.

"What do you think, Pilot? How much do you value your young friend?"

Idron swore. "You flogging goat-cracker! May dogs gnaw your wick off and the pox turn your insides to mush! I'll see you cursed! You'll wish you were dead."

"I think not," Edgar said, his voice cutting. "Calm yourself before I have no choice but to take offense. Now, your pretty Daniel will be perfectly safe if only you agree to my terms."

Idron's florid face worked. Finally he managed to speak. "What do you want?"

"I want you to pilot the Bramble ship to Bokal-Dur and back. Secretly, of course."

"To Bokal-Dur? But why?"

The Pilot's consternation matched Lucy's.

"The Bramble ship cargo is quite valuable in the Empire."

Slaves? Lucy gasped, unable to breathe. Marten rubbed her back, holding her hand tight against his chest.

"I need your decision, Pilot Idron. Do you want to see what *sylveth* makes of your lover?"

Edgar gestured at the creature inside the basin and Lucy realized that the black covering on the basin, floors, and walls was all designed to contain *sylveth* spawn and even *sylveth* itself. The entire room was devoted to just this spectacle. How many times had it been performed for the benefit of others? Her stomach clenched. Keros was more right than she'd ever imagined. Edgar Thorpe was a dangerous, sadistic man.

"Or do you want to go home with your secret and your lover intact? From time to time I will ask you to aid me. I am a generous man. The compensation for your efforts will be quite handsome, I assure you. But I require your answer now."

The silence frayed before the Pilot muttered, "I will."

"Very good. You may release him," Edgar directed the two footmen holding Daniel.

The young man wavered in place for a moment, then scrambled up the stairs into Idron's arms, sobbing loudly. The two lovers climbed up the steps and disappeared out the door. Now Edgar turned his attention to Marten. When he spoke, his voice brimmed with satisfaction.

"And now you, my brother. Have you learned your lesson? You agreed to helm this ship, and now you know what you'll face if you cross me. Do I have your word, such as it is, that you will stand the helm to Bokal-Dur?"

"Suck bilge," was Marten's angry reply.

"Watch your manners, Marten. Remember you wear the collar and I own your chain."

"I'd rather drink that bottle you've got there."

"Oh, no. This isn't for you. You are far too valuable to waste."

"You already murdered Jordan. I don't have anyone else you can hold over me."

"No? What about your man Baskin? Or"—Edgar walked over to the wall, stretching out his hand to point at Lucy's and Marten's interlocked fingers—"her."

Lucy felt Marten's recoil. He clutched his arm around her shoulders, pulling her close against his chest. As if he could protect her. As if he hadn't betrayed her and put her in this mess. Fury roared volcanically up inside her and she shoved out of his grip, leaping to her feet.

She felt the Koreion surging inside her. The cipher flamed, engulfing her hand and forearm in a gauntlet of fire. She pointed her hand at Edgar and *pushed* out the way she had with the ice. The flames leaped in a roaring plume, surrounding Edgar from head to foot in a burning veil. Lucy didn't move, pouring the flames over him like water.

Then something struck her from behind. She fell forward over the lip of the wall. Hands gripped her legs, flinging them into the air. She somersaulted and struck the stage, landing on her back, her head bouncing off the fabric-swathed stone floor. Pain fractured her head and jaw. She heard a cracking sound and the air exploded out of her lungs. She fought for breath, curling into a ball. Searing agony shredded her left arm. Her wits scattered. She keened, helpless to do anything else under the weight of such pain. Majick cascaded into her like an avalanche of glass. She *pushed* out, unfocused, uncaring where it went or what it might do. She just wanted to be rid of it.

Suddenly hands gripped her. She kicked, pain from the touch screwing through her. They lifted her and again she was dropped. She landed on a curved surface. Something sharp bit deeply into her thigh and stomach. Seconds later a heavy cloth dropped over her like a shroud. Majick roiled inside her. The Koreion thrashed, crazed. Agony flayed her. More sharp pain. Lucy became viscerally aware of the rat creature. Two of its legs were caught beneath her. The other two slashed at her. She heard chittering and then short, serrated teeth tore at her sleeve and skin. Lucy screamed and screamed. The corners of her mouth tore with the force.

She *pushed* away the majick again. It burst out in a single second of blissful respite. Then just as quickly it rebounded, crashing back into her with all the force of a tidal wave. The sound was deafening. Her mind shattered. Razor-edged nothingness swallowed her.

Chapter 28

Footmen held Marten back as Sharpel drove a boot into Lucy's back. She sprawled against the rail and Sharpel grabbed her feet and flung her the rest of the way over. She thumped onto the stage. The flames wreathing her arm roared to the ceiling in a fiery geyser. Lucy made a high whining shriek like ice breaking in the spring. The two black-clad footmen tossed her into the basin on top of the *sylveth* spawn. It chittered loudly, its free claws raking Lucy's thigh and stomach, flaying open her flesh. Lucy cried out inarticulately, her legs and arms thrashing.

Sharpel ran down the stairs, snatching up the long stretch of protective fabric and tossing it over the basin. Beneath the blanket Lucy bucked and convulsed. Her agonized screams ripped the air, raising the hairs on Marten's scalp. He fought the hands restraining him, shouting her name. One of his guards grabbed his collar and yanked. Marten choked and gasped. Then there was a powerful *boom!* The basin rocked wildly back and forth and the chairs surrounding the stage jumped and rattled. Acrid blue-black smoke billowed out of the basin, filling the room with an impenetrable fog.

For a moment all was still. Then Edgar moaned weakly. Others began to cough.

"Open the doors and clear this smoke! Watch out for the *sylveth*," shouted Sharpel.

The footmen restraining Marten shoved him back down into his chair. He strained to see Lucy, but could glimpse only shadowy movement on the stage.

At last the smoke began to thin. On the floor, Sharpel was kneeling next to Edgar, who lay crumpled in a heap. The two black-clad footmen hovered nearby, while the other two waved their coats to move the smoke out. There was no movement inside the basin.

"Call for a healer," Sharpel ordered, and one of the footmen dashed away. "Go find something to carry your master on. He's sorely wounded."

Marten couldn't help the burst of satisfaction he felt. The news that a sixteen-year-old Edgar had murdered his mother had not been dulled by the beating Marten had given him. Not to mention Edgar's threatening to pour raw *sylveth* on Lucy.

"Let him die," he called out. "He's got what he deserves."

The chilling look Sharpel turned on Marten was devoid of emotion. His eyes were like bottomless holes. The set of his face and body had altered. Ruthless command radiated from him as if by a word he could raze the entire city without a second's thought. A force of nature. Of gods and demons. Marten was reminded of the black waterspouts that formed out of nowhere on the Inland Sea. They were predators, hunting ships like cats after mice.

Marten couldn't help the gooseflesh that pimpled his arms when Sharpel said, "Come here."

He edged out into the aisle and down onto the stage, his guards trailing close behind. He stopped inches away from the other man, staring down at him.

"Your brother was of a mind to offer you your freedom in exchange for a future helming his ships to the Empire. Edgar is a sharp businessman, one of the best. But I think he's a bit blind when it comes to you. You're a mad dog. He believes he can control you, but I think you'll slip your chain. And since he's incapacitated at the moment, I am going to do him the favor of making sure you don't bite him." He looked past Marten to the waiting footmen. "Take him."

Marten jerked away from the hands that gripped his arms. "What about Lucy?"

Sharpel looked inside the basin. Lucy lay beneath a thin layer of fine ash. Baked blood crusted on the wounds on her stomach, thighs, and arms. Her hair was burnt away, leaving only tufts. Her skin was a patchwork of red and black. And there was plenty of it to see. Her clothes had been burned away, as had the majick-deadening blanket covering her. Marten's heart clutched. She was so still. Suddenly he was yanked away by his collar.

"What are you going to do to her?" he choked out past the metal crushing his throat.

Sharpel reached for another of the black fabric shrouds and flung it over her. "Dead or alive, she's going to the Bramble. You, on the other hand, are going to fetch a pretty profit in the Empire. It won't be terribly difficult finding another captain to helm the Bramble ship."

Marten spent the next three days climbing the walls in his room, alone with Baskin. No one came to bring them food or drink; no one answered their pounding and shouts. The slop jar overflowed and the room reeked of piss and shit. They drank the wash water, rationing it out. Marten brooded. Was Lucy alive? If she had lived through that explosion, had she survived the last days without food, water, and care? Damn, he'd like to see Edgar keelhauled.

On the third day, the door opened. Six footmen stood outside.

"Out," one ordered.

In the hallway, the two prisoners were pushed against a wall while manacles were fastened on their wrists and ankles. Then the footmen formed a box around Marten and Baskin and marched them up out of the bagnio.

Waiting under the portico was a pair of mules hitched to a flatbed cart with an iron rail down the middle. The footmen prodded the two men aboard, fastening them down to the rail. Two of them climbed up on the wagon box and the driver cracked the whip.

It was nearly dusk. The sky was sooty gray. Though the fire in Salford Terrace had been put out, the wind continued to spin the ash into the sky. The air held a sharp chill and Marten's breath plumed whitely. He braced his legs wide as the cart picked up speed on the rough cobbles. Baskin swore an unending litany.

The cart rolled onto Ashford Avenue and out to the Maida Vale. They crossed the river and wound down to the Tideswell Platform where the *Firedance* was moored. Throngs of onlookers mocked and jeered; the platform was nearly impassable. Hornets pushed aside the unruly spectators, making room. Marten saw some men he knew and quickly looked away.

He and Baskin were quickly unloaded and dragged up the gangplank and turned over to the mate and three hulking midshipmen. The mate was a tall, cadaverous man. His head was shaved and there was a green knotted-rope tattoo running down one side of his neck and up around his ear. Baskin was taken below, while Marten was hauled to the captain's cabin. He drew deep cleansing breaths of the briny air. Despite his shackles, he felt more free than he had in sennights. The rise and fall of the deck, the hypnotic shifting of the waves, and the salty taste of the air—it felt like home.

The mate knocked at the door. Without waiting for a reply, he pushed it open, looking over his shoulder at Marten. "Keep a civil tongue in yer head and if ye get any ideas, I'll cut yer throat." He pantomimed the action, motioning for the midshipmen to wait.

The captain was sitting at his desk. Marten knew him: Owen Creasely. He was a fair captain, losing only two ships in the last fourteen years. His eyes were tight; his mouth was a thin flat line. Whom had Sharpel threatened to get Creasely to take the helm? A shudder quaked through Marten. He could not blame Creasely for taking the job.

"Thorpe. Word is, you helped that Trenton girl murder Truehelm and now you got a berth on the Bramble ship. That so?"

"No."

"Well, you've been convicted with her. Lord Chancellor Truehelm made the decree this morning. They say he'd have liked to see you flogged to death, but he'll settle for the Bramble."

"And my brother and his minions are sending me to the Jutras instead."

Creasely gave a jerky nod, biting white dents into his lower lip. "We'll stop at the Bramble to drop the girl." His lip curled. "I put her in the mate's cabin, all crated up proper in a knacker box. Don't know if she's alive or not. But if she is, it's for you to keep watch on her. Sharpel says you've dibbled her. That's enough for me. You be responsible for her. Feed her if you want, let her rot if not. She does anything to endanger this ship or the crew, I'll toss you both overboard. Understand?"

Marten nodded. "Aye, aye, Cap'n." His pulse pounded. Was she alive?

"Keep to the cabin. Truehelm had a lot of friends, some of them in this crew. And the Trenton bitch—there are a lot of good people in the hold on their way to a life of slavery under the Jutras whips because of her. I won't speak to how the crew cuts their jib. They're not mine. If they want you, I'll have to let 'em have you to save the ship. Now go. Stay out of my way."

Marten began to turn and then stopped. "Did you hear about my brother?"

"He's got some sort of sickness. Majicar healers couldn't do much for him. Whispers say he's dying."

"Good."

The mate took him back out on deck, letting Marten into his cabin. "Askin' me, ye deserve t'be down in the bilge hole. But Cap'n says he wants her close t'hand case he needs t'toss her quick in the briny."

He shoved Marten inside and slammed the door, turning the lock.

Inside was dark. Marten unlatched the deadlight covering the window and flung it open. A dim glow illuminated the gloom, revealing the knacker box in the middle of the room. The deck was scraped where the box had been unceremoniously shoved inside. Swiftly Marten attacked the lid. It came off easily.

Lucy lay in an awkward heap beneath a black cloth. He pulled it away, tossing it in the corner. His eyes ran over her. Her skin was gray beneath her burns, and the *sylveth* spawn had cut and gouged her deeply in places. But she was breathing, if shallowly. Marten smothered a shout of relief. "Thank the gods," he whispered.

Carefully he slipped his arms under her, lifting her free. The mate had a rope bunk covered by a thin straw pallet with a tattered wool blanket. He laid Lucy down on it and fetched water from a bucket inside the door. He soaked a corner of his shirt, dabbing her face gently. She moaned and twisted, her mouth opening. He dribbled a few drops between her lips, and then a few more. She swallowed jerkily.

An hour later, she still hadn't woken, but he'd managed to give her half a dipper of water. She'd begun to shiver and he covered her with the blanket, lying down to lend her the warmth of his body. He hardly noticed when the ship cast off to a brassy fanfare and shouts of the gathered crowd. By dusk they cleared the harbor mouth and ran through the Pale. Marten was glad Lucy was asleep. Sailors got used to the effect of crossing the Pale—the blast was like a blow to the mind. Some people fainted and didn't wake for hours. Given Lucy's condition, Marten didn't know if she would have survived the crossing if she had been awake. But unconscious, she seemed to take no ill effect.

The seas were choppy and the *Firedance* rose and fell in short, swooping lunges. Marten held Lucy so that she didn't roll from the bed. He had no idea how to treat her burns. He washed the dried blood from the cuts and

gouges as best he could, stopping when she moaned and
thrashed in pain. She had a fever, shivering and sweating
alternately. He dressed her in his shirt to help keep her
warm, but there was little more he could do.

When food was brought, he chewed it to a pulp and
stirred it into the water, spooning the cold broth into
her mouth. The food was of a better quality than he
expected, a kindness of Creasely's perhaps, both of them
all too aware that they'd been poorly used by Edgar and
Sharpel. Or maybe it was that they were both captains,
lending them a special kinship. Whatever the reason,
Marten was grateful.

On the open sea, the air quickly turned cold. A thin
rime of ice crusted the deck and rails, sheathing the
ropes. Marten fastened the deadlight, but the cold permeated the cabin. He finally requested another blanket
from the mate when he brought food. The duty seemed
far below his station, but either the crew refused to
chance Lucy's wrath, or Creasely had made him responsible for their care. At Marten's petition, the mate stared
at him incredulously and then stalked wordlessly away.
But when he returned for the empty dishes, he brought
with him the requested blanket and a coarse shirt. He
handed them to Marten.

"Cap'n's compliments." His cheek bulged with a wad
of tobacco. He squinted up at the sky and then turned
back to Marten. "Seems the gods want t'be rid of ye
quick as can be. Making best speed. Be at th' Bramble
in less than a sennight." He smiled, revealing brown-
stained teeth. "Try as not t'freeze afore then. Crew'd
like t'hear the bitch's screams when we toss her
overboard."

He was still laughing uproariously when Marten shut
the cabin door.

It was another day before Lucy woke. She was deliri-
ous, lost somewhere between dreams and reality. She
cried out and wept, clutching herself close to Marten.
He held her loosely against his chest, stroking her back
lightly, trying not to aggravate her wounds. But even in

her delirium, she was hungry. He fed her and she fell back asleep, her breathing easier than it had been.

When she woke again, she knew him.

"Where are we?" she whispered.

He didn't mince the truth. "We're on the Bramble ship."

She caught her breath and said nothing for several minutes. At last she pulled away, struggling to sit up. Marten helped her, feeling her tremble and flinch from his light touch. When she spoke again, her voice was thin and uneven. Whether from the pain or from revulsion, he didn't know.

"What happened?"

Marten hesitated. "I don't know what you remember . . . ."

She knotted her fingers together, frowning in concentration. Then memory seeped up from the parched ground of oblivion. Her mouth twisted and her hands clawed the blankets.

"He was going to—" She broke off, her neck working. *"Sylveth!"* she spat out at last.

"You burned him." His voice inflected up in a question. *How?*

She snarled at the memory. "I did." She licked her lips. "Then someone hit me. I don't remember a whole lot after that."

Marten didn't press, but described the footmen throwing her into the basin with the *sylveth* spawn and then the explosion.

"They locked me up after that. For three days. You were in that box when I arrived on board. That was two, maybe three days ago."

Lucy sat very still, her head bowed. Her shoulders were hunched. "Not everything the papers said about me were lies. I collect—collected—true ciphers. That night I met you, when you found me in the salvage warehouse and I seemed injured, I'd just located another. It attached."

He wasn't sure what he was expecting, but this was

most definitely not it. His mouth fell open like a Pale-blasted idiot. "What?"

She lifted her head. "I've been attached by a cipher. A true cipher. That's how I started the fire in Salford Terrace. That's how I burned your brother. I only wish he hadn't been wearing knacker gear."

Marten scratched absently at the thick bristles sprouting from his jaw. "It may not have helped him much. Captain Creasely said the rumors are that he's dying. That the majicar healers couldn't help him."

"Good."

"Exactly so."

She glanced at him with raised brows.

"I was ready to gut him for what he did to you. But after hearing his confession to murdering my mother, after seeing what he was doing in that gods-cursed room—" His nostrils flared. "He can't die slowly and painfully enough."

It wasn't long before Lucy fell asleep again. Soon after she began shivering, her teeth clacking together. Her fever continued to burn, and soon it was clear that her wounds had turned septic. She woke for longer periods, huddling in the blankets. She did not protest Marten's touch, which worried him. Though she ate, her flesh seemed to melt away even as he watched. Her face lost its curves, turning almost skeletal. The bones of her arms and shoulders jutted through her skin, and holding her at night, Marten could count her ribs with his fingers. The fever and the infection were draining her and there was nothing he could do but watch and pray. He'd never felt so helpless in his life.

Every time she woke, he pestered her to eat.

"You're hardly eating enough to keep a rat alive," she pointed out.

"Which is just fine, since I am a sewer rat, or so I've been told."

"It's not like it matters. I'm going to the Bramble. You'll need your strength to deal with the Jutras. I'd just as soon die before Chance hits."

Marten had no arguments, but adamantly continued to force food on her. She was too weak to refuse.

It was eight days into their voyage when another snip of memory returned to Lucy. She'd been in a restless sleep, Marten keeping watch at the foot of the bed. She woke suddenly. "By the gods! The Jutras! Sharpel is a Jutras spy!" she shouted shrilly.

"What?"

Marten opened a deadlight, letting a stream of bright sunshine into the cabin. Lucy was sitting up on the bed, clutching the blanket. For the first time he saw how frighteningly thin she'd really become. She had no curves left; her bones jutted through her skin in sharp angles. Lucy shivered at the draft from the open window and Marten went to the bed, gingerly slipping behind her, extending his legs on either side of hers and pulling her back against his chest. The stench of her putrefying wounds nearly made him gag, but he ignored it. She drew a jagged breath as the cloth of her shirt pulled away from her seeping scabs. But she settled back against him despite her obvious pain. She did not speak, going so still he wondered if she was still awake.

"What do you mean, Sharpel is a Jutras spy?" he asked when Lucy had been silent too long. He could feel her shallow breathing, but he'd begun to fear she'd drift off to sleep and never wake again. The agony of that thought was appalling.

"I have always been able to sense majick," she said offhandedly. "I can feel spells. That's how I found my collection of ciphers." She lifted her left arm, turning it from side to side as if showing off a bracelet.

He went rigid with shock. "Are you saying . . . ?"

"Mmmhmm. It's still on my arm. If it wasn't for the fact that it won't come off, I'd think it was dead. I haven't felt anything from it since that night." She struggled suddenly to push herself up. "You shouldn't be here with me. If it should wake up—you should go."

He pulled her back gently, taking her hand in his and stroking her hair with the other. "We're aboard ship.

There's no place to go, even if I wanted to. Tell me the rest."

She sighed, whether from relief or pain, he couldn't tell. "You should know the whole story, starting when I first met him. I was nine years old. I didn't know who he was then."

She spoke for more than an hour, at one point drifting off to sleep. Marten waited patiently for her to wake, his mind churning. Edgar would never collaborate with the Jutras. Marten was sure of that. But there was no comfort in that knowledge; Edgar had proven how truly evil he really was. Yet underneath Marten's repulsion and fury was a child's love and worship for a strong elder brother. He swore softly, waking Lucy. He eased out from under her, fetched water, and sat on the edge of the bed to help her sip. Her hair was crisp as straw beneath his fingers.

"He was blackmailing me. He must have been watching me since I was a child. He figured out I was collecting the ciphers and made me retrieve a crate from customs. He didn't think I could break the protective spell sealing it up. Or he thought I'd figure it was just to protect the jewels in the box. But thanks to the cipher, I was able to unseal it and find the secret compartment with the contract. There were three copies of it. Two are still hidden."

She stiffened, gripping his arm with weak fingers.

"Keros! I told him about the contract and where to find them. I left him a letter to take to Cousin William if anything happened to me!"

"Keros?" His voice nearly cracked with his surprise.

"Didn't I tell you? He helped me." She went on to fill in the holes in her story. But pain fractured her mind and she wound about over the same ground several times, unaware.

"I would not have expected it of him. You got under his skin," he said when she trailed off.

She laughed softly. "Maybe. I thought it was guilt."

Marten took her wasted hand in his and lifted it to his lips. "It wasn't."

She did not answer. But neither did she pull away.

Marten became aware they'd reached the Bramble long before Lucy did. He felt the ship slowing as the sails were taken in, leaving only the main course, the forecourse, and the standing jib to move the ship along. The breeze was fresh and following. Marten said nothing to Lucy, savoring the time he had left with her. But he couldn't hide the slide of the anchor's chain through the hawsehole or the whir of the capstan spinning.

"We're here." Her voice was empty and distant.

"Aye."

Before she could say anything else, the key turned in the lock and the door was flung open. The mate filled the doorway.

"Out w' ye, then. No tricks." He shook the hilt of his cutlass. "Ye stay back, Thorpe."

"She can't walk on her own," Marten said quickly. It was true. There was no way Lucy could walk to the rail. Not with the roll of the deck and her weakened state. "I'll carry her."

The mate spat, the tobacco juice splattering Marten's boots. "Suit yerself. But I'll cut yer jackstays if her deck start to buck. Hurry now. Pilot says there be a *sylveth* tide rising. We don't want to run foul of it."

He waited as Marten retrieved Lucy. She was sitting up, her legs braced apart as she tried to stand. Her shirt—his shirt—barely reached the middle of her thighs. It was crusted with blood and pus. More of the filth ran down her legs. Livid streaks of red spread like spiderwebs beneath her skin, interspersed with putrid, weeping burns. Wordlessly, he wrapped a blanket around her and lifted her in his arms, trying to be gentle. He carried her out onto the deck.

She blinked and squinted, blinded by the brilliant sunlight. She looped an arm around his neck. Marten felt her muscles shake with the effort.

They made the walk to the rail in silence. Sailors hung from the shrouds in nervous clusters, watching with hostile eyes. They murmured epithets, but made no further overtures or outbursts. In the middle of the deck, Pilot Idron stood beside the compass post, just aft of the main hatch. The post was solid silver rising out of the deck. On top was a thirty-two-rayed compass, each ray made of *sylveth*. Idron's right hand rested on the *sylveth* dome in the center as he continued to scan the ever-changing depths of the Inland Sea for trouble. He met Marten's eyes for a grain, then flicked away. But the moment was enough to reveal that Idron was a roiling mass of rage and fear.

Marten continued his slow walk. The gate rail had been taken down. Spray spurted up over the bow, showering them in a fine mist. The captain stood at the foot of the stairs leading up to the forecastle. His face was impassive. He nodded to Marten, scowling.

"Just toss her down, then, and we'll hoist the sheets and be on our way," the mate said.

Marten stepped to the gap in the rail. His knees bent and flexed with the rise and fall of the ship. The water was glossy black and frothy white. A half a league away the Bramble rose blue and green, its mountains jagged and white like teeth.

"I can't swim," she said. "At least it should be a quick end."

His arms tightened and he made an animal sound in the back of his throat. She winced at the sudden pain and pulled her arm from round his neck.

"Thank you, for your care. You've made the journey easier than it should have been." Her lips pinched tight, but she did not allow her fear to color her expression. "If you see my family and Sarah and Blythe . . ." She broke off, her chin crumpling. She took a breath and blew it out. "If you see them, will you tell them I'm sorry for . . . everything?"

"I would. But I'm getting off here."

Her eyes widened. "What are you saying? You can't. The Chance storms! It's suicide."

"I'm not leaving you."

"You don't have to prove anything to me," she said. "We've both made mistakes. I don't blame you. Your brother and Sharpel were going to get me whether you helped or not. I'm dying anyway. Drowning is a mercy."

He pressed his lips close to her ear. "I'm not letting you go without me."

"Why?"

The mate prodded him with the tip of his cutlass. Marten grimaced, clutching her tight. It hurt her, but he didn't loosen his grip.

"Because I'd rather be with you in a vat of *sylveth* than without you on a throne of gold."

He didn't wait for her reply, but crouched and jumped, hearing shouts as they plummeted down into the night black waters of the Inland Sea.

Chapter 29

They struck the water, plunging deep underneath the waves. Pain raked her with steel claws. Lucy screamed, her mouth filling with water. She struggled wildly, kicking and thrashing. Marten held her tightly, dragging her up toward the surface. Then the pain was too much. She spasmed and went limp. Her mind ribboned chaotically. She held on to the thought that she shouldn't breathe. *Don't breathe. Don't breathe.*

"Lucy! Lucy!"

Marten held her chin, patting her cheeks with his fingers. She blinked at him. She was cold, so dreadfully cold. Down to the roots of her being. She thought of the cipher and its former fiery heat. If she could have laughed, she would have.

"Lucy, are you with me? We have to get ashore before the *sylveth* tide rolls in."

She nodded, still not quite able to believe he'd jumped into the water with her. He began to swim, pulling her along.

"Let me do the work. Relax."

But as thin as she'd become, Lucy was still a heavy burden to pull through the chop. And Marten had been days with little food. He struggled against the waves, his breathing guttural and harsh. The Bramble was half a league away and the *Firedance* a shadow running away across the waves. Lucy wanted to tell him to let go of her, to swim ahead to safety, but she knew he wouldn't.

He was insane of course. There was no other explanation.

She felt the *sylveth* coming before it overtook them. It was a burning, knifing sensation. She moaned, clutching at Marten and kicking her legs.

"Hurry!"

"What's wrong?" he rasped.

"The tide!"

But it was already too late. Streamers of *sylveth* unfurled through the waves like tentacles. Marten dived toward an opening, dragging Lucy after him. But there was no place to go. The *sylveth* caught him first. One moment he was holding Lucy afloat; the next he flung his arms wide, his back arching, his eyes rolling up into his head. His mouth jerked open in a silent scream. Then he sank. In a heartbeat he'd disappeared.

Lucy shouted weakly, kicking and splashing her arms awkwardly. Then she felt its touch. A whisper-soft caress. A feeling of bliss suffused her and she went limp. Her body dissolved into nothingness.

She came back to herself on a rocky shingle lying half in and half out of the water. She felt . . . perfect. There was no pain. No exhaustion. No hunger. No thirst. There was . . . want.

She sat up. Her toes curled, washed by warm, silvery waves. She scooped up some *sylveth* in her cupped hand. She lifted it up level with her eyes. *Shape*. The *sylveth* rolled itself into a ball, swirling with opalescent color. Lucy tilted her head. The ball changed into a face. Male. His eyes brown, his hair sun tarnished. Square face, strong, blunt features. Smile that infuriated. *Marten*.

The name trailed through her mind like sparks from a fire. They floated down, igniting flames. Memories. More sparks. More flames. They twisted into threads, winding and weaving together into a tapestry of a life. Her life.

Slowly she retreated from the web of memories. The *sylveth* had melted from her hand. But the face remained in her mind's eye. She stood, ankle deep in the shimmering tide. She looked down. She was naked. There was a silvery cast to her pale skin. Flecks of stardust sparkled in a seam between her breasts and scattered across her belly. Winding around her left arm was the cipher, its *sylveth* disks cobalt blue. The wind caressed her. It was, she thought, cold, identifying the sensation distantly, not truly feeling it.

Another thought and *sylveth* swirled up, arranging itself in a silky pair of twilight-hued leggings and a flowing tunic. She nodded satisfaction. Still, something was odd. She reached up to touch her head. The skin was smooth. Suddenly a thick wash of auburn curls cascaded down her back to her waist. She wrinkled her nose in distaste as the wind picked at it, teasing it across her face. Grains later, it wound up in an ornate braided coif. Better. She stepped out of the tide, fashioning soft boots around her feet.

And then she went in search of Marten.

Lucy wandered along the shore. The *sylveth* called to her; it celebrated her. She felt its presence in the beat of her pulse and the vibration of her chest when she breathed. It was soothing, invigorating. Like warm sunshine, cool water, and rich earth to a tree. It offered itself to her, a reservoir of power for the taking.

As she walked, she began to feel more like herself. Her senses grew more immediate. She was aware of growing hunger and thirst, and a need to relieve her bladder. She climbed higher on the shingle, finding a rock to brace against, and did so, wondering idly if she could create a slop jar to make it easier. She tried it. It was more difficult than molding the *sylveth* into Marten's face. She pulled dirt and pebbles up into a crumbling, lopsided, bulbous shape that had no lid nor wide lip to sit on. She scowled with concentration, pushing, pulling, molding. Sweat beaded on her forehead and upper lip. Gradually the jar grew taller, smoother, the lip widening. At last she felt done and stopped.

She examined her construction, panting with effort.

She reached out a finger and prodded it gently. The jar caved in with a puff of dust. She sighed, aggravated, and gave up. Marten was still waiting.

He was alive. The *sylveth* had told her so. She smiled, remembering his words before they'd jumped from the *Firedance*. *I'd rather be in a vat of* sylveth. . . . He'd had his wish.

She walked for hours. At midday, she stopped and frowned at the sun. Midday? It had been afternoon when they'd been forced from the ship. How much time had passed since? She shrugged and began to walk again.

It was dusk when she found him. Storm clouds had begun to pile up, their billowing tops white, their flat bottoms nearly as black as the waves. He was perched on a spur of rock protruding from the water. White-capped waves washed around him, spume spouting into the air to drench him.

He was naked. And like her, he was the same and different. He watched her approach up the shore with the patience of a lion stalking its prey. She stopped opposite him, the *sylveth*-streaked waves washing over her boots. Inside, her feet remained dry.

He stared back at her, examining her as she inspected him. He crouched on the rock, unmoving, a statue. His eyes had changed. They were black from corner to corner. Turbulent, like the waters of the storm-driven sea. Fine silvery scales traveled down his neck and spine to his buttocks. More spangled his cheeks and thighs, condensing into a dense, silvery net around his feet. Otherwise, he looked the same.

"I missed your hair," he called. There was a question in his voice. *Was she still herself? Was she afraid of him? Repulsed by him?*

"You lost your collar."

He touched his neck and shook his head. "I should still have it. I deserve it."

Lucy stood silently several moments. "No, you don't."

"No?" The question was wary.

"Unvarnished truth?"

"By all means."

She held out her hands in the air, palms flat. She lifted one higher than the other. "You stole my seals." She lifted the other. "You took me to Keros to help heal me. You tried to get information with Jordan to expose your brother, which led to your wearing the iron collar in the first place. You tried to protect me from Edgar in that dreadful room, refusing to be blackmailed. You cared for me on the ship, even after I'd incinerated your brother. You even helped me use the slop jar, which no doubt was the height of the journey. And then you jumped into the sea with me rather than abandon me to my fate." She rocked her hands in the air as if balancing scales, and then dropped them to her sides. "You are a good man. You are . . . my friend."

He closed his eyes, his head sagging forward. When he lifted his head again, his smile had returned, sharp and teasing. "Would you care to know my impression of you?"

She made a face. "By all means."

He stood, stepping down off the rock. The inky water hardened beneath his feet and he walked across it to stand beside her. His hands were warm as they framed her face. "You're infuriating. Brave. Obstinate. And I want to be far more to you than just your *friend*."

His mouth slanted over hers, his tongue tasting like wind and clouds. She kissed him back, sliding her arms around his neck to hold him firmly, her fingers delighting in the warm tension of his skin. At last he lifted his head.

"You smell much better than you did on the ship."

"You need clothes." She looked down between them. "You're being a bit impertinent."

He smiled suggestively, sliding his arms around her waist and pulling her against him. "I intend to be downright brazen."

Fat raindrops pattered down, sizzling on the water. He sighed noisily.

"I suppose we should look for shelter. And clothing."

He fingered her tunic, his brows rising. "Pretty. Find a shipwreck with a full hold?"

She shook her head. She looked down at the *sylveth* swirling in the waves around them. It answered her desire, sliding up to layer his skin. Grains later he was wearing knee-high boots, dark blue wool trousers, a cambric shirt, and a heavy wool frock coat. His hair smoothed back into a tail fastened at the crown of his head, the scrubby bristles vanishing from his jaw. He looked down at himself, startled.

"Won't Sharpel be surprised to see us?" he said with a razor grin.

"I can hardly wait."

They found shelter in a sea cave above the high-tide mark. But there was nothing to eat. Fishing in the Inland Sea was chancy—and even though *sylveth* had done all it was going to do to them both, Lucy wasn't eager to eat something that once might have been human. And it was too late in the year for berries.

"You're a majicar now. You created this fine clothing. What about roast lamb, potatoes, bread, and ale?" Marten waggled his brows at her hopefully.

Lucy thought of her failed attempt at a slop jar. "The clothes were easy. But food . . ." She frowned.

"It's worth a try. Fried rat would taste good right about now," he said, rubbing his stomach.

She sighed. She could feel the *sylveth* all around, running in thick veins through the length and breadth of the entire sea. It was powerful, raw majick. It tantalized. She knew she could form it into clothing. But then she'd been standing in the midst of it. She glanced at the mouth of the cave. The wind was howling and it had begun to sleet. She did not want to go out in that. Her stomach cramped painfully. Nor did she want to starve.

Marten came to sit on the sandy floor beside her. He lay down on his side, curving around so that she leaned back against his hips. He braced his elbow on the floor, resting his head in his palm, rubbing her shoulder lightly with the other hand. "The sea is . . . it's part of me. I can sense it, every drop, every knucklebone, every Koreion. It's like my heartbeat, like breathing. It'll answer my wants. I don't have to think about it. It's instinct. I just have to feel it."

Lucy met his strange black eyes, considering his words. She nodded, relaxing back against him. She closed her eyes, listening to the *sylveth*. Its reaction reminded her of a puppy left too long alone. It bounced and cavorted. It formed into the shape of a Koreion and wriggled happily. Lucy put an imaginary hand out to it. It nuzzled her fingers and rolled in a corkscrew of delight. She had the distinct impression that it had been waiting for her for a very long time. How long?

She began to think about food. Roasted lamb crusted with almonds, garlic, salt, and cracked pepper. Potatoes with brown crusty exteriors, drizzled with butter and cream. Steaming rosemary bread. Sugar-glazed custard. Tender spears of asparagus. Cold frothy ale. She could almost smell it.

Lucy opened her eyes. There was a feast on the sandy floor. The scent made her mouth water painfully.

"Is it real?" she asked, recalling the crumbling slop jar.

Marten sat up slowly, reaching for the bread. He broke off an end and bit into it. "Food of the gods," he mumbled, handing Lucy a chunk.

They settled down to eat. It was easier now to call up what she wanted. Knives, plates, forks, cups, napkins. She and Marten stuffed themselves until they could eat nothing more.

When they were through, she vanished the remnants of their meal. "I hope we don't regret that," she said as soon as she'd done it. "What if I can't repeat the trick?"

Marten put his arms around her, stroking his hands down her back and nibbling at her neck. "I'm not worried. Now . . . you've assuaged one of my hungers—how about conjuring a bed?"

*   *   *

The pull was inexorable. She could not resist. She crawled out of bed, putting on her clothes and going out the cave entrance. She didn't pause when tiny pellets of ice driven by the fierce wind pelted her face. She clambered over slick rocks and boulders. Tough bushes scraped at her as she pushed through, following a path she could not see.

The cipher on her arm glowed brilliant blue, giving her light to see by. She followed the coastline, going as fast as possible through the blustering storm. She was not startled when something bobbed up out of the waves. Marten strode ashore, falling into step beside her.

"Not the most favorable night to take a walk," he said, bending close to her ear so that she could hear him. "Should I be offended that you ran screaming into the night?"

"I did not run, nor did I scream."

"But you left me."

Lucy did not miss the rebuke in his voice.

"I knew you would come."

"Did you?"

"Of course."

"Where are we going?" he asked, accepting her declaration.

"I don't know. The cipher is at the helm."

Oddly, Lucy wasn't frightened by the imperious pull of the cipher. She'd begun to trust it in some perverse way. Or perhaps it didn't seem so frightening, not after bathing in *sylveth*.

They were led to a rocky stream flowing into the sea, and followed it inland as dawn broke. The storm did not let up and they took a short rest in a thick stand of conifers, Lucy conjuring porridge with molasses and a pot of hot, sweet tea.

"I wonder if all majicars can do what you do," Marten said idly. "They'd never want for anything."

Lucy shrugged. Using majick seemed easier than it ought to be. And only seemed to get easier with every attempt she made. It was not nearly as hard to do as customs work. The thought bothered her. She'd always had what she believed to be a natural talent and passion for her job. Like she'd always been meant to work in customs. And now majick had found her, or some lock inside her had been turned, and she wondered if she'd been meant for something else entirely. The idea made her cold in a way the sleet and wind did not.

They followed the stream up into the foothills. Ice coated the winter-killed grass, and conifers dotted the gray rock shelves thrusting up through the soil. They came to a steep ridge. It was seamed and cracked and oddly rounded, looking like the gods had piled together hot boulders, moulding them together in a fortress wall.

"Where to now?" Marten asked.

"Up."

They climbed. Lucy used majick to carve out hand- and footholds. Even so, the storm made the going difficult. Her arms, back, and legs ached and she left more skin than she wanted scraped off on the stone.

At last they cleared the top. Lucy wriggled up on her stomach, turning onto her back. Her ribs bellowed with the effort of breathing. Marten flung himself beside her. But the cipher wouldn't let her rest long. It physically pulled on her. Her arm extended over her head until the tendons in her shoulder stretched painfully. She obeyed the summons, rolling awkwardly to her feet, her arm straight before her. Marten followed.

"And you called *me* a gambler. Promise you'll give up collecting those," he said sardonically, steadying her on the icy rocks.

The ridge was narrow, dropping away before them into a deep chasm. With the rain, they could not see the bottom. The cipher tugged harder, dragging Lucy toward the edge. Marten grasped her around the waist.

"There has to be a way down, or across," she said.

"Or the whole point is to bring a victim up to the top of a cliff to dash his brains out below."

Inch by inch, they were jerked toward the edge. They were only two feet away when she finally realized she was going to have to try to use her newfound majick to attack the cipher itself. She snorted softly. *Choose your death. Six of one, half dozen of the other.*

Her mind was so scattered with rising fear that at first she couldn't focus enough to do anything. Then Marten skidded and she staggered forward. He snatched her again, hanging on her legs like an anchor.

"If this doesn't work, don't jump with me this time," she said.

Without waiting for his reply, she closed her eyes, concentrating on prying away the cipher. Instantly, a shock quaked through her. Her bones turned to taffy and she crumpled to the ground. Marten clung to her, but the strength of the cipher had increased a hundredfold.

"Let go!" Lucy hissed, plucking feebly at Marten's hands.

"I think not."

Then suddenly she felt the edge beneath her. She cried out, scrabbling for something to hold on to. She grabbed a tough gorse bush. It burned her hands as they slid down over its stems and she held nothing. Then she and Marten were falling into empty space.

Except . . .

They floated gently, drifting downward like gulls.

"Are you doing this?"

Lucy shook her head. "No," she rasped.

Marten was silent, turning his head to look below them.

"I'm beginning to think the cipher isn't actually *trying* to kill you."

The same thought had occurred to Lucy. She curled her hand in his. "Mutilation and torture are on the program, however."

Chapter 30

They sank downward, buoyed by majick. Lucy held tight to Marten, afraid if she let go, he'd plummet to the ground, unaided by the cipher. She could see green smudges below where evergreen trees grew, a winding riverbed, and expansive meadows. There was a herd of animals at the far end of the gorge.

"Do you see them?" she asked, pointing.

"Aye."

"What are they?"

He shrugged. "The Koreions don't care about *sylveth*. And a host of other sea creatures. They feed on *sylveth* spawn," he added quietly before shrugging. "Likely there are land animals that are equally unimpressed."

The wind lessened as they descended, blocked by the steep walls of the chasm. They'd dropped about halfway to the bottom when suddenly they stopped. In the same moment, the cobalt of the cipher began to fade. The chain loosened on Lucy's arm, and the air supporting them began to soften. They sank a few inches.

"I think it's taken us as far as it's willing to go," she said. "Up to us to get the rest of the way down, I think."

"We could always go up," Marten suggested.

She shook her head. "I think we need to finish this."

"Then allow me."

Suddenly the air hardened. The wind pulled into a tight spout, a whirling pillar. Below, chunks of mud and grass spun into the air. They dropped down quickly, the pillar shortening beneath them. Twenty feet above the ground, it began to disperse and they drifted down on a remaining updraft. They landed in churned black mud. Lucy staggered at the impact, lurching and falling to her hands and knees. The cipher dropped in a jingling heap beside her. Marten helped her up.

She wiped her hands on her leggings, strangely reticent to use majick to conjure a towel. She picked up the cipher. The *sylveth* disks were gray once again. It tingled in her fingers. It was done with her, but not dead.

"That's the cipher?"

She quirked a surprised brow at Marten. "You can see it?"

He nodded.

She slipped it into her pocket. "Come on."

He fell in beside her as she started walking west toward the center of the chasm. "Where are we going?"

"There's strong majick here. I can feel it."

"Some would take that as a sign to run in the other direction. Isn't that what got you into trouble with this?" He tapped the chain lumping in her pocket.

"It *is* a gamble," she said with an acerbic smile.

He touched his forehead in a mock salute. "By all means, let us go. I am loath to pass up a good game of chance."

The rain had stopped and the sun shone weakly. They'd walked more than half a league. Majick loomed ahead like a hurricane. The feel of it made Lucy's lungs hurt. It reverberated through her and around as if she were standing inside an enormous bell striking an infinite hour. Still she continued forward. There was something here she was supposed to find. She knew it. The cipher had *chosen* her for some reason, and it had not been one of Errol Cipher's cruel pranks. The pain and trouble that came with it was likely just an added treat for the ancient majicar's amusement.

The closer they came, the harder it was for Lucy to walk. She felt like she was pushing through a thickening wall. The dense vibrations grew stronger and faster. Her teeth rattled and her heart forgot its rhythm, beating wildly. Her chest hurt and her head felt as if it were being squeezed inside a fist. She was barely aware of Marten's fingers laced together with hers. Her vision blurred and she was as blind as if wandering through a tully fog.

At last she came to a point where she could hardly move. Sliding her foot forward hurt with such an intensity that she keened, unable to scrape together the words to voice her agony. But she wasn't about to give up. She had to find out what she'd suffered so much for. She pushed on. A step, another, one more.

And then suddenly she was free.

She stumbled forward, the release almost as unbearable as the pain itself. She slumped to the ground full length, pressing her cheek to the warm wet leaf meal, gasping for breath. Slowly her heart settled into its normal cadence, the lingering resonance faded, and her vision cleared. She sat up. Marten lay nearby, equally spent. He opened his eyes when she moved, jerkily pushing up to sit.

"Chance smiles," he rasped, and then spat dirt from his mouth.

"We are very lucky," she agreed, then looked about her. Her mouth fell open. "By the gods!"

They were sitting in an ancient grove of blood oak. The trees towered high above their heads. Their dark crimson boles were enormous; it would have taken fifteen people clasping hands to surround one. Majick thrummed in the air and vibrated in the earth. It felt as if the entire glade was . . . *breathing*. Diaphanous white mist curled and twisted in the branches. *Sylveth* mist.

Marten whistled low. "Am I dreaming?"

Lucy stood, approaching one of the trees. She pressed her palm against the warm, satiny wood. It twitched beneath her hand. She felt the power inside it. A volcanic force. She stepped back, her fingers curling.

The discovery was staggering. Blood oak. An entire grove of it. When a single branch was a treasure. This was . . . she rubbed her hands over her face, pinching her lips. Horrifying. Dreadful.

"I don't like this."

Marten came up behind her, putting his hands on her shoulders and rubbing gently.

"I don't think it matters if you like it or not."

She glanced back at him. "You think so too?"

He nodded. "You're the next Errol Cipher. No majicar could find this place without that cipher. And it chose you. Maybe only you in four hundred years. Which means you're *supposed* to be here."

She closed her eyes, shuddering.

He gave her a little shake. "Just think of it. Imagine what you can do. Soon they won't be called ciphers anymore—they'll be called trentons."

Lucy's lips pulled back in a predatory grin. "If he's alive, Edgar gets to have the first one. Sharpel the second."

Marten nodded, then sobered. He turned her around to face him. "This is a good thing, Lucy. The Jutras are invading Crosspointe. There are constant rumors about the Pale failing and the majicars can't fix it, not even working together. You're here, now, for a reason. You are Crosspointe's guardian."

She crossed her arms belligerently, wanting to argue. But she had a terrible feeling he wasn't wrong. "So if I'm the great guardian of Crosspointe, what are you supposed to be?"

"Me?"

She nodded. "Walks on water, molds the winds, funny eyes and silver scales—surely you're here for some great purpose as well."

"I am . . ."

Her brows arched. "What?"

"I am never leaving your side." He bent and kissed her.

She let it go on for a long moment, then tore herself away. His words had the ring of a promise. It loosened the tension squeezing her chest.

"Let's see the rest, then," she said, unsure how she felt.

"The rest?"

"There's something else here. Something . . . big."

It had been growing on her awareness for several minutes. A deep, churning power. The heart of the hurricane.

Water dripped from the branches of the blood oaks. The ground was covered in thick leaf meal with no bushes or flowers growing beneath the great trees. The invisible path Lucy followed took them up a low hill. She began to hear a rumbling as they neared the west wall of the great canyon. Dusk fell, but Lucy did not conjure light. She wasn't sure she ought to be using majick here. It felt too much like desecrating a holy place.

They crested the hill and stopped dead.

"By the gods," Marten murmured.

"I'm getting tired of hearing that."

"All right. Does *Braken's cods* make you feel better?"

"Yes."

"Then you may just be mad."

"I think you're probably right. Pale-blasted."

He crooked his arm at her. "Shall we go down?"

She nodded her head and slipped her hand through his arm.

They walked down into a wide shallow bowl. Almost immediately, they found themselves under the spreading branches of the largest blood oak Lucy could imagine existing in the world. It sat in a churning pool of *sylveth* fed by a cataract falling from the cliffs above. Mist rose from where it dashed against the rocks. The leaves of the tree were red-veined clusters. They shifted and whispered. Lucy thought if she listened close enough, she might be able to understand.

They stopped on the edge of the pool. It was really more like a small lake. The tree grew out of its depths, its bole easily eighty feet in diameter. How tall it was, Lucy couldn't begin to guess.

"You could build an entire ship from the timber," Marten said softly.

The leaves shook, as if reproaching him.

"I don't think she likes you talking about chopping her to bits."

"She?"

Lucy nodded. "The mother tree. Don't you feel it?"

He shook his head.

"What's that?"

He followed her pointing finger. "It looks like an entrance."

The oval opening was tiny in the side of the great tree. It shimmered, covered with a door of *sylveth*.

"I'll wait here for you."

Lucy glanced at Marten and then nodded. This was something she had to do alone. The cipher had chosen her, after all.

The pool roiled as she approached. Again she was reminded of a puppy left too long alone. She knelt, running her fingers through it. It swallowed her arm, running up over her neck. She stood, stepping out onto it. It firmed, but not before sliding up over her legs and waist. Soon she was entirely sheathed in the shimmering stuff. But she had no difficulty breathing, nor seeing.

She crossed to the door. She brushed her fingers over the surface and it dissolved. She stepped up into the tree. As she did, the *sylveth* drained away, returning to the pool.

The interior of the mother tree had been hollowed out to create a large room. The walls glowed with a soft pink light. Along a wall there was a bed, looking freshly made. Beside it was a table, a long workbench covered with all sorts of odd bits, a huge copper bathtub, and a tall mirror. Lucy caught sight of herself in it. She went closer, examining herself. She looked very much the same as she always had. Round figure, full breasts, freckles. She was surprised to see that the gold necklace signaling her royal lineage remained unchanged. Aside from the silvery speckles on her chest and belly, the only other outward sign of her change was in her eyes. The blue irises had turned silver. They shimmered and spun like raw *sylveth*. The pupils and outer ring were dark crimson. They would likely be very unnerving to others. Lucy rather liked the effect.

"Well, you will certainly turn heads, won't you?" she said to herself, returning to her examination of the room.

In the center was something resembling a Pilot's compass. It stood on a post of blood oak. It was living wood, Lucy realized, kneeling down to touch it. She stood again, examining the compass itself. The rays were each a different shade of red *sylveth*, and in the center bubbled a pool of the stuff. From its depths another red finger of *sylveth* protruded. Lucy reached out and touched it. Instantly the walls of the room flashed brilliant white.

"So you've come at last, have you? Took your time, too. Oh dear. A woman. Well, should have expected that. Pretty enough, though. At least that's something."

The low, scratchy voice was male. It reminded Lucy of a foghorn. It was also bad-tempered.

"Errol Cipher, I presume?" It couldn't be anyone else.

"What's left of him. What he left here to molder while you dawdled getting here. No senses—can't taste, touch, or smell. Nothing to look at. Nothing to hear but the gods-cursed wind blowing."

"Why did you bring me here?"

"*I* didn't. The trinket did. Made just to find someone strong enough to manage the blood oak. To be a proper heir to my knowledge."

His tone was pompous and self-impressed. He reminded her entirely too much of her elder brother Stephen. Lucy rolled her eyes.

"Heir?"

"Certainly, though I did not think it would be a woman."

"You don't like women?"

"Oh, no. I like women very much. Very much. But . . ."

"But?" she prompted.

He resolved out of the whiteness. He was slightly taller than she, with thick blond hair that flopped over his forehead, and a square, craggy face. His nose was broad and large, looking as if it had been roughly hewed from stone. His mouth was flat, his eyes the same red-ringed silver as hers. His chin had a cleft, and there was a gap between his two front teeth. He had a narrow waist and muscular shoulders. He appeared to be around forty-five years old, perhaps a few years older. He was dressed in antiquated loose trousers, low, slipperlike shoes, and a tight, short shirt with a wide studded leather belt. He was not handsome, Lucy thought. But something about him was tremendously compelling.

"Women have the capacity to do terrible things. Vicious things. Without hardly a qualm," he said. "They are quite reasonable right up to the point where they become unreasoning, and then they do exactly as they wish without concern for the consequences. Men, however, have hot fierce tempers that burn out quickly. They are more easily deflected from their stupidity. Women are single-minded about it."

"This from the man who set innumerable curses on his friends and enemies alike."

He smiled slyly. "Imagine if I were a woman. But there's no help for it. You are here and you are the one, so I must teach you."

"Teach me what?"

"Everything. Each ray of the compass contains journals, lessons, books—all that I've learned. It is for you. And for whoever comes after you. Touch the rays in order—box the compass, as it were. Only when you thoroughly learn what each has to offer will the next open for you. Guard the information well. It can be dangerous in the wrong hands. In stupid or weak hands. Is there still a Rampling on the throne?" he asked suddenly.

Lucy nodded. "Cousin William."

"Cousin? Ah, then, that is all right. Rampling blood is unreasonably loyal, stupidly steadfast, and revoltingly stubborn. Clever, too. Too clever by half, sometimes. Yes, you may just do."

"Just what do you expect me to do?" she asked, finding the situation more amusing than she ought to.

He put his hands on his hips, staring in disgusted disbelief. "Serve the crown, of course. That's what majicars do."

"They do?" Lucy thought of the guild. Certainly majicars were required to serve three months of every year. They did whatever was required, from healing to helping with customs, from building roads to providing majickal protections for the king. The rest of the year they did as they pleased. Though they provided regular service to Crosspointe, she wouldn't have said they served the crown.

"Of course. From the founding it was decided. Well, the first William and I decided. Trevor was only interested in amassing several fortunes. We overruled him," he said smugly. "After all, I could conjure a mountain of gold and jewels in my sleep. I have no need of money. Majicars really only have one true devotion, besides the gods, and that is learning their craft and using it for the good of the crown."

Lucy shook her head. "That's not the way it is now. Majicars have their own guild. They only serve the crown to pay a sort of tax on Merstone Island. Many charge hefty fees for the services they do otherwise. I have no idea what happens on Merstone Island. Experimenting and learning their craft, I suppose."

"That's outrageous," he sputtered, spots of color rising in his cheeks.

She watched entranced. He seemed so real.

"Well, that nonsense is about to change. *You* will serve. And you will bring them to heel."

"I will?"

He pointed a blunt finger at her, approaching so that

his insubstantial face was only inches from hers. "Do not play games, chit. I am not so dead that I cannot still curse you so that your skin sloughs off and your innards spill out your anus and your brain runs out your nose."

Lucy held up the charm on the end of her gold necklace. "I'm a Rampling, remember? Of course I will serve. I have all my life. But bringing the majicars to heel . . ." How could she do that? "Cousin William will have to decide."

He stood back and then nodded. "Well enough. Now"— he turned and walked, rubbing his hands together—"there is so much to tell you. Where to begin? The blood oak, I think. Yes, that's simple enough and—"

The tree shook and twisted as if someone was trying to uproot it. Lucy staggered, losing her balance and pulling her hand away from the hardened *sylveth* protrusion. Instantly the vision of Errol Cipher vanished. She caught the compass for balance, slicing her hand on one of the rays. Blood dripped to the floor.

Everything went still. Lucy pulled herself to her feet. Suddenly the walls turned brilliant red, the color of fresh blood. A pulse of majick rose up from the roots of the tree. It flooded Lucy, washing through her and beyond. For an instant she felt the tender tips of the leaves, the minuscule root hairs taking in nourishment from the *sylveth*, the tall, solid trunk driving deeply into the soil and sky. And she felt more. Sparks in a web, far away. And . . .

A void.

A wrongness.

A death.

Lucy's stomach turned over. Her hands shook with palsy. She braced her elbows on the top of the compass, grasping the *sylveth* finger with both hands. This time there was no white mist, no vision of Errol Cipher. Only his voice. Weak.

"What's happened?" she whispered, her voice cracking.

"The Pale. It's gone. The tree always knows where her children are. You must go. The *sylveth* rises. The Chance storms are already forming. Hurry."

His voice faded at the end.

"What do I do?"

"Make a new Pale."

"How?"

Lucy had a sense of annoyed amusement. "Conjure it, majicar. Anchor it to the Wall tree. Remember, it's *blood* oak."

"The Wall tree? What do you mean?"

But there was no answer. He was gone. She pushed herself upright, going to the doorway. The pool of *sylveth* churned madly, and she could hear the tree now. Its hum was echoed by the grove. An ominous sound.

Lucy patted its bark with her bleeding hand. "I'll fix it," she promised. Did the hum shift pitch for a moment? She couldn't be sure. She pulled her hand away, watching in fascination as her blood was absorbed into the wood and disappeared. *It's blood oak*, Errol Cipher had said. It was not named for its color.

Crossing back across the *sylveth* was far more difficult. It did not want to listen. She concentrated with everything she had, forcing it to hold her weight. She ran across, not trusting the bridge to hold. Marten caught her hands, helping her jump to shore.

"What's happened?"

"The Pale has been destroyed," she said, fleeing back through the grove.

Marten caught up with her. The barrier that had been so hard to cross did not hinder their leave-taking. They dashed through the trees and out into a meadow. Marten grasped Lucy's hand, pulling her to a halt. Feeling the stickiness on her hands, he examined the black stain in the moonlight.

"Can you fix this?"

She focused on her hand, imagining her flesh closing. Nothing happened. Instead she conjured a bandage. He wrapped it carefully around her wound.

"We have to get home," she said, her voice thick with worry. "Quickly. Chance storms are already building. We don't have much time."

Marten looked up at the sky, his face remote. Then he nodded. "It will take a few days for them to reach full strength and start sweeping across the sea."

"How are we going to get there? And in time?"

He flashed his most irritating smile. "Majick."

He called the winds again and lifted them back up to the lip of the chasm. From there they climbed down. He made her sit and rest at the foot of the great ridge.

"We haven't eaten all day. Let's try not to be stupider than we have to be. We'll need all our strength and wits about us."

Lucy assented, conjuring bread, meat, apples, and cream tea. They ate quickly. She recounted her visit with the remnant of Errol Cipher around bites of food.

"Errol Cipher's heir. Keros is going to have a litter of cats when he hears this."

Lucy grinned. "He'll rant at me for cutting up my hand again."

"Such a wet hen, isn't he?"

"I don't know. He watched me take a bath. He said all my fat was in the right places."

Marten lowered the sandwich he'd made, eyeing her darkly. "What was he doing watching you bathe?"

"Something about wanting to make sure I hadn't damaged myself more than I told him."

"And did you?"

"Not that time."

"I'd just as soon he kept out of your bathing room from now on."

"Really? Why?"

Marten hooked a hand around her neck, dragging her close and kissing her hard. He raised his head, snugging her close against his side.

"Because I'll blind him if he dares."

"He is a majicar, you know. That could be risky."

"He may be a majicar, but I am— Whatever I am, he'll find himself on the wrong end of a hot poker."

"I'll be sure to warn him."

"You do that."

* * *

It was nearly dawn by the time they returned to the shore. Lucy was exhausted, but she refused to rest.

"There's no time," she insisted.

"Then make us a boat. I'll do the rest."

She walked out into the water, closing her eyes. *Sylveth* coiled and swirled in the waves twenty leagues away. It lapped up against the Root and spread tendrils in a wide net near Normengas. It lay in a thick mass off the coast of Orsage and lingered deep under the waves west of Crosspointe. She tapped its power and thought of a boat. A customs cutter, with two masts and a sheltering roof. She opened her eyes. It rocked in the waves before her, exactly as she imagined, exactly as she'd remembered from every time she'd sailed across Blackwater Bay in one.

"You're getting very good at this," Marten said, lifting her aboard. He swung himself up easily. "A tight little craft. I'll set the sails and get under way."

He hoisted the sails, tying them off. Then he went to sit in the stern, one hand on the rudder.

"Ready? Hold on."

The wind rose. It bellied the sails. Soon they were skimming across the water. It was fast. But not fast enough.

"We won't get there in time," she told Marten.

He only smiled. Then suddenly the ocean surged. A tall wave picked them up on its crest. They thrust forward, racing across the ocean at lightning speed.

"Sleep," Marten ordered. "It will be hours before we're close."

Lucy nodded and went to the cabin. Just outside she stopped, looking out across the water. The eastern sky was streaked pink and orange. She narrowed her gaze, watching the water ahead. A Koreion rose up and sinuously dived back down, keeping pace with their boat. She smiled and went inside, conjuring a blanket and pillow and curling up on the floor.

Chapter 31

They rode through the day and into the night. Lucy woke, conjuring food, watching Marten while she ate. His face was remote and austere. His mind was far away, sunk deep in the sea and blowing swift across the waves. He took the fare she offered without a word or a look.

She was content to leave him be. Her own thoughts were tangled. She wanted time and peace to sort them out. She went to the bow, leaning against the rail and watching the Koreions. There were six of them now, diving and winding.

Her mind kept coming back to the Jutras. Sharpel had said Crosspointe's protections wouldn't last the month. Had he found a way to snap the Pale? But the Jutras wanted Crosspointe intact. They would want its Pilots and seamen and dockworkers. . . . Or it could just have failed. The papers had been predicting it for decades, saying its power was fading.

She stood for hours, finding no answers and only more questions. At last she gave up, conjuring warm brandy, and taking some to Marten. Then she returned to her nest on the floor of the cabin and slept again.

Marten shook her awake a couple of hours after dawn. "We're ten leagues out. I have to ease the wave or we'll swamp the harbor."

She returned to her vigil at the prow. Far ahead the headlands thrust steep and stark out of the sea. Merstone Island lumped blackly on the left side, marking the entrance to the strait and the harbor. What was missing was the glowing lights of the Pale. They would be blue by now, the wards shifting color as the storms built and the danger increased.

The cutter slowed, the wave subsiding beneath them. The wind remained steady and following.

"Where do you want to make landing?" Marten called from the stern.

"Straight up the mouth of the harbor. There's a private landing south of customs and north of the Weverton docks."

"They are going to want to stop us. Ask questions."

"They'll never know we're there."

It was harder to shield the cutter than Lucy expected. It moved swiftly and its speed resisted her efforts. Nor was majick easily accomplished on the water. But she turned her stubborn will on it. Soon she felt the spell take hold. But it would last only as long as she maintained her unwavering concentration.

Marten piloted them expertly through the strait and into the harbor. It was trickier maneuvering through the ships lying at anchor and between the wet docks. There was little space to pass through.

"Fools," Marten muttered. "The ships will be bouncing off one another when the storms hit. And the bumpers won't do a piss of good."

"They were supposed to be sent to Tilman," Lucy said. She felt her majick slipping and admonished herself for losing focus. She closed her eyes, reaffirming her hold. When Marten reefed the sails, she let the majick melt away and helped him. They bumped gently against the dock and she leaped out to secure the lines. Marten joined her.

"Up the ladder," she said, leading the way.

At the top, she paused, stretching her arm out, feeling in the crack for the oilskin-wrapped packet containing the remaining Jutras contracts. It was gone. She finished climbing up and crawled down to the exit, hoisting herself up with Marten close behind. There was an odd feel to the air. It was majick. She frowned. But it wasn't quite right. Like meat that had sat too long before cooking. A noise snagged her attention. It was both shrill and grumbling, like a distant roll of thunder.

"Do you hear that?"

He nodded.

"What is it?"

"Undoubtedly trouble."

"Undoubtedly. We'd better go."

Marten put his hand on her arm when she would have risen. "I'd feel better with my cutlass on my hip."

She lifted her brows. "Majick not enough for you?" But she conjured it and handed it to him.

"I could get spoiled."

Errol Cipher's voice echoed in her mind. *Serve the crown, of course. That's what majicars do. . . . I have no need of money.*

"Whatever your heart desires," she said.

He leered, grasping her hand. "I'll hold you to that."

Marten was too tired to use the winds to carry them across Sylmont, and Lucy was afraid to waste her majick and tire herself out. Hiding the cutter as they'd come into the harbor had been difficult. What would it take to rebuild the Pale? So they set out on foot.

They took as direct a route as possible, going across Tideswell and up through Salford Terrace. But they soon ran into an obstacle they had not expected. People crammed the streets. They spilled from the city center shouting and screaming, breaking windows, looting, and fighting. And they were headed for the castle.

Lucy and Marten watched from a doorway as the flow of people ran past. They carried torches, staves, pallet hooks, pitchforks, and whatever other manner of weapon they could scrounge. The one word that Lucy and Marten could pick out of the din was "Pale." Smoke billowed up several streets over as a building caught fire. Or was set on fire. The sounds of shattering glass and splintering wood whirled in the cacophony as shops were broken into.

"We have to get ahead of them," Marten said.

"The burn. They'll be too afraid to go there. It'll be the fastest for us anyhow."

They turned north in a perpendicular course to the mob. They ran, but soon a stitch in Lucy's side forced her to walk. When it released, they ran again.

The burn had crossed the Maida Vale, destroying a quarter-of-a-league stretch of the road up to the top of Harbottle Hill. The fire had burned everything. Sherborn Park had been completely obliterated. The flames had carved out a shallow hollow in the dirt that stretched easily four leagues east to west, and a half league north to south. It was filled with ash, made hard by recent rains. Lucy paused to look out along the horizon. Mare's tails and mackerels began to form, the first outriders of a storm. There was little time left.

The burn ended at Glamley Street not far from the castle. They crossed it, angling through the posh neighborhoods to rejoin the Maida Vale. The mansions here were surrounded by high walls and gates. All manner of hired police stood guard, from Hornets to Howlers, Eyes to Corbies. There were even a few of the Blackwatch interspersed among them.

Several people challenged their presence, but didn't follow when Lucy and Marten neither answered nor stopped.

The castle sat on top of a lazy hill. It was surrounded by a stubby curtain wall, anchored in place by regularly spaced square towers. Inside, the castle was a sprawling confusion. Each king and queen had added a bit here and there. Some more tastefully than others. Few people knew how to navigate it all, and the constant construction meant that anybody claiming to know his way around was questionable at best.

The castle was surrounded by lawns and formal gardens, and circled by a bridle path. There were several ponds dotting the park on the north side. The grandest feature was the Wall. It was the first thing one saw upon entering the massive gates. It wasn't just a single wall, but a triangular tower made of sparkling black granite. It sat fifty feet back from the entrance, rising high above the height of the curtain wall. The Rampling family tree was carefully inscribed around its three sides. Every living legitimate member of the family was recorded on the Wall. Hundreds of clerks worked assiduously to collect the information and reinscribed the tree on the Wall each year with the most current information.

Lucy eyed it as they approached, remembering Errol Cipher's admonition: *Anchor it to the Wall tree.* But how was the tower going to serve as a majickal anchor? She needed blood oak. Even witless children knew that much. The Pale had been created using blood oak in the first place, and she needed the same to re-create it.

The castle gates were closed. Marten pounded the hilt of his cutlass against the inset door. It was several minutes before it opened. Two Crown Shields stood inside, swords drawn. Lucy stepped forward, pulling her necklace out of her collar, holding the pendant out.

"I want to see the king," she demanded.

Her strange eyes unnerved them. They exchanged a glance.

"I said now."

The authority in her voice decided them. Grudgingly they opened the door.

"Ye'll have t'have an escort, miss. And *he* has t'wait outside."

"He's coming with me."

They objected loudly. Finally one went running for his sergeant of the guard. Lucy fumed while she waited. Every moment the storm drew closer and the mob grew more frenzied. The remaining guard watched them both, his gaze flicking from her red-ringed silver eyes to Marten's black orbs.

"Did I grow a third head?" he asked Lucy conversationally.

"A third one? Did you have two?"

"Not that I was aware of, but this lad's gape face has made me think perhaps I am mistaken."

The sergeant strode up, his pockmarked cheeks flushed. He examined the two visitors with a scathing eye.

"I don't have time for nattering. Explain your business."

"I want to see the king," Lucy said, once again showing her pendant. "And I want this gentleman to accompany me."

At the word *gentleman*, Marten snorted.

"No, miss. Necklace says you can come in. He stays out. Now, if that's all, I have work."

"It isn't all," Lucy said softly. She centered herself, focusing her majick. A sudden throb from close by made her start. She turned, ignoring the guards, staring at the Wall. She walked toward it. The sergeant shouted at her and she vaguely heard the scuffle of feet on the cobbles. There was a breath of wind on her neck, and then silence.

She felt a low hum vibrating in her lungs. She pressed her hands flat against the Wall. Majick sent questing tendrils over her fingers and up her arms. She sighed, leaning her forehead against the stone. The Wall tree. There was a living blood oak tree inside the monolith.

"Lucy?"

She straightened, turning around. The three Crown Shields were fixed in place, wrapped by tethers of wind. She met Marten's black gaze. "I can fix the Pale."

Marten stood guard over her as she settled down with her back against the Wall. She wanted to touch the wood of the tree, but there was no entrance in the trisided tower. She closed her eyes, centering herself. She breathed slowly, feeling the pulse of the tree's majick. She let her breathing match its rhythm. She extended her mind to it. It was alive in a way that was not entirely sentient. But something in it recognized her. Through it, Lucy could feel the mother tree, far away on the Bramble.

She began her conjuring. First the tidal wards to keep out the *sylveth* tides. But hard as she concentrated, she could not bring them into being. She gathered herself, reaching for whatever power she could tap. It was not enough. Her head aching, she slumped, clenching her fists. The hand she'd cut twinged against the pressure. She looked down at it. The bandage was ragged and dirty and blood had seeped through, making a black smudge against her palm.

Blood.

Remember, it's blood *oak.* Errol Cipher's last words to her.

Blood oak. She closed her eyes, smiling as she remembered the burst of majick when her blood had dripped onto the mother tree.

"Help me dig down to a root," she told Marten elatedly, conjuring a spade. "Be careful. Don't damage it."

She ran her fingers lightly over the ground, trying to sense the tree beneath the dirt. At last she found a place where the vibrations seemed to pulse more strongly. Marten began to dig. He scooped the dirt away carefully, making shallow scrapes. Several minutes passed before Lucy heard the telltale thunk of metal on wood. Hastily she pulled off the bandage, conjured a kitchen knife, and reopened the wound. She lay down on her stomach, stretching her hand into the hole and setting her wound against the root.

The surge of power was instantaneous. It filled her, threading through her bones, stitching through her flesh. She felt the tree's eager hunger. It had not tasted blood for seasons past remembering. It drew deeply from her well and returned the gift with a flood of singing majick. Far away, Lucy felt the mother tree, and then the entire grove. It was a symphony in her blood and bones. She clutched her hand around the exposed root, feeling like she might fly away.

Concentrating enough to conjure the Pale seemed ludicrous. Her teeth clacked together and her skull felt as if it were going to explode. She pressed her forehead against the ground, breathing deeply. She smelled the dirt, the rising storm, the sea, and the metallic green scent of the blood oak grove. Gathering herself, she thought about the tidal wards. This time there was enough majick to do what she wanted. She reached out, seeking the wards that Errol Cipher had set. Inside each was a fragment of the mother tree. Lucy called to them. One by one they answered, joining their tiny voices to the song.

She didn't have the slightest idea what Errol Cipher had done, nor how to re-create it. She didn't even try. Instead she trusted the instinct that had guided her since she'd emerged from the *sylveth* tide.

She wove her will into the song, adding a harmony of purpose. Of ownership. The blood oak responded eagerly. With triumphant satisfaction she felt the ring of tide wards snap to brilliant life. She repeated the process with the storm wards. When the Pale was complete, the song had increased in intensity. Instead of wilting with exhaustion, Lucy felt like dancing. Tears of uncontainable happiness seeped down her cheeks. She hated to pull her hand back and end the union. But she couldn't stay here forever.

Slowly she withdrew her hand. But the song didn't end. It merely muted. She could still feel it running through her blood. She rolled on her back laughing, clapping her hands together.

Marten watched her, extending his hand to help her up. "You're drunk," he said drily.

"I think I am," she said, hugging him.

He filled the hole back in, tamping it down. "What about them?" He jerked his head toward the three immobilized guards.

"Free them."

"Aye, aye, Cap'n," he said with a mocking salute.

The wind holding the three men immobile unwound and drifted away. They goggled at Lucy and Marten, caught between anger and fear. Shouts on the walls distracted them. A ragged cheer went up and someone rang the alarm bell.

"What's happening?" the sergeant demanded, turning

so that he could see the curtain wall and still keep an eye on the two intruders.

A guard pelted along the parapet at breakneck speed, ducking into the tower stairs. He emerged a few grains later, out of breath and flushed with excitement.

"Sergeant Digby, sir!" He plowed to a halt in front of the older man, throwing a salute. "The Pale, sir, it's back up!"

Digby stared in disbelief. "You stay here," he said to Lucy and Marten, then hurried up onto the ramparts. He stood and stared out at the harbor for a long minute, then thumped back down the stairs. He came to stand in front of Lucy and Marten, his arms crossed over his broad chest, the corner of his right eye twitching.

"Who are you?"

Lucy smiled wickedly. "I am Lucy Trenton. And this is Marten Thorpe. We're just back from the Bramble, and we want to see the king. Now."

The sergeant blanched at their names. He quickly gathered his composure.

"There gonna be trouble?"

Lucy wasn't entirely sure what he meant. Was he asking if she was going to cause trouble? Attack the king, maybe? Or . . . ? "There already is trouble. The Jutras are here. It may be we can stop them."

He scratched his chin, then nodded. He turned to the two men standing nervously behind him. "Fetch the cap'n. Tell him there's knucklebones in the throne room. Be quick."

The two men nodded and dashed away at a hard run. The sergeant turned back to Lucy and Marten.

"I'll take you to the king myself."

Lucy nodded; then foreboding struck her, turning her stomach to lead. "Tell me, Sergeant Digby, is there a secret way in?"

Chapter 32

Digby did not know a secret way into the throne room. But he was acquainted with the seneschal, who might, and so he took them to him. They entered through a servants' entrance in the north wing. The mishmash of decor as they passed through various parts of the sprawl revealed the various tastes of the previous kings and queens. One room was done up in brilliant orange, eye-scarring yellow, and puce. Another contained so much gold leaf that Lucy was nearly blinded.

At last they arrived at the seneschal's. The outer office contained rows of tables at which clerks scratched on parchments with careful pens. The master clerk overseeing them approached with a faintly disapproving crease between her brows.

"May I help you?"

"Need to see Master Whittier," Sergeant Digby declared.

"May I inquire as to your business?" she asked blandly.

"No," Digby said.

The clerk was taken aback. Her brows winged up in surprise.

"I'm afraid I must insist. Master Whittier is tremendously busy."

"I have to insist too," Digby said, and shouldered past her.

Lucy and Marten followed, unsuccessfully hiding their

grins. Once the sergeant had decided he was going to help them, he'd become as determined as a dog gnawing a meaty bone. He thrust through the far door, the clerk running to catch up, protesting vociferously. On the other side of the doors lay a library and the master clerk's office, and beyond was the seneschal's lair. Digby marched to the doors and thrust them open without knocking. Master Whittier looked up at the commotion.

"What is the meaning of this interruption, Mistress Harbine?" he asked severely.

"They refused to tell me their business, sir, and tromped on through like a herd of cattle!"

"Explain yourself, Sergeant Digby, is it?"

"Yessir." The sergeant looked pointedly at the clerk. "Be better in private, sir."

The seneschal sat back in his chair, his fingers steepling together. He was portly, with a fringe of brown hair around the dome of his skull. His face was doughy with rectangular spectacles perched on the end of his broad nose. He nodded finally.

"You may go, Mistress Harbine."

She sniffed and withdrew, pulling the doors closed.

"All right, then. Explain yourselves. I am quite busy. I've already squandered three hours waiting for my morning audience with the king, only to be dismissed without an explanation. Quite upsetting. There are signatures required. Today of all days he decides to break his schedule. Not since I've been in this chair has he neglected me in this way. It's put me quite behind the day and likely the entire sennight. Work doesn't stop because the Pale snaps. So be concise if you will."

Lucy exchanged a look with Marten. She didn't like the sound of the king's missing his regular appointment. It could be explained by a need to reestablish the Pale. . . . *Knucklebones in the throne room* . . . had Sharpel and his Jutras really made it that far?

"Pale's restored. Got reason to believe there's some trouble with the king," Digby announced baldly. "Need to get inside unannounced. Unseen, too."

Master Whittier just stared. He glanced at Lucy and Marten and recoiled, finally noticing their strange eyes. He looked back at Digby.

"What's going on?"

"Trouble." The sergeant slid a look to Lucy, but didn't elaborate.

Whittier tapped his fingers on his desk, and then stood abruptly. "Come with me. Are there more of you?"

"Sent for the cap'n to bring troops. He'll be here soon."

"I'll send Harbine to escort them."

He took them back to the outer office and sent his master clerk trotting off. "This way, please."

It would have taken a pack of bloodhounds and a month or so of seeking for Lucy to find her way through the meandering maze that led to a cluster of musty storerooms beneath the throne room. They contained a spectacular quantity of paintings, sculptures, musical instruments, tapestries, weaponry, and innumerable other riches piled haphazardly. The customs inspector in her longed to catalog and organize it.

Master Whittier stopped outside a plain door and inserted a heavy brass key in the lock. Majick made Lucy's nose tingle. The door was warded against unauthorized entry. It opened into a dark stairway. Whittier put a finger over his lips and crept upward with Lucy right behind. Sergeant Digby drew his sword with a quiet chiming sound. Marten followed suit. There was a small landing at the top of the stairs, illuminated only by cracks of light slipping between the heavy draperies walling off one end. Squabbling voices sounded from the other side. Lucy's mouth hardened as she recognized one. Sharpel.

She went to the corner where the drapes met the wall and pushed them open a hairbreadth. The invaders stood on the dais behind the two thrones. Or rather, behind where the thrones ought to have been. The massive chairs had been tumbled to the floor and smashed apart. Immediately Lucy recognized why. They were made of blood oak. Though how anyone could have figured that out, she didn't know. The thrones were gilded with complex inlays of enamel and precious stones. Until they'd been smashed, not a single speck of blood oak could have been seen. Even she had not recognized what they were, though she'd once even been allowed to sit on one, and her cousin William had dandled her on his knees when she was a child.

She saw him now, lying on the floor, bound like cordwood and gagged. Queen Naren was behind him, also bound. Her eyes were closed and she wasn't moving. A bruise spread across her forehead. Clustered on the floor in the center of the room was a group of terrified men and women, a mix of gentlefolk and servants. Stacked in the back against the wall was a pile of bodies from which emanated trails of blood. There appeared to be twenty or thirty altogether, and most wore the livery of the Crown Shields. Lucy pressed a hand to her lips.

Sharpel stood at the foot of the dais on the opposite side from Lucy, arguing with a slight man with straight, silky black hair that fell loosely to his hips. His skin was dark, his eyes yellow. A pattern of alternating red and black dots ran along his brow bone and his cheekbones just below his eyes. Additionally, there were two triangular slash marks in black on his left cheek, and a pattern of scars on his forehead and chin. Jutras. She glanced around the room. There were sixteen of them. Small, dark-skinned, with black hair and yellow eyes. Both men and women. Each shared the same loose, flowing hairstyle and tattooed dots around the eyes, but the ritual scarring and additional facial tattooing were quite different. Four guarded the main doors, and two more pairs guarded the side entrances. Others circled watchfully around the prisoners. And the last waited until Sharpel finished his diatribe before speaking quickly in a soft, unrelenting voice.

The words made no sense to Lucy. The language was

disconcertingly musical and guttural at the same time. The Jutras man gestured emphatically at the prostrate king. No, Sharpel was Jutras too, she reminded herself.

"There is nothing I can do about the Pale," Sharpel said loudly. "There is no majicar alive who can. Uniat and Cresset will protect us," he said with a slight bow of deference.

Lucy's hand knotted on the thick velvet drapes. They didn't know the Pale was restored. Which meant they didn't know that a very powerful majicar was nearby. She had the element of surprise.

The long-haired Jutras man began to speak again, switching unexpectedly to Celwysh. Lucy was startled at how fluent and elegant his mastery of Crosspointe's language was.

"If it is true that the Pale is beyond repair, then we have failed. But we will not go without honor."

"*If* it is true, Glaquis?" Sharpel's nostrils flared as he lifted his head, his lip curling as he stared narrowly down his nose. "Are you suggesting that I am lying? Or misinformed?"

The other man smiled, his teeth glittering white against his walnut skin. "I think that you should not be *picrit vendri*. But we who are *kiryat* will not permit your failure to stop us. You are correct. We will pray to the gods. But we must have sacrifices."

Lucy hardly saw him move. His hand darted out, splaying against Sharpel's chest. Glaquis muttered a long string of words in a quick staccato. He took his hand away and Sharpel dropped to the floor, unmoving, his eyes staring at the ceiling. The Jutras wizard squatted down, pushing the merchant onto his back. He smiled, saying something in his own language, then stood, calling loudly to his companions. They quickly cleared the floor, dragging the prisoners to a huddle near the shattered thrones. In the center, six of the Jutras, led by Glaquis, began some sort of ritual. They peeled away their clothing, naked except for yellow breechclouts. Their bodies were heavily scarred, the patterns stunning and some-how menacing.

They gathered in a circle, facing outward. In unison, they began chanting. The words were soft-edged and musical. Each said something different. Their words entwined around one another in a complex braid. As they spoke, each began walking an intricate pattern on the floor. Wherever they stepped, a pale gray line followed. They crisscrossed, weaving in and out in a stately dance.

Their movements were lithe and fluid. The gray lines darkened where they crossed and recrossed. Lucy became aware of majick gathering. It filled the room like a cloud, and wherever it came from, it was nothing she could touch. Fear prickled down her neck. What were they planning? Could she stop it?

After half a glass, the men stopped, standing equidistant around the edge of their creation. It was like a snowflake inscribed in the floor, the gray lines crossing so often that they'd become black. The Jutras stood silently for the space of five breaths, and then spun in place, and began again. This time they traced a larger pattern around the outside of the other. Their words changed, turning guttural. They stomped their feet, shouting the prayer, if prayer it was. Their skin gleamed with sweat as they tromped. The lines that followed them were dark red, swooping and sinuous. They reminded Lucy of the pattern a snake's belly made across the sand.

At last they finished, ending with thundering feet and sharp clapping hands. Then silence descended. They stepped back, dropping to their knees and pushing forward, foreheads pressed to the floor, arms spread wide. After several minutes, Glaquis rose. He motioned for his men to carry Sharpel and the king before him. Sharpel remained unmoving, stiff as a board. The Jutras man propped him like a rake against a garden wall. William struggled against his ropes, making angry sounds behind his gag. Glaquis pulled it away.

"Will you restore the Pale?" he asked. "Or do you wish me to offer you to the twin gods?"

"I can't restore the Pale," the king said. His red blond hair had gone gray and thin over the years. His skin was ruddy from being outside. His face was set, a bruise blossoming on his left cheek, his mouth swollen and pulpy. "I wouldn't if I could. I'd rather throw my people on the mercy of the gods than let you put them under the lash."

Glaquis shook his head. "Uniat will take pleasure in washing his hands in your blood. Cresset will taste your bravery sweet on her tongue. We rejoice to offer such a noble sacrifice. But this one—he has failed. Uniat will torture his soul until the forevertime ends in chaos. He will not forget that failure is betrayal."

He glanced at the prisoners. "With such sacrifice, Uniat and Cresset will hold us in their hands until the demon storms pass. They will guide us safely back off the Mourning Water, and your land and people will torment us no longer."

He returned to his place on the outer edge of the pattern. Lucy watched in fascinated horror as a long red knife materialized in his hand. The blade was as long as her forearm. It hooked at the end, resembling a tooth. He held it flat before him and bowed over it. Then he grasped Sharpel by the hair. He said something in Jutras, and the power clouding the room condensed sharply. Lucy gasped. Glaquis raised the knife and began to slowly carve away Sharpel's face, all the while chanting. His knife was sure and deft as he sliced away chunks of bloody flesh. He flicked them onto the prayer pattern. Where they landed, they sizzled and soon the smell of cooking meat permeated the room.

Sharpel's forced stillness was dreadful. He did not scream or struggle. Lucy could almost feel pity for him.

As the ritual dissection continued, the majick began to swell. It soon became difficult to breathe, the majick pressing against them like a heavy weight. Lucy pushed back at it, but with little effect. Her power was too weak.

Like throwing an apple at a ship to divert it. She didn't dare try to draw on the grove again. It might damage the Palc. She had to find another way.

Soon Sharpel's skull was bare of skin, flesh, and hair. A few bits of meat clung to his cheeks and nose, and he still retained his eyes, which were full of dreadful horror and agony. He was absolutely grotesque. Lucy could not look away. Her stomach bucked and churned and bile spilled onto her tongue. She swallowed hard, breathing through her mouth so that she wouldn't smell the burning flesh.

Suddenly Glaquis raised his knife over his head, shouting something. Then he sliced open the vein in Sharpel's neck and pitched him forward onto the prayer wheel.

The collected majick pulled back again, condensing tighter and tighter. It sucked the air out of Lucy's lungs and she could not find another breath. She gasped helplessly. The Jutras surrounding the circle began to chant again, pounding the floor with their hands. Suddenly the majick dropped, crushing Sharpel's dying body. Bones cracked and crunched. His flesh and organs squelched. Blood sprayed into the air and spurted out of his body in every direction. Still the majick pressed down, squeezing every drop from his body, the prayer pattern absorbing it like a sponge.

Lucy could not contain herself. She retched, covering her mouth to quiet the sounds. The seneschal did the same.

Then suddenly the dreadful pressure and drag of the majick lightened. It hovered in the room, dense and waiting. Already the next victim was being cut from the herd of prisoners. It was a matron of middling years with heavy jowls and fingers that glittered with rings. But it was the person sitting next to the woman that caught Lucy's horrified attention.

Keros.

What was he doing here? But she knew. He'd been trying to warn the king for her, and because of it, he was going to be sacrificed to the bloodthirsty Jutras gods.

She turned to Marten, her voice taut. "We have to stop this."

Already the second bloody ritual had begun. She felt the majick condense with the first shouted word. This time the drag was stronger. It made her teeth ache, sending nails of pain up to skewer her eyes.

"The storm's rising. Can you bring it faster? Stronger?"

Understanding flickered across Marten's face. He nodded, retreating to the wall. He sat cross-legged against it, turning his face upward. Lucy watched, helpless to do anything, wanting to urge him to hurry.

Footsteps sounded quietly on the stairs and the captain of the guard stepped up onto the landing.

"What's goin' on here?" he demanded in a low growl.

Sergeant Digby explained, his body tense and angry. His hands were bunched into fists. The captain peered out through the curtain, then spun back around, his long face white.

"Why don't she scream?"

"Majick," Lucy whispered.

"We gotta stop them mother-dibbling bastards." He sounded more angry than hopeful. "We can send for majicars. There's a couple healers in the south wing."

"There's no time."

"Just who asked you? Who in the depths are you?"

"Lucy Trenton."

His mouth fell open and he slapped for his sword. Digby caught his arm.

"She fixed the Pale."

The captain stiffened. His teeth dug white dents into his lower lip. He nodded. "All right. What do you want to do?"

"There's a Chance storm rising." She slid a glance to Marten. "It's going to be a big one. When it gets here, I'll use the power of the *sylveth* it carries to attack."

"Storm won't hit for hours. They'll all be dead by then."

"It will be upon us soon. *Very* soon," Marten said

dreamily. The loose tendrils of his hair floated about his head on an invisible current.

The captain started at the sound of Marten's voice, eyeing him narrowly. Lucy put a hand on his arm to get his attention.

"When I attack, you need to get the king and queen out. Get them to safety. And then the rest."

The captain nodded. "I'll bring some men up and send the rest around to bust in the other doors."

He disappeared down the stairs, reappearing within a minute, followed by a dozen dour-faced men. He lined them up. All was ready. Now she needed only the storm.

Lucy went to the curtain, standing between the captain and Digby. The woman was taking longer. There was more of her to cut away than Sharpel. What was left of the merchant spy lay on the prayer circle, a dried journeycake scarcely more than an inch thick. Lucy bit the inside of her cheek at the horror of it. She wouldn't have wished such a death on anyone. Becoming *sylveth* spawn would have been preferable.

"Why don't she scream or fight or somethin'?" one of the soldiers growled, his throat working.

"Majick," Digby muttered, echoing Lucy.

She felt the power of the *sylveth* gathering. It was clean and bright, like moonlight. It whirled up around Crosspointe on the wings of a gale wind. Marten pulled it into a coil until the entire island sat in the eye of a massive storm. The *sylveth* spun through it, pulling more and more out of the air and the sea.

The power was immense.

For a moment, uncertainty shook Lucy. Panic unraveled along her nerves. What if she couldn't manage the power? Or what if it wasn't enough? And then another fear struck her. What should she *do* with it? How should she attack?

And then there was no more time to dither. Glaquis peeled the last of the woman's face away and sliced through her vein, shoving her forward onto the prayer circle. Once again the wizards beat the ground and the accumulated majick descended, crushing the body flat, her bones turning to powder beneath its force.

They took Keros next. He did not go easily. He used his hands and feet, striking out with majick bolts of fire. He killed the Jutras guard who held him, but Glaquis deflected his attacks without effort, setting a palm on his forehead. Just like that, Keros's revolt was over. He went limp. He would have collapsed to the floor, but Glaquis grasped him by the hair, dragging him to the edge of the prayer circle. He raised his knife in the air, beginning the chant again.

Lucy could wait no longer. She opened herself to the power of the *sylveth* hurricane. She imagined a herd of angry Koreions. Help me, she said. *Kill!*

Her majick burst from her. Six great sea beasts filled the hall. They swept down on the kneeling priests and snapped them in two. One clamped its maw on Glaquis's head and shoulders, eviscerating him with its claws. The Koreions snatched and tossed, playing tug-of-war with the Jutras like dogs with rags.

The Crown Shields rushed in, ignoring the carnage and the terrifying beasts, and dragging out the terrified, weeping prisoners. They pulled them down the stairs. Queen Naren remained motionless. Lucy didn't know if it was a spell or worse.

The Jutras died easily. But the prayer circle and the blood majick did not.

Lucy walked out from the drapery to stand in the middle of the butchery. The collected power felt angry. It was still hungry. It had been cheated. It wanted death. It wanted worship.

She didn't know what to do. It would not remain quiescent long. If it was not fed, she had little doubt it would go hunting. But how to get rid of it?

For a grain she heard Errol Cipher's annoyed remonstrance when she'd asked about making a new Pale: *Conjure it, majicar.*

Could it be so easy?

She centered herself and gathered the power of the storm, holding it tight. She focused her mind on what she wanted, fixing it exactly in her mind. And then she let loose her will.

Filaments of raw *sylveth* unraveled in the air. They did not come through the Pale—Lucy created them using the power of the storm. They fastened on to nothingness, crisscrossing and weaving in and out in a lace web. It grew denser, the spaces in between growing smaller and smaller. Back and forth they wove, up and down. Soon a shimmering cloth made of raw *sylveth* floated in the air. Lucy held it tightly, readying herself. Then she lifted it, wrapping it around the mass of roiling Jutras majick.

When the two met, Lucy felt its touch on her skin like a vat of carrion. She screamed. She screamed all the screams that Sharpel had choked on, all those the woman could not voice. They were there inside the mass: the agony, the dreadful fear and horror as the knife sliced their faces away, as it peeled them down to the bone, as their veins were cut and their blood was crushed from them like juice from grapes, feeding the Jutras gods.

The pain was unbearable. But Lucy was too angry to let it stop her. Rage untied her reason. Her body collapsed, writhing, letting go of her bladder and bowels. But her mind remained relentlessly focused on its task. She would not let another soul die; she would starve this bloody hunger to death. She closed the Jutras majick in a pocket of *sylveth*. Then she *pushed*.

Slowly the mass collapsed. The shimmering ball shrank smaller and smaller, until it was the size of a head, a fist, an eye.

Then Lucy conjured the *sylveth* to harden, to seal in the Jutras majick so that it could not escape. She didn't know if it would work. She didn't know if it *could* work. But she wanted it. She wanted it, and so she conjured it.

The pain cut off as the seal closed.

She lay on the floor, weeping. The sensation of the

knife scraping at the bones of her skull lingered. She pressed her hands over her face, groping as if she couldn't be sure her face had not been carved away. Her clothes were clammy and cold. The smell of her own dirt mixed with charred meat and blood reached her and she retched, bile burning her nose.

Then Marten's arms circled her and he lifted her up. She clung to him, trapped in the memories of being flayed alive.

Marten carried Lucy out the main doors, kicking them open with a force no normal man should have. The hinges tore with a scream of metal and they hung drunkenly. Outside the Crown Shields waited. They stared, none trying to stop him as Marten strode past, ignoring their questions. If they had tried, he didn't know what he would do. He had to get Lucy away, somewhere safe where he could take care of her. He remembered how she was on the Bramble ship, so close to death. She seemed as broken now as then, only her desperate grasp on his neck lending him reason. If he lost her . . . The power of the storm was still in him, sparks snapping in his hair and crackling around his feet. If he lost her, he'd drive the Inland Sea over the Jutras Empire and drown it.

"Marten!"

Not even Keros's voice could pull Lucy from her hysteria. Marten didn't slow down.

"Is she all right? Where are you taking her? I won't let you hurt her again."

"I'm taking her someplace safe." The words were cold and black as the deepest depths of the Inland Sea.

But his pace slowed. Lucy clutched him tighter, as if afraid he was going to let her go. He lifted her higher, firming his hold.

"Bring her to me, to my house. She'll be safe there."

"It's too far. There's a mob."

"Then we'll find a place here. This maundering sprawl has hundreds of empty rooms."

"Your pardon, gentlemen. But I can help with that."

Vaguely Marten recognized the seneschal's voice. It trembled. He looked at the man for a moment, then nodded. The seneschal led them to a luxurious suite, leaving them there with a stammered thank-you. For stopping the Jutras. For saving . . . everyone. When he was gone, Keros sealed the doors with majick and Marten undressed Lucy and settled her in a bath, glaring murderously at Keros, who would have helped.

"She's my *friend*," Keros said, meeting Marten's unearthly black gaze unflinchingly.

"She's my life," Marten said, and shut the bedroom doors.

Lucy's tears slowly subsided. She did not speak, retaining a tight hold on Marten's hand as if he were the only thing anchoring her to sanity. When she was calm and clean, he lifted her out and toweled her off in front of the fire. He combed her hair dry and then helped her into bed, crawling in beside her and tightly wrapping her in his arms. She fell asleep with her ear against his chest, lulled by the beat of his heart.

Chapter 33

Lucy did not know how long she slept. When she woke, Marten was still there, stroking her hair, drawing the strands slowly between his fingers. She looked at him.

"Good evening. Welcome back to the land of the wakeful and hungry."

"How long have I been asleep?"

"All night and all day. It's past dinnertime. And I've been behaving like such a good pillow for you. But now I've got to use the slop jar."

He slid out of bed. Lucy rolled to the edge, sitting up and pulling the sheet around herself with a shiver.

"Is everything . . . all right?"

His back stiffened. "You are still alive."

"But the Jutras? King William? Queen Naren?"

He shook his head, turning back to face her. "I don't know. A very possessive woman has had me in her nefarious clutches and there's been a majicar guarding the doors, keeping out the nosy riffraff and gossips."

"Not to mention everyone wanting to talk to us to find out just what in the depths happened," Lucy said drily.

An impatient knock rattled the door. It thrust open before either of them could answer and Keros stormed inside. He glowered at Lucy.

"So, you're awake. It's about time."

"I'm hungry," she said. The horror of the events in the throne room was losing its grip on her. She smiled, ridiculously happy to see Keros unhurt and his usual grouchy self.

"They've been banging on the doors nonstop, wanting to see you. I'm surprised they didn't send for the Sennet to blast them open," Keros said, emotion pulling the corners of his mouth tight.

Lucy's jaw jutted in sudden anger. "I won't let them arrest you for being an unregistered majicar."

Keros froze, then gave a short, guttural laugh. "*You* won't let them."

"That's right."

He stared at her. "I'll send for food. And find you some clothing," he said harshly.

"Don't bother," she said with a merry smile.

A thought conjured a midnight silk dress with full skirts. Silver Koreions gamboled around along the cuffs, hem, and deep neckline.

Keros jerked back as if struck and then abruptly turned and disappeared. Lucy exchanged an uncertain glance with Marten, then followed. Keros was pacing in front of the door. The bellpull swung wildly.

"Is something the matter?"

He whirled around. "I thought you were dead. Or worse—*sylveth* spawn. You and Marten both. You were my only friends, the only people alive who I thought I could trust. Then Marten betrayed you. After that, I had to write him off—it was unforgivable. And now here you are, alive and well and snuggled up to Marten like nothing ever happened. And on top of everything else—" He broke off, his lips compressing.

"On top of everything else we've developed funny-looking eyes. But Marten has scales," she pointed out. "And he can call the winds. Not to mention control the waves."

He stared wordlessly.

"Lucy is Errol Cipher's heir. He said so. And we found a blood oak grove on the Bramble," Marten said. He walked in wearing a sheet wrapped around his hips.

"My clothes are ruined. Smell horrible. I could put them on, but I might be offensive to delicate noses. I could wander about in this very fine sheet. Or you could take pity and dress me." He waggled his brows at her. "Or I could go naked." He let his sheet slip a little.

She grinned. "I should like that rather more than Keros. But I think we'll have to go see Cousin William and explain ourselves. It would probably be better if you were a bit more circumspect."

Lucy conjured a pair of close-fitting black trousers, and a long vest and frock coat, with an ivory silk shirt. The vest and turned-back cuffs on his coat were embroidered in gold and cobalt thread in a pattern of scrolling curves and lines that suggested wind and waves.

"Very nice. Now how about dinner?"

"I've rung for someone," Keros said tightly.

"I'm hungry now. Aren't you, Lucy? You don't want to wait for a maid to fetch something and drag it all the way back here. It'll be cold and she'll hardly have more than a bowl of porridge and stale bread."

She gave Marten a withering look. "All right."

She conjured so much food that the table couldn't hold it all. They set some of it on the floor and chairs. Keros picked at his food, brooding as the other two ate ravenously. A maid came at last and he sent her away. When Lucy and Marten were too full to eat any more and she'd banished the remains, he confronted them.

"Now that you're sated, tell me what happened to you."

Another knock on the door prevented them from answering. Keros wrenched it open. Sergeant Digby stood there.

"Your pardon, but the king wants you," he said with a clumsy bow.

Lucy stood quickly. "Is there word on Queen Naren?"

"Dunno, miss. Best come now."

He guided them to the royal chambers, passing dozens of heavily armed Crown Shields. Their numbers increased the closer they came to their destination. Digby knocked at the outer chamber and they were let in by yet more Crown Shields, who directed the three into an interior sitting room. Lucy knocked on the door and the king himself answered.

"Lucy!"

He pulled her into a warm embrace. She returned it, moved. After all that she'd been accused of, that he could receive her so kindly.

"Come inside. We've been waiting for you. Your mother is here."

"Queen Naren?" Lucy asked hopefully.

William shook his head, a spasm crossing his face. The bruise was gone, healed by a majicar. "Her heart gave out. The terror was too much. I think she must not have suffered."

Lucy gripped his arm. "I'm so sorry."

He patted her hand and then motioned her inside. She went slowly. The knowledge of what had happened to the rest of the prisoners on the Bramble ship hit her with the force of a bludgeon. Her father, her brothers, Sarah, Blythe, James—slaves of the Jutras. What could she say to her mother?

"Lucy!"

Tears streamed down her mother's wan face. She stretched her arms out and Lucy went into them, kneeling down beside her mother's chair.

"I'm so sorry. It's all my fault."

"Nonsense," her mother said in her imperious voice. "This was not your doing and I won't hear otherwise." Her voice cracked. "Did you—did you see your father and Stephen and Robert?"

Lucy shook her head. "I didn't."

"But surely—when they came off the ship . . ."

"They didn't get off the ship," Lucy said, forcing the words out. "Marten and I were the only ones. Everyone else—" She broke off, biting her lips. She drew a steadying breath. "Everyone else was sent to Bokal-Dur. To be sold as slaves."

Shocked silence echoed in the room. William was the first to speak.

"Tell us the whole story. Everything."

Lucy settled into a chair. Marten sat at her feet. She took strength from his warm weight pressed against her legs. Keros retreated to the window, his face shadowed. Several of William's advisers were present and a majicar she recognized as a distant cousin. She told her story, beginning with the day when she met Sharpel, twenty years before. It took hours to tell, with Marten and Keros adding what they knew. Marten confessed his part in framing her, earning himself a sharp recrimination from William and angry words from her mother. He suffered these humbly, offering no defense. Lucy's obvious trust in him was all that prevented him from being hauled off in chains. Not that chains could have held him.

She did not reveal the discovery of the blood oak grove or Errol Cipher's majickal library. That information was for Cousin William alone. Keros already knew of course. She trusted him. But she didn't know William's advisers. Who knew if they too were Jutras spies?

When she was through, Keros explained that when he heard of her capture, he'd retrieved the Jutras contracts from her hiding place and brought them and her letter to the castle. "I told you it would not be easy to get an audience. It took nearly a sennight."

His tone was accusing. He was angry still and she wasn't sure why.

William rubbed his forehead. "I would that I'd seen you sooner. But the mess with the lighter and stevedore strikes and the pileup of the ships, not to mention the business with Lucy and the trials . . .

"They came out of nowhere. One moment they weren't there; the next the throne room was full of armed Jutras. They were all majicars, except Sharpel. There was nothing that could be done. They took everyone prisoner, killing every Crown Shield and anyone else who resisted. The one, Glaquis, was their leader. Their plan was to do something to me. A spell that would allow them to control me. I'd be a puppet and no one would ever know. Every king or queen from hereafter would have been under their control. Who knows who else they'd have gone after? The Merchants' Guild. Maybe even the majicars.

"I couldn't let it happen. I snapped the Pale. That upset their turnip cart. They didn't know I could do that. At first they couldn't believe I'd done it, or that I couldn't reverse it. It never occurred to them that the people of Crosspointe would rather die than live under Jutras domination. They thought us too fat, too complacent, too comfortable. And maybe that's true. But I carry the founding king's name so that I will not forget the principles this land was founded on. And we bend to no one."

"How did they escape from their prison?" Marten asked.

"Majick. Illusion. They had help from Sharpel. Knowing he and your brother coerced Pilots and captains with the threat of *sylveth*, it is not so hard to believe that he turned a majicar. Or put a spell on a majicar like the one intended for me. Or he could have turned every guard. I'll get to the bottom of this treachery, I can assure you."

"I don't understand how they could have gotten raw *sylveth* inside the Pale," the majicar said from her seat in the corner.

"I've been thinking about it. There are all those stories about worked *sylveth* that suddenly starts turning people into spawn."

"Fairy tales," the majicar said sharply.

"Maybe. But what if they were true? What if raw *sylveth* can be passed through the Pale in a worked *sylveth* container? I don't know, but it might be possible. But that's not the only way. It can be conjured," Lucy said.

"But . . ."

"Yes?"

"That kind of majick . . . you must be tremendously strong." He sounded both eager and frightened.

Lucy didn't answer.

Suddenly William stood. "Well, thank you, everyone. I shall call a council meeting within a glass to discuss these matters further. But now I'd like a few minutes with Lucy and her friends." He put a hand on Lucy's mother's shoulder when she went to ring for a servant to carry her out. "Laura, please stay."

The others bowed and withdrew. The king turned to Lucy.

"I have to know. How strong a majicar are you?"

"The cipher that attached to me was designed by Errol Cipher to find his heir—someone who could match his strength, and therefore be trusted with his knowledge." She explained about finding the blood oak grove and the room inside the mother tree. "He said that majicars are supposed to serve. I have served Crosspointe and the crown all my life. What I am is yours."

William nodded. "I know that, Lucy. And what about you?" he asked, turning to Marten. "Are you a majicar, also?"

Marten shook his head. "No."

"Then what?"

"I am . . . me. I am the Inland Sea, and the wind across the waves. I am the storm and the cloud and the drop of rain."

The king stared at him as if he'd sprouted wings. "What?"

"Like Lucy, I'm faithful to the crown. I always have been, barring my . . . former . . . love of gambling." His expression turned suddenly hard and remote, and a tightness pulled at the room like the moment before lightning strikes. "But make no mistake. What *I* am belongs to Lucy."

The king nodded, his expression unchanging. "And you, Keros. An unregistered majicar. What do I do with you?"

"Nothing," Lucy said softly. "He and I have no need to join the Sennet. We are the king's majicars. We serve no one else but you. Isn't that so?" she asked, looking at Keros.

"Exactly so," he said, his tone uninflected. She still could not see his expression and wondered what he was thinking.

"Then as your king, I must give you an unpalatable command. I expect you to obey. Do you understand?"

Both Lucy and Keros nodded slowly. Her stomach clenched.

"I forbid you to go seeking after your family or friends. For now, they are lost to us. Perhaps one day, but until then, you must abide by my command. I want your word."

Keros mumbled assent, his gaze boring into Lucy. She bowed her head. She couldn't just abandon them. Not knowing what the Jutras were capable of. She couldn't agree.

"Lucy," her mother said softly. "William is right. You are needed here. There may be corruption at every level. Who knows how many were involved in this plot? Not only that, but you are Errol Cipher's heir. You must bring back that lost knowledge to Crosspointe. You must help strengthen us. The Jutras will come again. It's only a matter of time."

Tears burned in Lucy's eyes and rolled hotly down her cheeks. She nodded. "I give you my word."

"Thank you. I must ask one more thing of you as soon as you can manage. I want you to restore the link that allows me to snap the Pale. I hate to think it will become necessary again, but I fear it will. Tomorrow will be soon enough. Now if you will excuse me, I must go see the children. They've been hit hard by Naren's death."

William withdrew, leaving Lucy alone with Keros, Marten, and her mother. The silence was awkward.

"Come here, young man," her mother said, directing a frosty look at Marten. He rose with liquid grace and went to stand before her. "Just what are your intentions toward my daughter?"

He gaped, taken aback.

"Mother—"

Laura Trenton waved an imperious hand at her daughter. "Quiet. Captain Thorpe, you have abused my daughter and betrayed her. Her father is away—" Her voice cracked and it took a moment for her to collect herself, her lips pinching together tightly. "Her father is away, and so I must act in his stead. Do you plan to marry her?"

Marten grinned. "Gladly. But either way, I will never leave her side."

"That's going to make using the slop jar rather awkward," Keros said crudely. "Not to mention when she wants to have a squeeze and a tickle with another man. Or even marry someone else."

Marten scowled at him. Lucy covered a smirk with her hand. Keros was getting back a bit of his own.

"You mind your manners," her mother said reprovingly.

"My apologies," Keros said with a precise bow.

"Pull the bell for me," her mother told Keros. "Sissy, Caroline, and the baby are safe in the castle, Lucy. They will want to see you. Jack is still at the shipyard. They kept him hidden."

The maids arrived and carried her mother's chair out, leaving the three friends alone. Marten prowled restlessly, while Keros dropped onto a chair.

"Your brother died," he announced to Marten suddenly. "Apparently it was quite a sudden illness. Unexpected. The majicars took him to Merstone to figure out what happened to him."

Marten didn't answer and Lucy wondered if he would mourn Edgar's death.

Again there was silence. Lucy watched Keros from beneath her lashes, trying to decipher his mood. He was unsettled, angry.

"Are you going to tell me? Or just stew about it like a boy who's lost his favorite toy?" she asked finally, tilting her head back.

Keros looked up, his cheeks flushing.

"By the way, Marten doesn't think you should watch me bathe anymore. Seems to find it objectionable."

He flicked a quick look at Marten, the redness in his cheeks intensifying. Suddenly he stood up. "I'd better be off."

But Lucy wasn't ready to let him escape so easily. She jumped to her feet and stopped him.

"Tell me what's bothering you. Something crawled up your chimney and died. What is it?"

He sighed, looking up at the ceiling, defeated. "Fine. Marten has been the closest thing I have had to family since . . . he's the closest thing I have to family. Then you came along. You were like a sister. A really annoying, bratty sister. And Marten—what he did to you made me feel sick. I felt like I lost a brother. Then you were both taken to the Bramble and I remembered what it was like to really lose a brother. And a sister. I wanted to rip my heart out of my chest. Then you turn up. But you're different. You are the most powerful majicar since Errol Cipher, and Marten seems to be Braken's son. Not only that, but ridiculously enough, you are lovers. *Lovers*, in every sense of the word.

"I have to wonder—how can that be possible when you hated him so much? The only answer I can come to is that you are not the same. Neither of you. The *sylveth* turned you into someone else. How can you still be my family if you are not you?"

Lucy didn't know what to say. Then she held up her hand. "I cut myself again."

He blinked, and then laughed. It was almost hysterical. He pulled himself together, wiping the tears from his face.

"Tell me you are still Lucy and that he is still Marten. Tell me I have not lost you."

Lucy narrowed her gaze thoughtfully. "I learned to conjure food so that I don't have to cook. And Marten . . ." She smiled. "Didn't you tell me we all make mistakes? If there's one thing I've learned, it's that

that is a singular truth. And I have discovered in him what you have seen in him. We have changed, Keros. But we are not different. In time, you will see.

"Now, if you don't mind, I'd like to go visit Merstone and make sure Edgar is quite as dead as he is supposed to be. Will you join us?"

"I wouldn't miss it. Oh, and I found this in the throne room. I'm guessing it belongs to you."

Keros held out a *sylveth* ball. Its hard, pearly exterior sheltered a red heart so dark it was nearly black. Lucy took it. The malevolence of the imprisoned Jutras power made her palm itch and sent a burrowing ache up to her shoulder.

"Yes, I suppose it is. I'll put it somewhere safe. It wouldn't do for it to fall in the wrong hands."

She slipped the ball into a pocket she conjured in her dress, sealing it in so that it couldn't fall out.

"Let's get going. I don't suppose it's polite to dawdle about in the king's private chambers."

Marten and Keros fell in beside her. She hooked an arm through each of theirs and smiled.

Some days, Lucy thought, deserved to be drowned at birth and everyone sent back to bed with a hot brandy, a box of chocolates, and a warm, energetic companion. Today was distinctly *not* one of those days.

Read on for a excerpt from
Diana Pharaoh Francis's next novel,

THE BLACK SHIP

Coming soon from Roc

Sylbrac rose early. It mattered not that he'd been out late the previous night. Nor that he'd put away the better part of a decanter of brandy all on his own. He disliked slovenly habits and kept a disciplined schedule regardless of his indulgences. He dressed with the aid of his valet and ate a sturdy breakfast of eggs, bacon, buttered potatoes, and strong tea.

As he ate, Fitch purred in his lap, gleefully kneading sharp claws into his thigh with the smug superiority that came with knowing there would be no retaliation. Sylbrac manfully ignored the pain, knowing that to interfere with the small cat's fun would only result in a snarling bite or bloody scratch across the back of his hand. Nor was that the worst of it. Fitch would then compound her revenge by shredding Sylbrac's favorite waistcoat. Or more than one.

After breakfast, he went for his usual ramble along the headland, leaving Fitch curled up on a cashmere blanket before the fire. He walked quickly, nearly running at times up the steep path and along the edge of the cliffs. He loved the briny smell of the sea, the whisper of the wind in the twisted pines along the shore, and the sibilant siren song of the water.

The sun was a glowing lemon peel, gilding the black waves with gold. He climbed up onto a jutting tor. The wind cleared the last vestiges of his headache. He breathed deeply, gazing longingly out at the horizon.

Frustrated anticipation coiled in his intestines. Chance was over, and riggers were scrambling to get ships ready for sailing. He'd get his assignment within a few days and would lay on deck by the end of Forgiveness at the latest.

His fingers flexed. It couldn't come soon enough. His eyes flicked to the Pale. The string of wards protecting Crosspointe from *sylveth* incursions and the Chance storms hung like fairy lights a quarter of a league offshore. They were entirely green now, the color of new grass, the color of safety. Sylbrac gave a short jerk of his head, roughly rubbing his hand over his jaw. He'd been too long ashore, watching the Pale fade from green to blue to green, waiting to return to the waves. He ached with the need to be free of the suffocating dirt and be out where he belonged.

The craving was blinding, and for a moment he swayed forward. He caught himself up short, climbing down off the tor.

He did not return home, but instead walked down into Blacksea.

The town girdled a forested cove. It was picturesque, with exclusive shops and quaint whitewashed houses made of brick and timber. Large manor houses shouldered through the trees in rising ranks along the low ridge surrounding the town. Below, a dozen coastal ketches lay at anchor in the harbor. They were painted white with crimson striping down the rails and keels. Banners floated from the tops of the masts, and crews bustled on the deck, readying for sail. Smaller pleasure boats filled the marina.

Sylbrac briskly strode along, paying little attention to the charming storefronts with their white window frames, blue shutters, and gingerbread trim. The air was redolent with wood smoke and baking bread. The scent of pine and salt overlaid it all. A dog nosed along the edge of the road and a pair of cats squabbled beneath a leafless lilac bush.

Just beyond the Exchange, Sylbrac turned up Petal

Avenue. At the end was a boxy redbrick building with white shutters and doors. Over the doors hung a wooden cutlass with the words FOR BRAVERY AND HONOR carved deeply into the wooden blade. A brass plate beside the door said merely TORSBY AND SONS. Sylbrac eagerly went inside.

He entered into a wide foyer. The walls were painted green with wood wainscotting the color of molasses. The floor was the same wood. Three of the walls were lined with racks containing several hundred swords of every design. The last contained daggers. Torsby was a master sword maker, the finest in Crosspointe. People came from far and wide to purchase his blades, and he was eccentrically choosy about whom he allowed to do so. Sylbrac was privileged to own three of Torsby's swords and five of his daggers.

He went through the archway down a wide hallway and into the spacious gallery beyond. Wide windows overlooking an overgrown garden ran the length of the back wall. The gallery was divided into three sections by low walls topped by brass rails. On the far right and left were two smaller enclosures, each thirty feet across. Within, three circles of different sizes had been painted on the floor in yellow, each divided into quarters. Round racks of wooden and iron practice swords stood in the corners. Beside them were bins of padded and unpadded cross staves, and a variety of targets. On the walls were rows of hooks holding gambesons of varying sizes. Also hanging on the walls were hobbles, wrist, waist, and ankle weights, and an assortment of other training blocks and tackle. Two pails of powdered clamshells hung on posts on either side of the practice areas.

The central section was far larger than the other two, being four times as wide. It also contained a series of concentric practice circles, but painted in different colors. The place smelled of beeswax, sweat, and leather.

Two women were sparring in one of the smaller enclosures. They'd been at it a while and were breathing heavily. Sweat gleamed on their cheeks and foreheads.

Will, Torsby's youngest son, poked the women with a staff, calling out instructions in a low growl.

Sylbrac watched them for a moment. Both were Pilots. He thought they might be Padrika and Shevritel. He couldn't be sure. All the Pilots' faces tended to blur together and he didn't bother learning many of their names. He'd not taken notice of these two before. His lip curled. A new hobbyhorse for them to ride until the next fancy struck.

"Fair morn, young Thorn."

The elder Torsby sat on a bench against the wall, running a soft cloth over the blade lying flat across his thighs. His grizzled hair hung in lank curls to his shoulders, his bald pate covered by a round leather cap. His doughy nose was red, his cheeks rough with stiff gray bristles. He eyed Sylbrac sardonically from beneath his shaggy brows.

"Been expectin' ye."

Sylbrac's black brows lifted. "Were you?"

"Aye. In a foul mood, too. Looks like I was right."

"Been reading tea leaves, have you? Does this mean you'll be putting up a booth at market day and start telling fortunes?"

"Nonesuch. 'Tis merely that ye be as predictable as Chance. The Ketirvan begins today. Truth be told, I expected ye afore dawn. Grind off a bit of the bitter edge."

Sylbrac's lips pulled flat. At the beginning of each year, the Pilot's Guild congregated under the guise of conducting the business of the guild. In reality, it was a vast chasm of putrescence with an overabundance of posturing, backbiting, conspiracy, and scheming. Inevitably, he'd end the week with a fiery pain in his gut and an insatiable urge to kill someone. Usually more than one someone. All told, there was nothing Sylbrac dreaded more. Not even being trapped between a gale wind and a knucklebone weir to the lee. At least the latter was a quick death, and far less painful.

He removed his coat, loosened his collar, and rolled up his sleeves. He stretched his arms over his head and bent from side to side. Torsby continued to polish the blade, chuckling softly.

"I think your hair needs a trimming," Sylbrac said, finding little humor in Torsby's amusement. "Perhaps a little off the eyebrows as well, old man."

"Thorn, me boy, ye couldn't scratch me ass if ye had ten swords and I had but one arm."

"In that case, I'd think you'd stop calling me Thorn."

"And call ye by that blasphemous name of yourn? I'd be struck dead. 'Sides, it suits ye better. Never met another such pain in the ass as yerself. Prickly bastard. Thorn in the side, thorn in the foot. But that has nothing to do with how ye swing a sword."

Sylbrac unbuckled his sword belt and drew his blade, tossing the scabbard down onto the bench before pacing around to the other side of the circle. He scooped up some of the clamshell powder.

"Shall we see what you have to teach me today, old man?"

Torsby was spry. In fact he was downright quick and nimble. Within minutes, Sylbrac was sweating. They went back and forth, swords flashing and clanging in rapid staccato. Torsby kept up a running commentary about Sylbrac's form, jeering at his pupil's growing breathlessness and stiff, angry moves.

"Gotta give up that soft livin', boy. Yer turning into a loblolly. And stop pounding like ye was beating the forge with a hammer. Ye know better. When yer in the circle with a blade in yer hand, yer head can't be anywhere else."

The reproof stung, the more so because it was true. Sylbrac laid in harder, forcing his mind to focus. Soon all thoughts of the upcoming Ketirvan faded like smoke in the wind and the nettles of tension that had been plaguing him since he'd become dirtbound unwound from his muscles.

"Aye, there ye go," was Torsby's only comment.

They sparred without pausing for well over a glass. At the end, Sylbrac was panting heavily, but relaxed. His body felt fluid. He returned Torsby's salute, touching his sword to his forehead before stepping out of the practice circle. He dipped a tin cup into the water bucket at the end of the bench and drank deeply. The water was flavored with mint and lemon. He gulped a second cup.

"You'll career yerself if ye keep drinking like that when yer so heated," Torsby commented, sipping from his own cup.

"Better a bellyache from this than the Ketirvan."

"Ye'll regret it when ye have both."

Sylbrac sighed, dropping the cup into the bucket with a splash. "There's no way around it. I am hulled. I shall have to attend and sit through the endless hours of talking and saying less than nothing. By Braken, couldn't they just cut out my eyes and tongue, lop off my legs and toss me to the wolves like the Jutras? It would be infinitely more merciful."

"Pilots' Guild isn't interested in mercy. Specially to a thorn like you. Ye takin' the cat again?"

"Most definitely. Fitch wouldn't miss a moment."

Torsby shook his head. "Ye invite trouble. Surprised ye never been tossed overboard, what with the cat, not to mention that whistling ye insist on."

"Can't sail the Inland Sea without a Pilot. No matter how much bad luck he carries with him. Besides, there's nothing unlucky about Fitch, and whistling is just music, not a summons for the wights of the world."

"Not a sailor on this island as would agree with ye."

"They don't have a choice, do they?"

"It's little wonder yer so much alone."

Sylbrac stiffened. Bleakness suffused him. It was hardly more than a month since Jordan's death. Torsby was more right than he knew. His brother's murder had left him completely alone. No friends, no family who would still claim him—no family that he'd still claim. Torsby was the closest thing to a friend he had. His lip curled in silent scorn. He made no effort at friends and reaped the harvest of his sowing. He had no right to complain. And yet he couldn't help the ache in his gut.

He sheathed his sword, buckling on his belt before wiping the sweat from his face with a towel.

"I choose to be alone. People annoy me."

"Do they now? And ye bein' such a lapdog. Ye'd think they'd cuddle right on up t'ye."

Sylbrac laughed. "The sea's enough for me."

"Some men like a tickle and a tumble from time t'time."

"As do I. But there's no need to worry. It's easy enough to find a skirt to twitch when I want one."

"Then it be a fine life ye got. No naggin' wife, no bawlin' kiddies, nothin' at all to disturb yer sleep or aggravate ye. Come home t'peace and everlovin' quiet."

"A fine life," Sylbrac agreed, but his jaw tightened. Jordan's death had left him adrift, no matter that he hadn't seen his brother in years. Now he had nothing, no one. And instead of free, he felt . . . lost.

He bid Torsby farewell and returned home to bathe and dress before the Ketirvan. But he couldn't shake the memories of Jordan and the attendant recollections of their parents. By the time he reached home he was fuming. He dismissed his valet with a snarl, throwing off his clothing and scrubbing himself vigorously before yanking on his formal clothing.

He wore a close-fitting black suit made of dosken and silk. It was light and easy to move in and bore no embroidery or embellishments. The jet buttons rose up to close tightly around his throat and he wore no cravat. He pulled on a short padded leather coat—a monkey-jacket like most sailors wore. The arms were ringed with silver bands with rows of *sylveth* studs circling between. Over it, he wore a sleeveless black robe. It was loose and flowing and shone with a silvery iridescence, like the moon striking the black waves of the Inland Sea. He stamped into his leather boots and tucked a stiletto into the top of the left one, and shoved a dagger into the small of his back. Weapons weren't allowed into the Ketirvan, but Sylbrac had grown up running wild on the docks. He never went anywhere without a blade of some sort.

He glanced in the mirror and ran a comb through his brown hair. Despite his efforts, it fell over his forehead in an untidy mop, the back of his hair hanging several inches below his collar. He rubbed at the bristles casting a scruffy shadow along his jaw and grinned crookedly at himself. He'd be damned if he'd shave. He slipped a heavy gold ring on his forefinger. It was shaped like a quadrafoil with a *sylveth* compass rose in the center. He ignored the matching broach, shoving it to the back of the drawer.

When he was ready to go, he poured himself a glass of red brandy and gulped it down in a single swig. He poured another and drank that and then set the glass down with a click and went to collect Fitch.

He settled the little cat on his shoulder. She curled beneath his ear, digging her claws in for balance and wrapping her tail around his neck. Sylbrac scratched her ears and then sighed as he departed for the Ketirvan.

The guildhall was located on the east side of Blacksea, requiring Sylbrac to cross through town. He took a route along the docks in the hopes that he wouldn't encounter any other Pilots. The air was sharp and the wind slapped hard. The cold cleared the murk of the brandy from his head, a fact he regretted. Fitch purred, clutching close against his jaw. He reached up and pet her.

He nodded to the sailors he passed. Most Pilots didn't bother to notice they were even alive. But Sylbrac respected them. He'd *been* them, long ago, before his gift was discovered. They lived hard, brave lives and most came to an abrupt end out on the sea. He liked their rough honesty a whole lot better than the haughty arrogance of his Pilot brethren. At least he didn't have to spend that much time with them. The Ketirvan occurred but once a year at the end of Chance when he was grounded anyway. The rest of the time he was onboard a ship where he belonged. Surely for these few days, he could put up with the conniving, gossiping, backstabbing, and blustering. Surely.

Sylbrac took a deep breath and blew it out, leashing himself tightly. It wouldn't bother him so much if not for Jordan—if not for the tide of memories that rose to drown him. Damn, but he'd put all that behind him! Put his family behind him, the priggish, sanctimonious lot of them. All but Jordan.

The story of his brother's death was murky. Murdered for certain—there was no doubt about that. At first it had been blamed on Lucy Trenton, a royal brat who had also been accused of smuggling and treason. But soon after Captain Marten Thorpe had been convicted as an accomplice. Sylbrac had never believed it. He'd sailed with Thorpe, had seen him and Jordan together. It just wasn't possible. And then the story shifted. A Jutras plot against the crown and Jordan caught up in it. Lucy Trenton and Marten Thorpe framed, and too late to save them from the Bramble. That story didn't seem believable either. But there was no way to get to the truth. That's what chewed his innards. Even if he could go ask his father, the lord chancellor was a liar. Sylbrac couldn't believe anything he said. And his mother . . . He'd as soon trust a Chance storm as a viper like her.

He climbed up along the headland, taking the cliff path through the trees instead of following the road. Below the tide was rolling in, the strand thinning with every wash of waves. Sylbrac broke into a jog. Fitch hissed her protest in his ear and dug her claws deep into the padding of his jacket. He left the path, pushing up the hill through the rhododendron bracken and broom bushes that cluttered the trees. He emerged just below the knob of a grassy hill, upon which perched the Dabloute. It was the most amazing building Sylbrac had ever seen. He never tired of looking at it. Carved from obsidian and alabaster, it looked like storm-whipped waves, rising high and falling, frozen in a timeless plunge. Sylbrac could almost believe that he might blink and the waves would finish dropping and be gathered back into the Inland Sea. There were no windows. The walls were cut so thin they were translucent.

He skirted around to the front of the Dabloute, feeling the tide rising higher in the bay. The Ketirvan would begin at the moment of high tide and the doors would be closed against latecomers. Much as he didn't want to be here, neither did Sylbrac want to be locked out. Too much idiocy was likely to be written into guild law if he wasn't there to lend a voice of reason. Or at least one of mulish obstruction.

The entrance of the guildhall was the upper half of a spectacular *sylveth* compass rose. The rays rose like a sunburst fifty feet in the air. The edges of each were gilded, and a dainty filigree overlaid the diamond glitter of the *sylveth*. Above them, twined in an erotic embrace, were Meris and Bracken, white on black. Their naked limbs grappled one another, though Sylbrac was never sure if they were cleaving lovingly to each other, or if Braken was restraining Meris to prevent her from running off to Hurn, her lover.

The entryway into the Dabloute was the center of the compass. Pilots moved through in groups, heads bent together, some laughing, some arguing passionately, others silent and stern. Sylbrac ignored them, striding ahead. No one called out a greeting, but several saw Fitch and made angry exclamations. Sylbrac smiled.

The inside of the Dabloute was as fantastical as without. The corridors were sinuous, the rooms oddly shaped. The ceilings disappeared into skurls and ripples, the floors rising and falling in soft undulations. There were no carpets or tapestries, no paintings or curtains. Rather every surface was carved into undersea shapes: knucklebones, fish, Koreion, vada-eels, celesties, and more. The sunlight from outside made everything seem to waver and move as if pushed by waves. Softly glowing *sylveth* lights set in the floors brightened the shadows. As soon as he passed inside, Sylbrac felt a soothing wash of peace. The Dabloute was the next best thing to actually being at sea.

He turned off from the main corridor, wanting a few minutes peace and quiet as he made his way to the Ketirvan. High tide was nearly fixed. He didn't have much time. He hurried along, turning sideways at one point where the passage narrowed and then opened up widely. The walls were heavily rippled here, with clefts and nooks like undersea grottoes. He halted abruptly when up ahead he heard the sound of raised voices— a man and a woman arguing. He took a step forward, and then there was a shark *crack!* and quick, angry footsteps.

The woman who stormed around the corner was short and heavy-boned. Her face was square, her skin coarse and tanned with years of exposure to weather. Her nostrils flared and red spotted her cheeks, her mouth pulled thin with fury. The cuffs of her sleeves and the hem of her robe were edged with small silver compass roses with *sylveth*-drop centers. She was Eyvresia, the Pirena-elect. When she saw Sylbrac, she stopped short, her gaze flattening. Fine black lines like cracks in fine porcelain crisscrossed her eyes, weaving like a web through the whites. Before either had time to speak, more footsteps sounded behind her and she gathered her robe, darting past Sylbrac into one of the grotto nooks. She ground one white-knuckled fist against her lips, glaring back at him as if daring him to expose her.

She was followed grains later by a man who hardly came to Sylbrac's chin. His short, curly gray hair was wild-looking, as if he'd been running his fingers through it. His black mustache and beard were clipped close, his brows set in a furious scowl. His eyes were also marked with fine black lines, only his bore far fewer than Evresia's. Those marking Sylbrac's eyes were darker and more numerous than either. By contrast to his own robes, however, the shorter man's black robes were weighted by compass roses stitched in gold thread, one covering each side of his chest from collarbone to hip, another on his back. *Sylveth* discs gleamed at the centers.

He stopped short when he saw Sylbrac, his mouth twisting. On his cheek was a scarlet imprint of a hand. Sylbrac grinned. What had Pirena Wildreveh said to make the Pirena-elect hit him?

"What are you doing here?"

As if he was manure someone had tracked in on his shoe. Sylbrac's smile flattened, his eyes narrowing as he reached up to stroke Fitch. Wildreveh's gaze followed his hand and his mouth puckered as if he'd eaten a mouthful of salt. It was that snide expression that made Sylbrac step to block Eyvresia from view. She had hit the bilge-sucking bastard, and so she'd earned a reward. Not that he ever needed an excuse to antagonize Wildreveh.

"I'm on my way to the Ketirvan."

"Not with that cat, you aren't."

"Oh, but I am. I'm not aware of any rules prohibiting cats. She's such a quiet thing, I doubt anyone will even notice her."

It was a bald-faced lie. Everyone would notice her. Her presence would be like a scream in the night, smoke in a darkened room.

"Then let me be clear. I forbid it. I want her out of the Dabloute. Now!"

Sylbrac's brows arched. "I don't believe you have such authority, Wildreveh."

The other man's jaw clenched. "I am Pirena of the guild. That's all the authority I need."

"I don't think so," Sylbrac said softly. He looked pointedly to Wildreveh's cheek, where Eyvresia's hand-print remained. "And anyway, you're only Pirena until the end of Ketirvan. You've got no fangs to hurt me."

The other man's lips slid apart in a death's-head grin. His square horsey teeth were stained brown and yellow. "Haven't I? We shall see."

With that he turned and marched away, his shoulders rigid. Eyvresia stepped out of the grotto, watching him disappear.

"I know you take great pride in antagonizing your fellow Pilots, but was that wise?"

Sylbrac glanced down at her. "What can he do?"

She shook her head. "I think it would have been better to know the answer to that question before you pushed pins into him. But it is certain that whatever it is he *can* do, he will." Her brow furrowed as she looked at Sylbrac. "Watch yourself. You've no friends here to cushion the blow."

Sylbrac only shrugged. He wasn't worried. He should have been.

ABOUT THE AUTHOR

Diana Pharaoh Francis has written the fantasy novel trilogy that includes *Path of Fate*, *Path of Honor*, and *Path of Blood*. *Path of Fate* was nominated for the Mary Roberts Rinehart Award. Her story "In Between the Dark and the Light" recently appeared in *Furry Fantastic*. Diana teaches in the English department at the University of Montana Western. For a lot more information, including where to read her blog, maps of her worlds, updated news, and other odd and fun tidbits, go to www.dianapfrancis.com.

One woman's choice will save a kingdom.

PATH OF FATE

by

DIANA PHARAOH FRANCIS

In the land of Kodu Riik, it is an honor to be
selected by the Lady to become an
ahalad-kaaslane—to have your soul bonded
with one of Her blessed animals, and roam the
land serving Her will. But Riesil refuses to
bow to fate—a decision that may have
repercussions across the realm.

"[FRANCIS] SWEPT ME AWAY WITH HER
MASTERFUL FEEL FOR THE NATURAL WORLD."
—CAROL BERG

"A STUBBORN, LIKEABLE HEROINE."
—KRISTEN BRITAIN

**Available wherever books are sold or at
penguin.com**

The stunning sequel to *Path of Fate*

PATH OF HONOR

by

DIANA PHARAOH FRANCIS

A year has passed since Reisil's arrival in
Koduteel, and her hopes of a happy life in her
rightful home are being dashed. Kodu Riik is
decimated by plague, famine, and war, and its
enemies are beginning to move. And Reisil's
power to heal has been lost, replaced with a
surging new ability—to destroy.

ALSO AVAILABLE
Path of Blood

**Available wherever books are sold or at
penguin.com**

THE ULTIMATE IN
SCIENCE FICTION AND FANTASY!